the matriarch

Witi Ihimaera was born in Gisborne, New Zealand, in 1944. He was a pioneer of Maori writing in English: the collection of short stories *Pounamu Pounamu* (1972) was followed by *Tangi* (1973), the first novel by a Maori. A hard-working writer and editor, his works include novels, short-story collections, children's books, plays and numerous anthologies. His book *The Whale Rider* has been made into a successful international film, which won the Toronto Film Festival People's Choice Award in 2002. Ihimaera is professor of English at the University of Auckland, teaching creative writing and indigenous literature.

WITI
IHIMAERA

the matriarch

RAUPO

A RAUPO BOOK
Published by the Penguin Group
Penguin Group (NZ), 67 Apollo Drive, Rosedale,
North Shore 0632, New Zealand (a division of Pearson New Zealand Ltd)
Penguin Group (USA) Inc., 375 Hudson Street,
New York, New York 10014, USA
Penguin Group (Canada), 90 Eglinton Avenue East, Suite 700, Toronto,
Ontario, M4P 2Y3, Canada (a division of Pearson Penguin Canada Inc.)
Penguin Books Ltd, 80 Strand, London, WC2R 0RL, England
Penguin Ireland, 25 St Stephen's Green,
Dublin 2, Ireland (a division of Penguin Books Ltd)
Penguin Group (Australia), 250 Camberwell Road, Camberwell,
Victoria 3124, Australia (a division of Pearson Australia Group Pty Ltd)
Penguin Books India Pvt Ltd, 11, Community Centre,
Panchsheel Park, New Delhi – 110 017, India
Penguin Books (South Africa) (Pty) Ltd, 24 Sturdee Avenue,
Rosebank, Johannesburg 2196, South Africa

Penguin Books Ltd, Registered Offices: 80 Strand, London, WC2R 0RL, England

First published by Heinemann Publishers, 1986
Reprinted 1987
Reprinted by Pan Books (New Zealand) Ltd, 1988, 1989, 1990
Reprinted by Secker and Warburg, 1996

This edition published by Penguin Group (NZ), 2009

Copyright © Witi Ihimaera, 1986, 2009

The right of Witi Ihimaera to be identified as the author of this work in terms of
section 96 of the Copyright Act 1994 is hereby asserted.

Typeset by Pindar NZ
Printed and bound in Australia by Griffin Press

ISBN 978 0 14 301092 0

A catalogue record for this book is available
from the National Library of New Zealand.

www.penguin.co.nz

MIX
Paper from
responsible sources
FSC
www.fsc.org **FSC® C009448**

contents

prologue

It was Uncle Alexis who started it all—this imaginative recon-struction of the woman who wore pearls in her hair, Riripeti, the matriarch who ruled the Mahana family for three generations. Poor Uncle Alex. The Italians would have called him *un superbo uomo*, a superb man, and so he was. But it was he who without knowing it started this journey into the past and into the dynamics of an astonishing family.

Father Blain said that all families are somewhat like jungles. So it is with mine, but I have made it even more of a jungle by mingling fiction with fact, like saprophytic vines twining the trunks of already dead trees. I think the matriarch herself would have approved of this. After all, she was the one who turned my own life into fiction.

⁓

The matriarch. She was sitting with the child on the highest terrace of Ramaroa pa, the ancient hill fort above the village of Waituhi. The hill was a gigantic crescent staircase of eleven terraces, like the poutama pattern, the wondrous Stairway to Heaven. Down below was the village itself and, beyond Waituhi, river flats widespread and country towns afar.

The child was listening to her telling him of his ancestry, his whakapapa. Her face, covered by a veil, was mysterious. Her beauty shone out with a gleaming light that he could almost touch and feel; it vibrated and electrified the air. Beneath the veil, shimmering like tears, were the pearls in her hair. Then the pearls gleamed with brilliance as she turned to him, and her voice thrilled with excitement. The clouds, swirling through the sky, cast strange patterns like fleeting kowhaiwhai designs across the earth, swirling, ever swirling.

'E mokopuna, but your life began even before you were born in Waituhi. You may have taken your first breath here but, ara, you have eternity in you also. Your life started even before the Stairway to Heaven was built. It began beyond the uppermost terrace of Ramaroa. Listen, and I will tell you of your creation and your beginning. Listen. Listen.

'At the beginning was Te Kore, the Void. Within the Void, the Nothingness, there came Te Po, the Night. After a timeless time, Te Po began to change. It changed twelve times—from the Great Night to the Extensive Night, from the Extensive Night to the Enveloping Night, from the Enveloping Night to the Intensive Night, from the Intensive Night to the Night Streaked with Light, from the Night Streaked with Light to the Night Streaked with Broad Light, from the Night Streaked with Broad Light to the Night of Unseeing, from the Night of Unseeing to the Night of Hesitant Exploration, from the Night of Hesitant Exploration to the Night of Groping, from the Night of Groping to the Night Inclined towards Day, from the Night Inclined towards Day to the Night that Borders Day. At this, the eleventh changing, the Night that Borders Day was divided by Twilight and Dawnlight, and beyond the Daylight arose the twelfth changing—Te Ao Marama, the Broad Daylight. All our rituals, mokopuna, acclaim the coming of Te Ao Marama, the World of Light.

'Look at the Heavens, mokopuna. At the same time as the coming of the World of Light the foundations of the Universe were evolving—of the earth and sky and waters, of the depths and heights, of the expanse of the skies and borders of the seas—and our own Maori home of the gods, the legendary Hawaiki, our Maori Olympus, was formed. Hawaiki nui, Hawaiki roa, Hawaiki pamamao, is how we describe this place, mokopuna, the place of greatness, of expanse, the place far away. All our Maori dead are still farewelled to Hawaiki in the ceremony we call the tangihanga.

'Then from Te Kore arose the first gods, Rangi awatea and Papatuanuku, the Sky Father Above and the Earth Mother Below. The Sky Father began to create the Heavens but, during his labours, he thought to make love to Papatuanuku because she was so beautiful. They pressed together in a close embrace, so close that they shut out the light. So it was that when they had children, who were gods themselves, the children were born into the darkness— Tane mahuta, God of Forests; Tangaroa, God of Oceans; Rongo ma tane, God of the Kumara Plant; Tu matauenga, God of Man and War; Haumia tiketike, God of the Fern Root; Ruaumoko, God of Earthquakes; and Tawhiri matea, God of Storms. At first the god children thought to kill their parents so they could live in the light, but it was Tawhiri matea who pitied his parents and argued that they should only be separated. One by one the god children tried to break Rangi's embrace from Papa, and one by one they failed. Then Tane conceived of the idea of standing on his hands on Papa and thrusting against Rangi with his feet. His manoeuvre was successful and, with great grieving, Rangi and Papa were separated until one was far above and the other was far below. Now, at last, the light came flooding across the land and there could be seen the great numbers of men who had been hidden between the bodies of the primal parents. Oh, it was so good to walk upright, and that is why our people, the Maori, still give salutations to Earth and Sky and the Separation which continues to allow us to live in the light. We say, "Ko Ranginui kei runga, ko Papatuanuku kei raro." Earth and Sky are our primal parents, mokopuna. Sky is high, sacred and male while Earth is low but fruitful, profane and female. Thus, so the old texts say, was the first setting apart of the roles of male and female. But I have always disputed this interpretation.

'With the coming of the Light, creation was able to be resumed. The children of Rangi and Papa completed the building of the Heavens, of earth and the water, of all things in them, animate and inanimate. Then because the children of Earth and Sky were male, Woman was created. It was Tane, instructed by his sky mother, who fashioned the first female from the red earth. Her name was Hineahuone, and she began to live when Tane breathed into her. Tane mated with her and, when his daughter was born, he mated with her also. His daughter's name was Hinetitama, Maid of the Flashing Dawn. But when she discovered that her husband was also her father, she fled in shame to the underworld, there to become Hine Nui Te Po, The Great Lady of the Night. She did this because of her shame that her husband was also her father.

'Now, mokopuna, up to this time none of your ancestors, the offspring of the gods, knew death. Thus they increased and multiplied upon the earth. Among them was Maui Tikitiki a Taranga, who was aborted by his mother and cast into the sea. Maui was half man and half god and it was he who tamed the sun so that it would go slower across the sky, who stole fire from his ancestress Mahuika and who, in his last adventure, brought death into the world. This occurred when he tried to destroy Hine Nui Te Po, she with the human body but whose eyes were greenstone, her hair sea-kelp, and her mouth that of a barracuda. He set off toward the red flashing light in the western sky where she lived. He took the smallest birds of the forest with him as companions. His plan was to enter her body at her vagina, make his way through it, and reappear at her mouth. "If I can pass right through her body I shall live," he told his bird companions. "But if Hine Nui Te Po is awakened, aue, I shall die." Thus, Maui began his journey. The watching birds kept as silent as possible—but then the fantail trilled into waiata. Hine Nui Te Po awoke, opened her eyes of greenstone and closed her thighs. Maui's body was crushed and he suffered the agonies of death. Because he failed in this adventure, all men became mortal.

'But before Maui died, e mokopuna, he had achieved a most important task. He went out fishing with his brothers and took with him an enchanted hook. He had no bait but what he did was strike his nose and smear the blood over the magic hook. With this hook Maui pulled up his fish, Te Ika a Maui, which we now stand on. It is known as the North Island of New Zealand and, as it rose out of the waves, Maui's canoe came to rest on the peak of Mount Hikurangi. The fish-hook became the cape which now forms the southernmost tip of Hawke's Bay.

'The fish of Maui became the land of the Maori, and we call it Aotearoa, e mokopuna. We are the tangata whenua, the people of the land. We have always been here—Ancients descended from the Time of Gods. Later, Maori voyagers also journeyed here from Hawaiki. Kupe was the first, around 700 AD, and Toi and Whatonga a few centuries later. Then, in tribal histories we are told of the arrival of legendary canoes from that same Hawaiki—the *Tainui*, *Te Arawa*, *Aotea*, *Tokomaru*, *Takitimu*, *Kurahaupo* and *Mataatua*. The *Tainui*, captained by Hoturoa, landed near Cape Runaway, coasted northward and rested finally at Maketu, spreading its people inland from Tamaki in the north to Mokau and Taumarunui in the south. The people of *Te Arawa*, led by Tamatekapua and Ngatoroirangi, landed near Cape Runaway also and travelled widely in the Bay of Plenty and inland to Tongariro, naming and claiming the land as they went. The people of the *Aotea*, sailed by Turi, finally settled in Patea. The *Tokomaru* began its voyage to Aotearoa in turmoil, made its landfall in the South Island and then in its voyage northward, settled the north Taranaki coast from Mokau to New Plymouth. The *Kurahaupo* scattered its settlers mainly along the western coast of the North Island. The *Horouta* landed at Ohiwa and peopled the Ngati Porou area from Cape Runaway to Whangara. The *Mataatua*, commanded by Toroa, is the canoe from which the Ngapuhi, the Rarawa, the Ngati Awa, the Whakatohea and the Ngati Tuhoe people are descended. The new Maori arrivals were fruitful and after a time about forty tribes developed and spread across the land. Within tribal groupings, rose sub-tribal and then kinship groups like ours of Te Whanau a Kai.

'Now, mokopuna. Listen and watch, because I must tell you of your lineage, and point out the land which is yours through me by birthright. Listen and remember.

'You are descended of the Ancients of Aotearoa. You are also descended of the canoe voyagers and, particularly, of the *Takitimu*. This was a very sacred canoe. It carried chiefs and priests, the repositories of the ancient lore, and it was they who brought much of the knowledge of Hawaiki to the new land. The captain was Tamatea Arikinui and you are named after him. Because of the precious freight of gods only raw food was eaten and cooked food was not taken on board. Many sacred ceremonies were performed to protect *Takitimu* on its voyage, and rituals were conducted to ensure that the winds and waves were favourable for its journey south. The canoe was escorted by a school of fish, with a taniwha named Ruamano heading it and another taniwha named Arai te uru behind. The god, Kahukura, in the form of a rainbow, guided the *Takitimu* by day. A lunar halo lit the way by night. When *Takitimu* struck rough weather, the sacred axes with which the waka had been made, Te Awhiorangi was used to chop a way through the waves.

'The *Takitimu* sailed the coast of Aotearoa for several years, settling different areas with its cargo of gods. One of these areas was the place called Turanganui, south of Hikurangi where Maui's canoe had rested, and north of his fish-hook at Hawke's Bay. Inland from this place is where we arose, mokopuna, you and me of Te Whanau a Kai, and all the people of Te Aitanga a Mahaki, Rongowhakaata and Tai Manuhiri.

'This is our land, mokopuna. Here. Now look: there, is the boundary between us and the Ngati Porou to the east. There, we have the Whanau a Apanui to the north. There, to the south, are the Ngati Kahungunu people with whom we have close affiliations. The Tuhoe, the Children of the Mist, are to our west. Now, within Turanganui, we have the Rongowhakaata confederation, Tai Manuhiri and Te Aitanga a Mahaki. The boundary of the Rongowhakaata confederation begins at the sea north of Muriwai and runs along the Oneroa Beach as far as Waikanae. There lies the boundary between Rongowhakaata and Te Aitanga a Mahaki, running to Makaraka, south-west across the Waipaoa River to, and up, the Waikakariki Stream, past Patutahi, then east to join the Tai Manuhiri tribal boundary. Watch even closer, mokopuna, for now

I must point out to you your lands of Te Whanau a Kai as they exist between the tribal lands of the people of Turanganui. Commit this to memory: we are on the western side of the Waipaoa River and opposite the Waimarie settlement near Ormond. We are washed by the Waipaoa River on our east and our north. We are divided from Repongaere by Tore o Haua. We are separated from Pukepapa by the Pouarua Creek on the west. We are five miles from Patutahi. Ramaroa Pa is our ancient hill fort. Taumata o Tumokonui is our highest peak. Our family marae is Rongopai, in the Waituhi Valley. Our closest kin in the valley are Nga Potiki.

'E mokopuna, we ruled here for over a thousand years and this was our land. This was our life. It is your life and land now. It was yours even before you took your first breath. It came to you beyond the time of men and gods to the very beginning of Night and the Void. A thousand years and further back, mokopuna, we had eternity in us.

'Then came the Pakeha.'

act one

1

It was July, 1974. Wellington. I had arrived late to see my Uncle Alexis who was going blind and after two hours I realised that I was committed to stay longer. It might have been better had I not gone to see him at all. But Regan, my wife, said I ought to go, and my father, Te Ariki, was expecting me to see his younger brother. Dad was cross that I hadn't made the effort before this. 'You've been back from London for a year now,' he had said the previous weekend when he'd telephoned from Gisborne. 'Surely you can get in your car and drive down the hill to Oriental Bay. Take your daughters with you. Your uncle's expecting you. He's wondering why you haven't been to see him. I told him last week that you must be busy. Well, Tamatea, try to un-busy yourself for a couple of hours. Go and see your uncle. It's not easy for him, being blind.' My father always called me Tamatea when he wanted to remind me of my family obligations.

It wasn't that Uncle Alex and I didn't get along together; just that the gap between the last time I had seen him and now was as wide as the ocean and as treacherous to navigate. Almost three years had gone by. How can you cross three years of sea in a few hours? On top of this we'd never really known each other very well and I was inclined to suspect that he didn't approve of my successes—the diplomatic career and public achievements had established a reputation which, for him, was all too good to be true. But I like to think that he admired me and, perhaps, was fond of me. I do know that he had always been amazed that I, among all his nephews and nieces, had never asked him for money—Uncle was wealthy, you see, though he never flaunted it. That hadn't stopped him from continuing to try to bribe me, and it was the same on that evening I went to see him. Alone.

Uncle's house was on a narrow street which wound down like a bandage into Oriental Bay. I had friends further down the street, James and Ilse, and I was almost tempted to drive past Uncle's and talk Russian literature with the wondrous Ilse. But I stopped the car and stepped out. The house was olive-green and there were no lights shining in the diamond windows. Then I saw my Aunt Roha, looking through the curtains at me. I ran through the rain, past the tall slapping shrubs, to the front entrance. The glass panels shimmered with a woman's shadow.

'Well look what the wind blew in,' my aunt said when she opened the door. Roha was an attractive woman, very slim and elegant. Tonight she looked sallow and waspish.

'I've come to see Uncle,' I said.

She kissed me. As her cheek brushed mine I felt the velvet of her skin. 'It took you long enough,' she answered.

She ushered me in and shut the door against the wind and the rain. The house was warm. Some of my cousins were home watching television. I saw one of them drifting past in a dream, a renaissance beauty with a bee sting for a mouth.

'Say hello to your cousin,' Roha said.

She turned to look at me. 'Oh, hello, cousin,' she whispered vaguely. She was like a somnambulist, a fairy princess sleepwalking her way down the dark corridor.

Roha took me to the main bedroom. It was dark. After all, what did a blind man need with the light? Uncle was sitting up in bed looking at nothing and listening to the wind and the patterning of rain against the window. 'Alex,' my aunt said to him. 'Your nephew's here to see you. Te Ariki's son.'

Uncle's face swivelled around in my direction, searching upward to where I might be. He looked bloated, with a greyness beneath the skin. His eyes were concealed behind large dark glasses, but the glasses could not completely hide the infectiousness of the welcome which spread across his face. I had always thought that Uncle Alex was devilishly handsome, a 1940s film star, a cross between Tyrone Power and Cesar Romero. When he and Roha were married they had been the most glamorous couple I had ever seen. I was supposed to be the pageboy at the wedding but at the last minute I decided I looked too ridiculous for words, and I wouldn't go ahead with it. Roha tried to get me into the velvet outfit but I made my body heavy and lumpy and she gave up in despair. Uncle laughed and ruffled my hair. 'Never mind,' he said to Roha. 'If he doesn't want to, he doesn't want to. Too stubborn. Anyway, there are enough stars at this wedding as it is,' he said as he kissed her, 'you and me.' He led her out to the wedding car. He looked like Escamillo and she, in beautiful white lace and satin like Carmen, in the last act of Bizet's opera. Later, at the church, they ran out smiling in a shower of white rose petals.

Thirty years later here they were, Uncle Alex and Roha. The white petals had long browned, shrivelled and dried in my aunt's memory book.

'You'd better stay for tea,' Roha said.

'No,' I answered. 'Thank you, though, for the invitation.'

'You can't expect to come here and then just leave,' she said. 'Your uncle's got a lot to talk to you about. You'll stay. You should have brought Regan with you.'

I walked over to my uncle. He was still grinning, and the grin kept growing larger and wider, the skin stretching and breaking over his teeth. 'I hope you brought a rifle with you, Tama,' he said pleasantly. 'I may as well be shot right here and now in this bed. I'd rather be dead than blind.'

I looked at Roha. Her eyes were shaded from me. 'Don't talk like that, Alex,' she said. 'What's the use of talking like that?' Her voice was tight.

'I'm no good to anybody now, girl,' he told her. 'I shot a bull once. It had gone blind. I put the bullet right here,' he continued, jabbing his fingers insistently at his forehead. 'Here. Here. Here. It was a kindness. The bull kept on blundering into trees and fences. Couldn't even find the cows. So Dad told me to take the rifle and go out into the paddock and shoot it.' Then his mood changed. 'Hey, have those kids said hello to their cousin yet?'

'Yes, Uncle,' I said.

He pierced me with his voice. 'Don't you do it to me too, boy. I may have lost my sight but my ears are as good as they ever were.' He turned to my aunt. 'Don't think I don't know what's going on in this house.'

Roha retreated, a sad smile on her lips.

I gripped Uncle's hands together in mine. The palms were so soft. 'I'm sorry I couldn't come earlier,' I said.

His hair was greasy and shot through with grey. 'Nobody likes to visit a blind man,' he said. He began to laugh again, a shocking sound. 'I think I must be going mad. I can't even sleep because the dark is all the same to me; I don't know what the time is unless the radio is on. I spend my time just listening. Listening. To what's going on. Only I don't know what's going on. Someone could be in the room and I wouldn't know. Your aunt has been trying to get me to go out, but I've seen blind people out on the street. Being helped across intersections. Onto buses. Friends come to see me, but what's the use? Someone's put a hoodoo on me, Tama. They stuck pins in my eyes.'

'It's good to be here, Uncle,' I said. 'Nobody has put anything on you. All your family love you.'

'Love?' he answered. He pulled my head to his and put his lips to my ear. 'Tell you what, though. If you love me, I'll make it worth your while. A thousand bucks, boy. If you shoot me.'

'Not enough,' I joked. I knew he wasn't serious.

'Make it ten thousand. And I'll throw in a new car.'

Uncle was one of the last of the big-time gamblers. Cards, horses, billiards, you name it and Uncle Alexis had at least $500 on it. And there'd be a new car in the street if the loser could not pay any debt to Uncle in cash.

I pushed him away. 'Hey, there,' I said. 'Don't tempt me. You know I'll never take your money now or ever. I'm proud of that, Uncle. It's a thing with me. I'll make my own way. My own money.'

He grew silent. Then he nodded his head. 'You were always too proud. I could never do anything with you.' His face grew gentle. 'Move closer to me, Tama, I want to know that you're here and that you won't make a fool of a blind man by sneaking out while I'm talking.' He seemed to be enjoying an inner joke.

Outside the rain was lashing at the landscape. He began to laugh again.

'You wouldn't remember this,' he said, 'but once I made a bet with Mum about you. You were eleven at the time and you were to receive an award from your school for being the top student in your class. Well, you know your grandmother—she said I had to drive her into Gisborne in the Lagonda to your graduation ceremony. It was such a nuisance. As usual, she got dressed up to the nines in a long black dress and grey fur coat, and she threaded pearls through her hair. "My grandson likes the pearls," she said. She looked really stunning and she winked at me and said, "Not bad for an old lady." So I took her in, and of course she was always good at making entrances with that walking stick banging on the floor. Everything stopped until she sat down. Well, it was so bloody boring, the whole thing. But when you came on to receive your prize, Mum seemed to glow and she changed the whole atmosphere of the place. It was almost as if she willed everybody, forced them to acknowledge your achievement. I was sick of it. She was always making you into something special. Somebody great. So I told her, I bet her, that I could bring you down, make you fall. Like Christ become Lucifer. She turned to me in the darkness and she said something I'll never forget. She replied in biblical language, "No Alex, you will never be able to do that because I have made him into a likeness as unto me." Uncle laughed again. 'I'm still not sure what she meant by that. But she can't say that I haven't tried.'

There is a photograph of the Italian diva, Renata Tebaldi, which suggests something of the look of Riripeti in later years. The face has a madonna smile which belies the strength of intellect and beauty that the soprano possessed. The brow is broad, the nose finely sculptured and aquiline, and the eyes are proud. It is a face which is fitting for such a patrician woman. The hair is lustrous, thick, and a cascade of auburn. My grandmother was like a diva herself and, in the style of her people she proclaimed her nobility with the beautiful moko on her chin.

The photograph of Renata Tebaldi, in colour, appears on the cover of a recital recording which the lyric soprano made in 1965. Curiously enough, the voice of Tebaldi comes even nearer to describing Riripeti than the photograph. It has a splendour which lies not so much in its range as in the evenness with which that range is negotiated. It has a singular beauty in the ravishing pianissimo floating tones that she produces so effortlessly. But there is also a singular strength. With her voice at the pitch of its passion, ah, that is Riripeti, the matriarch indeed, commanding and at her most imperious.

'*A costoro schiava non sono . . . della mia patria degna saro.* I am not a slave . . . I will be worthy of my native land.'

The matriarch. She was playing a game with the child. Her bracelets tinkled like oriental wind chimes as she bent down to his level. The family had just returned to the homestead at Waituhi from church— Riripeti, Grandfather Ihaka, the child's parents Te Ariki and Tiana, and uncles and aunts and their children. Ihaka had taken Te Ariki and the other uncles around the back of the homestead to look at wild horses to be broken in. The child's aunts were busy in the kitchen making family lunch. His cousins had gone off into the hills to play. His mother was nursing his two baby sisters. It was a hot, hot day.

'Let's sneak off,' the matriarch said. She still had on her long black dress and the hat with the veil. 'Let's run away from here.' She lifted the veil and he could see her eyes so dark green and deep that he felt he was falling into them. Tiny pearls glowed in her hair.

He paused. Running away was a very serious business. They had tried it before, he and Grandmother, and they had always been caught. For one thing, the matriarch couldn't really run, not even with a walking stick. In fact she couldn't run at all. For another, you needed a good plan and good timing. Grandmother always had good plans but her timing was really rotten. She always wanted to run away just before Sunday lunch when they most needed a good kai.

'Well, Tamatea, what do you say?' she asked. He was four years old. He was very hungry. He was in his best clothes from church and so was the matriarch. That's what church meant—getting dressed up and sitting in the dark with the family, watching grandfather nodding off halfway through the sermon, being prodded by his mother to keep still, and catching glimpses of the pearls in the matriarch's hair.

'Have you got enough money, Grandmother?' he asked.

She trilled with laughter and the pearls caught fire with the sunlight. 'I've always got money,' she said. 'You remember, don't you, what I told you before. Come to me if you need anything. Okay? Don't take anything from the rest of the family. Only from me, your grandmother. Now haere mai, let's go before they catch us. Kia tere. Kia tere.' She stood up, took his hand and led him swiftly through the willows toward the road. The shade from the willows was cool and welcoming. The bracelets twinkled at the matriarch's wrists as they fled through the shadow and the light.

They came to the gate. The matriarch leant on it for a while, catching her breath. 'Is anyone following us?' she asked.

He looked back at the homestead. He could hear laughter coming from it.

'Is there anybody in hot pursuit?' Smoke was curling from the kitchen chimney. No dogs were barking. He couldn't see his mother. He shook his head. 'Kei te pai,' the matriarch said excitedly. 'Good. Once we hit the bend we'll be safe. Oh, if only my friend Keita still lived around the corner. Then we could have knocked on her door and asked her to let us in. To hide us. Our pursuers wouldn't know where we were, would they?'

While she was talking, the matriarch was carefully removing the pearls from her hair. He put up his palms to receive them as, one by one, she dropped them like tears into his safe keeping. He remembered there had been a strange visitor at church today who had whispered to her companion, 'Look at the Maori woman, look at her! I've never heard of such a thing. Wearing pearls in her hair.' Naturally Grandmother wasn't going to let that go without comment. Right in the middle of the service she had turned to the woman and lifted her veil so that the pearls could gleam with more wonder. 'Oh yes, they're real,' she said loudly so everyone could hear. 'They come from Venice. Even Maori travel abroad. I wear them for the glory of God.' Then she had let her veil fall again. 'Stupid woman,' she had whispered audibly beneath it.

'There,' the matriarch said. 'All set. Just you and me, mokopuna. This time we'll escape forever.'

The dust swirled around the hem of her dress as she paused at the gate. He felt a stirring of excitement. Perhaps Grandmother was right. Perhaps this time they would finally make it and be free. Beyond the bend, that's where freedom was.

They began to hasten down the dusty road, an old woman and a small boy, past the houses of the village of Waituhi, towards the painted meeting house, Rongopai. On either side the maize grew thick and tall like soldiers at attention as they passed, plumes waving like feathers on military hats. Within the fields were the houses, most of them old and falling down. This was Falling Down Land. As they made their way along the road he would glimpse a curtain being lifted or a door cracking open enough for the people inside to stare out at them. Watching them as they fled from the homestead.

'Why don't they help us, Grandmother? Why don't they help us to get away?'

Her walking stick thudded heavily on the road. 'Because they are mortals, mokopuna, and they cannot help us. We are immortal you and I, like the patupaiarehe, the dream people who live in the hills. You know what immortal is? It means that we can never die, you or I. We were born of earthly parents, yes, but we were born different and we *are* different. So they can't help us, these people, can they? But we can help them, ah yes. It is our duty to help our people. To save Waituhi.'

He looked up at the matriarch. He knew she was an important woman in Waituhi. Her great-uncle once owned much of the land here which she inherited. People were very respectful to her not only because of her status but also because she was like a goddess.

She smiled at him. 'Not that you can help much at present,' she said. 'Too skinny and where are your muscles? Never mind, one of these days you'll grow up strong. But for the moment you trust in my strength, my grandson. One of these days, all this will belong to you.' She made a sweeping motion with her walking stick. 'You will need to be strong then.'

The sun did cartwheels in the sky. The crickets began to chirp a loud triumphant chorus. Grandmother knelt down to him and pinned him onto her dream wheel. 'Ah, mokopuna,' she breathed. 'I have strength because I know how to win. I was taught by the best warriors. On my Maori side I was taught to fight like a man. That was not unusual because i nga ra o mua, the women fought beside the men. On my Pakeha side, did I ever tell you that I was once the champion woman fencer here in Turanga? You should have seen me then, mokopuna. I would salute my opponent with the foil and then we would begin: en garde, attack, attack, retreat, parry, strike. My opponents didn't think much of me because I was a Maori you see, and what would a Maori know about the sword? Well, I fixed them. Not only the women but the men also. Their trouble was that they were always too polite. All la-di-da.'

He giggled as the matriarch did a pretend curtsy and tried to skip in a dainty fashion. 'I had the killer instinct, you see,' she breathed. 'That's what you've got to have if you want to win. The killer instinct. En garde, attack, attack, retreat, parry, thrust. Attack, attack, retreat, parry, thrust. But that was long ago.'

Dogs began to bark behind them. He heard voices calling. 'We're not going to make it,' he said.

'Of course we will,' she replied. 'All I have to do is hurry up a little more, that's all. Give me your shoulder, mokopuna. Quickly now.' She placed her weight on him. She was breathless with exhilaration.

Together, their shadows formed a huge misshapen beast, like a hunchback stumbling along the road.

'Hey! Old lady!' He heard his father, Te Ariki, yelling to them.

'Don't look back,' she said. 'If you look back you will lose speed and concentration. That's not how you win.'

They stumbled onward. The bend looked so far away. They would never get there. He could feel Grandmother's weight pressing down on him. Her walking stick was beginning to prod the ground slower. She was breathing heavily. Oh grandmother. The maize standing at attention. The houses falling down. The sun spiralling in the sky.

Then she stopped. The hem of her gown swayed to stillness. 'You go on,' she said. 'Quickly now. I will prevent our enemy from following you.'

'I can't leave you, Grandmother.'

'Obey me,' she said. 'Go, Tama.'

She pushed him away and he began running. He heard war whoops behind him. 'Keep running, Tama, run as fast as you can!' He heard his uncles laughing. He reached the bend. He looked back.

Attack, attack, retreat, parry, strike. There she was, the matriarch, using her walking stick as a sword, fending off her sons. Attack, attack, retreat, parry, strike. One by one she thrust at them, spinning and weaving black patterns with her gown. The veil fluttered across her face. Her movements were controlled and yet fluid as she kept them at bay. Attack, attack, retreat, parry, strike. Whirling and dipping and attacking and pirouetting like a dancer in the eye of the sun.

He ran back to her as one of his uncles disarmed her. She fell on his shoulders, laughing. 'I knew you wouldn't desert me,' she said.

They returned to the homestead. He pressed the pearls back into her keeping. In the distance he saw his mother, Tiana, watching and holding her face in her hands.

2

She said to Uncle Alexis, 'I have made him into a likeness as unto me.'

Over twenty-five years ago, somewhere in the 1950s, she said that to him. I would have been ten or eleven years old then and Uncle would have been perhaps even younger than I am now. Yet he remembered that mystical sequence of words, cast like runes all those years ago at a school breakup ceremony in Gisborne. They were scattered on his memory like pieces of a broken flute. Strange—why do we remember what we remember? Uncle had stumbled across the runes again, dried and splintered as they were, and put them together in their original sequence. The hesitant pursing of the lips, a trembling of fingers along the flute's length and then a slight breathing into the aperture: there had been no noise at first, simply a whistling of the wind through cracks in the bone and a conjuring of the ghosts. The sounds began to tighten, take shape and form. The breath from the throat stirred the magical powers so long locked inside the runes, and a whirlwind had been unleashed. The whirlwind stirred other runes, teasing and shifting back the dust in concentric circles, eddying outward. Something began to glimmer there. A wreath around a face. The face of a patrician woman. My grandmother, Riripeti.

En garde. Strike. Strike. Retreat. Parry. Thrust.

I was watching the flax bending across the bay window of the house that Regan and I had bought after our return from London. The flax was like an army of swords dashing against the glass. Behind, I could hear the occasional rustle as Regan turned the pages of her book—she was reading Lewis Carroll's *Through the Looking Glass* for the umpteenth time. Someone had written to the *New Zealand Listener* and quoted something about borogroves. Regan was such a pedant. It was crucial for her to know whether the 'r' was in the text of not. She was positive that it wasn't. But she was also irritated with me because I was too moody. Damn, damn, damn. She laid down the Carroll.

'This is ridiculous,' she said finally. 'Ever since you went to see your uncle you've been hell to live with. What's it all about?'

'My grandmother,' I replied. 'She said something to Uncle Alexis. He doesn't understand it. I've got an awful feeling that I might, though. Or maybe I don't. I'm all mixed up, and I don't like feeling this way. You know me, I like life all nice and tidy, all wrapped up without loose ends, where everything is easily explained, makes sense and is logical. For one thing, Uncle hinted about how Grandmother treated me as special. I can't remember that. But I've begun remembering other things about her. How she used to wear pearls in her hair. And a name. Paolo di Marchesi. And Venice.'

'Maybe that explains it,' Regan responded with resignation.

'Explains what?' I said.

'Oh, that family of yours. It's so . . . Italian. All this Sicilian passion. I used to think you inherited it from your mother. After all, she's the one you feared because of her murderous moods when you were a boy. But perhaps it comes from your grandmother after all.' Regan paused, puzzled. 'I didn't know your grandmother went to Venice.'

'I didn't say that she did,' I answered. 'But I remember once that somebody told me she had lived in Venice when she was a young girl.'

Regan sighed. She put her book down. 'The trouble with you is that you have a memory like a badger. Something comes into your head and you badger away at it. Badger, badger, badger. And everything else and everybody else has got to stop what they're doing until it's all sorted out. This thing about your grandmother now.' She got up and went into the kitchen. I could hear her putting on the electric jug. If all else fails, have a cuppa tea.

'But I loved Grandmother,' I said. 'I still do.'

'You all loved her,' Regan called from the kitchen. 'Your whole family. The entire Mahana clan, except perhaps your mother. But she married into your tribe, didn't she? Silly isn't it, but I've just thought of something. The one thing that your mother and I have got in common, except for you, is that we're outsiders.' Regan came back into the sitting room. 'I don't belong because I'm a Pakeha. Your mother doesn't because she's from Ngati Porou. That clan of yours is quite overpowering. If we lived in Gisborne it would take over our lives, I know it. I'm sure if your grandmother had been alive now she would never have allowed us to come to Wellington, let alone to marry.'

'We're no different from any other Maori clan,' I said. 'You don't understand.'

'What I understand is that I didn't marry only you, I married your tribe and family too. God, your people have been so prolific and your women so fertile, it's positively indecent. How many of you are there? Your grandmother might only have been one of two children but she had ten children and they had big families too. Your Uncle Manaaki had eight children and your father had nine. And that's only the immediate family.' Regan laughed and gave me her 'Lord Preserve Me' look. 'I guess in this case you're right, you're not too different from other Maori clans. But there's something else. Yes. Hmmmn.' She picked up her book again. Then she put it down. She knew I was waiting for her to complete what she had to say. For a moment I saw puzzlement in her eyes, and then fear.

'Well?' I probed.

'You'll take this all wrong,' she said. 'But there's something else. It's this whole business of being so Italianate. Your family is larger than life. It is a law unto itself. It's ruled by complete obedience by all to the clan. There's no such thing as being disloyal. Yet you people fight among each other such a lot. You tear each other to shreds. You're all so inconsistent. You say you love one another and yet you're always fighting over land or over each other. It's incestuous the way you all battle one minute and love each other the next. It's not ordinary. Not normal. And it is very tiring,'

I went into the kitchen to rescue the jug from boiling over. I tried to imagine the family as an outsider would see it and yes, the family code, Mafia-like, did demand allegiance particularly to the male line, the ascendant, at all cost. None of the Mahana clan had ever left it; instead, what we had all done was to bring our unsuspecting brides and stumbling husbands into it. And entry was only allowed if the family code was observed: whatever the family did was not to be questioned and, should its chauvinism ever place it under threat of law or morality, it was to be protected.

I remembered poor Aunt Helen who, like my Regan, had married into the family. Six years after gentle Uncle Manaaki died, Aunt Helen endeavoured to prevent another of my uncles, Pita, from seducing her daughter. Aunt Helen made a dramatic appearance at a family gathering to demonstrate against this gross indecency. A supplicant, she flew from Wellington to Gisborne to plead the case of her daughter. She asked the family to prevent my uncle from taking her to bed with him. She had been met with seeming sympathy—until my uncle himself had arrived. One by one the family members left my aunt, alone in the middle of the floor, to hug him and kiss him and welcome him into the protection of the clan. Aunt Helen made a direct appeal to my father as head of the clan, but not a word was said to my uncle, not even by Dad. My mother was in a smouldering mood. She strode across to Aunt Helen and took her away to our home. 'Te Ariki,' she said to Dad as she passed him, 'you have been weak. You should not have let this happen.'

Rebellious, my sisters and I sought out our father. We found the whole business disgusting. 'Keep out of it,' Te Ariki said. 'This is none of your business.' Our uncle wanted to say hello to us. My sister Teria told him she never wished to see him or speak to him again.

Our father gripped her arm and told her to be respectful. 'And will I be next, Dad?' she asked. 'And if I am, and if you are still living, will you approve? No, Dad. No.'

Afterwards, sitting alone with Te Ariki, I argued fiercely. 'You're the head of the clan,' I said. 'Why don't you put a stop to it? They would listen to you. Tell Uncle Pita to leave his niece alone. Order him.' While we were arguing, my mother came into the room.

'It's none of your business,' Dad repeated.

'Look,' I answered, 'I'm too old to be fobbed off as if I was still a kid. I used to believe everything you said. I thought everything you told me was the truth, but I now discover that it's only the truth according to the Mahana code. If the family does it, it is right, isn't it, Dad?'

My father blistered me with his anger. 'Don't you act so superior to me, son. Your fancy words don't mean anything. Live a little longer and maybe you'll get a little wiser.'

My mother was still, so still, in the room. I looked at her. I wasn't going to let my father get away with it that easily. 'This clan is always acting so holy and so God-fearing. Ah yes, such a praying family. Our Father Who art in Heaven. Well, don't you ever quote your bible at me again. And don't you ever try to tell me what's right and what's wrong because I don't believe you know. I think you must have known once, Dad, but not any longer. The family that sleeps together stays together, that's it, isn't it Dad?'

He hit me. I fell against the china cabinet. I waited for the next blow. It did not come. There was a flash of silver and my mother was there. She interposed herself between myself and Te Ariki. She looked large and strong in the light. Her eyes were so dark that I felt I was looking into murder. She stood there, unblinking, her face like a sphinx and without expression.

'Titiro ki au,' she said to Dad. 'Te Ariki, look at me. Look at me. You know the boy is right. Te Ariki, remember.'

My mother had a habit of tilting her face so that the light struck its planes with strength, with resolution. My father gave a deep cry, like a lost hawk in the night. He went to embrace her. She let him take her in his arms.

'That does it,' I thought. I took the tea back to the sitting room. Then I went to the telephone in the hall. 'Don't be too long,' Regan said. 'And don't speak too loud, otherwise you'll wake Bianca and Miranda.'

I looked up Uncle Alex's number. My aunt answered the phone. 'Oh, it never rains but it pours,' she said.

'Can I speak to Uncle?' I asked. 'It's about my grandmother.'

'Riripeti?' Aunt asked. 'Sorry, but tonight is the night he has to go to the hospital to have some tests on his eyes. One of the boys has taken him in. I'm not sure when he'll be back. Why don't you call him later. Better still, come around to see him.' She paused. 'I guess I can't help you, can I?'

'It's just that Uncle Alex said a couple of things about the family and Grandmother that have been puzzling me ever since. Could you ask him if he knows whether Grandmother ever lived in Italy? Venice?'

'Italy?' my aunt asked. 'What on earth would she have been doing in Italy?'

'I'm positive she said something about it to me when I was a small boy. Something about Venice. How she was taught to use the sword there.'

'The sword? I don't know anything about that. The old lady was a good sportswoman, sure. She was a crack shot too, and I did hear she was a champion rollerskater in Gisborne in the old days. That's before she had the accident.'

'This is ridiculous,' I whispered to Regan. 'My aunt says that Riripeti used to rollerskate. Surely they didn't have rollerskates in those days?'

'Then you know about the hockey trophies she won,' Aunt continued. 'I don't know about the sword. Oh yes, I heard she was good at the taiaha, too. But the sword? She was always telling you things that she never told us. It might be true. Then again it mightn't. You and Riripeti used to live in your own special world.'

'Well, do you know when she was born?'

'Alex's mother? Nobody really knows for certain. That's why she always used to joke about being immortal. I know that they put

1890 on her headstone. I think it was 1890, anyway.' Then she said, 'Look, I don't think Alex will know what you want. You should ask your cousin Whai. He might have the answers to all your questions. He's supposed to be the big shot with the whakapapa, the one who knows the family's history.'

I put the receiver down. Then I rang Whai.

'Kia ora, cousin,' I said when Whai answered. 'Do you know when Riripeti was born? Can you tell me anything about her?'

I heard him pause, and then a huge roar of laughter came down the phone. 'So the sleeper awakes! I was wondering when you would start asking about Artemis.'

'Artemis?'

'Your grandmother's Pakeha name,' he explained. 'You didn't know?' There was a pause. 'There'll be no stopping once you've started. Let's have coffee this Thursday. It's taken you long enough to start asking your questions. Are you sure you will be able to live with the answers?'

Bothered by Whai's veiled words, I put the receiver down. I walked back to the bay window. I took a sip of my tea. It was cold. En garde. Attack. Attack. Retreat.

Behind me, I heard Regan give a cry of triumph. 'I knew I was right,' she said. 'I knew it! It's borogoves without an r. The line in full is "All mimsy were the borogoves".' She looked up at me. 'It's from the poem called *Jabberwocky*,' she explained.

'What on earth is a jabberwocky?'

'A fantastic monster. It gets killed by a knight. In Lewis Carroll. I'll write to the *Listener* and point out that Carroll has been misquoted. Can't have that. I feel so vindicated. Want another cup of tea?'

I smiled across at her. Swords rattled against the windows like old ghosts.

Let us in, let us in. Oh, let us in.

༅

Sex permeated all aspects of Maori life. In the mythology of creation, it was the god Tane who sought to create a race of people who might live on earth. He therefore fashioned a mortal woman from the mud and earth and mated with her. Her name was Hineahuone, literally 'Woman made of soil' and she had a daughter, Hinetitama, whom Tane also mated with. This was the first incest and of it, the race of humankind was born.

Later, Hinetitama began to ask questions about who her father was. In those days, the house posts of the wharenui, the meeting house, could talk. When she asked them the question, they replied 'Tane the father is also Tane the husband.' Upset and ashamed, she fled, horrified, to the underworld and, transcendent, became Hine Nui Te Po, Great Mother of the Underworld. But in the early written texts, which my grandmother always disputed, Hine Nui Te Po was considered to be a malevolent Goddess of Death. In this incarnation, when the demi-god Maui tried to conquer her by entering her vagina, she crushed him with her thighs and thus death and destruction were brought permanently into the world. The female reproductive organs were termed 'whare o aitua' or 'whare o mate', the house of misfortune and disaster.

Woman was therefore non-sacred and destructive. In the traditional Maori society that developed, beliefs about women's activities, both prescribed and proscribed, wrongly emerged from this belief.

They are all gone now, gone into the Night, into Te Po, all the old people who knew Grandmother, all gone into Te Po Nakonako, Te Po Uriuri, Te Po Roa, the Night Endless and Unending.

The last to go was her childhood friend, Keita, who saw you coming from afar at a Maori gathering in Rotorua over a year ago. She began to call to you in Maori. Her voice was like Riripeti's and you could see Grandmother's look in her. The years ripped back between you as you stepped slowly towards her.

Grandmother had died over twenty-five years ago and this woman, her closest friend, had seen Riripeti and many others of the iwi go to the graveyard at Waituhi. She reached for you as you came, and you could see that she was old. Her eyes were lidded with yellow and her dark-pitted skin hung loosely on her face. In that gathering, with the modern world encasing you with its unnatural sounds, a world that must have seemed so incomprehensible to her, you embraced. 'E Tama,' Keita said, 'When I see you I see Riripeti's beloved. She loved you, yes, oh yes. She gave you a task. One of these days, return to it.'

Yes, even Keita has gone now.

As arranged, I meet my cousin Whai at a restaurant on The Terrace, Wellington.

'Yes, Aunt Roha is quite right,' he begins. 'Nobody, even these days, is too sure about the accuracy of birthdates of Maori people. There are still instances where Maori apply for the pension only to find that they have been registered in a different year, often under a different name and to a different parent.' He laughs. 'Do you know that old calypso song? "Woe is me, shame and scandal in the family?" It goes on about sisters not being sisters, and brothers not being brothers and so on. There's a lot of that in Maori birth registrations, I can tell you.'

Whai Mahana would prefer that I call him, more accurately, my uncle. He works as a senior librarian in the National Library, one of the very few Maori librarians in the country, and is highly regarded for his knowledge of Maori history. He is a fine man, tough, and some think him arrogant. I have always found him to be gentle and kind, a little lofty, but affectionate. He is wearing a pin-striped suit and is going bald. In his mid-forties, he is putting on weight.

'Anyway, what were we talking about?' he continues. 'Oh yes, Artemis. I never knew my auntie well, but there's no doubt she was a taniwha in the Maori world. She was on the same level as Apirana Ngata, Peter Buck, Maui Pomare . . . but, like Te Puea, she was one of only a very few women who were of the same rank as the men. And there was something about her, something extra, that only Maori women from Gisborne or the Coast possess. You can tell from the way they do the women's haka. The whole body is involved in the action. The stamping of the feet. The swing of the hips—nobody puts so much strength into the women's haka as our own women from the Coast. All other Maori women do it to look pretty. But our women do it like men.'

He sips his coffee. 'I hear Artemis was like that. A woman who, transcending her sex, was also able to function as a man would in the world. She never regarded herself as being less than them. If Artemis had been in the land wars against the Pakeha, she would have been in the front line of the attack, there's no doubt about that. And people would have had faith in her leadership and followed her, that's the important point.

'As I said before, a lot of our women are like that. Hana Konewa was one. Hine Te Ariki was another. You can see it in Whaia McClutchie today, in Te Mamaka Jones, Keri Kaa and Tilly Reedy. The interesting thing is that all these women were or are *unafraid*. And Whaia notwithstanding,' he smiles, 'all of them had and have amazing beauty. Look at Donna Awatere, that radical cousin of ours up in Auckland, and our other cousin Atareta Poananga. Pakeha tend to regard them suspiciously as being less Maori, because they are so beautiful. And they certainly cannot understand a person like Donna, where nothing fits. She's a university graduate, a psychologist for the Department of Health, trained overseas as a mezzo-soprano, and she gives it all up to return to Aotearoa to lead protests at Bastion Point or over the Treaty of Waitangi! And there's Atareta—the same thing, a brilliant degree in political science in Auckland, her father was with the UN Force in the Middle East, now she is with Foreign Affairs, looking like a Parisian model—she is probably more of a radical than Donna is. She smoulders. Nobody can dampen her fire, her passion. That's the kind of person your grandmother was—of that taniwha line of fearless women. In fact, these days, you look around and, huh, it seems as if all our men have gone soft. The women seem to be doing most of the protesting and jumping up and down these days. Certainly they are the ones who are taking Maori issues to the extremities of action.

'I guess beauty, of the amazing kind, has a leadership power of its own. But beauty is not enough, of course, in the Maori world where the power is mainly with the men—where women are not usually able to speak on the marae. They are not allowed. The arena of debate is the arena of men only. If you're a woman and you want to break the rules, you really have to know your stuff, the stuff that is usually taught only to the men in the whare wananga—the cut and thrust of debate, the historical and genealogical references, the protocol. A woman has to be a virtual superhuman to be able to do this and get away with it. Like the fabled taniwha of ancient times, the women must be both human and superhuman, natural and supernatural. And of course, in Artemis's case, she was able to call on the natural world to help her, particularly on her kaitiaki, the poisonous black spider with the red moko on its back.

'Beauty, intellectual skill, the ability to debate in a hostile arena and to obtain the support of the natural world—these are some of the things that Artemis had. She was a real Maori woman of the kind about whom legends are told. Boy, she wasn't afraid to stand up at a hui and let rip. And of course she looked so fantastic with those pearls and black gowns, quite out of place. She had a mystique, and I'm sure she cultivated it on purpose. And nobody, but nobody, was going to tell her to sit down until she was good and ready to. You know what it is like on a marae. Even if you're a man and you speak out of turn you get clobbered. Think how much worse it would be for a woman! But I understand that she was able to hold more than her own in any debate. And as I said before, she was able to persuade people to take faith in her leadership. To trust in her as leader of her people.'

He pauses and orders another cup of coffee, enquiring whether I would like a cup also. 'Then on top of all this she had the mana which was passed to her from her chief and great-uncle Wi Pere Halbert.'

There is a note of self-importance in Whai's monologue at this point—he sees himself as being very much in Wi Pere Halbert's mould.

'If you really want to understand your grandmother, I think you have to go back beyond the time when she was born, beyond 1890, back to when Wi Pere's father, Thomas Halbert, arrived in New Zealand in 1832. I say this because as you know your grandmother was a woman of extraordinary accomplishment. But she didn't just happen to be that way. It was cultivated in her. She had few peers, as a Maori woman in the Maori world—your father will be able to tell you about that. There was more—educated by Wi Pere, she was also able to be a taniwha in the Pakeha world, operating between both. Te Puea was the same. You wouldn't believe it now, but there was a certain grandeur in the Gisborne and East Coast districts which Artemis was heiress to. Not that Gisborne society was much, but there was the occasional ball or hunt. Artemis, by all accounts, was a fine huntswoman. Well, that part of her life is derived directly from the Thomas Halbert line, down through his son Wi Pere. I suspect that Wi Pere recognised her leadership qualities. He saw in her the kind of killer instinct, the power of arrogance, that he had himself. This may be why he cast his mantle on her.'

Whai looks me straight in the eye.

'And this might explain, also, the Italian connection. I know that in 1895 Wi Pere travelled to Europe in an effort to raise funds to buy Maori land back for Maori. He was rumoured to have stopped off in Venice. If he took Artemis with him, and left her there, she would have been five years old. What we know is that date coincides with the period from 1895 to 1911 when she disappeared. When she came back, she was ready to take on the purpose for which Wi Pere had prepared her. In 1909, seeing the relentless conquest of the land by the Pakeha, and himself being unable to stop it, Wi Pere made a declaration in the Upper House of Parliament that was implacable in its ferocity. "All the Pakehas," he vowed, "should be driven into the sea."

'All her life, Artemis was devoted to this kaupapa. Don't you remember what happened on Parliament Grounds in Wellington in 1949?'

~

Riripeti smiled through her veil. Above her the sky was grey, the cold winds storming from the south and shredding the clouds. She bent down and took the child's hands in hers. She pressed them, one to each side of her face, and kissed them.

'E mokopuna,' she breathed. 'Your hands are so cold.' She began to rub her face over his hands, back and forth, with tenderness. The pearls shivered as she did so. The veil tingled on his skin.

'Haere mai ra i te reo o te ra, haere mai ra,' came the high-pitched call of welcome from the forecourt of Parliament. 'Come in, the voice of the day, welcome.'

There was a rustle of anticipation in the ope, the group who had come from Te Whanau a Kai, Rongowhakaata and Te Aitanga a Mahaki and who numbered eighty or so. The travelling party had been hastily assembled and had travelled by buses and cars throughout the previous day and night to get from Waituhi to Wellington. Only yesterday had Riripeti found out about the meeting of all the Maori chiefs of Aotearoa at Parliament to work out a national settlement for Maori grievances regarding lands confiscated from them in the Land Wars.

But she had not been invited. Her anger was palpable. It was the last day of the parliamentary meeting. Her people's grievances had yet to be heard. She had even had to wait almost an hour before the Prime Minister and the other Maori chiefs would agree to admit her.

'E kui,' Aunt Floria said. 'We better start before they change their minds.'

Riripeti nodded. 'Then let us ascend the Valley of the Kings,' she said, 'and speak with Pharaoh, the Prime Minister, in his royal palace.' She called Grandfather Ihaka and her chief adviser, Tamati Kota to her side. 'We shall go forward in the shape of the female spider,' she told them. 'When Pharaoh sees the attack formation, he will know that his tireless adversary has come to confront him again.'

In an instant the ope coalesced and, shimmering with anger, the attacking spider appeared. Riripeti and her group of senior women were in front; they were the eyes of the spider. Immediately behind them were the elders, other members of the ope, men, women and children; they were the body. Maori warriors, stripped for action, were the legs—eight legs in all, with two kai taiaha, spear-carrying warriors—ready to spring forward and carry the spider to the gateway.

'Haere mai ra e kui ma, e koro ma i te Po,' came the call again. 'Come Riripeti, come with your people, come children, to the call of our ancestral home, standing here. Gather our dead to be wept over today, welcome.'

Riripeti gave the order. 'Timata. Begin.'

The two kai taiaha sped swiftly through the gateway and achieved maximum extension. The legs of the spider flexed, and it sprang into sight. Immediately there was a roar of acclamation.

'Anei. Look. It is Riripeti. It is the Matua. It is the Matriarch.'

And for the first time, the child saw Te Paremata o te Pakeha, the Parliament of the European, like a crouching sphinx four storeys tall. Beside it was another building, the General Assembly, the great library of European knowledge. Waiting upon a vivid red carpet on the stairway of Parliament was the Prime Minister, the chiefs he had invited to talk with him and other guests and visitors. They numbered over a thousand. Truly a triumphal display of pharaonic power.

'Haere mai ra nga mate o te tau, o te marama, o te wiki,' the welcoming call came for the third time. 'Come the dead of the year, of the month, of the week who have gone beyond the veil, haere atu ra.'

Still Riripeti gave no sign. She seemed to be waiting for something.

'Matua . . .' Aunt Floria said, 'we should respond to the welcome.'

'We are not all here,' Riripeti answered. 'The callers wish us to come bearing our dead? Our dead are not with us yet.'

It was at that moment that the south wind began to fade, become still. The clouds above Parliament stopped their flight across the sky.

The wind changed, blowing from the east, from the tribal lands of Te Whanau a Kai, Rongowhakaata and Te Aitanga a Mahaki. With it came the past with all its memories of those who had gone before. Riripeti bowed her head, in grief, at the remembrance of beloved elders, women and children which swirled around her. The pearls in her hair shimmered with sorrow.

Then she lifted her head. 'Now we are all here,' she said. 'Let the welcoming call be answered.'

Immediately four warriors, carrying trumpets made from ram's horns, lifted them to their lips and blew. The sound began to bray, powerfully, across the forecourt, louder and louder, until the child wanted to put his hands to his ears.

Riripeti looked at the buildings before her. 'What?' she smiled. 'Still standing?'

It was then that she removed her veil.

('Yes, I was there,' the retired journalist said. 'I was reporting on the meeting for the *Evening Post*. There'd been some concern by our Pakeha readers about what the Prime Minister would agree to in his discussions on the future of the Maori people and Maori land. Well, of course, everybody, all the rangatira Maori and Pakeha, were there—at least that's what we thought. Then on the third day of the meeting, this group arrived. It was led by your grandmother, Artemis. My God! How well I remember it! The Prime Minister and the Maori chiefs had almost reached an accord and there was some hostile reaction, I can tell you.

'The upshot was that Artemis was kept waiting for an hour, I think. Then she sent a message, "If you do not do me the courtesy of welcoming me I will come on anyway, welcome or not welcome.' Well, the prospect of an incident occurring on Parliament Grounds was not a happy one for the Prime Minister's officials, especially his private secretary, Bernard Scott, or Timoti, his highest-ranking Maori public servant. Timoti was dead against welcoming her but Bernard persuaded the Prime Minister it was better to let her join the meeting rather than gatecrash it. Even so, there was still violent opposition, so agreement was reached without consensus. You know more than I do about the status of women in your society, and the way in which they are not recognised as leaders.

'But the powhiri was done, and I can still remember how heart-stopping a moment it was when your iwi appeared. One second, there was nobody there. Next moment, a spider—that's the only way I can describe it—reached through, sprang, and when I looked again, there was Artemis, a woman in black veils, surrounded by her tribe, with warriors flexing and protecting her.

'I was standing next to an old Maori man. "So the elders thought they could get away with not inviting the Matua did they?" he chuckled.

'That wasn't all. Suddenly the wind died down. Then it began to blow, from the east I think. When that happened, the entire forecourt reverberated with the sound of ancient trumpets. It was at that moment that your grandmother removed her veil. I said before that Artemis was a striking woman, but none of us were prepared to see her like that—so extraordinarily beautiful.')

There was a roar from the assembly.

('I took a photograph of the occasion,' the journalist said. 'Regrettably, something was wrong and it did not come out. But I can still see that face in my mind's eye. The way the pearls, yes, pearls in her hair, glistened in the wind. The way her black gown drifted about her. And sometimes I still see her eyes and the clouds reflected in them. Oh, she was superb!')

The chief caller for the host assembly nodded her head in recognition. 'Ara, so the matriarch has arrived. Well, well, well. Time to start the karanga again.' She lifted her voice and together with the other women callers, they welcomed Riripeti forward.

'E Te Whanau a Kai, Rongowhakaata me Te Aitanga a Mahaki,' she sang, 'na taku potiki koe o Wi Pere i tiki atu i tahu atu o te rangi, i kukume mai, haere mai, haere mai, haere mai, haere mai.'

Riripeti nodded. 'That's better,' she said. She gave the sign that the karanga should be returned. Immediately, Aunt Floria and the other women began to reply. The sounds echoed and re-echoed backward, like one archway of sound being built upon another archway of sound. Great elemental doors opened in the sky, opening and opening and opening.

The whole atmosphere of the assembly changed. It was as if it had been charged with all the energy of heaven and earth. Then came the climax as, during the karanga, the powhiri began.

'Hei runga, hei raro,' the welcoming group thundered. The fronds of greenery moved up and down, in rhythmic actions to hit the thighs like cymbals. 'Kumea mai, te waka,' the group chanted. 'Toia mai, te waka. Haul the canoe. Drag the canoe. To the anchoring place the canoe. To the resting place the canoe. To the lying place to lie, the canoe.' The matriarch was standing with a madonna smile on her lips. Then the child saw that she was looking at him from the corner of her eyes.

Audaciously, she winked. 'This is for you, too, mokopuna, this welcome done to me.'

And Aunt Hiraina knelt down beside him and whispered in his ear. 'Trust your grandmother to put on a good show,' she giggled. 'These people got their beans today. She's forced them to acknowledge her in the appropriate manner. And now that it has been done in the proper way nobody is going to dare to stop her from taking her place as a chief among them. Not now that they have established her mana.'

The karanga and the powhiri came to an end. Riripeti stood there like a spear in the sky. Then she signalled to the ope that it was time to take their seats and to await the speeches of welcome from the elders of the assembly.

The child's mother, Tiana, came to take him to sit among the iwi.

'He sits with me,' Riripeti said, 'in his rightful place.' She brushed his forehead with her lips. Then she placed him beside her and Grandfather and other elders in the front row.

'He should not sit with us,' Ihaka hissed.

She ignored him. 'Now battle begins,' she said to the child. 'The Prime Minister and the chiefs of Maoridom thought I would not come, did they? Do they think they can represent me and my people? No, they cannot. Only I can speak for my iwi. I am the only one who is their mangai, their mouthpiece. Let them take my power at their peril. I'll really do what Wi Pere wanted to do—drive them all into the sea. And the sea will overpower them, just as it did Pharaoh when his cohorts tried to enslave Moses and the Israelites again.'

She pointed out the Prime Minister. 'Tamatea, remember. Always fight. Never give up. Your mana will help you. Fight fair if you can. But if you must, use whatever devices are at hand. Remember.'

The sky turned in Riripeti's eyes. A Maori elder was reflected there, standing to make ritual welcome to the ope. The matriarch turned to hear what he was saying. She was magnificent, alert and watchful.

The child turned and saw his mother, Tiana. Her face was a pale star in a dark heaven.

⌀

Thomas Halbert, the matriarch's great-grandfather, could not have been a prepossessing man. He was known to the Maori people in Turanga as 'Tame Puti' or 'Tommy Short'. Born in Newcastle-on-Tyne, the younger son of Robert Halbert, he was of Anglo-Scottish descent. I envisage him as being rather stumpy, with a barrel chest, bow legs and a lot of red hair. I say this because there seems to be a strain of this sort which the family has inherited and which is definitely not from the Maori side. It was from his wife, Riria, in other words, that the beauty of the family came, the fine aristocratic looks. (For all that, I am delighted that one of my daughters, Bianca, has inherited that red hair of Thomas Halbert.)

Why he and his older brother, James, left Newcastle-on-Tyne, nobody knows. Nor is anything known of his life there. I tried to find out when Regan and I visited England during our time in Europe, but Newcastle-on-Tyne was one of those places where we didn't want to dally. It had the look of a city still in the middle of industrial chaos—narrow cobbled streets, railway overbridges, and houses tightly terraced in dirty brick.

In his early twenties, a bit of an adventurer but basically honest, Thomas left home without regret. He had a little beard. His hair was cropped short. His parents did not shed tears at his going and neither did he. There was a ship at the docks on which he had a berth. He simply left, that's all there was to it. He had no sweetheart.

Thomas's brother James left the ship in Sydney; he sired ten children during his lifetime on that harsh continent. As for Thomas, he reached Poverty Bay in 1832, landing from a three-masted whaler, and went to trade at Mahia Peninsula for a short period before he settled permanently in Poverty Bay.

At the time the major trader of the area was John Williams

Harris, possibly the first European shore-trader in Poverty Bay—he has in fact been called 'the Founder of Poverty Bay' and 'Monarch of All He Surveyed' a typical piece of Pakeha egoism! But certainly there were a few Pakeha: in the Royal Geographical Society's Journal of 1832, p. 135, there is an item as below:

'Hawke's Bay: At Turanga, in this bay, is a flax establishment, with five or six white men resident.'

Born in Cornwall, England, in 1808, Harris was sent to New Zealand by J.B. Montefiore and Co., merchants, of Sydney, during the early stages of the flax boom to establish trading stations in the Gisborne–East Coast region. It is likely that Harris gladly welcomed Thomas Halbert and offered him the job at Mahia.

It was at Mahia that Thomas Halbert made the first of his six matrimonial contracts. His wife, whose name is not known, belonged to the Rongomaiwahine iwi; she had a son who died in infancy. At this stage cannibalism had not died out completely at Mahia and one day, Halbert and his assistant received portions of a human body which had been sent to them as a gift. The two men did not bury the remains because they felt that if the grave was found they might fall under suspicion of murder. I can see them debating the issue with typical Scottish deliberation. Thomas Halbert would have been very canny.

He left Mahia and moved to Gisborne, probably around 1833 or 1834. His first wife did not accompany him when he returned to Poverty Bay. I imagine that there was more comfort than love in the relationship and that, as when he had left Newcastle-on-Tyne, no tears were shed. He took up residence at Muriwai and his trading shop was in the location now known as 'The Willows'. Soon he began to do roaring business, selling muskets as well as tobacco, blankets and other assorted trinkets. But this venture was short-lived because his Maori (and Pakeha) customers had persistent cash-flow difficulties which meant that he had to over-extend their credit—a fact that his son, the matriarch's great-uncle, was able to use to political advantage. Wi Pere Halbert would often remind opponents of any of his deals or arrangements that they owed him for unpaid debts to his father.

Thomas Halbert's second wife was Pirihira Konekone of Te Aitanga a Mahaki. They quarrelled after she became pregnant, and she went to live with Lazarus (Raharuhi) Rukupo who, having no children of his own, gladly adopted her infant at birth. The child was named Otene Pitau, and he became a leader of the iwi at Pakirikiri. Otene Pitau married Mere Whiti Hone, and died at Manutuke on 13 August 1921.

The third wife of Thomas Halbert was Mereana Wero, also of Te Aitanga a Mahaki, but she was quickly displaced by a rival—my grandmother's great-great-aunt, Riria Mauaranui. As the story has it, Mereana was so disgusted at being slighted in such a manner that she took a Negro for her husband; there was no issue from the union. She then entered into another marriage and became the mother of Peka Kerekere.

Meanwhile, Riria Mauaranui swept onto centre stage and became the fourth wife of Thomas Halbert. She was a chieftainess, having great prestige throughout the Gisborne district, with descent lines that linked her closely to all ariki of Te Whanau a Kai, Rongowhakaata and Te Aitanga a Mahaki. So great was her mana that when she was captured with her people by the Tuhoe at Hauturu in 1826, she was released. Rather that, than face the wrath of her iwi in any battle to free her. She was escorted back to her own people.

Riria Mauaranui was therefore a woman with her own substantial land. Perhaps this is why Thomas Halbert was attracted to her. But why she agreed to the marriage with him, Tame Puti, the Pakeha with the barrel chest and ridiculous red hair, was a mystery. She was much younger than he was. Perhaps she was looking for someone from the Pakeha world who was of equal mana to her. There would have been very few white men to choose from.

It was Riria Mauaranui who bore the son, Wi Pere Halbert, who was destined to play such an important part in the political life of Poverty Bay and the East Coast. He told the Native Land Court (Gisborne minute book, No. 26) that he was born on 7 March 1837, and that date also appears in his own account of his life which was posthumously published in the *Gisborne Times* in 1916.

In that same year, Thomas Halbert and Riria Mauaranui moved

from Muriwai to Gisborne township on the Turanganui River. There, he returned to work for John Williams Harris, helping Harris to operate his whaling station. But he retained his home at Muriwai. Called Pouparae, the position of the dwelling is shown on a marine survey plan of the East Coast which was compiled in 1837 by Captain Wing of the schooner *Trent*. His neighbours then, according to evidence given before the Poverty Bay Crown Grants Commission in 1869, were William Morris, James Wilson and Peter Simpson.

Thomas Halbert returned to Pouparae in 1839 for the purpose of rearing pigs for export. During the hearing of his claim to the property he stated that Wi Pere Halbert was his only child at the time of the purchase. His omission of Otene Pitau can be explained only by the suggestion that, as Lazarus had adopted that child, he felt he had no further claim on him.

From the beginning Wi Pere benefited from being of both Maori and Pakeha descent. On his Maori side, he was raised under the tutelage of his mother, and priests and teachers of the whare wananga—the higher school of learning. He was clearly marked out to be a leader. On his Pakeha side, his father's position within the mercantile class enabled him to be embraced by them and to advance within Pakeha society. When Thomas Halbert acknowledged him as his eldest and heir, Wi Pere's ascent into the world of politics as a Maori–Pakeha, negotiating between both worlds, was assured.

How long Thomas Halbert and Riria Mauaranui were married is not known. After their relationship ended, he married for the fifth time. His fifth wife was Kaikere, of Rongowhakaata. This was a durable marriage which produced four daughters: Keita, who became the wife of James Ralston Wyllie and, after his death, of M.J. Gannon; Mere, who became Mrs Heany and, later, Mrs Donald Gordon; Maata, who became Mrs Cuff; and Sarah, who was the mother of Moana Paratene. A sister of Moana's married Rewiti Kohere, of East Cape.

The sixth and final wife of Thomas Halbert was Maora Pani, also of Rongowhakaata. She had been married previously and came to Thomas Halbert with a daughter. She bore Halbert a son, Thomas Halbert Jnr, twins who died in infancy, and a daughter called

Matewai who became Mrs Mataira of Nuhaka. She remarried after Halbert's death.

Death in a terrible form overtook Thomas Halbert one dark night in April 1865. He had been drinking on board a schooner that was lying in the Taruheru River near Makaraka. He would have been about sixty—paunchy, his red hair thinned and grey. He had made an interesting life out of nothing; a successful career in a country far away from home. To his contemporaries he would have been 'that stumpy Scot who has gone native like many of them', but I don't think he would have cared about his reputation. He had nothing to uphold except his allegiances to his children. I doubt that he had any allegiances to New Zealand—he simply lived, making his life as it came, accepting whatever it was with a shrug of the shoulders and a careless passivity.

So there he was, drinking on a schooner with two brothers named Yates. It was late, and they decided it was time to go home. They stumbled into their flat-bottomed boat and began to pole back to the landing place. Perhaps it was one of the Yates brothers who made the mistake but, somehow or other, the boat overturned in a shallow, muddy spot. According to the correspondent of the *Hawke's Bay Herald*, all three were wearing heavy sea boots. One of the Yates brothers got ashore, but the other and Thomas Halbert sank so deep in the silt that they could not extricate themselves. I can imagine Thomas Halbert laughing at the situation, being stuck there in the mud, and joking about the predicament. 'Hey, George' (the other Yates brother), 'gi'e us a hand will ye to extricate mesel' fram this muddy parritch.' And I can hear George giggling back, a bottle of whisky in his hand. 'Och, I'm up to me bluidy knees in the stuff mesel', Tom.' And perhaps Thomas Halbert yells back, 'Weel, if you're no help to me, lad, throw me the whuskie bottle so I can whet me whistle.' Maybe the moon is shining and making silver the incoming tide. Perhaps they knew that the end was near. I like to think of them passing the bottle and getting so blind drunk that by the time the tide finally came up past their eyes they were too insensible to tell the difference between water and whisky.

And Riria Mauaranui, you ask? Nobody knows why it was that

she separated from Thomas Halbert, but he did use Riria's influence to purchase tribal land, including some of her own, which he later sold. Was this what caused enmity between them? Whatever the reason, she re-established her ranking in Te Whanau a Kai and assured her son, Wi Pere, of his greatness. Perhaps she was the one of his wives—if the story is true—that Thomas Halbert took back to the Old Country on a short visit. If the visit did occur it would have been the one inconsistent act in his life, an act of passion, for a dark native woman would not have been welcomed in the Newcastle-on-Tyne of the late 1840s or 1850s. But I reckon that she would have given as good as she got, judging from family temperament. During the time that I was in England, as I wandered in the twilight of the hills or the city streets of London, I was often teased by the thought, 'Ha, Riria was here.' Or at least her scorn of that place.

All New Zealand schoolchildren are taught about Captain James Cook's discovery of New Zealand and his historic landfall at Poverty Bay in the *Endeavour* on October 1769. They are told that the event was quite glorious—that a lad at the masthead shouted 'Land Ahoy!' at 2 p.m. on that day, a curly-headed youth after whom the landform that he had sighted, Young Nick's Head, was named. They are then asked to imagine the sight as the *Endeavour* anchored off the mouth of the Turanganui River. They are told, to some amusement, that the reaction of the Maori people on shore was one of awe for the huge white bird, the floating island, and the multicoloured gods who had come on the bird. Ah yes, the stuff of romance indeed!

But what the schoolchildren are not told is that Cook's first landing was marked by the killing of a Maori called Te Maro, shot through the heart by a musket bullet, Monday 9 October 1769. Then on the morning of Tuesday 10 October 1769, another Maori called Te Rakau was shot and killed, and three others were wounded. During the afternoon of that same day a further four Maori were murdered in the bay merely because they had showed fight when molested, and three of their companions were taken captive.

Captain James Cook claimed New Zealand for Britain. The *Endeavour* finally left Poverty Bay on Thursday 12 October 1769. The glorious birth of the nation has the taste of bitter almonds when one remembers that six Maori died so that a flag could be raised, and that the *Endeavour* had lain in Poverty Bay for only two days and fourteen hours.

3

The matriarch was walking with the child along the banks of the Waipaoa River. The river was lined with weeping willows, the branches forming a lustrous canopy of green leaves falling, falling, falling into the slow moving water.

'*Piangea cantando, nell'erma landa, piangea la mesta,*' she sang, a sad waiata of willows, '*o salce, salce, salce.*' The hem of her long black gown was wet from the cold moss. Small puffs of wind scattered sun-stars across the water. Then, 'Come, mokopuna,' she smiled.

She took his left hand, stepped away from the riverbank and guided him into a forest where the trees were gilded by the sun. 'This is my sanctuary,' she told the child. 'All are forbidden to come here except for me—and now you.' Yellow and red leaves were falling, showers of golden and red like a benediction. Playfully, she began to run among the trees, playing hide and seek with the child. Gleeful, he chased after her as she ran from tree to tree. '*Cantiamo, cantiamo, il salce funebre sara la mia ghirlanda.*'

Tiring of the game, she took a seat on a fallen log in the middle of the clearing. The child ran after her and made to sit down beside her.

'Kia tupato,' she warned him. 'Be careful.'

In his haste to join her he had almost shredded a beautiful spider's web. A large black pungawerewere was in the middle of the web; on its back was a tattoo, a red moko. The spider was in an attack position, ready to strike and inject its poison.

The boy recoiled, but the matriarch reprimanded him. 'It is only my kaitiaki,' she said, 'my protector.' She put the cup of her hand to the spider and began to speak to it. 'Forgive the child,' she said, 'he is just a young boy and, like all young boys, boisterous and careless.'

She raised the pungawerewere to her face and breathed softly on it. 'The spider was only wishing to protect its young and its web,' she told the child. Only then did he see that the sanctuary was strung with spider's webs, like a cathedral. '*E dale ciglia le sgorgava il cor'amara onda del pianto*,' the matriarch sang. She placed the pungawerewere on the child's left shoulder. He giggled as it ran quickly up, through his hair, across his skull and down onto his right shoulder. It seemed to be sniffing him. Then it settled.

'This is why I have brought you here. It's the Place of the Willows,' the matriarch said.

She stood up. 'This is the child,' she said, her voice ringing through the sanctuary. 'As I have been your protectress, accept him as your protector also. It is not just the human iwi who must fight against the Pakeha. It is also all the iwi of the natural world. Have not your webs and homes been shredded? The Maori hawk, has it not lost its nesting place in the high cliffs? And the eels, where are their spawning grounds now?' Her voice seemed to ring out, out, out, into the world. 'Therefore your fight and mine are the same. Let it be so.'

The air was filled with spiders leaping on silver gossamer threads into the sun.

'*Ave maria nell'ora della morte, ave, amen.*'

⌐

Cantiamo, cantiamo.

Following my conversation with Whai, I planned to see Uncle

Alexis again. But Regan and our two daughters, Bianca and Miranda, had only been back from Europe for a few months and we were still settling in.

Life was difficult, for instance, at Foreign Affairs where I had begun my career as a trainee diplomat after completing my law degree at the University of Auckland. It was while I was in training that the Secretary of Foreign Affairs had said to me, 'I know you've only been with us for two years, Mr Mahana, but I'd like to recommend you for a secondment to the Commonwealth Office in London. They're asking us, the Australians, the Canadians and other foreign affairs offices in Commonwealth countries to send representatives to train in human rights. There's so much going on in Africa and Asia, let alone Polynesia, as black Commonwealth countries achieve their independence from Mother England and the white settler governments she established. A new kind of negotiator is needed, Mr Mahana, someone of—I hope you won't mind my saying this—your colour. Would you be interested?' I couldn't say no and Regan and I, together with our baby daughter Bianca, spent three years in England. Miranda was born in our second year living in London.

Since returning, my negotiation skills had indeed come in handy. I had been placed in South Pacific Division where I soon found myself holding down the desk for French Polynesia, dealing with the political unrest in the region.

It wasn't until the summer at the beginning of 1975, therefore, that I was able to visit with Uncle Alexis again. This time I took Regan, Bianca and Miranda with me.

Aunt Roha was happy to see Regan and the girls. 'You go on upstairs to your uncle,' she told me. 'Regan and I have a lot to catch up on and the girls can help their auntie do some baking, eh girls?'

Uncle's condition hadn't changed. He still lay in the darkened room, the curtains drawn. I kissed both his cheeks. 'Do you know that's what the Mafia do before they cut your throat?' he grinned, looking up at me with his sightless eyes. 'There's a thought,' he added. 'When you do it, make it quick eh?' But he seemed glad to see me and he smiled as he heard Bianca's infectious giggle and Miranda's youthful screams coming up from the kitchen. 'It's good to hear laughter in the house,' he said.

I sat beside Uncle Alexis on his bed. 'I love you, Uncle,' I answered.

He pulled me close, as if he needed to believe me, embracing me tightly with one hand. His other hand began to trace my brow, cheeks, nose, eyebrows and then my shoulders and chest.

At that moment, Aunt Roha interrupted us. 'I've brought you a cup of tea,' she said, 'and Tama's daughters have chocolate biscuits.' Regan stood at the doorway, ushering the girls in. They were nervous but, after a while, they became accustomed to the darkness and Uncle Alexis brooding in the bed. It wasn't long before they had clambered in beside him, guiding his hands to the biscuits so that he could grasp them and eat them.

'How old were you when Riripeti died?' he asked after a while. 'Eleven? Look at what you have achieved! Even though you didn't take over from her, and therefore didn't have a career in the Maori world, you confounded all expectations and made it in the Pakeha world instead! It's almost as if, when destiny was denied you, you were flung from the centre and found your life at the margins. But now you've come back to the centre again, eh?'

I looked at Aunt Roha, puzzled. 'Your uncle talks like this all the time,' she said. 'Trying to untangle the past. Most of the time I can't understand what he says.'

Uncle swivelled his face in her direction. 'Don't talk as if I'm not here,' he growled. His voice rose, loud, filling the room.

Aunt Roha pleaded softly with him, 'Alex, you'll frighten the children.'

Regan and I left Uncle soon afterwards. Despite Aunt Roha's insistence that we stay longer, it was way past the girls' bedtime and they were already nodding off to sleep. I wrapped Bianca in a shawl and took her in my arms. Regan carried Miranda.

'Goodbye, Uncle Alexis,' I said to him. 'I'll tell Dad that you're well.'

He looked quickly around and up, searching for me. 'Are you going up to Gisborne to see Te Ariki?" he asked.

'Yes,' I answered. 'I've got a diplomatic conference to attend in Auckland and I thought I'd fly via Gisborne on the way and spend a few days there with him, Mum and my sisters.'

I was halfway down the stairs with Regan and the children when I heard Uncle Alexis call to me, 'Nephew? You do know that you were supposed to take over from Riripeti, eh. When you didn't, that's when the *mate* came upon us all. That's why I have black holes where my eyes should be.' He began to laugh and laugh. His laughter followed us out of the house and into the night.

In the car going home, Regan looked at me, puzzled. 'I didn't know you were supposed to take over from Riripeti,' she began.

'Uncle Alexis doesn't know what he's talking about,' I said. 'When she died Grandfather Ihaka took over the leadership of the iwi. I was only a boy at the time. I was sent to boarding school. And from there I went to university.'

'It sounds like you were sent into exile,' Regan said.

'You're being melodramatic,' I answered.

'And what's a *mate*?' she asked.

I gripped the steering wheel. 'It's a curse,' I said.

↝

A few weeks later I flew from Wellington to Gisborne, en route to Auckland. It was a late afternoon flight and, as usual, I felt the sense of anticipation as the plane descended through the clouds. Below were the Wharerata Ranges, jagged spikes and spines like a pile of discarded and half eaten fish. To the right was the sea, impossibly blue, inviting, but deceptively dangerous. To the left was the impenetrable wilderness of Waikaremoana, southern gateway to Tuhoe country.

Then, ahead, I saw the Poverty Bay flats, being offered up as a chalice unto me, silvering in the sun. And there, in front, was Gisborne. The plane banked into its landing pattern and we were soon on the ground.

It had always been our habit, my father's and mine, to meet after long absences without anyone else in the family around. A formality attended our reunions and, today, nothing had changed. Despite the fact that he was a farmer, Dad was dressed in a white shirt, tie, suit and, on his head, he was wearing a snappy fedora—he looked like the conductor, the late Tullio Serafin.

'Hello Tamatea,' he said. We embraced with passion. There was a great love between us. It really began when Riripeti died. Who else had I to turn to than my own father?

'It's good to see you, Dad,' I answered. He was sixty now. The way he dressed also indicated that his was a nobleman's approach to life. He was like an Italian godfather, and he dressed to fit the part. Although his skin was burnt brown by the sun and slit with lines as deep as the ravines of the tribal land that he controlled on behalf of the iwi, he was still handsome, still strong, still with an aura of careless sensuousness.

Hugging each other, we waited for my suitcase to be unloaded, then walked out of the terminal to the car. 'How long are you home for?' he asked.

'A few days,' I answered.

He reprimanded me. 'Is that all? Can't you stay longer? What are you running away from, son? You should spend more time at home among the people. Some of them have already forgotten who you are.'

Te Ariki was, also, still authoritative. When I was growing up he was my exemplar of excellence in all things: masculinity, strength, wisdom and goodness. He had, like all the Mahana men, inherited Riripeti's dynamism and, with it, her charisma. But whereas Uncle Alexis was blind and wasting away, and his other brothers had succumbed to illness and death, nothing blighted Te Ariki's unbounded natural grace and vigour. He was a man's man, whom other men sought out. A model. A *ne plus ultra* person. No wonder then that I still idolised him and considered him the template for my own identity.

'I'm not running away,' I defended myself. 'It's better this way, isn't it?'

He gave me a keen look. He knew my answer was a veiled reference to my grandfather, Ihaka, and the huge gulf between us. There were some matters on which I held my own opinions and views, and my relationship with Grandfather Ihaka was one of them. Who would have thought that two people from the same family, grandfather and grandson, could despise each other so much?

We stepped into the car. 'Oh,' he began, as if he had just remembered something, 'your mother is up the Coast today but she should be back tonight. Your sisters are coming around home to cook us dinner.'

He started the motor and we drove home to Palliser Street. However, instead of taking the usual route along the main highway Te Ariki detoured along the long stretch of Awapuni Beach. Surfers were catching the last waves of the day. The road was busy with rush-hour traffic as the city closed down for the evening. When Dad parked the car among the sand dunes overlooking the sea and turned off the engine, I heard the faint bass sound of the town clock booming across the cityscape. Six o'clock.

I looked at him, puzzled. He was pensive and, when he turned to me, his gaze was direct.

'You've begun to ask questions,' he began. 'Whai told me.'

I caught a glimpse of something else behind his eyes, something that looked like fear. 'You've got some questions about Mum.'

Not my grandmother. His mother.

'Whai doesn't know anything,' Dad continued. 'Why didn't you start asking about Mum when some of the old people, especially her own sisters and brothers, were still living? What's the use of asking about her now? The best person to tell you about Riripeti is me. And although I'm the eldest of all her children, I didn't know her when she was young.'

He was right. I realised, surprised, that Dad was only seven years younger than Grandmother was when she died, aged sixty-seven, in 1957.

'The only other person you should trust to tell you about her is your grandfather.'

Ah yes, Ihaka. Once consort to Riripeti, he still lived on.

A long silence fell between us. Te Ariki seemed to be marshalling some further comment and, when he made it, he chose his words with care. 'You know,' he began, 'that when Riripeti died, the task of getting back the land was still unresolved.'

'Yes,' I nodded.

'Your grandfather and I took over,' he continued. 'We wanted to make Riripeti's great dream come true. But it's been difficult, Tamatea, you know that. I won't speak ill of my father, but he has been unable to keep the people together the way she did. As long as she was alive, everybody kept the faith—the Ringatu religion of which she was the leader. But since then, every year, more and more of the faithful turn to other religions or even turn from God.'

The sound of the waves washed through his words and, when they went back out, they seethed and hissed.

'It's happening everywhere to tribal people, Dad,' I told him, 'not just in New Zealand. Even in Riripeti's time, the world was changing. We can't keep the Pakeha out.'

'But her vision,' Dad insisted, 'it had logic, Tamatea. As long as the people kept together in their faith and as long as they had a valley in their lives to sustain them economically, we could maintain our sovereignty and achieve independence.'

Again he fell into silence. He stared out the car window, looking across to Young Nick's Head. When he spoke again his words were an admission of defeat. 'And the people have changed, son. Under Riripeti, they were obedient. But under your grandfather, well, he finds it difficult to keep them under control. I know you've always thought him to be autocratic, but it's the only kind of leadership that he knows. And then, of course, the last seven years' drought has been the worst on record.'

I nodded. Among Maori the drought had been almost biblical. 'Some people call it the *mate*,' I told Te Ariki.

He looked at me, fiercely, his eyes wild, his veins almost bursting from his skin. 'There is no curse,' he said. 'Did Whai say that? Or was it Alexis? It's the kind of talk that comes when they are trying to blame somebody or something else rather than themselves for their misfortunes.'

I pressed his arm, trying to comfort him. 'Aren't seven years of plenty to follow the seven years of hardship?'

He calmed down. 'Yes,' he answered, 'but the iwi battle among ourselves now, family against family. I won't let that happen with our family, the Mahana family, do you hear me Tamatea?'

'Yes,' I answered.

'Good,' he said, starting up the car. 'That's all you need to know.'

But I stopped him. 'Te Ariki, are the spiders still down in the grove by the Waipaoa River?'

'The pungawerewere?' he asked. 'Riripeti's spiders? Nobody has seen them for years.'

ᔑ

Disturbing as our conversation was, its resonance soon dissipated when we reached Palliser Street. We were hardly home for five minutes before my sisters Teria, Erina and Vanessa descended upon Mum and Dad's house in rapid succession.

My sisters liked to announce their arrivals from afar—a squeal of tyres in the distance, a growing crescendo as they zoomed down the driveway before throwing out the anchor, a slam of the car door, a crash in the hallway and bang as they opened the door.

Teria arrived first. 'I'm not at home,' I said to her as we kissed.

'Be thankful that I had the time to come and cook for you and Dad,' she answered. 'Make yourself useful, will you? There's a sack of spuds in the back of the car.'

I was opening the boot when, with a boom and a thud came Vanessa. 'What are you doing in the middle of the driveway?' she asked. 'I could have run you down, don't think I wasn't tempted.'

'Yes, it is a lovely day, isn't it?' I answered, watching as she picked up some pots and pans and took them into the house.

Finally, screaming blue murder about all the other cars cluttering up the driveway, Erina breezed in, the third sister of the formidable trio. 'Hello stranger,' she said as she kissed me.

By the time I got back into the house, they were already cooking up a storm—and targeting me with their lacerating wit.

'A little bird told me,' Teria said to her sisters, excluding me, 'that Tama thinks him and Grandmother are in the same image.'

'Him?' Erina chortled as she put a pot of puha and pork bones on the stove. 'But she was beautiful.' Well, thank you, Erina.

They giggled with each other. 'However there's nothing about Tama,' Vanessa added, 'that plastic surgery couldn't fix, eh.'

That set them off. Teria's mouth opened so wide with laughing that for a moment I hoped she'd fall into it. At the same time, however, I felt my usual admiration for my three sisters; when they were being comedic, they were a Maori version of the Three Stooges. I felt relieved that my fourth sister, Meri, and two brothers Hamuera and Mana weren't at home. Three against one wasn't too bad but six against one was an indecent assault.

'Ah well,' Teria said as she hastened into the sitting room to lay the table for dinner, 'time to be Tama's handmaidens again.'

The remark was made with a tinge of sarcasm. I intercepted her as she tried to pass. 'Yes,' I answered, aware of all the undercurrents that swirled around her words, 'and I love you too, sister.' I held her tightly in my arms.

At that, she stopped her work and looked at me fiercely. 'Don't think you can get around me with charm,' she said. 'It used to work when Riripeti was here to make everybody acknowledge you, but my sisters and I are only doing this because Dad asked us to.' At thirty, Teria was a handsome woman with that extraordinary silver plume in the shape of a feather in her otherwise thick black hair. Actually, all my sisters were handsome, having the kind of sturdiness and strength that comes from being women of the land with their feet planted firmly on the ground. Erina was twenty-eight and Vanessa was twenty-six, and like Teria they had married local Maori farmers who worked the iwi land.

But in Teria, there was something else. She was formidable too, and when she looked at me I could see all our troubled history— Teria's, Erina's, Vanessa's and mine—in her unswerving gaze. She still blamed me. Why? Because when Riripeti made me her beloved, taking me to Waituhi during the weekends—and then bringing me up for two years away from my family—she set me apart from my sisters. And when she guided me through school, grooming me for tribal leadership, she gave me everything and my sisters were given nothing. They were to serve. I was to be served.

I let her go. She turned to the stove again. 'Dinner won't be long,' she said. 'Erina, how about getting on with those potatoes, eh? They won't peel themselves. And Vanessa, did you bring a pudding?'

She looked at me again intensely. 'You owe us,' she said. 'Our cousin Sammy reminded me of how much.'

'Sammy?' I asked. He and his younger sister Raina were the children of Uncle Pita and Aunt Hiraina. I had to smile at a memory of childhood when Sammy had pushed me off my trike because he wanted to have a ride on it; much later, when we were going through school, he had become one of my main defenders in fights with other kids. 'I have to look after you,' he said. Oh, the changing loyalties between childhood and adulthood.

Teria nodded. 'I met him at the River Bar last weekend. We were talking about Grandmother and especially one Christmas when she made all her grandchildren line up because she wanted to give us all ten shillings. Except in your case, she gave you twenty shillings.'

I looked at Teria, puzzled. 'You don't understand, do you,' she said, noting my blank look. 'And you owe our mother too.' She turned to Erina and Vanessa. 'We all do, don't we, sisters.'

Hearing them affirming their love for Tiana, I couldn't help remembering that night of the First Telling, when we were children, and she told us how she met our father, Te Ariki.

Son giunta! . . . grazie, o Dio! Estremo asil quest' e per me . . .

24 September 1950. It is at the end of a very bad winter for all of us. We are living in a one-bedroom bach in Crawford Road, Kaiti, Gisborne. Dad has been away from home for two months. He has gone to Mataura, in the South Island, on a shearing contract. Although he is regularly sending money back to us by telegraph, his last payment hasn't come through. We are running out of money.

Tonight, a huge thunderstorm has come up from the south. My mother is sleeping in the bedroom with Vanessa in the cot beside her. Teria, Erina and I are in the room which is both kitchen and dining room, sleeping on mattresses on the floor. Frightened by the thunder, Teria has her fist against her mouth. I see by the blue light of zigzag lightning that Erina is afraid also. She puts her head under the blankets. I feel her trying to burrow into the space between my chest and thighs.

'Don't be afraid,' I tell them, 'I'll always protect you. Always.'

Dad told me I had to protect the family while he was away. It's been difficult. The electricity was cut off last month; that's why we are using candles. Then Mum had to go to hospital to have her teeth taken out. It was very painful. She wore a scarf over her face but the blood seeped through, and we thought she was dying. To top it all off, the man from Maori Affairs came last week when Mum telephoned for welfare support. Instead of helping, he touched my mother. She had to fight him off with her knife. I've stopped going to school and now I stay at home with her, just in case he comes back. But that's only made matters worse. Yesterday, the school sent an inspector around to check up on me. The inspector told Mum that my sisters and I might be taken away from her.

The thunder booms again and more lightning flashes across the sky.

'I want to see Mummy,' Erina weeps.

The candlelight is shining under the doorway of the bedroom.

'Me too,' Teria says.

'Okay,' I nod. I help them out of the blankets. We hold each other as we step slowly through the dark. There are kehua, ghosts, lurking there, ready to snatch away any stragglers. Teria pushes the door open.

Our mother is lying in bed. She is cradling our baby sister, Vanessa, in her arms. She is, herself, like a little child in a big double bed in a little box of a bedroom. She has never been conventionally attractive but she has a way of angling her face to the light which makes her look almost beautiful. Looked at straight on, you simply see her Ngati Porou ancestry at its most ordinary—the fullness of the flesh and the softness of the contours that shape her cheekbones.

'You children should be asleep,' she says.

'It was Erina's idea,' I answer.

'She was frightened of the thunder,' Teria adds. Talk about ganging up on the youngest.

'And your light was still on,' I say.

The candlelight flickers. Our mother shivers. 'Well, you children better sleep with me then, eh, because I'm a bit scared too.'

We run to the bed and leap onto it before the kehua can get our ankles and bite us.

'Mind baby Vanessa,' Mum warns.

It is so warm in the bed. It feels safe to be close to our mother. The thunder and lightning can't hurt us now.

After a while, Teria asks, 'Mummy, when will Daddy be coming home?'

'Oh, when he's finished his work. Next week perhaps. But if he's not back by then we'll go picking blackberries and maybe I can get a cleaning job. We'll be all right. Don't you worry, children.'

A pause. Then Teria asks again, 'How did you and Daddy meet each other? Did you fall in love with him straight away? Was he as handsome as a prince? Did you live happily ever after?'

My mother's laughter trills through the bedroom. She is a good storyteller. 'You children are so funny,' she says. 'And Teria is the funniest of all.' Her eyes glow wide in the candlelight. "All right, I'll tell you.'

We settle down to listen.

'Well, I was in Hastings, which is three hours by train from Gisborne. I was very young when I met your father. I went to the pictures one night with my girlfriend, Mereira; I don't know where she is now, and I haven't seen her for ages. We were both working in a fruitpicking gang among the orchards. Anyway the movie was one with an actress called Joan Crawford in it and Mereira said my shoulders were like Joan Crawford's. Oh the movie was so sad and Mereira cried, she was such a baby. Well, at halftime we went outside so that Mereira could have a smoke. I said to her, "You enjoy your cigarette while I get us some chocolates." I went next door to the cafeteria and there he was.'

'Who?'

'Your father of course, who else? I didn't notice him at first because he had a mate with him, one of the Meha boys. Like me, your father came from Gisborne, and he and Charlie were in a shearing gang. Anyway, I wasn't going to speak to a man I had never met before. But as I was leaving the cafeteria Charlie Meha tried to pick me up. I gave him the brush-off but him and your father followed me back into the picture theatre. Well, as soon as Mereira saw Te Ariki she fell for him. That Mereira loved boys. As for me, I was stuck with Charlie Meha and his hands started to wander. I said to Mereira, "I don't like this fella so I'm going back to the camp." She tried to dissuade me and then sighed, "Tell you what! If we swap boys, will you stay? One boy is like another to me." So we did! And that's how I met your father. All because Mereira decided to do a swap.'

'And was he handsome? And did you love him?'

'Oh yes,' our mother breathes. 'I thought he was the most handsome boy I had seen. The trouble was that he knew he was goodlooking and, after the movie, he didn't know whether or not he wanted to keep going out with me. After all, some of his other girlfriends were much prettier. But, for some reason, we continued to go out, even if his attitude was rather arrogant. For instance, he asked me to go to a dance and I said yes. There I was, waiting at the front door when he came along—and he had another girl with him! He'd forgotten all about the date with me. When he went to apologise, I socked him in the jaw.'

My sisters and I gasp with amazement.

'I think that's when your father began to fall in love with me,' Mum laughs. 'So we decided to get married and to have you four children. He rang his mother—your grandmother, Riripeti—and she wasn't happy about it. She considered me a woman of no account, without the appropriate lineage to marry into the Mahana iwi. As for me, I got in touch with my mother and she gave me her blessing. We got married in a registry office in Hastings. Mereira was my bridesmaid. Charlie Meha was the best man. Mereira bawled her eyes out.'

The candlelight flickers in the night. Our mother's voice grows hushed and mysterious.

'We had a short honeymoon and when your father's shearing gang finished their contract, we decided to return to Gisborne to start our life as husband and wife. We booked on the train on Saturday 11 June 1943. In fact, the weather that night was really awful, as bad as it is tonight. There were a lot of slips on the track and whenever we went over a railway bridge we could see that the rivers below were really high and swollen. At one point, as the train was going along a cliff, we could see the water rushing down the hills, and we thought it would sweep us away. The journey was really frightening. But I was with Te Ariki and he protected me. We were very much in love. I wanted nobody but him. We must have arrived at Gisborne about 11 p.m. I know it was very late. And guess what?'

'What, Mummy?'

'Your grandmother was there to meet us. I had never seen her before, I didn't even know Te Ariki was her son until that moment. I screamed at him, "Why didn't you tell me that Riripeti was your mother?" I thought that Fate was playing a trick. But it wasn't a trick.' My mother's voice drifts away into silence. She begins to rock back and forth with Vanessa, humming a lullaby.

Teria and I look quickly at each other. We see that our mother's face has tilted upward, the planes flattening out. Her eyes, nose, lips and chin are brought into sharp relief. The irises have shrunk to a pinpoint. Her eyes are wide, dark and staring.

Our mother is spiralling out of the lovely story of meeting Te Ariki. If she goes any deeper it will be difficult to pull her up.

'Teria, take Vanessa from Mum,' I tell my sister.

Whenever she spirals, Mum's whole body becomes rigid. Her toes paddle as if she is swimming. Indeed, whenever Mum dreams, her toes always start to paddle; she is a dream swimmer, swimming throught the veil of wakefulness into her strange dream world beyond. Often, my sisters and I have watched from the foot of the bed as our mother swims away, her face still and remote, but her toes circling furiously. There is an epic quality about her when she swims. Where does she go to? Is it to combat some cruel foe at the other end of the universe?

But as soon as Teria takes Vanessa from our mother's arms and returns her to her crib, Mum's face whips around to confront us. Her lips curl back and she snarls, reaching for the knife that she always keeps in her bedside cabinet.

'Tiana, no.' I say the words sharply, insistent. It is the only way to snap her out of her spiral.

Then I place my hands over her feet to stop them from paddling. She struggles, but Teria and Erina join me. Grimly, we imprison her feet, stopping her toes from circling, until Mum stills again and ascends from the sea of her dreams, gasping for air.

Quickly, I bring her back to her story. 'So Riripeti came to the railway station to meet you and Te Ariki?' I ask. 'What about your own mother?'

'Oh, yes, she was there too,' Mum begins vaguely. Our mother is back with us. 'And guess what?'

'Tell us, tell us.'

'Riripeti took your father away in the Lagonda. My mother took me away on her buggy. And I didn't see your father again for eight months.'

'But why!'

'Riripeti didn't approve of your father getting married to me,' she whispers. 'She had her own plans for him.'

The rain dashes against the window. Teria plucks at Mum's nightdress. 'But where's the happy ever after? There has to be a happy ever after.'

Our mother smiles in a distracted manner.

'Why, of course there was a happy ever after. Because my son, Tama, came along and, when he arrived, that made all the difference because Riripeti allowed your father to come back to me. And then, later, we three pretty daughters and, yes, we lived happy ever after. But there was a price to pay.'

'Yes?'

My mother looks directly into my eyes. I can't escape her.

'Tamatea was the eldest grandson,' she says. 'By right of tipuna wahine, Riripeti claimed him for her own.'

My mother's life too, just like my sisters' lives, has been irrevocably affected by my grandmother's actions.

Pieta di me, Signore ... deh non abandonar.

Later that night, it must have been just after one o'clock, I heard Tiana's car coming up the driveway. I listened as the door slammed, and then heard my mother entering the house. The moon was full, so Tiana didn't bother to put on any lights. I watched from the doorway and saw her go past to the bedroom that she shared with Te Ariki.

She knew I was there, watching.

Dad was already asleep. Tiana must have only gone to the bedroom to get her nightdress and dressing gown because she soon drifted past the doorway again to the bathroom. As she turned on the shower, I heard the water rushing softly through the pipes. Then it stopped. I sensed Tiana moving back down the hallway again to the bedroom. I closed my eyes quickly.

I felt her presence and her breath as it disturbed the air.

'I know you're awake, Tamatea,' she said.

My mother was always a person who waited in shadows. Her face emerged out of nowhere, the orbits of the eyes as dark as the shadows she stood in.

'Hello Tiana,' I answered.

Then the moonlight, shining through the window, struck the planes of her cheeks. With an expression of hope, she reached out to caress me.

I averted my face. I knew she was hurt by my gesture. My shame at rejecting her like that battled with my yearning to trust in her love—and I quickly reached out for her hands and kissed them. After all, she was my mother.

'Your sisters are glad to see you home,' she said. 'So is your father.'

'And you?'

'I am always glad to see my firstborn,' she said. 'How long are you home for?

'Only for a few days.'

Immediately, her mood changed. 'It's always only for a few days, isn't it, Tamatea. What use to us is that?' She pulled her hands away from my grasp. 'And while you're back you act like the lord of the manor. Why can't you have a greater responsibility to your family?

But you can't wait to get away again, can you. In particular, you can't wait to get away from me, eh.'

A friend once said to me that sometimes you have to listen not to what is being said but to what is *not* being said. He found Maori people fascinating because their non-verbal communication was so complex. There was so much behind my mother's words that she was not saying.

An angry rejoinder flamed in the darkness. 'You're a great one to talk about responsibility,' I answered. 'After all, you were the one who gave me away to be brought up by Riripeti. And I was your firstborn, eh, Tiana?'

It was a callous, arrogant, mocking thing for a son to say to his mother.

Imperceptibly, she swayed. 'It was the custom,' she answered. 'You were the eldest son of an eldest son of an eldest son for more generations than anyone could remember. ('Oh darling,' Regan wept when our first child, Bianca was born. 'I am so sorry. I know I should have been delivered of a son for the tribe. So sorry.') The eldest grandchild was always brought up by the paternal grandmother. And I was an outsider when I married your father and married into his tribe. I had no say.'

My friend was right: if you listened closely to what was *not* being said, then and only then would you discover the truth.

'And then your grandmother, well, she was a law unto herself when she took you. She had a dream for you that came from her own life and from the tribe and all the ancestors that had gone before her.'

The darkness was rich with the mystical sounds of a bone flute, conjuring ghosts, whistling in the night.

Tiana tried to soften the anger between us. She bent down and kissed me on the forehead. 'Let's not quarrel on your first night back home,' she said. Then she added something very strange. 'I don't blame your grandmother for being the way that she was. It was her inescapable destiny. Goodnight, son.'

᠗

Ah yes, inescapable destiny.

If we take 1890 to be her birthdate, Riripeti's times were strange and turbulent and filled with the whirlwinds of change in the Maori world. There's a story told of her, that at her birth the midwife saw one eye, swimming in blood, staring out from her mother Waiputa's vagina, as if she was in a haste to be born. What would she have seen?

She came into a world already colonised by the British Government. A number of chiefs had signed a worthless treaty at Waitangi in 1840; when she grew to womanhood she disclaimed its rights over her—none of her chiefs had put their marks to the treaty—but she knew she was a colonised person, a slave. Her people, on the Maori side, inhabited the rich alluvial lowland of Turanga. They lived in small family units in passionate conflict with the region that Captain James Cook had called 'Poverty Bay'. She was of Te Whanau a Kai, Rongowhakaata and Te Aitanga a Mahaki descent. Her people were already, at that time, endeavouring to repudiate land transactions earlier made between Maori and Pakeha.

It was a world which had seen the gradual coming of the Pakeha—first as whaler (not only of British descent but Spanish, Portuguese, Italian, black American, as many of the Maori genealogies will today testify), then as flax traders during the flax boom, tree fellers, evangelists and, finally, settlers and farmers. All these Pakeha strode through the villages, the hundreds of pa sites, smothering the Maori fires and razing the temples of pagan religion. Yet, at the time, the Maori of Poverty Bay were already equals: renowned fishermen and agriculturalists of whom Joseph Barrow Montefiore, Sydney merchant, said in 1838, 'Their potatoes are cultivated better than those grown by many of the settlers in New South Wales.' However, then came sheep farming and, with the change of land use from agricultural to pastoral production, the aggregation of the small tribal holdings into large sheep runs. The agricultural basis of the people collapsed.

Riripeti's own great-great-uncle, Thomas Halbert, was an agent of this collapse. He became one of the first Pakeha to own land in the Gisborne district, the block known as 'Pouparae' which he acquired on 18 December 1839: 1004 acres in exchange for £80 cash, four double-barrelled fowling pieces, 40 shirts, 36 axes, 32 plane irons, 60 blankets, 36 iron pots, 24 hoes, 400 lbs of gunpowder, 10 pieces of print, 500 lbs of tobacco, 36 hatchets, 130 razors, 30 knives, 40 spades, and 22 pairs of scissors. When the transaction came before Commissioner Bell in 1859, the Maori witnesses were adamant that the sale only went through because of his wife, Riria Mauaranui, and that the beneficiary was supposed to be her son, Wi Pere Halbert. His father rejected the suggestion and later sold Pouparae in 1841, the father disowning his part-Maori son.

The first European census of Poverty Bay, including half-bloods, had been taken almost forty years before Riripeti was born. The statistics were compiled by W.B. Baker of Tolaga Bay; where the wife was a Maori, her name was not shown. The return enumerated forty-four adults including fourteen women, thirty-five children and twenty-five half-blood children ranging in age from one year to seventeen years. 'Halbert, T., Trader' appeared first on the list. At that time there were twenty weather-boarded houses in the district, most of them surrounding the then small settlement of Gisborne. There were also barns, stores, sheds, stables and other wooden buildings. Thomas Halbert had thirteen acres under cultivation; no information was given as to the amount of land cultivated by the Maori people of the district. (The half-blood children were listed with only the father's surname. There were two boys and three girls listed for Halbert.)

There had already been many violent clashes and slayings: Maori and Maori, Maori and Pakeha. The former were continuations of earlier conflicts in line with the concept of utu. Those between Maori and Pakeha were frequently caused by the violation of the laws of tapu—even by evangelists. Increasingly, there were many quarrels and armed raids over land and business transactions. Turanga, as Mr (later Sir) Donald McLean said in February 1851, was certainly as reported to him—a fine rich country, with 40,000 acres of deep, alluvial soil: '. . . A Veritable Paradise for Pastoralists'. The land was rich and fertile, in pleasing contrast to the barren Wharerata Ranges which enclosed the Bay. You descended from the ranges and obtained a splendid panoramic view of the lowland and the glittering blue-green sea curving like a sickle towards the harbour. The plain was intersected by rivers which struck their serpentine course through handsome clumps of kahikatea and puriri forests and beside numerous wheat cultivations and groves of peach and other varieties of English fruit trees. The clear blue sky was scrawled with the smoke from many pa fires, and the nearest rose from the Maori settlements on the banks of the Te Arai and Waipaoa rivers. There, the Maori villagers reaped their fields, some leading horses and others driving cattle and pet pigs before them. Through the rich grass and across the river or woodland they greeted visitors with 'E hoa pakeha, tena koe,' presenting them with fruit and honey fresh taken from the hives. They were very numerous, in general lean and tall and well-shaped. Some had dark-coloured eyes, black hair and beards of middling length. Most of the men were tattooed; some of the women had the moko curling on their chins. The clothing of both men and women was an admixture of Maori woven cloth and cloak, and Pakeha trousers or bright fabric wrapped around the waist in the case of the women. Some Maori wore hats and smoked pipes. Almost all were barefooted.

Visitors might have got close enough to look into the eyes of these people. They might have even seen the outer perimeters of their villages. But beyond that, beyond the darkness, they would not have wished to venture. After all, they would have heard that Maori ate human flesh. They killed wantonly. They were savages ruled by superstition and beliefs in carved wooden idols. It hadn't been too long ago that fierce intertribal warfare had occurred when Hongi and Te Haupa sailed from the Ngapuhi region to north of Tokomaru Bay. Hongi had obtained the musket from the Pakeha; the tribes of the Bay of Plenty and of the East Coast had few firearms. He burnt 500 villages during his relentless progress. He took two thousand men, women and children as prisoner. Seventy heads were carried back. Many of the slaves were slain and cooked.

Following in Hongi's trail came another raiding party from the north, led by Pomare, Titore and Te Wera (also called Hauraki). This expedition reached as far down the East Coast as Te Whetumatarau stronghold—the Star of One Hundred Rays—which overlooks the present township of Te Araroa. As with the siege of Troy, the invaders occupied the Te Araroa Flats for some time, living on the plantations and the contents of the storehouses, then packed up and seemed to sail away. But instead, they hid behind Matakaoa Point. (Pomare said darkly in retreat, 'Enjoy your wife tonight for tomorrow she will be mine.') Stealthily they returned and fell upon the unsuspecting residents who had descended rejoicing to their homes. Many were slaughtered and taken prisoner.

Further raiding expeditions criss-cross the years with astonishing frequency—focusing on Poverty Bay and the East Coast—from all points south, west, north and from the sea in the east. The Mahia Peninsula, for instance, became a place of refuge for very large numbers of southern Ngati Kahungunu who, for many years, had had to endure the harassing attentions of Urewera, Waikato, Taupo, Hauraki and Bay of Plenty invaders, and who now also feared Te Rauparaha and his Ngati Raukawa from further south. Among the pa of the Mahia that were assailed stood a superb stronghold on lofty Moumoukai, near Morere. The defenders could neither be driven out nor starved out. The people of Moumoukai, a mountain over 600 metres high, never fell to invasion.

So visitors would have felt it best not to look into the eyes of the natives or into their villages; and they would have made the sign of the cross in thankfulness that religion, Christian religion, was coming to change their ways and the rule of British law was being imposed. Better still, at least Maori were still mainly fighting one another and not yet the Pakeha. And the Pakeha, thank God, still had the musket.

But not for long. Traders began selling firearms to the Maori and among them, again, was the ubiquitous Thomas Halbert. Mr Donald McLean, in that same February of 1851, received a petition at the first court sitting ever held in Poverty Bay, complaining that gunpowder was being sold by certain residents to the Maori and that, only on the previous day, there had been a transaction involving 15 lbs. The petition, signed by J.W. Harris, T. U'Ren Snr, R. Espie, J.H. King, and J. Dunlop, urged that such sales should be stopped as 'they are not only a violation of the law, but may be the means of seriously endangering the lives and property of the Europeans'. Upon Espie swearing to the truth of an information charging Thomas Halbert with selling gunpowder to a 'native' named Paraone te Wae, Mr McLean issued a summons requiring the accused to appear before him. He swore in U'Ren as a special constable and provided him with a search warrant authorising him to use any munitions of war he might find about the premises of the said 'Thomas Halbert'. A fine of £20 was imposed. Mr McLean made it known that a reward of £5 would be paid to any native who furnished information concerning any future sale of powder.

(Let me address you, my Pakeha ancestor, Thomas Halbert: you married into the Maori people of Turanga and you had children of mixed blood. Could it be possible that, in the burgeoning years, you disowned your Pakeha heritage for the sake of the Maori? Did you relent about the sale of your son's land, obtain his forgiveness and take up the cause of the oppressed? Ah yes, I divine the seeds here, my Pakeha ancestor. Sympathiser. Pro-Maori. Gun runner.)

This was the flux of Riripeti's world, a world being pressed upon by a Pakeha thumb, pushing on the tattooed temple and relentlessly cracking and crushing the skull. It was a time when the British system of law and order clashed with age-old customs and deep-rooted rituals, a period when Poverty Bay Maori still steadfastly refused to acknowledge Queen Victoria as their ruler; their paramount chief, Te Kani a Takirau, had not been a signatory of the Treaty of Waitangi and, therefore, the mana remained with the Maori. (One hundred and five years later, as a five-year-old boy, I sat with Riripeti at a Maori land meeting and watched as her eyes flashed like paua and she pounded the table in frustration and anger that the taking of land by the Pakeha was still continuing on the East Coast. 'We must fight back,' she told the gathering. 'And it is not only the land that needs our protection but the sea also. Our fishing grounds are being surveyed. Very soon they too will be denuded of our ika, as the land has been of the iwi.' Beyond the meeting, I could hear the call of the sea, pounding like Riripeti's words. I thought to myself that there must be many others in other countries who felt the desolation of being landless and colonised in their own lands also. Yes, it was true, the land was being taken and where there was no land the people had to leave and find new livelihoods in strange, alien cities. Gone, gone, they have gone, the many iwi from the land.)

So the decade of the 1850s opened with symptoms of grave unrest. There was further opposition to the sale of any further land to Europeans and the advocacy of repudiation of past sales. Here there was fertile soil for the weeds of dissatisfaction. Some of the local Maori were encouraged to rebel by rumours of sales repudiations in other parts of New Zealand. However, other Maori presented a remarkable picture of resilience as they attempted to fight their exploiters. 'The natives,' the Rev. T.S. Grace wrote in his report to the Church Missionary Society for 1852, 'have attained a degree of [business] intelligence beyond what might have been expected in so short a period. Their motto is now: "Ploughs, sheep and ships," to establish a civilisation like unto that of the Pakeha. I have had much conversation with some of them individually, but now they appear in a body to lay hold of these ideas with a giant grasp, and, so far, I must say they have continued to work them out with a steady determinations such as I never thought them capable of.'

But interrogate that phrase: Like unto that of the Pakeha.

There is an inequity here, a basic obscenity. The Paheka did not want the Maori to be equal. In the 1860s they did not wish the establishment of anti-selling land leagues throughout Aotearoa. Nor did they view the setting up of a Maori King in the Waikato as anything but an affront to their British monarch. With relentless speed, war broke out in the Taranaki and then the Waikato. Hauhauism, a fervent religious movement, spread as an anti-Pakeha ferment across the land. And to Turanga came the Te Kooti revolt.

Possessed of Maori and Pakeha blood, Riripeti was born thirty years later. She was already at war with herself. The midwife saw, at her birth, not only that eye swimming in blood. She saw also that Riripeti had her hands at her own throat as if attempting to strangle herself.

4

The matriarch's laughter trilled from the direction of the old homestead. 'Mokopuna? Mokopuna, haere mai, save me.'

The child looked up. He was playing in the back paddocks with his sisters and cousins. He loved tumbling and running with them in the long grass, and Sundays were the only days when they were all together. Every Sunday it was traditional for the family to come to lunch at Riripeti's homestead.

'Mokopuna? Mokopuna.'

Far off he could see the back courtyard of the homestead. The matriarch was there, and she was riding Blue Mist. She was wearing a riding hat and a long black gown, and she had a crop in her hand. On the ground, Grandfather Ihaka, Te Ariki and the child's uncles were laughing and leaping and trying to catch hold of the reins of the stallion. The matriarch was sitting sidesaddle and trying to get away from them. Tiana and the child's aunts were standing on the verandah of the homestead, watching as the matriarch wove patterns of escape in the sunlight. The stallion danced and reared at her direction, backing and turning and clattering over the uneven bricks of the path. Some of the dogs were barking loudly; there were small squealed appogiaturi from the pups.

Then she saw him. She spun Blue Mist quickly and the men and dogs scattered away from her. She must have said something to Grandfather because he yelled back at her, 'No!' But she did not heed him. She took her crop and slashed at the stallion. It reared again. Grandfather tried to pull Grandmother from Blue Mist. He was too late. The stallion leapt away from the courtyard and began to thrum, thrum, thrum towards the paddock where the boy was standing. He watched as she spurred the stallion on. There was a fence between them.

At first the child thought that the matriarch had changed her mind because she seemed to slow the stallion on its approach to the fence, and then she came to a halt. She made as if to turn Blue Mist towards the gateway and then halted again. She shaded her eyes from the sun—and that was when he knew she would try the jump.

The fence was very high, designed to keep the cattle penned into the yard. It was made of long rough-hewn slabs of timber and topped with barbed wire.

Grandfather cried again, 'No!'

The matriarch looked at him with scorn as he yelled words at her. She pulled at the reins and returned Blue Mist to a point halfway between the fence and the homestead. Then she turned the stallion's head to face the fence again. The child heard his Aunt Floria scream with a high piping sound. He saw his uncles running towards Grandmother, waving their hands at her.

Thrum, thrum, thrum. The matriarch spurred the stallion towards the fence.

'No!' Grandfather yelled for the third time.

Even before Blue Mist was twelve lengths from the fence, the child knew that his grandmother would not make it. He began to run towards her. He felt that if he opened his arms he might be able to catch her as the horse crashed into the fence and unseated her. Then he had to stop and just watch. He could feel the terror of the stallion—the way in which its eyes jutted from its head, the veins almost bursting from the rippling skin. He could see into the face of the matriarch. It was purposeful. Intent. Her black gown was billowing in the wind. Her riding hat fell from her head. The stallion reached the fence.

The matriarch cried out, 'Mokopuna.'

A flock of starlings scattered like a rain of arrows in the sunlit vault of sky.

He closed his eyes. He clenched his fists. He compressed his lips. Perhaps if he tried hard enough he would be able to turn time back. The matriarch's laughter trilled from the direction of the old homestead. 'Mokopuna? Mokopuna, haere mai, save me.' All he wanted to do was to look into blackness. The matriarch slammed into the ground like a broken doll. A moment went past. An eternity. Blue Mist was tangled in the barbed wire and trying to get up. The child felt tears in his eyes. The matriarch lay still.

Something nudged him. The flanks of a stallion. He felt the sharp point of a riding crop prodding him.

'E mokopuna, did I frighten you?' Grandmother asked.

He opened his eyes. She was sitting there. On Blue Mist. Her face was calm. She smiled.

Then Grandfather Ihaka slammed into him and threw him bodily to the ground. Furiously, he looked into the matriarch's face. 'Must you always show off to the boy?' he said.

Her eyes were veiled. 'Don't you touch him again, Ihaka. Ever.' She flicked him dangerously with her crop and turned the stallion back towards the old homestead.

The child saw his mother, Tiana, striding towards him in the sunlight, coming to help him up from the ground.

࿉

The matriarch cried out, 'Mokopuna.' Grandfather slammed into me and threw me to the ground. 'Must you always show off to the boy?' I saw Tiana, striding towards me, striding, striding, striding, but never quite reaching me.

I lifted my arms to her and called her name, 'Mum.' Suddenly there was the sound of a horse's hooves thrumming and silver laughter, and the air was filled with a ghost stallion flailing the air around her. Its hooves flashed like silver knives. Undaunted, she strode through them and—

My mother reached through my dreams, helping me up, and I awoke to a blood-red dawn. She brushed her fingers hesitantly through my hair.

'How long have you been here by my side?' I asked, suspicious. I had the feeling that she had been watching the flickering and darting of my dreams, and the way in which the silver knives flailed the darkness beneath the folds of my eyelids.

'Not long,' she said. 'You still have the bad dreams?'

I relented. 'Sometimes. Not too often,' I answered.

Tiana kissed my forehead. 'Your father should give you a blessing before you return to Wellington. That might calm your dreams.' Then she became alarmed. 'Or maybe something has happened to you meantime? Has someone touched your head? Or a woman walked over your body? You must be careful, son. Be on the watch. Someone may wish to harm you.'

'Tiana,' I answered, 'I'm always careful.'

She nodded. Then, 'Your sister Teria telephoned earlier. She wanted to know if you are going out to Waituhi to visit the meeting house, Rongopai. If you are, can you leave it till tomorrow? She wants to go with you.' She stood up. She tried to joke, 'Now I've got to go to work. No rest for the wicked!'

I looked at my watch. It was almost 5 a.m. My mother was a kitchenhand at a local hotel, making breakfast for the early morning travellers before they checked out. Such a normal job, and this was yet another day like any other day of her life.

Soon after Mum left, Te Ariki came in to see me. 'I'm already late,' he said as we kissed. 'You don't feel like coming to Maera Station with me, do you? We're shearing out there. How about doing some real work for a change!'

'Sorry Dad,' I answered. 'I've got some appointments in town.'

My cousin Whai had organised an appointment for me to see Miss Maud Rivers, the chief librarian at the Gisborne Library. He had also given me the name of a research historian at the Gisborne Museum and Art Gallery. ('Go and see John Lawrence,' Whai said. 'He'll tell you more about Riripeti.')

'No?' Dad said. 'I didn't think you would. Ah well, it's good to have you home, anyway, son, even if you do sleep in. We'll talk again tonight. Ka kite, e tama.'

For my parents, 5 a.m. starts were normal. Up with the sun and down with the sun, that was *la dolce vita* (My little daughter Bianca screamed with joy one morning when we were driving to the airport to catch an early flight. 'Look at all my cousins,' she said. The streets were crisp and clean but filled with Maori workers, a surreal vision of bottom-barrel people tramping with leaden feet on their way to factories and the first shift.)

Then, at 8 a.m. my two younger brothers, Hamuera and Mana, and my sister, Meri, jumped on the bed. There were ten years between myself and Hamuera, and twenty or so years between myself and Mana and Meri. Teria had been absolutely disgusted with Mum and Dad when Meri had arrived, but she was positively appalled that they could compound the situation by having Mana. I was at boarding school at the time, and Teria was attending the local high school. She wailed, 'Oh, Mum, what will my friends say?' Following Mana's birth, Teria told me grumpily that our mother had better get her tubes tied or else Dad should, as she put it, 'get the cut'.

'How's it going, brother?' Hamuera asked. He was grown so tall and handsome now. A regular Don Juan. We wrestled for a while, happy to see each other, but I could tell that he was still feeling the wounds of ten years of knowing and hearing that his older brother was better than he would ever be. And I wanted to say to him, 'Hey, you've got a lot going for you, brother. Go out into the world, take it like the warrior you are. Don't try to emulate me. Be yourself, because you're great just as you are, and I'm proud of you.' But the moment was lost and the words were not said, and the wounds remained between us. He was working at Dalgety's as a trainee stock and sales agent. Apparently, Grandfather Ihaka had high expectations of grooming him to take on the same selling position in the tribe's farming portfolio—especially now that 'Your older brother, Tamatea, has done a disappearing trick on us. Foreign Affairs? What use is that to the iwi?' But before he left I had to ask him, 'Hamuera, how has Tiana been with you younger children?'

He looked at me curiously. 'She's been okay,' he answered. 'All that stuff that happened when there was just you, Teria, Erina and Vanessa, there's been none of that with me, Mana and Meri. Nothing.'

Mana and Meri departed soon after Hamuera. They were both still at school, though Meri hated it and wanted to leave. 'Please speak to Mummy for me?' she asked. 'I know Mummy will listen to you.' As for Mana, all he could do was sit and watch me and I knew that he adored me and that there was nothing I could do about it. I wanted to say to him, 'Oh Mana, don't.'

And finally they were gone, they were all gone, and I was left alone in the house at Palliser Street. This was the second house that we had owned; the first was at Crawford Road.

First things first: breakfast. Then a swim at Waikanae Beach—I needed the calm of being by myself and absorbing the therapeutic heat of the sun. The morning was brilliant. The sea was deep green and still. Young Nick's Head looked like a sharp white adze slicing deeply into the water. Further out, an oil freighter traced a widening oil slick which curled like a taniwha in the slow moving currents.

‿

It was 10 o'clock when, relaxed, I presented myself at the Gisborne City Library and asked for Maud Rivers.

'Oh yes, your grandmother could well have been on hunts,' she smiled primly. She was a middle-aged woman, a little wary about why I wanted to know about Pakeha society in Gisborne at the beginning of the twentieth century. 'Gisborne wasn't all that far behind the times in our part of the world!' she clucked, as if offended by my question. 'Now let me see,' she continued as she leafed through a blue-covered volume. 'Ah, here we are. Hunting. Well. It says here that hunting was first engaged in in Poverty Bay on 9 July 1882 at Lavenham. That is not very far from where your grandmother lived, is it? A Mr H. Mason acted as master and a Mr Hassell filled the role of whip. Recalling the initial meet, Mr Hassell in 1947 wrote "I have vivid recollection of the first meet in Poverty Bay . . . As the ground was greasy, falls in the slush and mud came thick and fast . . . Between 400 and 500 riders turned out on the most amazing variety of horseflesh one would ever see in a lifetime." Apparently there was a Hunt Club Ball. No doubt your grandmother would have been there, waltzing away the night!' She sighed. 'Gone are the old days. Gone, gone, gone. Do people still waltz, I wonder? Or have we all moved on to rock and roll? What? Oh, it's disco now is it? Hmmmn.'

Thoroughly vindicated, Maud Rivers led me down another aisle of books, selected one, and then another. 'Now let's see what we can do about that other enquiry of yours. Rollerskating. Aha! As I told you, Gisborne hasn't done too badly at all.' There was a further sense of self-satisfaction in her voice. 'It appears that we actually had rollerskating, or rinking as it was known then, in Gisborne in 1876. It was introduced by a Mr Burland of Napier. The skating rink was in a wooden-floored hall in the city and speed skating events were held for both men and women.' She turned the page. 'The City Rink was built in the 1880s. Now this is interesting—several mishaps occurred at the revival in 1910. A young woman, a young girl and a man each broke a wrist, a youth fractured a foot, a lad had both bones in his forearm broken, and another young man broke his arm.' She gasped in horror. 'That doesn't sound like skating to me! More like a massacre.'

I made the mistake of trying to joke with Maud Rivers. 'Riripeti didn't get back from Venice until 1911. But those mishaps sound like just the kind of things she would have been involved in.'

'Why, what a thing to say about one's grandmother,' she answered. 'Not very charitable, are you?' She showed me firmly to the door. 'Do come again.'

The Gisborne Museum and Art Gallery was only five minutes' walk from the library. Time enough for me to reprimand myself and hope that I would be more diplomatic in my next appointment. Suitably meek, I asked for John Lawrence at the reception desk.

The building was looking very attractive, but I couldn't help thinking how at odds the European architecture was with the history of the region. After all, Poverty Bay was steeped in Maoritanga and the museum itself was notable mainly for its Maori artefacts. Yet here they were installed in a European-looking building, like memorials to a people who no longer existed.

I was staring at the model of an ancient pa site, expertly done in plastic and clay and wooden matches, when John Lawrence arrived. 'Are you Tamatea Mahana?' he asked as he vigorously shook my hand. 'Very nice to meet you! It's always a pleasure to meet a descendant of Artemis Pere.' He was a genial man, stooped but excited about my visit to the museum. 'What do you think of the model?'

'I don't think Riripeti would have liked it,' I admitted. 'She would never have liked to have our culture miniaturised to mere plastic in this manner. Made small like this, a reduction to the absurd.'

I could have bit my tongue. But unlike Maud Rivers, John Lawrence accepted my observation in good grace. 'Whai told me you would be forthright! You and I are going to get along very well.'

I tried to visualise the pa as it must have appeared in its original situation overlooking the Turanganui River. The fort would have been built to maximise the advantages of the terrain, strategically situated with the sea on one side, the river on the second, the buttress of Kaiti Hill as protection to the left flank, and open only to the broad Turanga plains on the right flank. Here, the stockades as well as the trenches and ramparts would have been solidly built to protect the pa from enemy attack. A wooden pahu, situated on the highest point, would have been built to warn of any approaching enemy. Fighting stages over the carved gateways and other vulnerable points gave protection and from these stages darts and stones would be thrown down on an enemy. Inside the pa the villagers would have been alerted from their sleeping huts, ready to douse the flames that a hostile force might have started to cause panic among those within.

'In later days,' John Lawrence explained, noting my interest, 'the pahu would also have been struck to warn of the coming of Pakeha sailing ships to Turanga. The native council, the runanga, was in control of Pakeha trading and it set the price of products, not the Pakeha. The runanga charged vessels a fee for entering the river at this point.' He indicated the place on the model. 'For instance, the schooner *Wellington*, on 10 December 1851, was not allowed to provision itself with fresh water until it had paid 2/7 per bucket. Oh yes, your people were very much in command of the situation. They even began to acquire fleets of small schooners and cutters so that they might transport their produce to Auckland themselves. Te Kooti Arikirangi was at one time reputed to have owned such a schooner. You can be sure that the Pakeha settlers did not like these developments at all!'

He shook his head and motioned me into the small room where he did his research work. Gesturing me to a seat he seemed to drift off into a reverie of his own.

'Oh yes, they were very strange times for us here in Gisborne, the 1850s and 1860s, leading up to the Matawhero Massacre. Your grandmother's great-uncle, Wi Pere, would have been thirty at the time of the massacre. Te Kooti Arikirangi, the other important ancestor in your life, would have been ten or fifteen years older. Isn't it interesting that you have these two men in your whakapapa, to all intents and purposes seeming to be on different sides? Or were they?'

I shrugged my shoulders. 'I guess I will only be able to decide for myself,' I answered, 'once I get to know the times better. That's what Whai told me anyway. He said that there was no other way to understand Riripeti. But I didn't think I would have to go so far back to do it.'

John Lawrence pursed his lips. 'Well, Whai's correct. You can't fully comprehend unless you look at what happened before Artemis's ascendancy. The prelude to the Matawhero Massacre and the Te Kooti revolt are absolutely important in this context. And you cannot look at the massacre itself without understanding the dissatisfaction that caused it. The whole conflict, of course, continued to be over the land and the business of having a British Queen.' He reached for a document in a large glass case. 'As you know, most of your people in Poverty Bay and East Coast denied allegiance to Queen Victoria. On the other hand, they saw no point in joining the Maori King movement in 1856 and 1857 which attempted to set up a Maori royalty. Some researchers say that Te Kani a Takirau, your ancestor up the East Coast, was approached to be the Maori King. Apparently his response was that it would be impossible for anyone to confer on him a title greater than that which was his birthright and therefore he could not accept any new and hollow award.' John Lawrence laughed. 'Now there was a man who was secure in his mana.' He unfolded the document. 'But this is interesting, too, because there was a third element at work which was causing great inner turmoil—the work of the Christian missionaries. I have to confess my bias about Christianity; I've never made it a secret that I am an atheist. I think it was intolerable that Christian ministers could equate your people with savagery and paganism and therefore quite blithely establish a religion that was as savage and as pagan. The ironic thing is that Europeans today are amused at the Maori versions of Christianity as set up by the Ratana and Ringatu movements. For Maori, the Pakeha God was not adequate; fine for Pakeha, but not so fine for Maori. Who can really say which is the right way to God? Christians have been arguing about that point for years—be they Roman Catholic, Ringatu, Anglican, Ratana, Presbyterian, Mormon or Seventh Day Adventist. Well, they can have it.

'What I'm trying to say—and this is why I wanted you to see this document—is that the conflict was not only over the land, the tinana, but also over the spirit of the Maori, the wairua. The document is a letter by Mr Wardell R.M. to Governor Gore Browne.'

He handled the document carefully. It was beautifully penned in large circular lines. One could imagine Wardell composing the letter by flickering candlelight.

'The letter is about a huge runanga, held in Poverty Bay on 21 May 1858. Wardell describes it as being "the most influential and most numerously attended that has taken place since my arrival". First, in none of the speeches at the runanga was there any support for the Queen's authority. All that the leaders were prepared to receive from Europeans was Christianity. Yes, that is an admission that the missionaries were doing well. They used their Bibles as swords to split the people in half' (he smiled bitterly), 'and to divide them, so that when the conflict between Maori and Pakeha came in the 1860s they had the majority of Maori right in their pockets, singing hymns and asking God's forgiveness upon those other Maori who had gone astray like tattooed sheep. But I'm sorry. I'm getting away from the point of the document.

'Second, although the leaders were prepared to accept Christianity, a certain Rutene Piwaka complained about the changes that had been made in the prayer book. "The first prayer book," he said, "contained a prayer for the rangatira Maori and their families. In the second edition the prayer was for the Queen and the rangatira Maori. The prayer in the third edition was for the Queen and her family alone. Let the Pakeha pray for the Queen if they like, but we will not call her our Queen, nor will we recognise her authority."'

John Lawrence paused before returning the document to its glass cabinet. 'Of course, things were deteriorating between Maori and Pakeha. In April 1859 I think—I should check my dates—there was another runanga in the Hawke's Bay in which all tribes were advised to cancel all leases to Pakeha and to repurchase lands that they had parted with. On 11 January 1860, when Governor Gore Browne paid a visit to Poverty Bay, not one speech of welcome was made to him by the Maori people. Instead, Lazarus got up and told him that the Maori people of Poverty Bay did not recognise Queen Victoria's claim to rule over them; the Queen's flag should not have been hoisted on the magistrate's courthouse and the lands which had been obtained from the Maori should be returned!' He shook his head at some inner thought. 'Can you imagine how His Excellency must have felt at having his nose put out of joint? In a dispatch to the Duke of Newcastle he wrote that the natives were lacking in courtesy to him. He said that they had told him, "Unless you have come to restore the lands which the Europeans have cheated us out of, you may return whence you came and take your English magistrate with you."

'Then the Land Wars broke out. In the Waitara in 1860. In the

Waikato in July 1863. At first the Maori tribes of Poverty Bay and the East Coast declined to send help to the rebels and, for a time, the Land Wars did not really affect our region. But then came the Hauhau, in 1865.'

Certain allowances need to be made for John Lawrence's statements. I am sure that under less informal circumstances he would not have let his own atheism show through as bitterly as it did here. Again, when he refers to the 'Matawhero Massacre' what he is really referring to is Te Kooti Arikirangi's retaliation against a whole history of Pakeha abuse of Maori people, custom and land. He is referring to an attack made by Te Kooti in return for his false arrest and imprisonment on the Chatham Islands—Wharekauri. He is referring to an act of utu. And after all, is not the doctrine of an eye for an eye, a tooth for a tooth, enshrined in the Old Testament? In the flux of the times the Matawhero incident is surely no more horrifying than the atrocities committed on the Maori people in the name of civilisation. Of course, the difference is that white people were killed at Matawhero. The blood of a white man, woman or child, spilt by natives, is called an atrocity. The blood of a native man, woman or child spilt by a white man is called an act of self-defence.

But there is one point in John Lawrence's delivery which I agree with and which needs further amplification. This is the role of the church in extending the conflict between Maori and Pakeha over the spiritual domain. It wasn't good enough to take away our lands. The Pakeha had to take away our souls too! Not only did we have to give up our physical world; we had to give up our spiritual world as well. Although Christianity was not forced on us, I am nonetheless disturbed by the rapidity of the conversion process, the evangelical zeal with which the early missionaries could blithely sweep away the Maori's own religious customs. The first missionary visit to the Poverty Bay district occurred in 1834. By 1841, only a year after William Williams set up the Poverty Bay station, Maori people were attending services in their thousands—3200 at Waiapu and Tokomaru, 2500 at Uawa and Turanga. Three years later, it was estimated that 4300 of the 6000 inhabitants of East Cape and Waiapu, 2300 out of the 4000 at Uawa, and 6000 out of the 10,000 at Turanga and Mahia were Christian. 'A great work has been accomplished, in which the hand of the Lord has been signally manifest,' wrote Williams. 'It has not been through the labours of your Missionaries for the Word has only been preached by Native Teachers. We have literally stood still to see the salvation of God.'

Was this why conversion was so successful? By placing the cross in the hands of Maori dupes and telling them to go forth and let the cross so shine, is this how the people were dazzled and hastened to be baptised? And what occurred at baptism? The Maori name was suppressed and replaced by a new, English name. The Maori atua were similarly suppressed and replaced by the one Pakeha God.

So the missionaries gathered in Maori souls. They also gathered in land. Witness the Reverend Archdeacon Henry Williams, Missioner of the Church Missionary Society: principal advisor to the Ngapuhi people, Reverend Williams advised them to sign the Treaty of Waitangi. But at the signing the finger was pointed at him and James Busby, the Resident appointed by the British Government, by the Ngati Kawa chief, Te Kemara, who said, 'My land is gone, all gone, the inheritances of my ancestors, fathers, relatives, all stolen, gone with the missionaries. They have it all, those men there, Busby and Williams, they have my land.' The Reverend Williams felt constrained to reply to this and other accusations by saying that the missionaries had done sterling service in New Zealand, they had laboured long hours in the service of others, that he himself had a family to support—eleven children in all—and, why, surely the land he had was not excessive given the fact that it would have to be divided eleven ways on his death?

The Reverend Williams was followed in similar vein by James Busby, who said that the purchase of land was a necessary insurance against old age on the part of Europeans like himself. (He had grabbed 50,000 acres for his golden years.) Yes indeed, there was a ruffling of feathers and no doubt relief when the Treaty was duly signed and sealed. With the signing, the very Reverend Williams was then able to convert his occupancy of many thousands of acres of Maori land given to him by the chiefs into a proper title under British law. Much later, after Governor George Grey had made allegations about his land deals, the Church Missionary Society dismissed Williams from his post as missionary. His brother, the Reverend William Williams, was able eventually to secure his reinstatement. Was Jerusalem built in New Zealand's green and pleasant hills? Some Maori people thought so, but others did not. Among those who didn't were the Hauhau led by their prophet, Te Ua Haumene.

About the Treaty of Waitangi, the Reverend Kingi Ihaka has said that it was 'only but paper, yet troublesome, causing prestige to decline and land to be confiscated. As a result was the saying "Titiro ki te rangi tahuri rawa ake, kahore he whenua e . . . Kua riro." We looked up to heaven and before we knew where we were there was no land left . . . all gone.'

The Treaty was signed between the British Government and some Maori chiefs on 6 February 1840. It was the instrument by which the British decided to extend their sovereignty to New Zealand. From the Pakeha point of view the British Crown was surprisingly accommodating, given the colonial imperative by which all the major white conquerors were motivated. The Crown said that all property belonged to the Maori and could not be taken without our consent and without payment. Land was made available for European settlement, but the interests of Maori owners were protected by restricting to the Government the right to purchase their land. Other intrinsic rights were also guaranteed. The Treaty has therefore been praised for its High Mindedness, its Attempt at an Honourable Solution to Accommodating the Needs of the Pakeha (and Maori), its Integrity. The trouble is that the Treaty has never had any status in domestic or international law. The Pakeha signed it knowing it was worthless.

Now, from te taha Maori, the view is different. The British Crown has consistently broken its contract (and all you Pakeha lawyers can argue until the cows come home that the Treaty wasn't a legal document but we believe it is). Maori tribal lands from the very beginning, even before the ink was dry on the document, have been illegally taken, granted, sold, leased and wrongly withheld, misused and misplaced. There have been losses of forestry rights, mineral rights, fishing rights and Maori tribal cultural rights. What contentment is there for Maori, knowing how our forefathers fought and died last century to rectify the inconsistencies and injustices that the Treaty embodies? Are we to continue to ignore, in these modern times, the struggle they endured to prevent land from being swallowed up by the greedy Pakeha speculators, and to prevent our customs and traditions from being trampled on by the Pakeha?

For most assuredly you, Pakeha, began taking the land from us as you were signing your worthless Treaty. You, Pakeha, began taking away our culture. You said at the time that we were now one people, he iwi kotahi tatou. What you really meant was that we now belonged to you.

That was why we went to war.

~

Te Paremata o te Pakeha, 1949.

The wind was in abeyance on the forecourt of Parliament Buildings, Wellington. The eastern wind was on one side, the southerly on the other. In between was calm, like the eye of a cyclone.

But Riripeti was not calm. The child felt her fingers clasping his upper arms, almost hurting him. She was watching, intense, the consultation that was occurring between the Prime Minister and the chiefs of Maoridom, waiting on the red carpet. 'Kia tupato,' she said. 'Now comes the time of the mihimihi, the speechmaking. We must listen carefully when the speeches are made to welcome us, because we must respond in kind. If we do not hear all that is said then we cannot reply with all that must be said. So be alert because, after all, this is Pharaoh's territory, not ours. For instance, it was an earlier Pharaoh to the one who stands before us, who prepared the ground for the building of Te Paremata o te Pakeha when, in the early 1800s, he gave a hundred muskets, a hundred blankets and a pile of pretty baubles to Maori who he thought represented the tribes of the lower North Island. They didn't.'

She directed the child's gaze across Parliament Grounds to the inner harbour of Wellington, the sea storming along the waterfront. 'And regardless of the groans of the Maori, it was Pharaoh's ships, the *Tory* in 1839, *Aurora* in 1840 and four later vessels, that brought the Pakeha to the harbour that had first been discovered by Kupe a thousand years before, and founded by Tara. They raised Wellington as the capital of New Zealand and, shortly thereafter, began to build their edifices of governance here, within the Valley of the Kings. And the highest shrine of power is Te Paremata o te Pakeha. It is a place of dread, mokopuna. From its halls all the laws which control the lives of all Maori are promulgated.'

The pearls shimmered in her hair as she glanced across the forecourt at the Prime Minister and the chiefs of Maoridom. The Prime Minister's chief official, Timoti, was conversing with Maui, one of the elders. 'They are up to something,' Riripeti warned the child. 'But they had better be careful for they will get as good as they give—' she winked at the child '—and perhaps more than they expect.'

There was a murmur of amusement from the ope. 'The Matua's in a fighting mood. Those old fellas better watch out because she only had a little breakfast today.' But behind the joking was a darkness, a fear, because in any encounter like this the forecourt was a marae, the courtyard of Tu, God of War. Any person, man or woman, who proposed to do battle there needed to be well aware of their weapons. For a moment, the child also felt fearful for the matriarch. He looked up and saw the sky turning in her eyes, the eyes that took colour from the elements and which were on this day as dark green as the pounamu. He wanted to say something to her but, almost as suddenly as the wind had died, so too did the tumult and the ecstasy following their entry onto Parliament Grounds.

'Now it really begins,' Riripeti said. 'See? Whai is to be their first speaker.'

He stood on the red carpet, tokotoko in his hand, a walking stick, which he raised in a dramatic gesture. His voice boomed across the forecourt, his tokotoko pulling the wrath of the heavens down, down to earth.

'Tihei . . . mauri ora,' Whai began, the words thrusting out, pushing out, into the world of light. 'I sneeze . . . it is life. Tihei uriuri, tihei nakonako, it is darkness, it is blackness. Lay, ha, set in its place, the sky above. Lay, ha, set in its place the earth below.' The words were rapid and recited in a rhythmic incantatory manner. 'Ka tau, ha, whakatau ko Te Matuku mai ki Rarotonga. Trace back to Te Matuku from Rarotonga, who dived to the spirit within, who dived to the spirit without.' Whai strode up and down the red carpet in time with the cadence of his chant, gesturing and brandishing his walking stick. 'Fix firmly, Te More from Hawaiki, rising and falling. Rise and stand up to the sky. Aua kia eke, eke panuku, eke Tangaroa. Whano, whano, haramai te toki, haumi e, hui e . . . taiki e.' With each arching phrase his voice climbed higher in the sky. 'Rise, rise together, up, Tangaroa. Go, go, bring me the adze. Bind it, join it . . . it is done.'

The words were ancient and obscure. Right at the end, a giant tidal wave of voices joined with his. 'Taiki e. Yes, let it be done.'

Riripeti nodded with approval. 'Whai was always a great orator,' she told the child. 'One of these days, mokopuna, you must learn some of the ritual chants, the tauparapara and the patere. Such chants dignify your speech. But, hush, mokopuna, we must hear what else he has to say.'

Whai had paused, looking back at Timoti. Was that a nod that was exchanged between them? Imperceptibly, his stance altered and so did the quality of his korero. 'Whakatau mai, whakatau mai, whakatau mai, whakatau mai. Land here, land here,' he welcomed the ope, 'land here, land here. Come tribes, come the voices, the canoes of the island from beneath the four winds. Welcome the tribes of that coast, of this coast, of the interior. Haere mai nga rangatira o te motu. Welcome, chiefs of the island—'

('At this point,' the journalist said, 'I sensed that something was amiss. I can't put my finger on it, but it was as if the electricity in the air had turned from positive to negative. There was a strange unease—Bernard Scott picked up on it too—and some of the Maori people waiting on the red carpet were whispering to one another. The old Maori man I was standing next to explained it to me. "There's been a jack-up between Timoti and some of the chiefs of Maoridom. They must be in a hurry to get back to their meeting to treat the Matua like this." When I asked him what the problem was, he told me, "A chief is always welcomed in a chiefly manner with chiefly korero and speechmaking. But Whai, the chief who is welcoming the Matua, treats her almost as if she has no mana." I asked him, "What's mana?" He answered, "It is the power of her office. Just as you would honour your king, we would expect Whai to acknowledge her rank. It is the same with Maori and rangatira Maori. He is not recognising her rank. He is speaking to her as if she is a commoner. No references to genealogy. No drawing of descent lines together. But worse than that, he is doing it deliberately, treating her, to all intents and purposes, as an outcast."

'And it was clear,' the journalist continued, 'that Artemis recognised the slight and had taken offense. You know, sometimes distances seem deceptive. But when the sun came briefly through the clouds, it illuminated her extraordinary face, and brought her so close to me that I could almost touch her. The sunlight gleamed like fire on the pearls in her hair. I will never forget what she did. She looked up at the sun and her face was so deathly calm. And then—')

The child heard Riripeti whisper to herself. 'Alas, Whai, must you treat me in this unseemly manner?' She looked across at the other elders where they sat on the red carpet. 'And you, Henare, and you Maui, and you, Timoti. This is not the way, my dear friends. Not like this. Are we not Maori and therefore on the same side? Or have you joined Pharaoh against me?'

Whai's voice spun itself out into the air, spinning, spinning, spinning. Riripeti lifted her head, as if to watch the words ascending. Spinning, spinning, spinning, and the sun shafted through the words as they ascended into heaven.

She stared straight into the sun and did not blink. Instead, she absorbed its power.

'Aue, e kui,' Aunt Hiraina said. There was confusion, anger, sorrow and embarrassment in the ranks of the ope. To stand here, like this, on the forecourt, without due acknowledgement given to Riripeti, their rangatira, required strength. And then their rage began to mount.

'Kia kaha,' Riripeti breathed. 'This is my fight, not yours. Nevertheless, close your ranks, all of you, stand close, closer still, for it is my great honour to feel your aroha for your Matua. Be one group and let us have the one heart and one purpose.' Her voice rose with authority. 'The red carpet of the Pakeha is before us and let nobody, Pakeha or Maori, stand in our way.'

Immediately, the ope began to acclaim her. 'Ae! Ae! Ae!'

'We are not the first petitioners to come to the Paremata o te Pakeha to make our case to the Prime Minister, e hoa, give us back our land, and we will not be the last. The carpet is like unto a river of blood into the House of the European. It is like the Red Sea which Moses parted so that the Children of Israel could walk through it and reach sweet Beulah Land.' She smiled her madonna smile. 'Do you not remember our history? After our land was taken following the Te Kooti Wars in 1869, so many of our ancestors have walked this same red carpet. Riperata Kahutia in 1878 offered up her plea; it was rejected. Wi Pere Halbert, in the early 1900s, pleaded in the very House before us; his petition was thrown out. A Commission of Inquiry in 1919 could not resolve our grievances. In 1923, Heni Materoa spoke again on our behalf. In 1938, again, our tribal representatives came to plead with the Parliament. And subsequently I have come again and again and again. And is not what is happening to us, right now, the same as when Moses went up into the mountains to obtain the Ten Commandments and, while he was away, the Children of Israel became divided one tribe against each other? I do not blame my brother chiefs.'

The child watched as Riripeti imprisoned all eyes into hers. She lifted her hands to her head and began to pull her dark black veil back down and over her face.

'If this is what they want,' she said, 'then this is what they will get.'

('The atmosphere was so tense,' the journalist said. 'The Prime Minister was watching, bemused, as Bernard Scott hastily consulted with Timoti but, clearly, the elders of Maoridom were adamant.

Better to put Artemis in her place now and not allow her the opportunity of appearing as an equal, with equal authority, among them.')

'So be it,' Riripeti said. She looked up at the sun again, full, glorious, a gigantic glowing orb of immense power.

She lifted her right hand up to her veil and began to pull it down across her face.

('But I have yet to tell you of the most extraordinary incident,' the journalist said. 'I guess it will never, ever be explained. On reflection I think it was entirely coincidental, but who knows? I have heard that some of your people have the power to make such things happen—')

The veil slowly descending. As it did so, the clouds began to join across where once had been a brief space of sunlit sky.

'So be it,' Riripeti said again.

With a ponderous rumbling, like iron gates closing, the sun began to go out.

⁓

The Land Wars began in Waitara in 1860. By 1863, the Waikato had taken up arms against the Pakeha. All over Aotearoa the sun was going out.

As for Poverty Bay and the East Coast, the wars began with the arrival at Opotiki on 28 February 1865 of Pai Marire emissaries led by Kereopa. There, at the command of Jehovah, they put the Reverend C.S. Volkner on trial—he had always maintained that the Waitara War, in Taranaki, was just, and that the only way to save the Maori people was to subjugate them—and then hanged him.

But while the conflict on the Coast was clearly related to events in Taranaki and the Waikato, neither its beginning nor its end was dependent on them. 'The East Coast, in a word,' wrote W.H. Oliver, 'had its own war for its own reasons, and they were considerably Maori reasons. Outside influences, whether Pai Marire emissaries or government troops, acted as catalysts precipitating the unstable elements of Maori society into hostile groupings.'

What were these unstable elements? Primarily, the Maori of Poverty Bay and the East Coast were already divided into those who were pro-Pakeha and those who were anti-Pakeha. It was the Maori with his hands around his own neck. The Pakeha convinced some Maori that it was still possible to come to advantageous terms with settler and government about Maori needs. They turned those tribes sympathetic to Pakeha against those who wanted to lead a total resistance against the Pakeha. It was the latter group which saw all Maori as united in victimhood and tried to create a Maori nationalism in resistance and, hopefully, in victory. And it was to these upstarts and troublemakers, embracing an already hopeless cause, that the miraculous teachings of the Hauhau appealed.

'Hapa, hapa, paimarire hau!' was the cry which gave the Pai Marire Church its name. This was the chant of the warriors as they ran into battle with their right hands raised to give them immunity from bullets. The church was revealed to the prophet Te Ua Haumene by the angel Gabriel. The Maori people were one of the Lost Tribes of Israel, living in 'New Canaan', and the angel said that they would be delivered from bondage from the Pakeha overlords. If they had complete faith in the power of the karakia, in the prophecies of the High Priest, Te Ua, in the ceremonies involving the Niu pole, and the conscious willing of the expulsion of the Pakeha, the Maori would be saved—not only from original sin, but also from the Pakeha himself. O yea, the Pakeha would be destroyed, rire, rire, hau, hau.

The Pakeha called them fanatics, these Hauhau. But they touched a chord in the Maori heart, that of aroha ki te iwi, love of country. In particular, the people of Te Whanau a Kai responded with ardour. Who among us could resist the tangi, the weeping for our Aotearoa, and for those of us who had already been slain by the Pakeha in our lands of the Taranaki and Waikato?

This was why the ancestors of Riripeti, she who was to become the matriarch, took the Pai Marire emissaries as our guests when they arrived from Opotiki on 13 March 1865. Two days later, we also took the Hauhau contingent: they brought news of the bitter struggle in the Taranaki and had come to us from Ruatahuna, from the country of the Tuhoe people. We took them into our hearts and we had a karakia at Patutahi, near our village of Waituhi. There, we set up the Niu, the tall pole, eighty feet in length, and crossed the yardarms with two curved knobs representing nga atua, Ruru and Oiki, and topped by the Hauhau flag. Rope streamers descended from the pole and we took them in our hands because this was how Jehovah's angels would enter our bodies if we believed in Him. Then, as we chanted, we marched around the Niu, our eyes fixed with a steady gaze on the pole itself. Round and round and round, the pace increasing, the hundreds of us weeping for the loss of our land and our iwi. And that is why many other dissidents from Ngati Porou, Rongowhakaata and Te Aitanga a Mahaki embraced the new faith. This is why we became angry with the Pakeha and when we saw him closing his mission stations and his settlements—he was fearful of the increasing Maori tensions—we could only feel elation in our hearts. We saw the Reverend Williams and the Reverend Clarke leave with their families, departing the Pakeha mission station at Waerenga a Hika—and this was a victory for the Maori Jehovah—and sailing on the SS *St Kilda* on the evening of 3 April 1865. We saw the European settlements in Poverty Bay become completely disorganised. They were helpless, these Pakeha, to stand against us, because their government's troops were already committed to the wars in the Taranaki. They were leaving the district and there were now fewer Europeans than in 1840.

Ae, but many Pakeha remained and they had the support of Maori loyalists of Ngati Porou, Rongowhakaata and Te Aitanga a Mahaki. They cleaved unto the Pakeha God and denied Pai Marire. And so the pattern of the fighting was confused, for just as many Maori supported the Pakeha as fought against them. On 7 May 1865, Ngati Porou loyalists even erected the Queen's flagstaff at Turanga. Why did they provoke Te Whanau a Kai and other Maori nationalists in this manner? Our symbol had become the Niu, not the flag of the British Crown.

This was why we built Waerenga a Hika fortress. It was our fighting centre on the bank of the old riverbed near the Waerenga a Hika mission station. The building of the pa consolidated the optimism of the Hauhau nationalists as we took one pa after another from the loyalists in our progress to recover Poverty Bay and the East Coast and drive the Pakeha back into the sea.

But, aue, what was this? The wind swept the good signs from the dust and brought with it the portents of doom. Cast the spells again upon the earth!

Alas, the Ngati Porou. They saw not our purpose or the purpose of the Hauhau but rather the spectre of their old enemy, Taranaki. They scented not the freedom of the new nationalism but instead smelt the fear of conquest from their traditional foes from the south. So they fought back against our incursions into their lands.

Aue. Again, cast the spells. Now thrice throw the spells. Aue, aue, the third casting!

The Pakeha in Poverty Bay doubled, trebled their numbers as military forces and arms consignments were brought into the battles against us. Fifty Hawke's Bay Volunteers. Forty-five Forest Rangers. And there, too, in the dust's new patterning, was a gunboat, HMS *Eclipse*, at the battle of Te Hatepe.

Cast the spells quickly again. Aue!

We had made successful conquests in Ngati Porou, but suffered our first defeat on 2 August 1865 at Pa Kairomiromi, and we were beginning to be pushed back. And aue, there was another victory against us at Pukemaire on 9 October 1865, and at Pukeamaru on 11 October 1865 where 200 of us were forced to take the oath of allegiance against our Hauhau faith. And, aue, Hirini te Kani declared himself on the side of the Crown.

The pattern. The pattern. Alas, it was a new pattern!

See the British Queen, riding to victory against us on the tattooed back of the loyalist Ngati Porou, Rongowhakaata and Te Aitanga a Mahaki. Around and around she rode, stamping our rebellion with the bare feet of her loyalist people, and pushing us back, back, back, to our central stronghold at Waerenga a Hika.

So cast the spells once more and divine the final stand at Waerenga a Hika. Once. Twice. Thrice. Again. Again. Again. Ah yes, now look. See. Watch. Listen. Hapa, hapa, paimarire hau. Rire, rire, hau, hau.

Oh it was all so strange, the ebb and flow, the very flux of war. As the noose tightened around Waerenga a Hika pa, the Hauhau became more like victims than perpetrators of aggression. With news of defeats, like portents in the sky, the Poverty Bay Hauhau, including Te Whanau a Kai, began to seek for peace and to extricate themselves with honour from a war of nationalism. But their Pakeha opponents wanted blood. They refused to discuss any terms of surrender and began to wantonly spread rumours of Hauhau atrocities so that when the final blooding was made there would be no sympathy for the insurgents.

More and more European troops arrived. On 26 September 1865, twenty-six Military Settlers arrived from Hawke's Bay and built a stockade at Kaiti: on 27 September 1865, this force was augmented by thirty members of the Hawke's Bay C.D.C. under a Captain La Serre. Loyalists of the Rongowhakaata assembled at a pa at Oweta on 14 October 1865; Henare Potae and thirty Ngati Porou friendlies joined them, reaching Poverty Bay on 30 October 1865. In the following month, orders were given that all European troops on the East Coast should be drafted to Poverty Bay; on 9 November 1865, HMS *Esk* landed the Ngati Porou leaders Ropata, Mokena and Potae and 260 followers at Turanga. On that same day, the ship *Sturt* arrived from Waiapu with a hundred Forest Rangers under a Major Frazer. The order was made: the moment had come to confront the rebels at Waerenga a Hika.

The time had come for the blooding. Mr Donald McLean, on 9 November 1865, issued a simple ultimatum: the Hauhau must come in and submit to the Government or they would be attacked and deprived of their lands. The attack, according to the ultimatum, would take place at noon on the 15th. The Hauhau chiefs told McLean that they were willing to surrender but wanted him to come to them in peace. McLean refused. ('The Hauhau, clearly, were not to be allowed to make peace,' says W.H. Oliver, 'and so remain powerful and capable of disturbance in the future. Their power was to be broken.') No surrender was made on the 15th so the period of grace was extended for twenty-four hours. At the expiry of the time limit, the Government, settler and loyalist troops were instructed to move out and engage the enemy. 'Go straight at them,' said Major Frazer.

The hedge was the first defence of the pa. Between the hedge and the pa was a cleared expanse, about 150 metres wide. At the inner edge of the clearing was a double palisade about four metres high—the uprights were large puriri posts and they were joined together by closely woven stakes of manuka. To the north of the pa was thick scrub. Extensive forests stood to the south. At the rear of the pa was the lagoon.

On the first day of the attack, the troops settled into position at the front of the pa and to its left and right. The rebels chanted a defiant haka. The fighting began the next day. Attack and counter attack. Parry and riposte. The bugles of life and of death. Somewhere in the middle of it all, white flags were hoisted. Flags of surrender or flags of the Hauhau religion, nobody really knows. Then towards the end of the siege, a six-pounder howitzer was trained on the pa.

The date was 22 November 1865. It was the day of the fall of Waerenga a Hika. The Niu pole with its flag toppled in the place called Turanga.

The Pai Marire revolt on the East Coast and in Poverty Bay was over. During the rebellion, which lasted less than eight months, seven fortified pa were destroyed. Close upon 1300 rebels surrendered or were captured, 600 stands of arms were given up and 223 Maori rebels were killed as against thirty-one members of the Crown. No number exists for the loyal Maori who died.

At Waerenga a Hika pa itself, 800 rebels were forced to surrender. Rebel dead and wounded exceeded 130. The Crown forces lost seven to death's embrace and seven were wounded. 'Never before in the history of the colony,' said Premier Stafford on 19 August 1868, 'has there been so memorable and so creditable a series of military operations as those which were carried out by Colonel Frazer on the East Coast in 1865. European forces, which had totalled in all rarely above 130, had, with native allies, subjected the whole of the country between Cape Runaway and Hawke's Bay in less than twelve months.'

Yes, it is so strange, so strange, the fortunes of war, all so strange, the casting of patterns, the *fatalitá* of events. Throughout all of Aotearoa, the Land Wars were coming to an end. Victory was with the Pakeha and his loyal Maori people; defeat was with the nationalist Maori upstarts and renegades. Even more bitter was that defeat brought with it a further loss of land—not only to the Maori who had fought against the Pakeha but also to the Maori who had fought with him. Ah yes, a bitter irony indeed.

With a ponderous rumbling, like iron gates closing, the sun began to go out. But it was not yet total eclipse. There was still a further divination to come, a stirring in the shadow of the fall of Waerenga a Hika. The pa was the hinge of fate for the Maori coast, but the gates were not yet closed.

Cast the spells one more time. Who waits in the shadows of the pa?

Standing there, pushing the gates open, was a man and another religion: Te Kooti Arikirangi te Turuki was the man; Ringatu was the religion.

Pakeha, we did not belong to you yet—not yet.

Nine years after the fall of Waerenga a Hika pa, in March 1874, some Maori dwellers in Waiapu were foraging near Te Hatepe. They found a large device in a lead casing.

Reports are confusing about what happened next. Official sources believe that the Maori who had discovered the object decided to build a large fire around it in order to obtain the lead. Local information suggests that the fire was built without any real understanding of the danger of this act, or of what the device was—an unexploded shell fired from HMS *Eclipse* in early July 1865.

A large number of Maori sat around the fire, talking and laughing about love and life and, perhaps, fate. The heat from the fire glowed upon the projectile's casing. The shell exploded, a tragic coda to the battle nine years before. The irony is underlined by the name of the gunboat from whence the missile had been fired.

Twenty people were killed in the explosion and a number of others were injured by the flying shrapnel.

The sun had not yet gone out.

5

*L a luce langue, il faro spegnesi ch'eterno scorre per gli ampi cieli.
Notte desiata, provvida veli la man colpevole che ferira.* Light weakens, and the beacon that eternally courses the far-flung heavens is spent . . .

That second night at Palliser Street, I thrashed in my sleep again. After all the years of closing the door against my memories, I had begun to dream about Riripeti.

'Matua . . . Riripeti . . .'

When she died seventeen years ago I had been totally bereft. I was uncontrollable at her tangihanga, shouting at the funeral that she wasn't dead; after all, she had told me that she was immortal, and I believed her. Just before they took her to be buried, I reached a point of emotional collapse, especially when the lid was placed on her casket. 'Why are you doing that? How can she breathe?' It was only when she was being committed to the earth, and I saw the wet clay covering her casket, that I fully realised: she was dead and she wasn't coming back. I fainted at the graveside. I spent two months in hospital in a mental delirium that was complicated by pneumonia. I would wake up, thinking that it was me, not she, who had been buried alive in the casket. Screaming, I would thrust my arms up and about me and, if I ever felt something—cloth, sheets, blankets, anything—I would collapse into my delirium again. The old priest, Tamati Kota gave me blessing after blessing. My boyhood mind could barely cope with the enormity of the loss. An entire year is missing from my memory. The best way to handle my grief was to shut the doorway to memories of Riripeti—and keep it shut. But now it was opening again. Perhaps I would be stronger this time.

Even so, when I woke up, I was drenched with sweat. And when I saw Tiana sitting beside me, I drew back. 'You are watching me again,' I said. 'You know I have never liked you watching me while I am asleep.'

Her hair, unpinned, was around her shoulders. She was wearing a white nightdress. 'You were groaning, son,' she answered. 'What mother can let her child continue in his nightmare without wanting to help him?'

I saw that she was pleading with me, but I did not want to soften my heart. 'I don't need your help,' I said. Although I was now an adult I still didn't trust her.

Her expression became still. 'So things are still the same between us?' she asked. She lifted her face to the light. 'No matter what happened, Tamatea, you were my eldest son,' she began. Her voice was not without tenderness. 'You were the only thing I had ever truly owned. Whatever I did, I did because of that and if love is a crime I stand upon mine own act and confess it. It's time to forgive me, Tama.'

My heart was racing. I felt both anger and love but, before Tiana and I could continue our conversation, Te Ariki appeared at the doorway.

'Grandfather Ihaka wants to see me,' he said. 'He's out at Te Karaka this morning, at Takipu marae, supporting a case that they have against the Waikohu County Council. The council wants to change the course of the Waikohu River. Over your grandfather's dead body.'

The moment of reconciliation between Tiana and me was gone.

Forgiveness? I could never give Tiana the absolution she wanted. Not yet.

'Your sister Teria will come by at eight to pick you up,' she said. 'Have a good day at Waituhi, son.' She turned to Te Ariki. 'Can you drop me off at work? I'll leave you two alone.'

For a moment, Te Ariki and I were silent. Then, 'And you'll be leaving Gisborne for Auckland this afternoon?' he asked. My father and I have always hated saying goodbye to one another. Goodbyes are too final with their fears of 'Will we ever meet again?' So we cover up our emotions as best we can. It was unfair of me to have come for such a short visit.

'Yes,' I nodded.

'Don't worry about us,' he said. 'We'll be all right. By the way, your Uncle Pita and Aunt Hiraina went down to Wellington last week to pick up your cousin Raina. They say she's back on the drugs again. They want to bring her back here where they can look after her. If they telephone for your help, you know what to do. Come home to Gisborne for longer next time. And bring Regan and Bianca with you. Are you ashamed of us or something? I want to see my mokopuna soon. So don't forget to give them a kiss from Grandfather. Ma te Atua koe e manaaki. You know I love you.'

We embraced. He turned, but I restrained him.

'Dad,' I asked, 'why did Tiana hate Riripeti?'

'What kind of question is that?' he answered. 'Your grandmother and Tiana may have had their differences, but after we were reunited and you were born, they made peace with each other.'

'What about when Grandmother decided to bring me up?'

'Your mother was always obedient to Riripeti,' he said.

Soon after he left with Tiana, my brother and sister Hamuera and Meri dashed in to say goodbye. Mana began playing his disco records. There was a splash and a flurry of activity as he got dressed, in time with the music, in his school uniform. He came in and wrestled me awake.

'I'm off now. Footie practice. I might make the first fifteen this year. Can I come down to Wellington during the holidays and stay with you? You really mean it? Great. Well, take care brother, see you around. You know, the kids at school think you're really neat. They don't believe me when I tell them you and me are brothers. Oh, and Teria said she'd pick you up at 8 a.m. on the dot.'

At 8.15 a.m. there was a squeal of brakes, a zoom down the driveway, a slam of the back door, and Teria breezed in, yawned, and draped herself around my neck.

'I thought I'd let you sleep in a little,' she said. 'You need all the beauty that you can get. Ready to go to Waituhi? All set? Right. Exit stage left running.'

I followed my sister out to the car.

~

Teria and I sped out of the city. We crossed the city limits at Makaraka, went past Matawhero, over the concrete bridge spanning the Matawhero River, and took the road arrowing towards the foothills where Waituhi was, fifteen kilometres west of the city. We were halfway there when she decided to turn off the road. She stopped the car.

'Hamuera told me what you asked him yesterday,' she began. 'About Mum, and whether she had been the same with him, Mana and Meri as she had been with us—you, me, Erina and Vanessa.'

The sun came out from behind some clouds and the light flared, hurting my eyes.

'She's not like that any more,' Teria said. 'All those times when she used to lash out at us, they're gone now.'

Gone? They may have gone but the memories were still as clear. I remembered that even as Tiana was lashing out at us, me and my sisters, we knew in our heart of hearts that our mother really did love us. After each lashing, or stroke of the knife—she would score our skin lightly, just enough to make the blood well out like tiny rubies along the cut—we would chant in unison in the darkness of our bedroom, 'Mummy loves us, she loves us, she really does, but we've been bad and we have to be punished, and that's why she hurts us, but she loves us, yes, she really does, Mummy loves us.'

'If you say so,' I answered Teria.

We would resolve to be better children because, often as not, our mother's punishments were justifiable: we had, indeed, been late with the milking or in setting the table for dinner or we'd forgotten to look after baby Vanessa or, after they were born, Meri, Hamuera and Mana—or committed some other misdemeanour. In the world of the rural Maori community of the 1950s and 1960s, such discipline was commonplace. But in Tiana's case, her attacks on us came as senseless reactions to her own upbringing. Something had happened to her when she was a young girl that had destroyed any illusions about the nature of love and being loved. She had been owned in some terrible way. Somebody had controlled her. Whatever it was, something done to her from that time had marked her behaviour and imprisoned her within its cycle so that she could not help but do it to us.

In particular, she wanted to own me. The knife marks were the marks of her ownership. We soothed our bruises and smeared ointment over the trails made by the knife and resolved to be better children without never really knowing what 'better' was. We yearned to love our mother. Perhaps she knew this. Perhaps she was trying to teach us the most important lesson of all about love: love is inconsistent, it is cruel as well as kind, it is not to be trusted. It uses people and is used by people. Even so, we devised strategies to win love from her. Sometimes we won. Sometimes we didn't.

'I say so,' Teria said grimly. But then she began shaking. 'You promised to protect us, always. But when you grew up you left us. And when you went to stay with Riripeti, you never came back during the weekends. Then you went to boarding school. You promised, but you broke your promise. Why did you leave us Tama? Why didn't you ever come back for us?'

Teria always presented a tough exterior but not even that could stop her remembering how she had to protect Erina and Vanessa because, yes, after Riripeti died, I had left Waituhi, the iwi, and my sisters too. I had gone forward. I never glanced back.

'How many times do I have to say sorry, sister?' I asked her.

She looked at me angrily. She started the car. 'When you've said it enough times, I'll let you know.'

We approached Patutahi, the small township just before the village of Waituhi. Teria wanted to get some more cigarettes, so we stopped at the corner store. Patutahi hadn't changed much. It was still four blocks of hotel, school, unused community hall, garage, corner store and the ubiquitous New Zealand war memorial.

Then Teria returned. She hesitated. She looked at me in a strange manner and said, 'Oh yes, one other thing. At the River Bar, when I met our cousin Sammy, he had quite a few drinks in him. You've heard what's happened to Raina, haven't you, and her drug addiction?'

'Yes,' I nodded.

'He said that what's happened to her, everything bad that's happened to the Mahana clan, is all because of you.'

'Me?' I was getting a little angry.

'He said it was about mana. Inherited power. When Grandmother raised you to be her heir, she gave you everything. That's why your own life and career have taken you to the heavens. You have been protected. Whereas others, like Raina, have been without protection.'

'Uncle Alexis has a different view,' I defended myself. 'When my career in the Maori world was denied me, I had to make it in the Pakeha world. I had no other option. I did it myself.'

'Denied you?' Teria asked, puzzled. 'What did Uncle mean by that?'

'I don't know. He didn't actually say it in those words but the implication was clear.' I paused. 'Whatever has happened to others in the family is not of my making. And it is not of Riripeti's. She loved all the iwi, not just me. Her life was devoted to the people of Te Whanau a Kai. I may have been her favourite grandchild but I was not the only one to feel the warmth of her aroha. She would have been greatly upset to hear talk like Sammy's which divides the family and the iwi.'

Teria made as if to say something further, but then dismissed it with a shrug of her shoulders. However, as the car sped across the bridge and through the maize fields bordering Waituhi I could sense that she was wrestling with some inner turmoil.

Then there it was, the gateway to Waituhi, the once-palisaded hill, its crumbling steps incised in dark silhouette against the sky. My heart began to swirl with the same maelstrom of past and present, of light and darkness, of elation and sadness. Every approach to Waituhi was a rebirth. At the same time it was also an acknowledgement of loss, for this was the womb of my life and it had given life to the family of the womb, generation after generation. I felt my blood sing with their welcome at my return, and my eyes glistened at the song in the blood. I wanted to call back my own acclamation to the people and the land from where I had come. I placed my hand on my sister and she slowed the car.

'I'll walk from here,' I said.

She looked at me. 'Which way will you take?'

'This time, I'll circle the foothills,' I said. 'It shouldn't take long. I'll meet you at Takitimu Hall. It will take me a couple of hours.'

We were silent for a moment. Then Teria remembered something. 'Oh, by the way, I came across that woman who was a friend of Mum's in Hastings. You know, when Mum got married to Dad?'

'You mean you found Mereira?' I asked, astonished.

'That's her. Yes. I've got her address somewhere. I'll send it to you in Wellington.'

I had remembered something too. 'It was wrong,' I said to Teria, 'for Riripeti to give me that extra ten shillings.'

Her eyes moistened with tears. She smiled gratefully. Kissed me.

As her face drew away I saw myself in her eyes. 'Mana,' she said. 'It's all got to do with mana.'

~

'So be it,' Riripeti said.

She pulled her dark veil down and over her face.

On the forecourt of Parliament, the Prime Minister, chiefs of Maoridom and all who were gathered there looked up into the sky, crying out in alarm. The clouds were joining across what had once been a brief space of sunlit sky, like viscous liquid poured, spreading and streaming into the blue gap of air. It was as if Ranginui, the Sky

Father, so long separated from Papatuanuku, had finally wrenched free of his heavenly imprisonment and wished to embrace the Earth Mother again. With relentless power he descended, blotting out the sun in his inevitable embrace of earth.

'Grandmother,' the child cried out.

Like everyone else he was afraid. He felt the warmth withdrawing, and the light being sucked away, as the moon slowly began to bite into the edge of the sun. He looked up and saw the black cutting edge across the sun's glowing face, and tears sprang to his eyes because the light was still blinding in its intensity. He averted his gaze a moment. He heard people screaming, even members of the ope, the group which had come with Riripeti. Through his blurring vision he looked at the group.

They were all staring into the sky. Only Tiana's face was averted from the sun and, for a brief moment, the child saw his mother looking across at him. Her face was expressionless, immobile, yet it had intensity in the gaze. Then the child saw his mother's eyes shift, almost imperceptibly, to the matriarch. Her responding glance was autocratic and triumphant.

The light lessening, lessening. The black disc of the moon closed like a gate on the sun. The pearls in Riripeti's hair began to change colour. The lustrous pale of the pearls became drenched with blood.

The child looked up into the sky again. The sun was almost out now, but around the black hole where its light had been was a bright circlet of light and, from it, there erupted bursts of flame, spectacular, wondrous, curling into the black universe.

The clouds were completely joined, and the upstaring faces and the marae itself were bathed in a wan light. The sun seemed to stand in blackness for eternity. There it shone, a beacon smothered by the clouds, still, forbidding, angry, with its corona of fire. It was like looking through a piece of smoked glass. The effect was powerful and brooding.

Riripeti looked across at the elders where they sat on the paepae. She nodded at them. She inclined her head to the Prime Minister.

'So it is done,' she said. The crowd on the marae was still in a state of alarm. Some were crying out to her.

Then the child saw that the pearls in her hair were changing colour again, assuming their usual sheen. Whatever was happening would soon be over. Alert, he listened as Riripeti called to the ope and pulled them together with her presence.

'It will soon be time for us to reply to the speeches of welcome,' she said. 'When the sun comes, I want us to be ready. As soon as the fullness of the light returns, I will give the sign, and our first speaker will begin. But we will not now reply in kind to our welcome. We will not lower ourselves to the unseemliness of the speeches which have been given to us. Let's show these people how it should be done. And if it's a fight they want, a fight they will have, for this is the courtyard of Tu, the God of War. But the fight will not come yet, not until we have replied to the welcome. So, wait for my sign.'

The sun, black and awesome. Then, gradually, the moon moved away from the sun's face and the intensity of the light increased, ever increased, and, as it did so, Riripeti lifted the black veil from her face. The clouds opened. The sun hurled its light like a hammer to the earth. Ranginui, the Sky Father, returned to the heavens. Riripeti seemed to blaze on the marae.

('Well,' the journalist said, 'the sun going out like that was a brilliant coup de théâtre, and Artemis's sense of timing was absolutely impeccable. What a flamboyant trickster she was, such a charlatan, such a sorceress! I'm sorry if you object to my using those terms but, after all, you can't believe that it was she who made the sun go out. It was a total eclipse, of course, and it lasted about seven and a half minutes, maybe less. I'd read that it was going to occur but I had forgotten the timing of the event. So had most other people. Your grandmother, clever woman as she was, must have known about it all the time. There is no other explanation. She certainly used it to her advantage, my oath she did.

'Oh, the pandemonium when it happened. I've not been one to believe in witchcraft and all that, but when that sun started to go out I was struck with fear. Of course it didn't take me long to realise what was happening. Artemis knew all along. Later, after the welcomes were over, Timoti and some other elders in the paepae refused to have anything to do with her. They were apoplectic with rage. But one of them, I think his name was Whai, roared with laughter and complimented her, "Legends will be woven of this day when the Matua made the sun go out."

'She had beaten them all, you see. But more was to follow—')

With the return of the sun, the mood on the forecourt of Parliament turned to elation. Smiling, Riripeti turned to Grandfather Ihaka, 'Come, let us start our replies to the speeches of welcome which have been given to us. Let us be the best that anyone has seen or heard.'

She motioned him forward. 'Kia hiwa ra! Kia hiwa ra!' Grandfather Ihaka began. 'Be careful. Be wakeful. Ka moe araara ki te matahi tuna . . . You have to stay awake to catch eels. You have to stay awake to catch a war party—'

His speech was taunting. It brought images of sentries patrolling the stepped terraces of ancient hill forts in the red light of dawn.

'—Ka tiritiria, ka reareaia a tama tu ki tona hiwa ra. Scatter, rise up, stand in your places. Kia hiwa ra. Be watchful. Be wakeful. Be alert on this terrace. Be alert on that terrace, or someone will wound you and make you bleed—'

He patterned the ground like a sentry, springing back and forth, swaying, probing, seeking out the enemy on the horizon.

'—Papaki tu ana te tai ki Te Reinga. The tide is beating to Te Reinga. Eke panuku. Eke Tangaroa. Hui e . . . taiki e.'

On the last words, the ope and the people gathered on Parliament Grounds joined in a huge shout of acclamation. 'Taiki e!'

('Your speakers were superb,' the journalist said. 'I understand that your grandfather was the first speaker. The second was Tamati Kota, the priest who was known as Artemis's Left Hand of God. The third was your father, Te Ariki. From all accounts, they were so proficient that everyone kept on roaring with the pleasure of their imagery and wit. As you know, I can't fully understand your language, but I can gauge when a good show is put on. Your speakers had the crowd with them all the way. Oh, they were so glorious to listen to, and to watch. They made references to genealogy and land and everything they said was appropriate and correct. The old man near me, well, his eyes were gleaming with the pleasure of it all. "I haven't seen or heard such a fine display of oratory for years," he said. One after another, your speakers followed upon each other, representatives from Te Whanau a Kai, Rongowhakaata and Te Aitanga a Mahaki. It was just brilliant. Then it appeared as if the last speaker had spoken.')

The excitement on Parliament Grounds had reached fever pitch.

'You have all done well,' Riripeti said. 'Our mana has been sustained. Kei te pai. Ka nui te honore kua homai ki au. It is a great honour to serve you.'

But the iwi knew that the Matua was still angry at the slight done to her.

'Now it is my turn,' she said.

Instantly, there was a murmur in the ope.

'No, don't do it,' Grandfather Ihaka said. 'The Prime Minister, chiefs of Maoridom and the tangata whenua await us.'

'Haere mai koutou ki te ruru,' came the call.

('Well, you know,' the journalist said, 'we thought it was all over. Everything seemed to be calm enough. People started to chatter among themselves again and to talk over the events of the welcome. You know, to relax.')

'Don't do it, no, don't,' Grandfather Ihaka said again.

('The elders in the paepae called Artemis and your people over to meet in the hongi. But your grandmother didn't move. And Timoti began to get angry again. "No, she wouldn't do it; she's a woman; she wouldn't dare." Everywhere, conversation began to fade, and silence fell. It was quite uncanny.')

Riripeti turned swiftly to the child. 'Listen, mokopuna, listen to me. This is a very dangerous and difficult course that I am embarked upon, but it must be done. Do you think the chiefs of Maoridom will let me say what our iwi has come here to say when this is the last day of the hui? No. I have to speak now, while our people still hold the ground.'

('You know your customs better than I do,' the journalist said. 'Oh yes, the role of women must be difficult in your society. I must say that I felt an immense respect for Artemis.')

'Mokopuna, you must pray for me. For while I have done what

I am going to do in my own land, I have not done it outside the home ground. There may very well be a price to pay.'

'Haere mai, haere mai,' the call from the tangata whenua echoed across to the iwi again. One second, then another went past.

The child heard his grandmother's bracelets tinkling like oriental wind chimes as she gripped her walking stick.

'No, don't,' Grandfather Ihaka said for the third time.

Her knuckles went white as she pressed on the walking stick. Her long black gown rustled and swept into the wind. The pearls in her hair were shivering like drops of water on a web.

'Te Whanau a Kai hei panapana maro,' she said. 'Our people never retreat, whether they be men or women.'

There was a roar of anger, like a whirlwind, as Riripeti levered herself to stand on the marae, her body climbing higher and higher against the backdrop of the sky.

6

The marae as we know it today is taken to mean a complex comprising a meeting house, courtyard and dining hall, although this is a relatively modern innovation. Originally the marae was the earthen courtyard in the village, and it was situated immediately outside the chief's house. Nowadays a marae can be any space where Maori gather, including the forecourt of Parliament.

The marae is the domain of Tumatauenga, God of War, while inside the house is the domain of peaceful pursuits, Rongomatane, God of Peace. The marae may be any shape or size. The meeting house is almost without exception traditional in form: single-storeyed, rectangular, consisting of one large room with a deep gabled porch across the front, and a single door and window in the front wall. The façades and interiors of many meeting houses are richly decorated with traditional carving, reed panelling and rafter patterns. Many marae and meeting houses have names of their own.

Visitors to the marae, during Maori gatherings, are separately welcomed with a formal ritual which includes calling, chanting, wailing and oratory. In earlier, more warlike times these rituals were observed to manage encounters in peace, but they were not always peaceful. Right throughout the rituals nobody could be certain whether the outcome would be peace or war.

There is no fear of warfare today, but suspicion and hot pride, grievances real or unreal, can still be powerful underlying factors in the mihimihi that takes place between tangata whenua and manuhiri. Although there are no longer likely to be physical attacks on visitors to a strange marae, there may still be baleful spiritual influences about. In the old days, distant tribes were thought of as sorcerers and witches, and this attitude has not entirely vanished.

༄

Ka tu nga taumata korero o aku tupuna ki Maunga Haumia, ka heke ki nga wai o Paoa, e Te Whanau a Kai, ko Mahaki, ko Rongowhakaata e.

I began to climb Ramaroa, the high ancient hill fort. Below, I heard Teria sounding her horn in farewell and watched as her car sped into Waituhi. I turned skyward and heard the karanga of the land as the ancient hill called me to ascend.

'Piki mai, kake mai, haere mai.'

It was from this point that my grandmother and I always began our walks around Waituhi. My father, Te Ariki, would bring me here from Gisborne in the car because, at the time, the inevitable drift by Maori to the cities to find paid work had already begun and we lived at Crawford Road. Riripeti strenuously objected to his living in the city, of course, saying, 'How will I be able to raise my mokopuna so that he can fulfil his destiny?' She saw in my father's departure the beginning of the dissolution of the family which she had fought so hard to keep on the land. She only tolerated the separation, in my case, on one condition: that I would be returned to Waituhi and into her care every Friday evening for the weekend. That was over twenty-five years ago, and my memory is still attuned to the rhythm of those car journeys to the village. If Te Ariki couldn't do it, Riripeti sent one of my uncles to get me—and woe betide any of them if they were late.

'Kua reri koe?' she would ask when I arrived. 'Are you ready?

Then let's go.'

Even though she used a walking stick and often found the climbing and walking difficult, nothing would stop her from firmly taking me to walk every inch of our proud land. And as we did so, she would begin her korero.

'You are descended from many tribes, but this is your turangawaewae, your footstool. From your grandfather, my husband, you have lineage with Tuhoe, Whakatohea, Kahungunu, Te Aitanga a Mahaki, among others. From my line, you can lay claim Te Whanau a Kai as your papakainga, and ancestry with Te Aitanga a Mahaki, Rongowhakaata, Kahungunu and Waikato. Through your mother, even though Tiana is a woman of no account, you have lineage with Ngati Porou and Te Whanau a Apanui and, again, to Waikato. But this is where you belong. And because this is your land, you must know it like it knows itself, and you must love it even more than it loves itself. You must get to know its very boundaries, e mokopuna, and every part of it, because without this knowledge you are lost. Without it, you do not possess the land. You become a person without a homeland. You are a man who will never know aroha ki te iwi, love for your people and for the land. You will never know why it is important for you to fight for it against any person who might wish to take it.'

'Climb towards me, climb on,' came the karanga.

As I climbed there seemed more and more of sky and less and less of earth until there I was at the lowest terrace of Ramaroa pa. Once, the pa commanded the area with an impregnability that must have been envied by all the iwi of Turanga. Although still imposing, its gigantic staircase of eleven crescent terraces could only suggest the grandeur of the poutama it had once been—the wondrous Stairway to Heaven.

I began to ascend the terraces to the top. I was possessed of the same exhilaration that always came upon me whenever I was here among the elaborate and extensive earthworks. I witnessed the intimacy of the huge single and double pits which had once been roofed dwellings of the pa settlers. I felt the thrill of the defence system with its deep and wide entrenchments and circular walls of earth.

As in the past, I kept my eye on the top and highest terrace, where the karanga came most clearly down to me as I ascended.

Finally, I reached the summit. I did not want to look out across the landscape of Waituhi yet, for to do so would be to die a little and not to know the ecstasy of the heart at seeing the greenstone country from the top of Heaven's stairway. Then I took a deep breath and, with pounding heart, I opened my arms upward and outward to embrace the land. I answered the karanga.

'Tihei mauri ora! I sneeze and it is life!'

I looked down the slope to the village below. Beyond were river flats widespread and country towns afar.

This had been Riripeti's kingdom. And her glory. She had been the ariki here, having the responsibility of protecting the land and the iwi. By virtue of the role she took as a tohunga—priestess for the Ringatu religion, based on the Old Testament—she was also the spiritual leader of the people. But whenever I was too much in awe of her, she would caution me, saying, 'I am only a servant. I do the bidding of the Lord and I serve the people as best I can.'

And when we came here together, resting on the summit of Ramaroa, she would sometimes wink at me and say, 'And on days like this, with the sun shining brightly and the wind like a zephyr, I am simply Tamatea's grandmother, ne?'

Then, sitting together on the Stairway to Heaven, she would tell me about the genealogy of the land and the iwi. Without whakapapa, how can you know who you are in the present? Without genealogy to bind it together, there can be no iwi. An iwi without whakapapa cannot feel the aroha for the land that they live in.

'I have already told you of the time of the gods,' Riripeti began, 'and of the times when the gods communed with mankind, whom Tane had made in his own image. These first men, the ancient ones, lived in the mountains that surround us and particularly around Hikurangi Mountain—the first place in the world to greet the sun. Then, with the arrival of Maori who came by canoes from far-off Hawaiki, was developed the numerous and constituent tribes of Poverty Bay and the East Coast.

'As far as Te Whanau a Kai is concerned, it was Paraki, back in the mists of time, who was our first settler. It was his grandson, Tui, who marked out our ancient boundaries. One of his descendants was Ruapani, who became paramount chief of Turanga. In him converged all the lines of Maori greatness in Aotearoa. But Ruapani's story was not as strong or colourful as that of the great chief Kahungunu, who lived to the south, but passed through Ruapani's land. One of his descendants was Rakaihikuroa, who married Te Orapa, who was a descendant of Ruapani. But did the mana go to Kahungunu? No, it stayed with Te Orapa! Even though, today, fathers and sons are still regarded as more important than mothers and daughters, here in Te Whanau a Kai, the mana is with the women. And because of this, I am able to claim my superiority to any male line. My authority, my mana, comes from the matriarchy. And sometimes it is better that women rule than men. Let me tell you a story of men and their jealousies—'

'The very autocratic chief, Rakaihikuroa, lived in Waituhi at a hill fort at Repongaere. His eldest son, Tupurupuru, lived near him at a pa named Pukepoto.

'Both were very proud, secure in their mana. If either visited any particular area, planted their taiaha in any piece of ground, or left their belt there, the people of the surrounding countryside would bring them food and gifts and respond appropriately to men who believed that they ruled by divine right. However, Rakaihikuroa had a cousin whose name was Kahutapere. He was more popular than Rakaihikuroa and, to make matters worse, he had twin sons—Tarakiuta and Tarakitai—who were more greatly loved than Rakaihikuroa's own son Tupurupuru. Rakaihikuroa and Tupurupuru therefore began to feel the gnawings of fear and jealousy for their own prestige and power. In the manner of the great Italian power struggles between rival citadels and aristocratic houses, the aged Rakaihikuroa and his arrogant son plotted to murder the young and beloved twins of Kahutapere, and thereby establish their own bloodline and succession in their own royal house.'

(If you wish to, you might imagine all this happening against the background of tall castellated cities, and dress the actors in the rich costumes and accents of the courts of Renaissance Italy. Imagine it in Siena. Or Venice. Or Modena, with all the trappings of intrigue and violent clashes between rival factions in cobbled streets, of courtesans watching from high balconies, and the *cortegiani* divining the ebb and flow of events.)

'The twins, beautiful and youthful, were fine sportsmen; even when they lost in competitions of strength, agility and intelligence, they were adored. They were boys, in their early teens perhaps, and they showed great proficiency and adeptness in the art of whip top spinning. In this sport, competitors would line up at the top of a hill, down which the course would slope like a slalom run to the bottom. The competitors would hold their spinning tops in one hand and a flax whip in the other and, at the word of the starter, they would place their tops on the ground and whip them, to keep them spinning; in this manner would begin the race of the spinning tops to the bottom of the run. Sometimes various obstacles like jumps or pits or fences would need to be negotiated, and the competitors would then have to show their dexterity in whipping the tops so that they leapt, soared, pirouetted, retreated and veered to left or right of whatever was placed in their paths. The twins were so proficient that they were usually the only ones who reached the bottom of the slope, the full extent of the course.

'On the days when the competitions were to be held it was usual for the twins to start practice very early in the mornings. It was on the night before one of these competitions that Rakaihikuroa plotted their murder with his son. The jealous father said to Tupurupuru, "Go tonight to the course and, right at the bottom, build a huge pit; then, make yourself a whero-rua, a double-ended top, and challenge the twins to beat you during the practice; when they reach the pit, you will know what to do."

'That night, Tupurupuru went out and did as he and his father had agreed upon, dug the pit and made himself a double-ended top. The next morning he went to the course and was on the ground by daylight. Not long after, the twins appeared. Tupurupuru dropped his top on the ground and began to whip it down the slope. Down and down it spun, a toy of evil weaving its murderous intent and luring the twins to join the competition. They too placed their tops on the ground and whipped them into movement so that the tops skimmed and danced a downward descent in the dust. Around and over obstacles the tops sped and soared and the twins were caught up in the excitement of the chase. They drew nearer and nearer to Tupurupuru; suddenly before them was the pit which he had dug in the night. It was so wide that not even the boys' tops could have soared over it. Tupurupuru lashed at his top and it spun into the pit. The twins whipped at their tops which soared, almost reached the other side of the pit, and then teetered and fell into the wide hole also. Laughing, Tupurupuru asked the two boys to retrieve the three tops. They did so and without knowing placed themselves at their cousin's mercy. He jumped in after them, slipped out his mere, and dealt them both the death blow by jabbing the edge of the mere at their foreheads and levering the club upward so that their craniums were opened up like lids. Tupurupuru then buried the twins in the pit and levelled the ground so that little evidence of the murder could be seen.

'"Is it done?" his father asked.

'"Yes, it is done well," Tupurupuru answered.

'Now the scene changes to the pa of Kahutapere, the father of the murdered twins. When the boys did not return home, a long search took place which lasted several days. Kahutapere began to grieve for he knew that his sons were dead. But he wanted vengeance. He therefore constructed two kites, named after the twins, instilled magic into them, and sent them into the sky. His priests chanted incantations as the kites dipped and swung on the currents of the wind. "Show me the place of your murderer," Kahutapere cried. The two kites, rising to a great height, stopped over the pa of Rakaihikuroa. There, they hovered for a while and, slowly, twice dipped in the air.

'Kahutapere then knew that someone from Rakaihikuroa's pa had killed his sons. He went to speak to the aged man, saying, "Friend, have you killed our children?" Rakaihikuroa replied obliquely from his royal chair, "Waiho ra kia tu takitahi ana nga whetu o te rangi;

Let there be only one star shining in the sky." His meaning was that only one heir should rule over the land, and that heir should be Tupurupuru. Kahutapere was then set upon and, although he escaped, many of his party and two more of his sons were killed.

'Kahutapere called for assistance to his other relatives, saying, "I am at war with Rakaihikuroa and his son Tupurupuru." His cousin, Mahaki, who was living at Pa Werawera in Waikohu, readily acceded and, with Taururangi and their armies, advanced on Pukepoto where Tupurupuru challenged any of the opposing warriors to meet him in single combat. Now, what Tupurupuru had done was to make spears of manuka and he named the spears, giving them the names of warriors who would accept his challenge. Therefore, he was able to drive the foremost warriors back, always back. But this could not last, for the fates were against him. For that morning, when preparing himself for the battle, the flax his servant was using to bind his hair into a topknot had several times broken, a bad omen.

'So it was that Mahaki's youngest son, Whakarau, was able to kill the murderer of the twins. He arrived late at the battle and had not yet killed the first person who had crossed his path and consecrated him to Tu. Thus the fates were with Whakarau, for Tu, the God of War, had higher priority than Tupurupuru's magic. Tupurupuru threw the spear at Whakarau, with his name on it; Whakarau was able to parry it and it glanced to one side. Tupurupuru could only watch with a sense of impending doom as Whakarau darted at him and speared him through the head. An elder of Whakarau said, "Keep clear, keep clear, do not touch the staggering fish of the hook of the last son of my mother."

'Tupurupuru's body was taken by the victors and hung by the plaited hair on the end of a swaying kahikatea bough across the stream opposite his father's pa. The account between Rakaihikuroa and Kahutapere was equalised. Rakaihikuroa left the land and it was therefore divided up between the sons of Mahaki. One of those sons was named Kai, and it was from him that our tribe, Te Whanau a Kai takes its name.

'But never forget. The mana has always been with the women. Kai was from the migrant line and his two wives, Te Haaki and

Whareana, were from the local iwi. They in no way gave up their rights of take tipuna—their rights to hold the land based on continuous occupation and ancestry—to their husband.

'The land is therefore ours. We flourished upon it.

'Then on 7 October 1769 reports came to the village and spread right throughout the lands of Turanga of a huge white bird anchoring in the bay. It carried a cargo of gods, like the *Takitimu*, but these gods brought death, not life.

'One hundred years later, the Pai Marire religion was established in Turanga right in the shadow of Ramaroa pa. A few years after that, in 1868, Ramaroa again towered above the events of the Matawhero Retaliation.'

⌒

Walk the proud land.

It was my custom, whenever I was at home in Gisborne, and no matter whether I had the time or not, to go out to Waituhi. This was the one ritual that could never be broken, and my family knew it. Most times I would simply say to Mum and Dad, 'I'm just going to spend some hours at our meeting house.' At other times, like today, I would follow one of the boundaries. For, oh, how we walked this land, Riripeti and I, and how fearful I was that I might forget some small yet significant detail of what had been told to me as a child.

'Okay, Tamatea,' I said to myself, 'let's follow the western boundary.'

In the old days, the boundaries between the neighbouring canoe areas or tribal grounds were mutually arranged and decided upon. Natural features like Ramaroa pa, the Waipaoa River, or sea coasts, cliff escarpments and the like, were taken to define boundaries. Where natural features were absent, a mound or cairn of stones, post pole or a hole dug in the ground would be used as a marker. These boundaries, and the stories attached to their making, would be memorised. In this way, the entire land was made into a living geography text and history book. The minutiae of life, ah yes, all was imprinted and still living, inscribed on the land. And to ensure the continuity of the tribal memory, the people would traverse the land from time to time and from generation to generation.

('You are very fortunate,' a friend once said to me. 'Those tribal walks are not common these days. I am surprised that a woman should take it upon herself to instruct you. She must have been most unusual, for many of the things she would have shown you and told you would have been tapu. They would have been the kind of instruction you normally received in the whare wananga, the sacred house of learning. But then, I guess, these are modern days and, yes, you are right, even the holding of the whare wananga is not common.')

Full of resolve, I followed the low-lying hills from Ramaroa pa by way of the peak of Taumata o Tumokonui, named after one of Waituhi's ancient settlers. The settlement must have been quite large because many terraces and pits could be seen on the three main spurs which radiated from the top of the mountain. As I paused there, I remembered the story that Riripeti had told me about Tumokonui's two wives. His first wife was called Hekeiterangi and was seduced away from her husband by occult means. The name of the seducer was Mokaiohungia, and the enraged husband raided the seducer's settlement at Te Arai. He discovered the two lovers hiding in a kumara pit and, in a rare act of generosity, spared their lives.

The second wife of Tumokonui was a fascinating woman. She was an uri taniwha, a woman descended of the mermen and mermaids who lived in the Waipaoa River. Her name was Hine Te Ariki and she loved her husband very much. When he died, she returned to her people in the river and migrated upstream into the mountains near Te Karaka. There, in the river known as the Waikohu, she lived until her own death. The dark green waters still sing with sirens and the surface still occasionally swirls with the swimming of the mermen and mermaids beneath.

Indeed, just as the spider with the red moko on its back was Riripeti's protector, so was Hine Te Ariki, the merwoman, the kai-tiaki of my mother, Tiana. It was often believed that at moments when your human form could not perform some task thrust upon you, you could transform into your kaitiaki to do it. The distinction between the real and the unreal, the natural and the supernatural, the human world and that of taniwha, allowed such shapeshifting. I had never known Tiana to take on the form of Hine Te Ariki but Riripeti was rumoured to have done so. It may have been fantasy but it added to her charisma.

Perspiring, I headed for the eastern corner of Waituhi and there, on the flat, acknowledged the small mound called Pa Whakarau. This was the place where Whakarau, who killed Tupurupuru, put his mark to the land. Riripeti had told me that Waituhi had prospered under Whakarau and the flow of life was relatively peaceful. The original village firmly established itself around a settler by the name of Taritonga. Even in those days the village was associated with a religious purpose because its original name was Te Waituhi a Taritonga, which means The Baptismal Water Owned by Taritonga. This was in the period around 1750, and the people were secure in their lives and on the land.

Smiling to myself, I struck across hillside farmland and small plantations and around the spongy swamp perimeter of Lake Repongaere. The lake grew to its present size because of the thrashing and twisting of the huge eel which lived there and wanted more water to live in. The wild ducks cried to me as I passed through the toetoe, and occasionally I saw the turmoil in this water, filled with the thousands of descendants of old Ancestor Eel. ('Did you know that a Pakeha wants to put an eel farm on the lake?' my Uncle Manaaki once asked me. 'You better speak to your father about it. That lake belongs to us and its food is for us. It should not be commercialised. It is our food basket.')

I washed myself in the lake. 'I'm home,' I shouted. Then, I set off, following the Repongaere Stream and cutting across the Tangihanga Road to the Pouarua Stream. The stream would then return me to Lavenham Road, the main road running through Waituhi.

Our western boundary, of course, continued much further than that, incorporating the Wi Pere Estate right through to Humphreys Road. If I had had time, I would have traversed Tangihanga to look down upon the main farming station. This was the estate set up by the family's ancestor, Wi Pere, to provide the people with a livelihood on their own land. Many of my cousins, uncles and aunts worked there, shearing, handling the cattle and, in recent years, erecting the racks upon which the rich vines of burgundy grapes ripened under the hot hill-entrapped sun.

Nor was there time to walk by the Waipaoa River, heading for the old ferry pont. Across the river from the pont was Waerenga a Hika, the place of the last Hauhau stand, and following the bank was the old Maori track used by warring parties on their ways back and forth to claim utu. It was along this same track that Te Kooti led his people against the militia at Matawhero.

The Waipaoa River ruled our lives; its waters irrigated the valley. It demanded respect, this river which had washed Waituhi over for centuries, this place of the baptismal fount of Taritonga. Riripeti and her priest, Tamati Kota, often brought the Children of Israel to the water to be immersed and blessed unto God. But the river also frightened some people, mainly because it was always moody, never quite at rest. In winter, it raged and flooded the land with its swollen anger; I liked to think that it was even angrier now that it had been contained in a series of flood embankments. But its flood times were welcomed today because of the silt it brought down from the hills and spread like a rich fan across the river plains. And again, the village had learnt to use the river's bounty by establishing horticultural produce of all kinds—maize, kumara, potato, pumpkin, peas, kiwifruit, the vine—and a system of irrigation that certainly beat the old days, during Riripeti's time of leadership, when water had to be carted up from the river in ten-gallon drums.

Such a strange river with its uri taniwha swimming in the depths and swirling with the currents as they stirred beneath the overhanging willows.

Below the small settlement of Pakowhai was the Place of the Willows. Despite the strangeness, there was nothing to fear about it. As long as you respected the spider clan that lived there, the pungawerewere with the red moko on their backs, you would be all right.

I should have been uplifted by being back in Waituhi.

But all the memories that had been created since I had seen Uncle Alexis spilled over and I felt a huge sense of grief. What had my cousin Whai said about me?

The dreamer awakes.

The clouds swirled across the sky, casting strange patterns like fleeting kowhaiwhai designs across the earth.

My heart thundered with longing for Riripeti. I wanted her to be there with me again, taking my hand, telling me the stories of the times of gods and men, and filling my life with splendour.

'Where is the mana?' I asked. 'Where is the tapu? Grandmother? You said you would live forever.'

Trembling with sorrow, I sank to my knees. The clouds were swirling. It was so difficult to keep walking the proud land without her.

'Grandmother?'

And suddenly, the clouds changed.

The child was walking on a long ago day with Riripeti. They were looking across the greenstone land. The kowhaiwhai in the sky swirled a pattern of calm, such calm.

'Kia kaha,' she whispered. 'Kia manawanui.'

Her voice struck the reverberating drum of the land. Her face, veiled, was mysterious. Her beauty was awesome. It shone out of her with a gleaming light that you could almost touch and feel. It vibrated and electrified the air.

She had been telling the child of his ancestry, his whakapapa. Of the time of Te Kore, the Void. Of the twelve changes of Te Po, the Night, and the coming of Te Ao Marama, the World of Light. Of the primal parents, the Sky Father above and the Earth Mother below and the Separation so that all might live in the light. Then, of the times of gods and man, when both were one and the same until Maui brought death into the world. Of the coming of legendary canoes to a land to the south called Aotearoa. And of ancient people and of *Takitimu*, the canoe of the gods.

'We had eternity in us,' she said. 'You began your life back then, e mokopuna, many thousands of years before you were born in Waituhi.'

That was when it happened, and the child felt it happen.

'Don't be afraid,' she whispered. 'Kia kaha. Kia manawanui.'

The elements were coming alive, the long silent dynamo of creation beginning to hum. The earth began to breathe. The sky took the form of a giant tattooed god. The mauri, the forces of life animate and inanimate, stirred in the wind and flooded through a widening cleft of light.

The veil between day and night lifted, and they were in some otherworld where gods and men commune. Where timelessness begins and there is no separation of past and present. A world energised with glowing forces and creatures of light fading in and out of the hills, the plains and the physical landscape of Waituhi.

The child saw into the essence of things. He saw the gleaming sap ascending the trees, and the sap and the dark red blood coursing his transparent body were one and the same. He saw into the geological structures of the earth, and the diamond sparkling structure of the mountains was one and the same as the gleaming cellular structure of his body. He saw the movement of light and wind and cloud, and they were one and the same as his own life forces.

Then he looked up into the heavens and saw worlds being created beyond this earth; and the creation of new suns and new nebulae were the same as the worlds in his blood. He looked into the faces of the gods and was not blinded. He was in the universe and the universe was in him.

But he began to spiral out beyond the reach of gods, and he grew afraid and wanted to cry out. He felt himself falling back through Te Po, and the twelve Changings of the Night. The light began to diminish, ever diminish, until all was utter and complete darkness. So dark it was that he felt as if he had no form or shape at all. The quality of the darkness changed, and he knew that he had descended into Te Kore, the Void. The Nothingness.

'Kia kaha, kia manawanui,' Riripeti said again. She was a voice a million aeons away.

He did not know how long he was in the Void. He thought he was going to die, for the feeling that he had was like he thought death must be. He could not cry because he had no tears to weep. He could not call out in fear because he had no voice. He could not reach out because he had no form.

Then he heard voices chanting, softly chanting in the pit of blackness. The voices seemed to reach around him, like a cocoon of sound, and he felt, more than knew, that he was being lifted from the Void. From out of Te Kore he came, journeying back through the twelve Changings of the Night. The chanting grew stronger and louder as he voyaged in that timeless time.

He saw creation. He felt the first ray of light.

He was part of the cauldron of energy which laid the foundations of the universe—of the earth and sky and waters, of the depths and heights, of the expanse of the skies and borders of the seas.

He saw the gods. He saw the creation of woman. He saw legendary canoes glittering in emerald seas and escorted by fabulous creatures of awesome power. He saw a huge fish being pulled out of the sky by a magic hook, transforming itself into a cloud-streaming land.

He heard the karanga, calling him to come forward, to return, and the sound overwhelmed him with its glory. Then he felt many hands caressing him, fluttering over and across him. Anointing him. Bathing his gleaming body. Loving him. Whispering to him. Creatures of light filled the air with their songs and their light. They ferried him forward, ever forward, through benediction after benediction.

And he felt himself returning through tribes and tribes of man, generation after generation, and gentle tears falling like soft rain upon him.

The clouds, swirling through the sky, cast strange patterns like fleeting kowhaiwhai designs across the earth. 'E mokopuna, listen,' Riripeti said. 'The mana and the tapu still remain, in the land and in Waituhi and in the iwi of Te Whanau a Kai. It is in Rongopai also. It is not something that can be seen with the eye, e mokopuna, but with the heart and the soul and the intellect.'

The clouds ever, ever swirling.

Riripeti, a woman and therefore not tapu, was standing where men only stood.

Yes, she was high-born, and she had spoken on marae in her own lands, but on Parliament Grounds she was outside her tribal boundaries and therefore could not rely on any genealogical and spiritual protection. In the old days, standing like this, she would have been killed. Her act of assertion would have been regarded as a violation of the tapu of the marae and the tapu of the male. In most other tribes, excluding her own and a very few others, the art of whaikorero was the province of the male. Even in her own lands, her rank had to be absolutely impeccable to allow her to speak. Wisely, on the forecourt of Parliament, a place strange and dangerous even to her mana, she had at least followed the male orators of the ope—Grandfather Ihaka, Tamati Kota and Te Ariki.

Nevertheless, as Riripeti took a few steps forward to face the people, even she was unprepared for the physical, mental and psychic force of the reaction. It was as if blows were being rained down upon her, wave upon wave of hostility and outrage. They stopped her completely in her tracks, and the child saw her reel back and put her arms up to fend off the attack. It seemed to the child that she was fighting for her life, not just against the antagonism of the marae but against the spiritual forces which made the marae more than a place of the present. In the past were powerful forces, perhaps even more tapu than his grandmother's own sacredness. They were not baleful or malevolent. Rather, they were exerting their authority against this woman who had dared to stand where she should not unless she could demonstrate that her power was equal to theirs.

('Oh, it was terrible,' the journalist said. 'Artemis stood up. Instantly, people began to yell at her, and their fury consumed the forecourt of Parliament. It seemed to revolve around the forecourt; it came from everywhere, even from the ground itself, and you could put your hands to your ears and stop the sound but it shrieked inside your head also. People were shouting down at Artemis. "You are trampling on the tapu of this marae," they said. "You should die for this insult," they called. "Your neck should be wrung because it is only the rooster which crows," they yelled.

'And, you know, the really awful thing was that the anger and the shouting seemed to awaken the forecourt itself as a living entity. I'd never thought that inanimate objects had lives at all. You read about houses being possessed, and natural locations having spiritual forces; well, that's what appeared to happen here. The forecourt in front of Parliament started to live, to breathe.')

It was then that the child saw them. They appeared out of the air, out of the ground. They were mauri, creatures of light and creatures of darkness, circling and spinning around Riripeti, weaving a dizzying and dazzling skein of attack. They had no shapes and they were without form. They seemed not of the world, not human, and their brilliance was breathtaking.

Riripeti staggered under their assault. The luminosity of her spirit lessened at each dazzling attack. She looked across to the child. Although her lips did not move, he heard her call to him.

('I know this might sound fanciful, but it was almost as if supernatural forces of the past had come to join with the living and to confront Artemis with their anger. Yes, she still stood in as proud a manner as ever. Such a stunning sight, standing there, but I don't think that I have ever seen a lonelier sight in my life than at that moment, that grandmother of yours, standing there. Alone. So desperately alone.')

'Help me,' she said.

Her face seemed so close to his, so close. Her eyes were dark with pain, as if she had been dealt a mortal blow and was dying. Around her, the creatures of light and creatures of darkness ever circled and, more and more, struck her with their sacredness and power.

Desperately, the child looked across to Grandfather Ihaka, Tamati Kota, Te Ariki and others of the ope. Surely they could see what was happening? Surely they could help Grandmother?

'Help me,' she said again.

An invisible force had imprisoned her hands and was forcing them up to and around her throat. She was struggling against the force, tearing her fingernails so that the blood began to trickle down her arms. She looked across at the child again and spoke to him, her lips not moving. 'No, e mokopuna,' she said, 'you are the only one who can help me. Only you, for the manner of our births was the same and we have been created one and the same. Listen. Hasten. Do you recognise what is happening to me? What are these mauri, these beings of the supernatural? Tell me, tell me.'

'I do not know them,' he answered.

She closed her eyes. When she opened them again they were as one eye swimming in blood. 'E mokopuna,' she began again. 'Listen, then, to what I ask. Our own mana, yours and mine. Is it the equal? Your own tapu, is it the equal? For if they are, I might yet survive, Hasten. Hasten.'

The mauri were spinning and encircling Riripeti with a net of deadly brilliance. The creatures of darkness were shooting shafts of elemental energy into her soul.

Then the child looked up into the heavens and saw worlds beyond this earth, and the worlds spinning into darkness, and the creation of new suns and new nebulae, were the same as the worlds in his blood. He looked into the faces of the gods and was not blinded. He was in the universe and the universe was in him.

And he realised. 'Yes,' he said. 'The mana and the tapu are equal.'

'Why, e mokopuna?'

He told her.

('Yes, I really felt sorry for Artemis,' the journalist said. 'She looked quite lost. Tragic. The old Maori man nearby said, "Well, she's had it, she is defeated. She thought she could do it, be a man on the marae, but she had neither the tapu nor the mana. Courage, yes, but that is not enough." Until the old Maori man told me, I hadn't realised how difficult it was to live in the Maori way. All your protocols and etiquettes and spiritual restraints. It's much easier, surely, to be a European. Anyway, at the same time as he was speaking, I caught a movement happening down on the marae. There had been a young boy sitting beside Artemis all the time that the ope was being welcomed. Well, quite suddenly, he simply—')

All the child knew was that he had to stand up and go to save his grandmother. He started to walk towards her. The mauri became motionless, glowing with brilliance. Slowly they advanced towards him.

He opened his mouth and began to sing.

('—got up from his seat and walked towards her. I'm not too sure why he did it. I was told, later, that it was the only act that saved her. My own feeling is that he was related in some way and couldn't bear to see his grandmother being abused by the people. Yes, I guessed it was you. Were you crying? No, I don't think so. But the action was so surprising, the more so because we were not prepared for it. I suppose that even on a marae, children tend to get away with some things that adults can't get away with. Well, apparently you managed to turn the defeat into victory. You began to sing a chant. The whole thing was quite audacious, from what I understand. But as you started to sing, and as the crowd began to get the gist of your meaning, they started to roar with the boldness of it. What you sang, and what you said was—')

The creatures of light and the creatures of dark were advancing. The child sang, calling out to them in a clear voice.

'In the beginning was Te Kore, the Void, the Nothingness, without shape or form, limitless and unending. And after Te Kore was the Night, Te Po, the Great Night, the Long Night, the Dark Night, Te Po nui, Te Po roa, Te Po kerekere, Te Po tiwha, Te Po tangotango, Te Po kitea—'

Singing, singing to creatures above the marae. Far off, Riripeti understood and, in the understanding, gained the strength to ward off the spiralling attacks; her mana generated its own dynamic force, making luminous her soul. Her voice sang out like the child's, telling the creatures of darkness and the creatures of light why she should live.

'From out of the Night arose Ranginui, the Skyfather, and Papatuanuku, the Earth Mother, who lay together, the parents of all creation, and to them were born children. In darkness they were born. Wishing to live in the light, they separated their parents and, in that widening cleft, began to stand and to walk together. And when the light came flooding across the land—'

The creatures of light and darkness were spinning, spinning. The voices of the child and the matriarch climbed toward them. The people congregated on the red carpet leapt to their feet with the boldness of the song.

'—could be seen the great numbers of men and the creatures of darkness and light.'

('—a chant about the creation of the world. And the gist of the message? Oh it was so simple. You sang about the Void. Then about the Long Night. You told of the Sky Father and the Earth Mother. You sang how they were separated and the times when men and gods communed. Then you told of how the Maori came to this place where the ancients already lived. By that time, the people at Parliament were in an absolute uproar. Such a furore—')

The child walked across to Riripeti. Together, they looked up into that shining cloud, radiant and tremulous with brilliance.

'We are descended of the ancients,' they sang.

('—how the crowd roared—')

'We are descended of Takitimu.'

('—Oh, the boldness of it,' the journalist said. 'The cheek of it took everyone's breath away. The magnificence of it—')

The creatures of light and the creatures of darkness shimmered in acknowledgement. As they did, the shimmer enclosed the child and the matriarch in a communion of soul with soul, mana with mana, tapu with tapu.

('You said that your mana was equal to theirs because you, also, were descended from the gods!')

And Riripeti smiled her madonna smile, and knelt down to the child. He had, again, looked into the faces of the gods and not been blinded.

'E mokopuna, you have done well,' she said. 'Listen to the acclamation. This is for you, mokopuna, as well as for me and our iwi.'

('Well, after that, things happened quickly. The elders of the paepae could do nothing except continue the powhiri. When it was over, that was when Artemis really ripped into them! She stated why the people of Te Whanau a Kai, Te Aitanga a Mahaki and Rongowhakaata had come to Wellington. "Give us back our land,

Pharaoh. Let us enable it to blossom into our own sweet Canaan. Deliver us from our bondage."

'She absolutely demanded to be able to put her claims to the Prime Minister, even though the gathering of chiefs was almost over. "I will stay until I have my say," she said. What could the Prime Minister do? He could only say yes. So she got her way. He agreed that the hui could adjourn to a nearby marae where a huge feast was being prepared. That's where the fireworks really started! Meanwhile—')

The creatures of light and the creatures of darkness began to depart from the child and his grandmother. They were wondrous to look upon.

Suddenly, there was a flash of black light, like a spear of obsidian.

It struck Riripeti.

'Uh,' she groaned. She pressed her palms tight against her heart. The child was alarmed. He watched her luminosity as it faded; but then it surged again. 'No, I'm all right,' she whispered. All the child could think of was what she had said before standing:

'There may be a price to pay.'

Alarmed, he looked around for assistance. He saw his mother Tiana and realised that of all the people who had gathered, only she had seen the attack.

She lifted her face to the light.

act two

7

The matriarch was watching the night sky with the child. This was the first night of their return to Watuhi from Parliament Grounds in Wellington. The elation of the victory had calmed now.

'*O patria mia mai piu, mai piu ti rivedro*,' she sang, a reflective song to the people and to the land, 'oh blue skies, oh soft native breezes, where the light of my youth shone in tranquility.' The moonlight etched her profile with beauty.

'Grandmother, we won, didn't we?' the child asked.

She nodded and the pearls shimmered in her hair. She smiled her madonna smile. The moon was full and flooding the darkness with its light. There were three luminous circlets around the moon, and a small star within the second and third circlet. There was no other night light, no stars with their twinkling sparks of coldness.

'*O verdi colli, o profumate rive. O fresche valli, o queto asil beato*,' she sang in the night. Her voice soared with such strength that it seemed to bring the sky to life. A comet flamed like a sign across the face of the moon. Below lay Waituhi, a scattering of fires flickering in the bosom of the moon-drenched land. '*Or che d'amore il sogno e dileguato, o patria mia, non ti vedro mai piu.*'

'We did it for the land and the people,' the matriarch said.

A haze began to cover the moon. The matriarch took a deep indrawn breath and cried, 'No!' The circlets started to dissolve into the black night. She pressed the palms of her hands to her heart. '*Padre, pieta, pieta.*'

'I must live forever,' she cried.

In great pain she opened her arms and turned full circle to the night sky, the dark hills and the flames flickering. '*O patria, o patria,*' she sang, '*quanto mi costi,*' her voice challenging and echoing away, away, away.

⌐

The plane from Gisborne flew in to Wellington on the wing of a giant southerly blowing from the depths of the Antarctic. The wind made of the sea huge dark spikes like icicles relentlessly nailing themselves onto the land. Wellington itself was a city huddling one house close against the other to escape the crushing numbness of the cold. From the air it looked like a huge pack of cards scattered over the hills, just managing to stand upright. But you had the feeling that if God wanted to, all He needed to do was to touch one house with His finger, and slowly but surely, all the cards would start tumbling down, tumbling down, tumbling down, towards the sea.

Regan, Bianca and Miranda were waiting at the airport. They had caught an earlier plane from Auckland. I cradled Bianca close to me and kissed her cold cheeks. She beamed with delight; she had always been a gorgeous child, glowing like a rich, golden apricot. When she was born, a journalist friend took one look at her and said, 'Ah, this lassie was delivered by caesarean section.' We were astonished and asked, 'How do you know?' He laughed and said, 'It's the shape of her head and the look that she has. She's a very lucky girl not to have suffered the trauma of birth.' And Regan said, pulling a face, 'Well, she mightn't have, but I certainly did.' She had been in labour for over twenty-six hours before the doctors decided to deliver Bianca by caesarean. 'We think you've had enough,' they said. 'I certainly have,' she snapped back. At that stage she was in no mood to continue in pain. But she was upset when her own doctor couldn't do the delivery. When Bianca was born and Regan was being wheeled from the delivery room she was conscious enough to ask, 'Is it a boy? Is it a boy?'

'How was the flight?' Regan asked me as we walked through the airport terminal. 'Ours was awful. We had delays in Auckland because they weren't too sure whether the airport down here was open. Then, of course, when we finally trooped out to the plane, there was a further delay because of engine trouble. And Miranda wanted to crawl along the aisle but the flight was too rough. The landing was horrible.'

The terminal was packed. Wellington airport was always like this when there were delays; lots of people jammed into a building which looked more like a packing crate.

'You should have let Miranda do her crawl,' I said. 'Or better still, let her loose under the seats.' I grinned to myself as I remembered the first time our younger daughter had done that. It was so funny watching row upon row of people bobbing up and down as she went past, looking down at her and saying, 'Ooh,' and moving their legs like skittles to let her through.

But Regan didn't hear me. 'And I was sitting right next to a racist pig who heard the air hostess say my Maori surname, and he was so obnoxious to Miranda. You know how friendly she is. She wanted him to cuddle her and he would move away. I was so glad when, before landing, Miranda sicked up into his uptight lap.'

Regan, the mother protector. Nobody, but nobody, could abuse her daughters and get away with it. She could despatch people with such marvellous scorn. Once a French anthropologist asked her, in all innocence, 'What is it like to be married to a Maori?' She found the question offensive but contained herself and responded with a superb and withering reply, 'As I have not been married to an Eskimo, an Englishman, a Pygmy in an African jungle, an Australian, an American, a nomad who might live in the Gobi desert, let alone a Frenchman—' she paused and drew breath '—I have no basis for comparison.' End of sentence. End of question. Touché. Attagirl, Regan.

'Oh, my dear,' she said in the car, 'but how was your family? How was Tiana?' She had suddenly realised that she had been talking all the time—about her father William, mother Betty, sister Anna, Uncle David and Aunt Kay and the daily sagas of life in the bosom of the Wright family. 'They send their love by the way. Mother wants me to thank you for letting me go up there with Bianca and Miranda. You know how they love the girls; they're the only grandchildren, after all.'

I wanted to answer, 'Yes, I know, Regan, but they are Maori too, and must understand about their Maori ancestry, because that is the part that they're going to miss out on. Wherever they go they are in a European world. Both they and we must make the effort to take them back to Gisborne more often. And I'm not blaming you, dear, because I'm partly to blame also.' Instead, 'Mum's fine,' I said. 'She and Te Ariki would like to see you, Bianca and Miranda some time soon. Perhaps we can go up there next Christmas. Mum is still working hard. Dad is just the same. He wants me to go back for a longer time. He hates these short visits that I make, but they're all I can manage at the moment. I think he's right though. It isn't fair to them. Oh, yes, and Teria has found Mereira.'

'Really?' Regan asked. We were driving around the seafront at Evans Bay. The wind was lashing the waves so that they leapt across the roadway. The drops splattered against the windscreen, rattling like spears: Let us in. Let us in. 'Why, that's wonderful! You'll be able to go to see her sometime.' She took my hand and pressed it.

'What on earth for?'

Regan shrugged her shoulders. 'Don't you want to see her? She was very important to your mother. She might be able to tell you a little more about how Tiana and Te Ariki met. It's such a wonderful romantic story, their meeting like that in Hastings and falling in love so quickly! Then the marriage itself, and the return to Gisborne by train. It's so exciting, and sad too, when you think of what must have happened when they arrived in Gisborne. I mean, in all the tellings of the story, the climax comes with your grandmother taking

Te Ariki off in one direction, and Tiana being taken away by her mother. But haven't you ever wondered why they didn't approve? And why Tiana and Te Ariki were separated for eight months? There's a mystery there. It's a romantic story, but Tiana is not a romantic person. There's something missing in the telling of it. I can't explain, but it sounds too much like Georgette Heyer. It's . . . too romantic, that's all. It's not real.' She paused. We were coming to the bottom of Roseneath. 'Them's my sentiments anyway,' she said as we started to grind our way up one of the steepest streets in the city of Wellington.

It was so good to be back home. As is usual when people have been away from each other, there was a lot of catching up to do, the sharing of two lives and the knitting together of the common elements so that there is no sense of being apart. As Regan made dinner and I unpacked, and she put Miranda down to rest and I went up into the ceiling to fix a leak, and she took the dinner out of the oven and I set the table, we talked. We often talked without really hearing what the other had to say. We said things at cross-purposes, cutting into each other's monologues, taking the flow of conversation in so many different directions—and all at the same time, too—so that if you strung everything that we said together it would sound something like this:

'—and Anna has decided to go back to university next year though goodness knows why she'd want to take psychology—I'm sure I took my suit pants to Gisborne with me—No you didn't but it's getting a bit old and why don't you give it to Mana—Mana? Oh, he's doing so well at school and I think he's got a girlfriend—and speaking of friends I think that Anna's found somebody and I don't know who but she's promised to write and let me know—What was in the mail while I was away? Oh this bloody roof I think we'll have to get it repaired by a professional—Dad and Uncle David are planning to build a yacht and of course you know where they want to do that. Right in the middle of Mum's garden. Naturally she's not happy— And Teria took me out to Waituhi but I didn't get to Rongopai —What a shame but never mind. The mail wasn't much but you've got a letter from Rhys in Geneva—Have I? And is that chicken I can smell burning—Oh no. Look, why don't you write to Rhys—What about?—Your grandmother. Damn, it is burnt. Never mind. Is the table set?—Yes. So your father is building a yacht, huh?'

So it went on, like eight tennis players all playing the same game on the one court. Until it was over: game, set and match.

'Gosh, that burnt chicken was nice,' I said. The remnants of the meal were scattered around us, bones, wings, legs, flung here and there on the table as airily as our conversations.

'I would prefer the emphasis to be on the chicken,' Regan answered, 'and not on its condition.' She was cuddling up against me. Very soon it would be time for bed. Meantime, it was nice to be slothful and to let our gluttony digest in an easy who-cares fashion. 'Were you able to find out anything more about your grandmother? Whether or not she'd been to Venice?'

'No.'

'Why don't you write to Rhys? I'm sure he'd be willing to help. You know Rhys. He loves mysteries.'

'I suppose I could. Do you think he'd mind? Perhaps I should forget about the whole business. Tiana said I should. She said that I should leave the dead to rest. She wasn't at all happy with my questions. The worst thing is that the more I remember, the more I keep on remembering. Some of the moments I remember just add to the puzzle. It's quite frightening. I keep recalling things that perhaps I shouldn't. Unlocking doors. And each door leads to another and another and another. It's like a nightmare. I open a door on a question, and the only answer is another door.'

'But you can't stop, can you?'

'It's too late.'

She got up and kissed me. 'Well then, write to Rhys. I'm having a shower and then we are going to bed. You write to Rhys while I'm in the bathroom. And don't take too long. I don't want to be kept waiting.'

So I wrote to Rhys Rickard, a diplomat friend of mine who was living in Switzerland. I told him about Riripeti, the pearls she threaded in her hair and gave him a name: Paolo di Marchesi. I asked him for his help. Rhys was a bit of a madman, working for the United

Nations, Lord help them, and he owed me a few favours. I asked him to see what he could find out about the di Marchesi family. If he was going to Venice, I wrote, perhaps he could endeavour to discover if they existed. I added that I felt I could count on him.

The letter didn't take long to write; I would post it tomorrow. I would also ring my cousin, Sammy, and find out where Aunt Hiraina and Uncle Pita were.

I walked down to the bedroom. Regan had been late getting into the shower. I walked into the bathroom, took my clothes off and joined her. 'Hello,' I said as the water thrummed onto us, 'I thought I'd save some water and shower with a friend.'

But that night, all of the ordinariness and warmth of the return to Wellington could not save me. I had a dream, a terrible dream, in which I was walking across the courtyard towards the painted meeting house, Rongopai. A light was burning in the house and when I opened the door, I saw the matriarch there. She was sitting under the harsh light and she was veiled in black. I walked over to where she sat. But when she lifted the veil, it was not the matriarch at all but my mother, Tiana. Her face was that of the Medusa. The orbits of her eyes were filled with snakes. Her voice hissed like a basilisk as she sprang upon me and plunged a knife into my heart.

'See? You can bleed. Tell me, when Bianca was born, what was the manner of her birth? Tell me. Tell me.'

My blood made more serpents arise out of the dust. But there was another door and, opening it, I saw the matriarch. I ran towards her but, when she lifted her veil, it was Tiana. The knife sliced the air again.

'See? You can bleed. Tell me, when Bianca was born, what was the manner of her birth? Tell me. Tell me.'

I escaped again and ran through another door. And another. And another. And always there was a woman standing there who looked like the matriarch but was Tiana, Tiana, Tiana. And her knife kept on slashing into my heart.

I screamed a long timeless scream, until I felt my jaws breaking apart. Regan woke me, saying, 'Darling, it's all right, it's all right.'

I was drenched with sweat and the blood was pumping fast

through my heart. 'Help me, Regan,' I said.

She held me close to her and rocked me in her arms. Gradually, I started to calm down.

But the light slashed like knives at the window and at my eyelids. I woke with a start and began to shiver. The dawn was coming. I turned to Regan and waited for her eyes to flicker open. I asked her, 'Regan, when Bianca was born, was there anything strange about her birth?'

'Well, her head was very large, much too large for her to enter the world through my birth canal. That's why she had to be delivered by caesarean section.'

'Was there anything else?' I remembered listening to the heartbeat of the child through the doctor's stethoscope. It sounded like someone swimming, swimming out of the depths towards the world of light.

'She was the wrong way up. Her head was twisted around the wrong way. Her left elbow was in a strange position.'

'Was the eye swimming in blood?'

'Darling . . .'

'Were her hands around her neck?'

'My dear . . .'

'Were they?' I must have looked quite frightening with my relentless, insistent probing. Regan stared at me with fear in her face.

'No,' she said.

I felt the tension draining from me. I slumped back onto the pillows. Without really knowing why, I began to cry. Softly. In the dawn.

I took another shower that morning. 'I have made him into a likeness as unto me,' Grandmother had said to Uncle Alexis. And now a dream had come to me and I knew the manner of my birth had something to do with that strange pattern of words.

Regan came into the bathroom. I saw her shimmering on the other side of the shower curtain, not quite human. When she began to speak, her voice was troubled. 'About Bianca's birth,' she began. 'That's the second time I've been asked about the manner in which she was born.' The water hissed through her words. 'I haven't told you before, but your mother rang the hospital. She didn't want to speak to you. She wanted to speak to me, only me. She asked me the same question about the eye swimming in blood. And the position of the hands. I told her what I've told you. I know your mother never cries but this was the first time I've ever known Tiana to come close to weeping.'

She left me then, in the bathroom, filled with the steam of the rushing water. Again I remembered the matriarch and the child, and the world which encircled us. The steam seemed to be alive with spears, and each spear had my name on it: 'Let us in, let us in.'

'Oh, let us in.'

8

The matriarch took a fighting stance in front of the child. She had put her hat and walking stick aside. She took off her jacket because it was so hot. The pearls shone in the sun. In her hands she held a taiaha, a carved fighting staff.

'Titiro ki au,' she said. 'Look at me, mokopuna, and listen.'

He nodded his head. She was teaching the child how to fight so that next time they would escape from Waituhi and never be caught. They were on the side lawn at the old homestead. The hens were scrabbling in the flax, pouting, clucking and pecking at one another. Far off he could hear his grandfather, his father and two of his uncles, whistling in the dogs. The men had gone out shepherding grandfather's sheep. It was almost lunchtime and they were due to return for kai.

'The first lesson,' she said. 'You see the way I am standing? With my left foot forward? That means I am right-handed. If I was a boxer I would lead with my right fist and protect myself with my left arm. You understand? But I am not teaching you boxing. I am teaching you the taiaha. Now, you show me how you stand when you fight.'

He looked up at the matriarch and copied the way she was standing.

'Aha!' she said. 'Your right foot is forward of your left foot so that tells me that you will lead with your left. See? You know your left from your right, don't you, boy?'

He didn't really, but he nodded up at her. She was standing silhouetted against the sun. Her lustrous hair tumbled loose from the long pins she always used to keep it off the nape of her neck. She saw him shading his eyes and nudged him with the broom until they had circled and reversed positions and it was she who was looking into the sun.

'That's your second lesson,' she said. 'When you're small like you are, you have to be more cunning. You must use every advantage you can get, ne. Make me the one to look into the sun! Or me the one to tread in the cow's poop!'

He began to giggle. This was a good game. The matriarch frowned and hit him on the legs with the fighting staff. He looked into that patrician face of hers, gleaming in the rays of the sun, and saw an expression of seriousness. Her forehead beaded with tiny pearls of sweat.

'Never mind about laughing,' she said. 'Pay attention to me. See? I am standing more side-on than you. That's so my enemy can't hurt my heart or my stomach. It will still be painful when his blows land, but I won't get winded or badly hurt. Side-on, he hits me here. Here. Here.'

She began jabbing at him with the taiaha. The side of his face. The shoulders. His hips, his legs. The blows were sharp, stinging, forcing him to back away.

'E koe,' she said. 'Now listen again and watch. See my eyes? Most times when your enemy wants to make his move his eyes give him away. He might blink. He might make his eyes grow big. He might make them small. Again, whakarongo ki au, listen to the breathing. Your enemy likes to take a big breath before he strikes. Like this! And this! And this!'

The matriarch feinted with the fighting staff. At his body. His head. His legs. Each time she did so, she blinked her eyelids and expelled her breath forcefully from her lungs. Her feet stamped patterns in the dirt. The taiaha skimmed the air, its shadow flashing like a dark wing across the sunlit lawn. At the back of the old homestead he heard the sound of approaching horses and dogs, and the graunching of the sledge on the brick path. Grandfather Ihaka appeared with his father and uncles. His father laughed.

'Kia tupato, Te Ariki,' the matriarch warned him. 'You'll be next.'

'You look so hardcase, old lady,' Dad said. 'You and that fighting staff in your hands. Whoever taught you to do the taiaha?'

'Ae,' Grandfather Ihaka agreed. 'Women do not know of such things. Warfare is for men. The kitchen and the bedroom are for the women.'

He went to run to his father. The matriarch barred his way.

'E tu koe i reira,' she said. Her eyes were lit with determination as she pushed him back into position. 'You're not leaving until you get this right. Forget that the men are here. They know nothing except to boast how men should be and how women should be. They forget who I am. I'm the king here.'

Grandfather said something to her in Maori. 'Well, I wouldn't need to do this if you did it,' she replied. 'This mokopuna needs to know how to defend himself. He's too soft.'

She turned to him again. 'This is not play,' she warned. 'This is not pretend. So take some deep breaths like I am doing, and be alert. Now, when I lunge with the fighting staff you parry the thrust with the outside of your arms. When I lunge to the right, you push the taiaha to the side with your left arm as if you're sweeping a blowfly from your face. When I lunge to the left you do the same thing but with your right arm. When I lunge straight at you, turn your body sideways so I miss. If you get the chance to hit me, you hit me, because I shall be hitting you with the fighting staff every chance I get. You understand? Kei te pai. Let us begin. Take up your position. Watch my eyes. Be alert.'

'You show the old lady,' Uncle Alexis called. 'Don't let her beat you, boy.'

He glanced over at his uncle and that was when the matriarch made her first lunge at him. The pain shocked him and he backed away.

'Hey, old lady,' Te Ariki called. 'Go easy on my son.'

He looked into her eyes. They were hard. 'I told you to be on your guard. I warned you. Take your position again. Never mind about the men. Concentrate on me. Concentrate on the fight.'

She lunged again. The blow caught his left thigh. 'E koe,' she said as she thrust to his right and the fighting staff slammed into his left shoulder. He could feel tears in his eyes. 'No good just standing there, mokopuna,' Grandmother said. 'No good crying. Start defending yourself. Be alert. Kia kaha.'

She thrust again, and again and again. 'E koe,' she shrilled as she scored hits on his body. 'E koe. E koe. E koe.'

Grandfather Ihaka, father and uncles were silent. He wondered why his father did not intervene. His heart was pounding with fright. His body was stinging from the blows.

'Fight back,' the matriarch screamed. 'Fight back, you soft kid.'

Her hair was entirely loose of its pins. There were sweat stains at her neck and armpits. Her athletic body wove patterns between the darkness and light as she took advantage from the sun.

By luck, he managed to parry one of her thrusts.

'That's it,' the matriarch cried. She lunged at his chest, and he turned side-on so that she missed him. 'Kei te pai,' she said as she turned and slammed the taiaha at his neck. 'But next time, hit me in the stomach as I pass you. E koe. E koe. E koe.'

He got the hang of it. He watched his grandmother's eyes. He listened to her breathing. He tried to ascertain her weaknesses. The matriarch saw his understanding. Her voice was triumphant.

'That's it, boy,' she cried. 'You show me. You show your grandfather too. And your father. You've got it mokopuna. Kei te pai. Good. Good.'

Her voice soared into the stillness of the sky. Her thrusts were more serious and more calculated. She was a warrior queen, but her movements were becoming laboured. She was breathing heavily, sucking the air strongly into her.

She lunged. He sidestepped. He watched her looming over him

and twisting to his left. Her eyes caught his, dazzling like diamonds. Yes. Yes.

He lifted the taiaha and punched it at her heart.

The matriarch gave a hoarse, agonised cry as she fell. He stood over her. 'E koe,' he shouted. 'E koe. E koe.' Te Ariki came over to him and slapped his face. 'Don't you hit your grandmother like that, ever again.'

'She hit me,' he answered. 'She hit me.'

The matriarch reached up for his father. 'Leave him alone, Te Ariki. I asked for it. He did well.'

All he could feel was the pain of the bruising from the fighting staff and the anger for his father and grandmother. As the matriarch rose from the ground he bunched his fists.

'You hate me now, ne?' the matriarch called.

'Yes!' he shouted.

'I hurt you, ne?' she asked.

She let her taiaha fall. She came to him and put her arms around him. 'Don't cry, boy. Don't cry. Nothing to cry about. You won.'

'What a good fight,' Uncle Pita laughed. 'Better than going to see Errol Flynn.'

The matriarch led the child into the homestead, ignoring the men. She whispered her dreams to him in that low, thrilling voice. She was always a dream spinner, spinning dreams of many colours on the dream wheel. 'It was important for you to learn how to hate.' She said. 'You have learnt well.'

⌇

'Kororia ki To Ingoa Tapu,' the matriarch said.

She held her hand, upraised, as a homage to God. She had taken the child to the place of healing, to Rongopai. It had been deserted for many years and from the dusty road in front of it, looked drab and desolate. Yet, open the door and walk in, and you are in the Sistine Chapel of the Maori nation.

The matriarch and the child sat in the darkness of the deserted hall. The paintings—for the interior was entirely painted—were dimly lit with daylight seeping through the open doorway. They seemed like living creatures of the night. Fantastic vines and trees took root in the dirt floor, tracing sinuous limbs to the ceiling. There, exotic birds and phantoms glided among the painted heavens.

The matriarch soothed the bruises on the child's body and arms. She had not realised how much she had hurt him in the taiaha lesson. She knew, also, that he did not yet understand why she allowed him to cause her pain. He had not yet forgiven her for the one or the other and she could feel the anger, the puzzlement, still inside him. She looked down both sides of the meeting house towards the front doorway. The painted ancestors seemed to spring to life from the pillars. The light began to fade and there was only the wind swirling, like a dream within the hall. The time of healing was nigh. Now was the time to begin.

'E mokopuna, listen to the Song of Te Kooti. You will learn in the listening why you have to hate and, then, why you have to learn to forgive. What happened to Te Kooti is what has happened to all of us and will continue to happen unless we fight on and hold to the truth.

'Glory to Thy Holy Name. His name was Te Kooti Arikirangi Te Turuki and Jehovah chose him at birth to lead his Children of Israel, the Maori nation, out of the land of the Pakeha, out of slavery to Egypt. This he did do, as Moses did also, when Moses opened the Red Sea and led his people to Canaan. It was of Te Kooti that the tohunga, Toeroa, said to Turakau, the mother of Te Kooti, "Your unborn child will be a son whose fame will reach to the four corners of the earth for good or evil." Indeed, so it has come to pass that his fame for goodness spread as foretold. But so also did his fame for evil. Yet this was not of his doing, this evil, for it was the Pakeha themselves who first began the evil by denying Te Kooti his blessedness; after the fall of the pa at Waerenga a Hika, during the Hauhau wars, they wrongly imprisoned him and exiled him to Wharekauri. When he escaped from Wharekauri, the Pakeha wished to hunt him down like an animal. Only then did he take up arms against Pharaoh and against all Egypt.

'Kororia ki To Ingoa Tapu. His father was Hone te Rangi Pataihi.

His hapu was Ngati Maru of the Rongowhakaata Confederation. From his father's mother, Waikura, he had the blood of the Ngati Ruapani iwi. Two other male children were born that year, Hui a Kama and Whanau ua Rerea. The third was Te Kooti. But nobody knows the year of his birth or the circumstances attending it.

'And the Lord was with the child and wished to use him for goodness and the Pakeha's sake. So Te Kooti was sent to the mission school at Whakato and his holiness shone from him in his reading of the scriptures and of the psalms of David, the same David who slew the giant Goliath with a stone from a sling and brought him down to the ground. Therefore, Te Kooti was baptised by the Pakeha and thereby consecrated to Jehovah's great purpose for good. He wished to be trained as a mission teacher but the temple was unclean and had unclean thoughts. And Pharaoh grew exceedingly jealous of the holiness shining forth from Te Kooti. It was the Bishop W. Williams who denied the request.

'Glory to Thy Holy Name. The Pakeha hardened their hearts against him and would not see his goodness even when the vision was given unto them. They saw only their own evil, accusing the boy of their own sin, the sin of pride and of arrogance. They persuaded his parents likewise, and the parents imprisoned him in a kumara pit and left him to die. But lo and behold he escaped when the Lord sent an angel in the form of a man. Te Kooti was close to death. The angel said to him, "Arise! Let us go forth!" A path opened in the covering of the pit. And Te Kooti came forth.

'He came forth into manhood and he lived in the land of Egypt with his people, but knew not that he was chosen. He worked for Pharaoh, in the bush and on the farmland. He was a fine horseman and, like Moses, was well respected. He went to sea, became super-cargo on the schooner *Henry* and, later, captain of the Maori-owned *Rua Whetuki*. He visited Pharaoh's palace at Auckland and, like the prodigal son, fell into ungodly ways and vice. When he returned to his people of Turanganui he brought his evil ways with him. So much so that his own people began to turn against him.

'Then came the wars with the Hauhau and the Maori nation was split between those who sided with Pharaoh and those who did not.

Although his brother, Komere, and others of the Rongowhakaata Confederation joined with the Hauhau, Te Kooti did not. He was in the thrall of Egypt, and he was a loyal warrior of God, and he therefore fought on the government side at the siege of Waerenga a Hika in November 1865. But then it happened that his eyes were opened to the uncleanliness of the temple, and the sin of pride of Egypt. For he was in the Bishop's house, the house of Bishop W. Williams, when he was placed under arrest. He was charged with treasonable communication with the Hauhau, in that he had visited the Hauhau camp at Pukeamionga. He had done this in an attempt to persuade his brother to leave the Hauhau. His principal accuser then said that he had seen Te Kooti withdraw the bullets from his cartridges during the fighting. This was not proven, so he was released.

'Kororia ki To Ingoa Tapu. And so Te Kooti was set free, but some months after the siege he was rearrested by Pharaoh. This time it was Captain Read who charged him with spying, made him a military prisoner, and sent him to Napier with the Hauhau rebels. While he was there, he saw Donald McLean and appealed to him, but Pharaoh would not listen to him, saying, "Send him away with the rest to the Chatham Islands." It was Captain Read who instigated it all to prevent Te Kooti from hurting his own trade in the Land of Egypt. The Pakeha also wanted to remove all those who were troublesome and persisted in disturbing the peace of Egypt. In their own parliament questions were asked whether rebels could be deported without trial. It was rumoured that one of the reasons for the deportations was so that the Government could move quicker to confiscate Maori land, and do so without the lamentations of Israel. It was Major Biggs who was responsible for the prophet's exile.

'Then there was a wailing throughout the land as the prisoners were sent into exile. This was in 1866, and in total seventy men, women and children were taken by their guards on 3 March to the Chatham Islands. The second lot of prisoners, numbering eighty-eight, were sent on 27 April. On 10 June, one hundred and sixteen prisoners were sent in the third batch. And a fourth lot of prisoners, fifty-six in number, got to the island prison on 26 November. Te Kooti was in the third batch of prisoners; he was innocent.

'Glory to Thy Holy Name. The place of exile was a place of desolation. The prisoners suffered humiliation and indignity from Pharaoh's gaolers. They were in exile for a span of two years. But Jehovah was merciful and He at last revealed to Te Kooti that he had been chosen.

'"The spirit of God aroused me, saying, 'Arise; I am sent by God to heal you, that you may preach His name to His people who are living as captives in this land, that they may understand that it was Jehovah who drove you all here.' I said, 'Speak, O Lord.' He answered, 'Be not afraid, for your cry has come unto God, and He has given heed to your crying. Hearken; I will strengthen you and make known to you the words which I spoke to your fathers, to Abraham, Isaac, and Jacob, and to their seed even down to David. The understanding of man is but the "letter"; it is from the outside only, and is not the truth; mine is from within, and is known by none other. Now, therefore, speak my words and make them known to my people: Speak my words, and mine only.'"

'Kororia ki To Ingoa Tapu. And Te Kooti the man became Te Kooti the prophet and he established his church, Ringatu, as the power of the people in bondage in Egypt. The spirit moved him to study the psalms, the books of Joshua and Judges, to compose scriptural verses and hold religious services twice daily. "O God, if our hearts arise from the land in which we now dwell as slaves, and repent and pray to Thee and confess our sins in Thy presence, then, O, Jehovah, do Thou blot out the sins of Thine own people, who have sinned against Thee. Do not Thou, O God, cause us to be wholly destroyed. Wherefore it is that we glorify Thy Holy Name. Amen."

'But at the end of the two years at Wharekauri, the prisoners had not yet been released. This is the period of imprisonment, no longer, that Mr Donald McLean had promised them. But he was Pharaoh, and hardened his heart, and the prisoners and the prophet remained on Wharekauri. During this time, by the power of the spirit, the Hauhau were turned to the Ringatu religion.

Then on 1 July 1868, the prophet received a vision. He saw a ship anchoring at the Chatham Islands and that he, and his people, would take it, return to the Maori nation and lead his people out of the land of Egypt.

'Glory To Thy Holy Name. So it came to pass that a ship, the *Rifleman*, reached the Chatham Islands on 3 July. The next day, rain came down, interfering with the loading of the cargo. While the captain and some of the crew were ashore, that was when the prophesy was fulfilled. Alas, during the fulfilment, one of the Egyptians took an axe, threw it at one of the prisoners and, in the fight, he was killed. But nobody saw who had killed the Egyptian. For this reason, lots were drawn and it fell to Te Kooti to make sacrifice, in the biblical manner, of his uncle. With this sacrifice, the escape was made successfully.

'Verily, this was the God-sent deliverance. It was the Passover. The prophet and his followers had prayed and it was done. "O Jehovah, O Christ, O Holy Ghost, remember me, now awakening on my bed; for Thou hast watched over me during this past night. O Christ, deliver me from the land of the devil. Forsake me not throughout this day. O my Lord, turn favourably towards me; draw me up out of the depths; let me be ever as Peter, who was taken up by Thee out of the raging sea. Take me up from within the net of death. Wherefore I glorify Thy Holy Name. Kororia ki To Ingoa. Amine."'

The Chatham Islands lie some 800 kilometres east of Lyttelton, about latitude 44 degrees south and longitude 176 degrees west. At the time of the flight from Wharekauri, they were seven days sailing from Turanga. In 1861 the total population was estimated at 413 Maori, 160 Moriori, seventeen half-castes and forty-six Europeans. Today the present population is some 400 souls. The Moriori have disappeared. Skies are often overcast.

The stuff of romance and desperation attends the prophet Te Kooti's escape from the Chathams and the voyage of the *Rifleman* through the grey swelling seas northwards to Gisborne. Here's a contemporary account of it:

Guard Michael Mullooly: 'At 2 p.m. on 4 July 1868, the prisoners filed into the redoubt on the Chathams. It was wet outside. The landing of cargo from the *Rifleman* had been delayed.

'At about 2.45 p.m. I walked out of the barracks room; it was so full that I could hardly move. I had not gone more than seven paces when I was seized by three or four prisoners, laid face down very gently and bound hand and foot, my hands being tied behind my back . . . I saw them break open the magazine, roll out the ammunition, take possession of the rifles (which they loaded and capped in great haste) and the bayonets . . .

'When I left the barracks room I met an old fellow who had been sick for six months and I remarked to myself: "What business has he here? . . ." They left me on the ground for about five minutes and then carried me into the barracks room. I saw Constables Cotter, Muirhead and Johnson, who were also tied hand and foot. They told me that Constable Michael Hartnett [a single man, whose father was a pensioner at Onehunga] had been tomahawked. I saw them open all our boxes. They took all the money they could find, but nothing else, out of the barracks room.

'About three shots were fired, and then they brought in Captain Thomas and laid him down. He was tied very tightly and, I believe, suffered very much. I saw them drag in Constable Hemmington with his trousers torn off his back [sic]. He looked rather fierce; I saw them handcuff him. As I was suffering a good deal of pain in my wrists, I got them to unbind my hands and handcuff me also. Captain Thomas also asked them to handcuff him, but they took no notice. He called out to me to ask them to handcuff him. The man in charge said that he had got no more handcuffs, so I showed him where he could get a pair.

'A fellow then came in and told Captain Thomas that they wanted him at the courthouse to talk with Alick [Mr Shand, the interpreter]. They took him away, well watched. One fellow followed him with a long rope. I thought they were going to hang him . . . A few minutes afterwards the prisoners commenced to karakia [pray] in Elliott's room. They then formed a circle in the barracks square and began to pray again. I think it was a Hauhau karakia, for I heard them say: "No. 1; No. 2, etc." They had another prayer at the gate, then shouted and left.

'Two civilians came in and loosed us. We saw they were all on board the *Rifleman*. They cast the *Florence* adrift and she went ashore on the beach. I do not know who the fellows were who tied me up.

I saw Te Kooti walking about doing nothing . . . I did not hear him speak. He seemed quite pleased. I saw Pohipo No. 4 on the parapet, apparently doing sentry . . .'

Throughout the voyage, a Maori sentry armed with a sword stood over the helmsman and sentries patrolled the deck day and night. The captive ship landed at Whareongaonga, about eight miles south of Young Nick's Head, at dusk on 10 July 1868. She carried the prophet, 162 men, sixty-four women and seventy-one children; three men and one woman had remained behind. Among the cargo were large quantities of flour, sugar and general stores and some barrels of beer. The followers of Te Kooti had also thirty-three rifles, eight double-barrelled guns, seven revolvers, twenty-nine bayonets, three kegs of powder, 4584 cartridges, 6670 percussion caps and some swords which they had taken from the redoubt. In addition they had £522 in notes and coin. All the voyagers and cargo were landed during the night and most of the next day. Then the *Rifleman* was released. It sailed to Napier where the news of the escape from the Chatham Islands was telegraphed to Wellington.

Two hundred and ninety-eight people, standing on a beach in their homeland. Not many to start a religious movement! What were their thoughts? After all they were finally back on their native land, from which they had been cruelly and unfairly separated without trial or any recourse to judgment. Perhaps they held a tangi, a weeping, on the sand. Certainly, they prayed to Jehovah, thanking Him for His deliverance of them. Then, they must have looked to their leader, the prophet Te Kooti Arikirangi Te Turuki.

Over the next five days, it was he who dealt with emissaries from the Government who requested that he and his followers should surrender both themselves and the cargo they had brought with them. Who among us would not have sympathised with their refusal to give themselves back into the hands of Pharaoh and the Egyptians? All they wished to do was to set up a religious community, based on the teachings of their prophet.

On 15 July 1868, Te Kooti therefore led the Ringatu inland on the long journey to seek the land of Canaan. So began the Te Kooti Wars. Everywhere his people went they were pursued.

'Upon looking back upon this extraordinary incident,' wrote G.S. Cooper in his report on the flight from Wharekauri, 'it is difficult to say whether one's wonder is excited more by the precision, rapidity and completeness with which the enterprise was planned and executed than by the moderation shown in the hour of victory by a gang of barbarous fanatics, who, in a moment, found their former masters bound at their feet and their lives entirely at their mercy.'

Ah yes, the prophet and the people were merciful, but they themselves were not shown mercy. They sought the land of Canaan; instead, began the time of war, the wandering in the wilderness of Israel and their religious persecution at the hands of Pharaoh.

'Kororia ki To Ingoa Tapu,' the matriarch said.

Her upraised hand cast a shadow across the earthen floor of the place of healing. The bracelets beneath the folds of her long black gown tinkled like oriental chimes. She unclasped two of them; they were of curious design, and as the child watched, he saw that there were two silver pendant-shaped vials suspended from the bracelets, about the length of his small finger. The matriarch uncapped one of the vials and touched her palms to the opening. Then, speaking in Maori, she imprinted her fingers and palms upon parts of the body of the child. As she did so, her breathing altered:

'Kssss. Kssss. Kssss. Kssss.'

He felt the liquid, so cold, yet also hot, tingling on his skin. He watched the shadow of her motioning arms make the sign of the prophet against the painted pillars of the meeting house. She cradled him and kissed him and for a while was silent. The child looked into her face. The veils across her face seemed like a curtain and beyond the curtain her eyes shone like a spider's. He could see her thoughts springing like silver threads through each dark iris, through the forests of the tribal memory.

'E mokopuna, the Song of Te Kooti tells us that the man called Te Kooti came back as the prophet Te Kooti, and he brought with him the Ringatu Church which he had established while in prison on Wharekauri.

'Glory to Thy Holy Name. And upon landing at Whareongonga,

the prophet told the people that he would be like unto Moses and that, with the guidance of Jehovah, he would lead us out of bondage of Egypt. He called the hill at the southern end of the beach, Mount Moriah, and he named the two shelving reefs of the beach, the Tablets of the New Law. He said that when the prophet and the church had triumphed against Egypt, yea, he would touch those rocks with Aaron's Rod and the New Revelation would spring from the earth.

'Then the prophet told the first worshippers of the church, the two hundred and ninety-seven who had escaped with him, that they must establish the Ringatu religion; the Urewera country was chosen as the place of the building of the church. But on 14 July 1868, just before they were to travel inland, the cohorts of Pharaoh, Major Biggs and eight militia, appeared to demand the surrender of the prophet and their guns. This the prophet would not do, saying, "We did no wrong, yet you put us in prison. We will not be returned to gaol for we remain innocent, and never will we return to you the rifles with which you might then slaughter us. God has given us the arms and we are not going to give them up at any man's bidding. We wish to go on our way unmolested."

'Kororia ki To Ingoa Tapu. It was then that Pharaoh came down like the wolf on the fold, attempting to scatter us, but the Lord was with us and we turned Pharaoh away. The next day, the 15th, the prophet began to lead us from Whareongonga towards the Urewera. But at Paparatu, on the 20th, Pharaoh came down upon us again with his cohorts of 140 soldiers, Maori and Pakeha, and surrounded our camp while we were sleeping. We fought for seven hours and again, Jehovah was with us, and we turned Pharaoh away. We cried for our dead and asked the Lord to take them unto Him. Te Kooti again told Biggs, "We wish to go on our way unmolested."

'But again, on the 24th, Biggs attacked us at Te Koneke Ridge. The Lord remained with us, and we turned Pharaoh away, crossed the Hangaroa River and began to traverse the Ruakituri Valley. And after the fight, the prophet wrote a letter to the Government that they should not destroy us and that we were not desirous of fighting. He wrote that the people wished only to go to the protection of the

Maori King and to settle the Ringatu in the Urewera.

'Alas, yet did Pharaoh's soldiers still pursue us. But Jehovah sent snowstorms to our aid so that the Egyptian cohort of two hundred and thirty-six men were cast into disarray and could not come upon us in the night. The people were sheltered by the Lord until the 8th of August when the wrath of Pharaoh again descended. The place of the battle was the Ruakituri Valley and we were encamped at Tuahu under cover of the bank opposite the rock known as Te Wero a Tohe. The snowstorms that the Lord had sent made torrential the Ruakituri River so that the soldiers could not get to us and defeat us. Hard frost and more snow came down upon Pharaoh and he retreated with great lamentation. We ourselves cried for our dead and entreated the Lord to take them unto Him.

'Glory to Thy Holy Name. It was then that the prophet gathered the people together. He said unto us, "Three times we have been attacked since we left Whareongaonga and three times I have entreated the Government not to kill us. I have written to the Government also, once at Whareongaonga and the second time after the attack at Te Koneke. But Pharaoh still pursues us and does not let us continue our pilgrimage to the Urewera.

'"For this reason, and in the name of Jehovah, the people must be protected. The Egyptians will never leave us in peace. We will never be unmolested. If it is war that they want, it is war that they shall have. Let us therefore leave this place and settle the church and the people at Puketapu Mountain. And from the Mountain, let the voice of Jehovah go out to the children of Israel in bondage to Egypt. Let all know that we are at the mountain for, yea, if the Lord speaks to their hearts, then they will come to us. For we will need them in the war."

'Kororia ki To Ingoa Tapu. After the prophet had spoken, the people cried out in sorrow not for themselves but for the Egyptians. They followed the prophet to Puketapu Mountain where Te Kooti sent the declaration of war to the Government, both Maori and Pakeha. He said, "Friends, I agree that we fight, for I have been followed up by you three times." Then he said, "I will fight you in November. That is the month when trouble will arise."

'And the people journeyed to Puketapu and established the church at the Mountain. Many were the Children of Israel who came to join us and the prophet; we were there for three months preparing for the war. And Pharaoh grew sorely afraid and sent emissaries unto the prophet and posted sentries even at Ramaroa Pa where a watch could be made on the ford over the Waipaoa River; he assembled his own troops against the stronghold at Puketapu Mountain.

'It was too late. As he had promised, and three months after he established the church at Puketapu Mountain, Te Kooti issued the word. He said, "We wished to go on our way unmolested. We were attacked three times by Pharaoh. We have made our declaration for war for the month of November. That month has now come. We would have much preferred peace. It is now war. It is time to lead the Children of Israel from out of the bondage of Egypt."

'And Te Kooti led us in karakia, "Here is Thy servant lying on his bed, much like a dead man, without thoughts or desires towards my Creator. Alas! While I was thinking of error and confusion, suddenly there came love from my Father in Heaven, and then I broke forth into wailings and lamentations for myself, that I had not been mindful of my heavenly Father. O my Deliverer, remember me; drag me out of the net of death, and place Thy Holy Spirit within me this night. Glory to Thy Holy Name. Kororia ki To Ingoa Tapu. Amine."'

ᕑ

THE MATAWHERO RETALIATION/PRELUDE:
9 AUGUST TO 9 NOVEMBER 1868
He had all Poverty Bay, the East Coast and Hawke's Bay to choose from. He could have made his act of war against any of the towns of the three regions; instead, Te Kooti Arikirangi Te Turuki chose to make this act upon the small settlement of Matawhero, just outside Gisborne.

Some historians have puzzled over this and, ultimately, have decided that Te Kooti was too afraid to attack any of the well garrisoned settlements. But the prophet could have taken Gisborne if he had wanted to. No, the reason for not razing Gisborne itself is that

Te Kooti was not interested nor directed to do this. If there was to be an act of war, let it be a small act, and let it be directed against those who had in fact fired upon the prophet and thereby on Jehovah. Yes, let it be against Pharaoh, Major Biggs, the man who had exiled the prophet to Wharekauri and then, on Te Kooti's return, had pursued him through three battles to Puketapu Mountain. Let it be against Pharaoh's cohorts, the militia who, with Major Biggs, were stationed at Matawhero. Let it be between the two armies of war.

Major Biggs, Major Biggs, you walked three months in the valley of the shadow of death. You felt the chill, on first entering, and you wrote to Mr McLean on 18 August 1868—'Is there any likelihood of our having any protection here [Poverty Bay] in the shape of an organised force, either Native or European or both? Our population is decreasing rapidly, from five to ten leaving by every vessel for Auckland. If the ex-prisoners come down in the summer (as the natives of this place expect) we shall not be able to protect ourselves without assistance.'

Alas, Major Biggs. You wanted, over the three months between August and November, to mount an attack on Te Kooti's stronghold, but the government forces could not be spared to aid you as they were still needed in the Land Wars on the other side of the island in the Taranaki. All you could do was to mount patrols around the mountain and throughout the area, continue to enlist the support of the loyal Maori, try to prevent more Maori joining the prophet, and watch, wait and listen. You knew that November would be the month of the attack. Your strategy was to withdraw all outsettlers into the towns at first word of Te Kooti's leaving Puketapu Mountain. You did not know that it was not any of the towns that Te Kooti wanted; what he wanted was you and your outsettlement.

They are so strange, so strange, the fortunes of war. As promised, the fires of a Maori war party began to creep down the flanks of Puketapu Mountain in the early days of November. The fires scorched a trail towards Poverty Bay. On 8 November, it was confirmed to you that Te Kooti had indeed left his mountain stronghold. The fires crept closer, but your sentries and scouts, watching all the tracks, reported no oncoming. Then on 9 November, the Reverend

Williams himself told you that Te Kooti was on the way. Your reply was that your scouts would soon be reporting to you on the matter and would give sufficient warning to enable outsettlers enough time to move to Gisborne. That's where you thought the attack would take place; so you guarded the Te Reinga track to the township. There was another approach, down the Ngatapa Valley, and a vigilante group of settlers watched the ford over the Waipaoa River at a point above Patutahi, a hill patterned on the poutama.

Ah, the *fatalitá* of events. Major Biggs, you thought this action unnecessary. The settlers stopped their watch two weeks before 9 November.

The fires loomed closer, burning your eyes, Major Biggs, but you still kept watch on Te Reinga and not Ngatapa; Mrs Wyllie herself told you that Te Kooti was moving down Ngatapa but you said that was absurd. You could have moved settlers into Gisborne at that stage but you didn't; that would have saved lives, certainly, but it would not have put Te Kooti off his trail.

Major Reginald Newton Biggs, I wish to give you a lyrical and rhapsodic interlude, something to balance the cruel reality of death, the smashing of your head to pulp during the dawn of the 10th of November. Let me conjure up a family picnic, yes, by the banks of the Waipaoa River. You are there, thirty-eight years of age, with your wife Emily, aged nineteen, your child George, just one year old, and your child's nurse, Jane Farrell, a sweet twenty-six. You have been showing off your prowess with a gun and now, you are stripping down to longjohns to swim the river. 'No, Reginald, darling, you will drown,' Emily protests. But she knows that you are a good swimmer. Her breath catches in her throat at the sight of your manliness in the sun and the strength of the loins which have taken her night upon night. You dive into the river, and the nurse laughs and pulls her dress away from the cascading splash. Your sweet son reaches up to catch the splashes as they fall. 'No, Reginald, darling, no.' The sun is hot, and willows drape themselves along the banks; a chiaroscuro of light shimmers gently around you all.

So swim, swim out, swim for the last time, Major Biggs. You will be dead tomorrow. So will your son. So will your son's nurse. So will your sweet, sweet wife, your Emily, who watches you as you reach the shadows cast by the underwater valleys of the Waipaoa.

Many people met Te Kooti but no genuine photograph of him has come to light. His appearance remains an enigma, and all we have to assist us to visualise the prophet are the written records of people like that of Mr Firth, a Waikato farmer.

'As I approached Wi Tamehana's monument, a Maori advanced to meet me, raising his hat and saluting me as he approached. I dismounted on learning that Te Kooti stood before me. He was attended by two half-caste youths, fully armed, Te Kooti himself being unarmed. His height is about five feet nine inches, he is about thirty-five years of age, stoutly built, broad shouldered and strong limbed. His features are not repulsive, and rather large development of jaw and chin conveys the idea of a man of strong and resolute will. He has no tattoo; hair black and glossy, wears a black moustache and short black beard. His dress consisted of woollen cords, top boots, and a gray shirt, over the latter he wore a loose vest with gold chain and greenstone ornaments. I noticed that he had lost the middle finger of the left hand.

'I urged him to surrender to the Government but he refused, saying, "If they let me alone I will live quietly. If not, I will fight."'

The name 'Arikirangi' was tattooed across his chest. The name 'Te Turuki', an old family name, was tattooed on his right arm.

ᶜ

THE MATAWHERO RETALIATION/CLOSE UP:
FRIDAY 6 NOVEMBER 1868, 11 A.M.
. . . and the fires of Te Kooti began to move down the flank of Puketapu Mountain.

Lieutenant Gascoyne watched intently as the old Maori quickly sketched a map in the dust of the road. The Maori was gesticulating in a frustrated manner and his voice rose and fell in agitation. Beside the old man, one of the native scouts was listening and, every now and then, the scout interposed a question which only seemed to make the old man angrier. The argument reached a pitch; the old man compressed his lips into silence and began to rock on his heels.

'Well?' Lieutenant Gascoyne asked. 'What do you reckon?'

'The old man has no reason to lie,' the scout said.

'So what does he say?'

'He reckons that we're watching the wrong track. Look, he's sketched it for us. Here's our chief camp, about twenty miles from Gisborne, where we are on this point descending to the Hangaroa River. But here, a long way to the right of us, is a very ancient track. The old man reckons this is the one that Te Kooti will take. Look.' The scout began to trace the route. 'From Puketapu Mountain there's a track down the Ngatapa Valley but we are watching Te Reinga. At this point, the Ngatapa Valley spills into Patutahi. The old man reckons Te Kooti will come down the valley to the settlement. From Patutahi the ancient track goes along the western side of the Waipaoa River and, then, down to the lower ford at Matawhero. No Pakeha live along this route. That's why I think the old man is right. If Te Kooti follows this track he can get right to Matawhero and Turanganui unseen.'

'Better look at it tomorrow,' Lieutenant Gascoyne said. He threw the old Maori man a stick of tobacco. The old man put a piece in his mouth, chewed, and then spat on the ground. The spittle trickled slowly down the dust representation of the Ngatapa Valley.

SATURDAY 7 NOVEMBER, 9.30 A.M.

. . . towards the Ngatapa Valley the fires spread for this was the time of war.

In Napier, Mr McLean was waiting for the telegraph office to open. That devil, Te Kooti, was finally on the move. Intelligence received from friendly natives of Hawke's Bay had come in yesterday: a war party from Puketapu Mountain was definitely moving on Poverty Bay.

'Come along man,' Mr McLean shouted at the telegraph operator. 'Quickly now. I want to follow up on a message I sent yesterday. That one was to the Hon. Mr Richmond, but this one must go to the Defence Minister in Wellington.'

He stayed to watch until the message was finally transmitted. He felt pangs of guilt. It was he who had sentenced Te Kooti to the Chatham Islands. If the devil murdered any white people, their blood was on his conscience.

'Is that it, Mr McLean?' the telegraph operator asked.

'Yes, let me check.' He looked over the text of the telegram, nodded his head, and strode out of the office. The telegram read:

HAUHAUS SAID TO BE GOING TO POVERTY BAY STOP ENEMY SHOULD HAVE BEEN FOLLOWED UP TO PUKETAPU AND POVERTY BAY STOP PROPOSE THAT THE SS ST KILDA PROCEED TO POVERTY BAY TO ASCERTAIN THE WHEREABOUTS OF THE HAUHAUS STOP MCLEAN

10.47 A.M.

Lieutenant Gascoyne guided his horse carefully along the ancient track. Dammit to hell, he needed more men, more scouts, to watch the trails in this wild country, at least six scouting parties.

'Te Kooti could come along here,' he swore, 'and nobody would know.' He had two native scouts with him. The three men had followed the deeply worn track for eight to ten miles along the valley. It was heavily overgrown with manuka, perfect cover for a raiding party to sneak in under, attack, and retreat.

Lieutenant Gascoyne and his two men rested on a saddle overlooking the Mangakaretu Stream.

'I don't like it,' one of the Maori scouts said. 'I can feel death approaching.'

'So can I,' Lieutenant Gascoyne said. 'I'd better go to see Major Biggs tonight. I can do that on our way back to camp.'

He wheeled his horse back down the track. In the far distance he saw smoke curling into the blue sky. About six miles away.

'Pighunters,' his Maori guides said. 'Must be. There've been signs of pigs all along the track. Te Kooti wouldn't have come this far so soon.'

Lieutenant Gascoyne's eyes narrowed into slits against the sun. His horse stumbled on the track, almost unseating him . . .

and the fires flickering, flickering.

The telegraph operator in Napier rapped on the door to Mr McLean's office. 'A message has come from Wellington,' he said.

The message read: AGREE SS ST KILDA SHOULD PROCEED TO POVERTY BAY STOP REQUEST APPROVED STOP HAULTAIN

Mr McLean smiled hollowly. Too late, too late. A gale had come up and it was unlikely that the *St Kilda* would leave for at least a few days. On top of that, her damned engine was playing up again and she was liable to break down.

'Thank you,' he said.

He turned to the window. Far to the north he could see the gale approaching, its storm clouds broiling across the mountains.

7.01 P.M.

Lieutenant Gascoyne stood watching Major Biggs and his family at dinner. He had refused an invitation to join them. He was conscious of smelling like a native in front of the women, Mrs Biggs and the nurse, Jane Farrell.

'Speak up, Mr Gascoyne,' Major Biggs said. 'Don't mind the ladies, they're well used to military talk now.'

'We're scouting too far to the southwest,' Lieutenant Gascoyne said, adding, 'Sir. If the band of Te Kooti's comes down the Ngatapa instead of the Te Reinga, we'll be the last to know. Sir.'

'Preposterous,' Major Biggs said. 'Te Kooti will not come down the Ngatapa. Did Mrs Wyllie tell you that? No? Well let me tell you what I told her: I have scouts out and I will receive twenty-four hours' notice before anything happens. The story is absurd and you are all in an unnecessary state of alarm.'

'Sir,' Lieutenant Gascoyne interjected, 'at least let me post three men in the valley. I inspected the track today and I . . .'

Major Biggs waved him into silence. 'A vigilante group of settlers has already wasted their time keeping watch there, and I told them so. I told Wi Pere the same thing.' He waved his fork conspiratorially. 'Let me tell you, in private, that I know Te Kooti's advancing but—' the ladies gasped in fright '—he doesn't realise that I know how, when and how many men he has.' The women began to clap. 'He's coming down Te Reinga,' he announced with the voice of authority. 'You keep watching there.'

Lieutenant Gascoyne stood still and straight. Major Biggs looked at him, annoyed.

'Now get back to your post,' Major Biggs said, 'and be sure not to leave it. Keep a sharp watch every night and scout towards Wairoa daily. If you see armed men, or are fired on, you are to come in at once and give the alarm by scattering, but come yourself to me as quickly as possible.'

Lieutenant Gascoyne nodded. Major Biggs saw him to the door.

'I know I am right,' Major Biggs said.

In another room, a baby began to cry. Lieutenant Gascoyne heard the nurse singing to it as she cradled the child in her arms, '. . . for me and my true love will never meet again on the bonny bonny banks of . . .'

SUNDAY, 8 NOVEMBER, 12.00 NOON

. . . and the flames began to leap, to scorch, to blaze with the thrill of war.

The Reverend Williams saw the native mailman, on his arrival from Wairoa, approaching the mission station at Whakato. The mailman was on his way to Gisborne but the Reverend Williams went to the door and threw out his arms in a gesture of Christian welcome.

'What news?' he called heartily, for this was the day of the Lord, and a proper day to be glad of life.

'Aue, e pa,' the mailman replied. 'Te Kooti has come to Poverty Bay.'

The Reverend Williams was having guests for luncheon. He bade the mailman enter the sitting room where he assembled his guests.

'The first we knew about it,' the mailman began, 'was when Colonel Lambert assembled a large force of friendly Maoris to go to Whataroa Pa. As you know, some of our own Maori people have gone to join Te Kooti, not many, but enough, and there was suspicion that Chief Te Waru from Whataroa Pa would join him also. First of all, we sent four emissaries to Te Waru pleading him not to join up. They never returned. So, nine days ago, this large force went to the pa to see what had happened to our emissaries. When they got there, the pa was deserted. Aue, our four emissaries had been murdered. One female of some age, who was left there, told Colonel Lambert that Te Waru's people had gone off with Te Kooti and intended to attack Turanga, Wairoa and Napier in succession. Thus has Te Kooti come to Poverty Bay.'

A guest interjected. 'Didn't Colonel Lambert's force pursue the rebels?'

'Kaore. No.'

'Why not?'

The mailman, not knowing the answer, was silent.

3.00 P.M.

The gale hit Napier with a vengeance, unleashing its power with considerable force. The *St Kilda* could not leave her berth.

6.07 P.M.

The Reverend Williams ushered Major Biggs to one side. The clergyman had completed afternoon service at Matawhero. Attendance had not been good. Alas, more good souls were leaving the district. How could one blame them? These were not peaceful times.

'I thought you should know,' said the Reverend Williams, 'that word has come from Wairoa that Te Kooti is on his way to Turanga.'

'Thank you,' Major Biggs replied. He was in a hurry; his wife was waiting for him at the buggy.

'I am most concerned,' the Reverend Williams insisted.

'I have my scouts watching the country,' Major Biggs said. 'They will warn me in ample time to enable the outsettlers to be withdrawn to Turanganui.'

'But the news—'

'I am aware of it,' Major Biggs said. 'Indeed, I have also heard from Major St John and Major Mair that Te Kooti has been urging his sympathisers to Opotiki to join him on a raid of Turanga. The devil seems to be attracting followers from all points north, south and west. From Wairoa. From Opotiki. From the Tuhoe, and even as far away as the Waikato.' He could see that the clergyman was becoming agitated so he added, 'But, let me assure you, Reverend Williams, that I have the matter well taken care of.'

He shook the Reverend Williams' hand and walked down to his waiting wife, child, and the child's nurse.

'Rumours, always rumours,' Major Biggs muttered. 'I shall not let them spoil our picnic by the river tomorrow.'

He gave Emily a kiss on the cheek.

MONDAY, 9 NOVEMBER, 8.56 A.M.

. . . and now the fires dancing in one spot, waiting for the night. Dancing, quiet, and waiting for word from the prophet. War. War.

The mailman reached Turanganui and, there, was pleased to see the Reverend Williams. 'Aue, e pa,' he said. 'Here is a letter which I should have given you at Whakato. I give it to you now.'

The Reverend Williams received the letter. It was from his brother, the Reverend S. Williams, of Napier. Upon reading it, he went post haste to Wilson's Redoubt. A court sitting was being held and Major Biggs was in attendance.

The clerk at the door tried to bar entry to the Reverend Williams. He pushed past. 'Major Biggs,' he called, waving the letter.

9.05 A.M.

The *St Kilda* began to leave the dock at Napier. The gale had now passed the township. The vessel eased slowly out. Then it stopped. The engine had always been contrary, having a life of its own. The engineer, inspecting it, sent word from the engine room. 'We must return to berth. The engine has broken down, necessitating repairs.'

9.07 A.M.

The Reverend Williams was in a state of apoplexy in the face of Major Biggs' imperturbability. He tried again. 'With all due respect, Major Biggs, my brother tells me that he has it on authority which he could not doubt that Te Kooti has started for Poverty Bay. My brother suggests that all settlers should at once get into as secure a position as possible. He says that this information has also been conveyed to Mr McLean and the Hon. J.C. Richmond.'

'All rumours,' Major Biggs replied. 'I myself have heard nothing official from Wairoa or Napier.'

The Reverend Williams was surprised. 'Even so, Major Biggs, I suggest that it is time for all outsettlers to be told of the impending danger and that they should come in to Gisborne. Now.'

Major Biggs smiled at him. 'I have my scouts and they—'

12.05 P.M.
'Emily, my darling, I'm sorry I'm late. Is the picnic hamper packed? Our son ready? And Jane? Come on, nursie, come on now.'

3.05 P.M.
'O no, Reginald, darling, you will drown.'

The fires, the fires, burning steadily, awaiting the fall of night.

So swim, swim out for the last time, Major Biggs to the shadows cast by the underwater valleys of the Waipaoa. As you swim, take care not to look downwards into the black waters because if you do, you will see there a taniwha, in your likeness. White, almost scabrous, it is a thing of prophetic power as it imitates your movements, stroke by stroke. And now it rises to kiss you with its deadly lips and to welcome you in your slow, slow swimming towards your death.

'Kororia ki To Ingoa Tapu,' the matriarch said. She took up the second vial and let the amber drops of oil spill into the chalice of her palms. As with the first liquid, she began to anoint the child again. Her voice and her breathing gathered strength at each impression upon his limbs and body that she made:

'Ksss. Ksss. Ksss. Ksss.'

She raised her hand and began to pray again. Her prayer echoed through the painted house, stirring through the painted forest and the people, natural and supernatural, who lived therein. It was like a whirlwind, passionate and filled with the inevitability of war.

The child observed her looking towards a panel on which was

painted a large Scotch thistle. This was the sign of Te Kooti, the prophet. And this house, Rongopai, was built for him. But he had never visited it, this meeting house, one of the cathedrals built unto his likeness, for his wanderings had been long and bitter, and when the war had begun, no forgiveness was granted him.

The matriarch's face grew wan and distant, as if she herself was physically withdrawing into that time of the Te Kooti retaliation. With a quick motion, she grasped the child by both hands and, suddenly, it seemed as if they were both being taken up in the whirlwind beyond the dimensions of the place of healing and into the realm of despair and hatred.

'Hold tight my child,' the matriarch said. 'Hold tight and do not let go. And listen, for this is the song, the Song of Te Kooti, without end, without end. E mokopuna, so it came to pass that in the month of November 1868 the prophet came down from Puketapu Mountain and fell upon the cohorts of Pharaoh, Pakeha and Maori. And as Pharaoh had done unto the prophet, so did the prophet do unto Pharaoh. Just as God had done unto the Egyptians when they would not let his people go, by sending death to the first born of the Egyptians during the time of Moses, so did the prophet do to the Pakeha because they would not let the Maori nation go.

'Glory to Thy Holy Name. And the prophet came down and swooped upon the Egyptians residing in the land of Turanga at the place of Matawhero. Many were the Pakeha who went unto their Maker, and many were the Maori who went unto their Maker. Then did the prophet retreat, for he did not wish more killing but rather the sign to be given when Biggs was sent to his Maker. So he said, "Enough," and entreated the Egyptians, "Will you now let my people go? Will you let us go so that we may build our temple to the Lord in Canaan and live there in peace?" But Pharaoh hardened his heart and he said, "No, I will not let your people go." And his Egyptian subjects cried out to him to kill the prophet and to destroy the Maori nation.

'Thus began the flight of Israel into the wilderness. For fifteen years we were pursued by the cohorts of Pharaoh and the chariots of his armies. We suffered much suffering and we buried many of our dead in our flight. But always we cried out to Jehovah to succour us.

'Kororia ki To Ingoa Tapu. And our flight began when Pharaoh sent a huge army against the Children of Israel. This was on 10 November 1868, and it was commanded by a small number of the Pakeha and many Maori troops: two hundred and seventy of the Ngati Kahungunu; sixty of the northern Kahungunu; one hundred of the Rongowhakaata. On 22 November, three of our nation were slain at Patutahi. We therefore fled to Makaretu and entrenched ourselves on the far side of the valley. And God spoke to us and said, "Build a fire between yourself and Pharaoh and I will send it down upon the Egyptians." For nine days we were succoured by the Lord. Then on the ninth day, the Egyptians were joined by three hundred and seventy-six Ngati Porou, and his cohorts therefore numbered up to one hundred against our men, women and children. We began our retreat from Makaretu to Ngatapa, and twenty-eight of our nation were killed by the blood lust of the Egyptians.

'And at Ngatapa, three and a half miles from Makaretu, the Maori nation rested, but on 5 December, we were set upon again by Pharaoh. Our hill-fort was strong, comprising three inner courtyards, and steep flanks, and the Egyptians were faint-hearted and failed to defeat us. The Lord sent bad weather to our aid and drove Pharaoh away. But fifty of our people were killed in that battle, and there was lamentation among us. And there was no forgiveness in the hearts of some of the people, so a lightning retaliation was made on Opou on 12 December and four Egyptians went to Jehovah.

'Glory to Your Holy Name. Then Pharaoh became exceedingly angry and mustered a large army against us at Ngatapa. He built a chain of small forts up the valley under the command of Colonel Whitmore and began his siege on 27 December; he had seven hundred troops and his equipment included two mortars which bombarded our pa. Death rained upon us and one hundred and twenty-five of the Maori nation were struck down during the siege; the pa was sweet with the smell of death. The attack went on for ten days and nights. Finally the prophet said, "We must go from this place and resume our flight." Jehovah cleared a way for us, for the back of the pa was a steep cliff which could not be ringed by the cohorts of Pharaoh. The prophet said, "Let us build flax ladders, cast them down the cliff, and climb down them during the night." The women began to make the ladders, and the death rained on them, but it was done. And some of the women and the suffering made of themselves a sacrifice saying, "We are weak and wounded and will only make slow your escape. Let us stay behind to hold the ladders and destroy them when you have gone; let us delay Pharaoh's pursuit, for we would gladly die that the Maori nation might live." The people wept together, farewelled each other, prayed to God, and with heavy hearts the escape was made during the dark night. The prophet himself, on the white horse Poukai Whenua, a stallion of great spiritual powers, escaped the government soldiers.

'So it was that Whitmore, the next morning, discovered that the pa was defended only by the women and the wounded: fourteen men and sixty-six women and children. He waxed exceedingly angry. And while the women tried to keep him at bay, even attacking him although they were wounded, he sent his forces to pursue the prophet and the people. £20 was the price put on every capture and £1000 was the price for the prophet. The pursuing cohorts of Pharaoh were like a dark cloud which could be seen by the Maori nation. Again, the weak and the wounded wished to make themselves a sacrifice for the prophet and the safety of the Maori nation, saying, "We will defend your retreat; go and build our religion and remember us when you have come unto the land of Canaan." And again the people wept together and farewelled each other and prayed to God.

'Kororia ki To Ingoa Tapu. And one hundred and twenty was the number of the defenders of Ngatapa who caused Pharaoh to fight them, and they were captured and made to kneel before Pharaoh. They became martyrs to the Maori nation, for Pharaoh was angry and ordered their execution.

This is how the killing was done: the people were taken to the verge of a cliff. They were stripped and ranged in a line along the cliff. Then the firing party raised their rifles and executed them, their bodies falling over the cliff. When news of this came to the prophet, he led the people in lamentation, crying, "Pharaoh, let my people go!" We prayed for our dead for they had died to save us.

'So it was that the prophet and the people escaped, and over the next two months were at rest at the place known as Koraha. Our numbers were only one hundred and forty, but many came to join the Children of Israel. In March 1869, the people made small retaliations against the Egyptians to keep them at bay so that the wounded and the sick might recover from the wounds of the flight. Then, when we were fully recovered the prophet said, "It is time for us to resume our search for the Promised Land. Let us therefore be of stout heart and good spirit and, praising the Lord, let us journey to Ruatahuna." And so it was done and, when we reached that place, we were received by the people of the Urewera. Many saw the justice of our cause and joined us in great numbers.

'Now mokopuna, at the same time as Pharaoh was pursuing us, he was also still fighting his Land Wars throughout the rest of Egypt. We gained respite until April 1869. Then it was that a rumour reached us that Pharaoh would attack us. Because of this, we tried to dissuade Pharaoh by a sign at Mohaka. And Pharaoh himself was beset by rumours of war and stationed a mixed force of eight hundred men, including three hundred and fifty armed constabulary, at Onepoto, Lake Waikaremoana. This was in May 1869, but we had already given our sign and did not attack; Pharaoh withdrew. We became exceedingly glad of heart that the sign had been sent to Pharaoh.

'Glory to Your Holy Name. But alas, Pharaoh again hardened his heart and pursued us still. All that year of 1869, we continued our flight across the country, and the Egyptians came upon us twelve times. But Jehovah was with us and sustained us. During 1870 and 1871, the pursuit increased when Pharaoh's cohorts from the East Coast, Hawke's Bay, Rotorua and Wanganui were brought to the aid of his armies. At each attack, our people suffered and many went to God. On 23 March 1870, Pharaoh attacked us at Maraetai Pa and twenty-five of the Maori nation were executed and three hundred and seventy-five taken prisoner. Two expeditions were mounted against us at Te Wera in April 1870 and our citadel of the hills, Motuaha Pa, but Jehovah was with us. In July 1870, Jehovah saved the prophet when Pharaoh pursued him from Tolaga Bay to Waihapua and thence to Mangatu.

'All this time, the prophet kept crying unto Pharaoh, "Let my people go." He entreated Pharaoh to make peace with the Maori nation. But year after year the Egyptians pursued us and our numbers were sorely reduced. The prophet saw this and prayed to Jehovah for guidance saying, "O God, we are so long wandering in the wilderness and we are still pursued by Pharaoh. Thy people have suffered intense hardship but we do not despair. Yet our numbers grow small and faint of heart. Succour us, O Lord. Show us the way and take us up from within the net of death. Wherefore I glorify Thy Holy Name. Amen."

'Then Pharaoh engaged the Maori nation on 14 February 1872 and Jehovah was with us. The prophet gathered us together and said, "Alas, our numbers are growing small and we will die if not for God's deliverance. We must therefore go separate ways for where Pharaoh can follow one, he cannot follow the many. So I say to you to take His teachings with you and establish the Ringatu religion. As for me, I will take the main body of the Maori nation to the King Country to live under the protection of King Tawhiao."

'Kororia ki To Ingoa Tapu. So it was that we went our different ways to establish the Ringatu, and the prophet pilgrimaged to Te Kuiti. Lo and behold, Jehovah cast his mantle over the prophet so that no harm could come upon him. His teachings spread throughout the land, so much so, that the church grew and many people visited him at Te Kuiti. This was between the years 1872 and 1883. Many were the Maori people who were given the sight by God to witness the wrongs that had been done to the prophet. People began to flock to him like locusts to the honey of the truth, for they saw the truth in him.

'And it came to pass that Jehovah caused Pharaoh and the Egyptians to grow old and weary of the fight against the Children of Israel, not only against Te Kooti but also the other prophets and leaders throughout Egypt. Jehovah caused Pharaoh to say to the Maori nation, "Let us have no more troubles; let us have amnesty between us." And it was through Rewi Maniapoto that the Native Minister, Hon. J. Bryce, came to visit Te Kooti at Manga o Rongo in February 1883 and a pardon was agreed upon. The prophet told

Pharaoh that he had never wished the strife, and he forgave Pharaoh. But he warned, "If you molest me, beware, for if you do, what I have done in the past will be nothing compared with what I will do in the future."

'Glory to Your Holy Name. With great rejoicing and tears, we ended our wandering in the wilderness. Pharaoh acknowledged his wrong in keeping the people in bondage without just cause. And although there were still those among Egypt who protested mightily at the pardoning of the prophet, the prophet forgave them, yea, even though they had killed and slaughtered many of the Maori nation. Land was granted to the prophet and the church, verily, at Wainui at Ohiwa. This was freely given by Pharaoh.

'And the Children of Israel came joyously to the land. We sorrowed for our companions who had died for the sake of the coming to the land. We praised Jehovah for his blessings and for bringing to pass the settlement of the Children of Israel in the land of Canaan.

'Glory to Thy Holy Name. Kororia ki To Ingoa Tapu. Amine.'

9

Matawhero is one of many small settlements which now surround the city of Gisborne, like embers to the larger fire that have been strewn across the Gisborne flats. It is eight kilometres from the city, just a bit further out from Makaraka.

At the time of the Matawhero Retaliation, most of the homes of the settlement were within the bend of the Waipaoa River stretching from Matawhero Point to the spot where the old Ngatapa railway bridge stood. The church was almost in the middle of the settlement. Some of the homes were not a great distance apart. There were forty-five Europeans and half-castes resident in the settlement at the time of the attack and as many Maori settlers. In nearby Makaraka, the number of Europeans was fifty-six, including half-castes, and a greater number of Maori farmers.

Today, of course, the population is much larger, and Matawhero is gaining fame as a wine-growing and rich horticultural and orcharding area. (Every wine buff should visit the vineyards on the old road where the ancient bridge superstructure can still be seen.) As well, Matawhero remains notable for its seasonal sheep and cattle sales at the Matawhero saleyards. Not far from the saleyards is a huge barn of a hotel, and Friday and Saturday nights are boozy, lusty affairs. Maori and Pakeha congregate in the public bars in an impossible change-partners kind of dance to and from the all-powerful dispensers of the brown ale.

On the face of it, Matawhero presents a portrait of placidity, of calm seas, of green vines and orchards rolling rich breakers into the warm wind, disturbed only occasionally by a Friday night assault or Saturday night fatality at the crossroads. Nothing much assails the scatter of homes, except for the droning of commercial aeroplanes as they land at nearby Gisborne Airport or the train as it traverses the Gisborne flats and, oddly enough, also runs right through Gisborne's airstrip. Or perhaps there is the occasional clacking and clanging of vineyard machinery and tractors along the road which cuts the flats into neat and tidy little squares.

Sound doesn't travel far in this place. Perhaps that is why the Te Kooti attack was so successful. None of the survivors claimed to have been warned either by seeing a home in flames or by hearing the cries of neighbours. With the exception of Mrs Alice Wilson, who died of wounds a few days after the attack, all saved themselves only after they had been informed by friendly Maori or having heard the familiar sound of musketry or actually seeing the war party. From that moment, the word spread throughout the other settlements on the flats so that they all could make haste into Gisborne itself.

'Te Kooti is here. Save yourselves. Go to the redoubt on Kaiti Hill.' From all points on the flats they hastened, from Matawhero, Makaraka, Muriwai, Whataupoko, Waerenga a Hika and elsewhere, seeking to escape the criss-crossing path of the raiders.

The second thing you notice about the small settlement is that nobody likes to talk about the Matawhero Retaliation. Maori people appear to be embarrassed about it as a sign of the old bloodlust and paganism and, anyway, the past is past and they are now getting on very happily with the Pakeha, thank you very much. They should not be so riddled with guilt; they were victims too, with over thirty Maori killed during the raid, as many as the European dead. When you ask Pakeha people they, also, begin to shift from the left foot to the right foot. It's almost as if, in the asking, you are challenging their right to be there; you are making them remember that once not very long ago there was a 'massacre', whether they like to admit it or not. You begin to see them looking grim-faced towards the church where it was all supposed to have happened. According to popular belief, the white settlers were at prayer when the raiders made their attack on the settlement. A raid of this sort is much more indictable and much more of an atrocity if it is perpetrated before the face of God.

Perhaps the reason for being tight-lipped is that Poverty Bay citizens now pride themselves on their good record of race relations, and rightly so. But they need to be told the truth: the Matawhero Retaliation was part of a religious war which the Pakeha himself began. When religious fervour is engaged, the primary question during any attack is whether you are for or against. That is why there were both Maori and Pakeha victims. The death roll would have been longer had Te Kooti cordoned off the settlement; only five homes in Matawhero itself were successfully attacked. That at least should reduce the scale of the assault in the popular mind.

Nor was there any slaughter of innocents in the church at Matawhero. In war there are no innocents. No right or wrong. Only the living and the dead.

ৎ

THE MATAWHERO RETALIATION/THE ATTACK:
MONDAY, 9 NOVEMBER, 6.30 P.M.
It was at dusk that the word was given by the prophet and the war began. The war party emerged from the Ngatapa Valley and followed the old track which led past Repongaere Lake on the run owned by Lieutenant George Neville Dodd, 40, and Trooper Richard Peppard, 25. The band diverted along the bank of the Waikakariki Stream to Patutahi Pa.

'Keep silent or you will be killed,' the twenty Maori residents were warned. 'Some of you we will take back to Pukepuke pa to be our hostages and to be kept there with others of our people. The rest of you we are placing under guard here at this pa. We want no warning given by you to Major Biggs or the settlers. We want only to ask one question: will you join us or will you not? Be careful as to the way you answer.'

In the corner of the pa, Hoera and Meri Taiapu resolved to answer yes to the question, but then to try to warn the settlers at Matawhero.

'Which of you is Karepa?' Te Kooti asked. 'I wish intelligence as to the settlers' homes and to their movements. Your life is in my hands.'

'I wish to join you,' one of the Patutahi residents said. 'I suggest you burn down the settlers' homes as well as kill the settlers.'

For the rest of the evening, the raiders planned their attack on Matawhero and the strategy of the attack.

'Shall we cordon Matawhero and slay all?'

'No,' Te Kooti answered. 'The lives of the people are in God's hands. If their deaths are willed, then they will die.'

'Some of our raiders have old scores to settle with the Maori and the Pakeha who fought against us when we were Hauhau.'

'I say again, if the deaths are willed, then the deaths will be,' Te Kooti said. 'We will now wait till morning. Then we shall attack.'

TUESDAY, 10 NOVEMBER, 12.01 A.M.
The attack commenced. A small wing of raiders was sent back to the Dodd and Peppard home on Lake Repongaere. The dogs began to bark. Trooper Peppard rose from sleep and went to awaken Lieutenant Dodd.

'Something's happening out there.'

Their cook, Richard Rathbone, was also roused. He watched as Peppard and Dodd walked out into the night. A volley of shots came from the bush and the two men began to jerk and to blossom with blood. Silence fell, even the dogs became silent.

Rathbone's heart was beating like thunder. He slid away from the front door and hid in the shadows of his bedroom. He heard shrill whooping sounds outside and then the silence descended again. He counted to fifteen and slipped out the back door. He felt for other presences in the dark and when he was confident that he was alone, he went up to the bodies of his two friends. Both were dead. He thought he would head for Toanga. There he met a Maori who told him he must hasten because the raiders were after him.

'Thank you,' Rathbone said.

He began to pass by. He looked back and saw the Maori take up his rifle and point it at him. The shot shattered his backbone and he fell down dead.

1.30 A.M.

The schooner *Success* and the schooner *Tawera* were both in trouble on the Turanganui River. They had been taking on board cattle from the mission station property, and became stuck on the bar as they attempted to leave the river.

'Sailor, go aloft and loosen our sails,' the master of the *Tawera*, Captain Trimmer, ordered. 'With the wind's help we might be able to get ourselves off the bar. Up you go now.'

The night was clear and starlit. The sailor noticed a fire, but it was to the south of Matawhero. It did not arouse his suspicions. He loosened the sails. In the distance, he saw Robert Atkins, head stockman at the mission station, riding off to his home at Waerenga a Hika.

2.20 A.M.

Robert Atkins rode past Major Biggs' home at Matawhero. He noticed that there was a light in one of the rooms. He wasn't sure, but he thought he heard a baby crying. Perhaps it needed attention.

'. . . for me and my true love will never meet again on the . . .'

3.05 A.M.

The wing of the raiders returned from Dodd and Peppard's. One of the raiders reported to Te Kooti that they had seen J.R. Wyllie at his home near Waerenga a Hika. The lamp was on in his window and he was writing at a table.

'He was a party to my exile,' the prophet said. 'We will return to him after we have settled with Biggs at Matawhero. Meantime, we have another score to settle with another traitor.'

His men brought forth Pera Kararehe, the elder brother of Matenga Taihuka, who had deserted the prophet and sworn allegiance to the Queen and to the Pakeha Christianity.

'Are you like your brother?' Te Kooti asked.

'Yes.'

'So be it.'

The axe bit deeply. Pera Kararehe cried out in pain. He fell quickly to the ground, the blood gushing from his body like a wild river.

3.30 A.M.

Fired with the passion of war, the war party proceeded quickly from Patutahi along the western side of the river to the lower ford at Matawhero. Here it was much broader and shallower. The horses waded across to Matawhero, making serene arrow patterns, pointing upstream, from the water flowing around them. On the other side, the raiders split up into attack groups. Like shafts loosed from a bow, they descended on the settlement.

3.45 A.M.

Lieutenant James Walsh, 33, his wife Emma, 26, and their infant daughter, Nora Ellen, were asleep in the main bedroom of their cottage near the lower ford. The front door was open, and the raiders slipped in quietly. They were filled with passion, so much so that when Nora started to murmur in her sleep she was instantly decapitated.

'Who's there?' Emma called at the noise.

The raiders axed her and James Walsh as they were rising from sleep.

'Help us,' James Walsh screamed through the wall to the smaller bedroom where his partner, Sergeant James Padbury, 32, was sleeping. Padbury leapt to his feet. He ran from the bedroom. He saw the raiders standing by the bloodied cradle, and the axes still rising and falling on the bodies of James and Emma Walsh.

'Padbury,' a raider said. 'We met when you were our guard on Wharekauri. Go to your death.'

The raiders surrounded Padbury. He managed to retreat back into his bedroom before he was killed.

3.55 A.M.

Piripi Taketake awoke quickly at the entry of raiders into the whare.

'Who goes there?' he demanded.

He heard the muffled sounds of his three children, Pera, Taraipene and Te Paea. He roused his wife, Harata, and she began to call the children. Even before Piripi could stop her, she was out of bed and on her way to them. Before she got to the door she was axed.

With a cry, Piripi leapt at his wife's attacker. He was pinned back by many hands, and his face was wrenched upward so that he could see the futility of his struggles. Harata was already dead, the blood oozing from the cleft in her head. The children were screaming.

The sentence was given. 'You were against us,' Te Kooti said.

He heard chopping sounds cutting off the lives of his children. Then he felt a sharp warmth as his throat was slit.

4.00 A.M.

There was a noise outside the house. Major Biggs listened to it again. Emily stirred beside him. 'What is it, dear?' she murmured.

He kissed her gently. "Perhaps it is one of the scouts,' he said. 'Maybe two, by the sounds of it. I'd better go out and see.' He swung himself out of bed and did not try to cover his nakedness as young Charlie James, a boy in his employ, walked past the bedroom to the front door. 'No, no,' Biggs said to him as he slipped into his trousers. 'I'll see to it. You go back to bed.'

He walked to the front door. He looked out into blackness. A shot rang out and ripped into his foot. For a moment he was stunned. 'Oh my God.' Tears of grief welled into his eyes for he knew what was going to happen. He shut the door quickly and called to Emily, 'Emily, dear, the Hauhaus are here. You, Jane, and Charlie, take our son and make your escape into the bush. Oh my wife. Quickly. Quickly. Oh my son, George.'

It was too late. The raiders had entirely circled the house. Charlie James saw them approaching the front door and the back door. There was a grating under the back door which led to an outbuilding. He opened it and looked for his mistress Jane to follow.

The war party burst into the house. Charlie James closed the grating quickly.

'Biggs, my old enemy, my nemesis,' Te Kooti said. 'This is the end for you. You sent me away without trial. You have pursued me and killed my people. Why, Biggs, why? No answer, my old enemy? It is of no account; you may give the reason to your Maker for you will meet him soon.'

The raiders took Biggs outside and made him lie spreadeagled on the ground, facing up so that he could see the night sky, so clear and starlit, but becoming light with the approaching dawn. Then the sky began to get crowded out with the dark faces of the raiders. One of them stepped more closely into Biggs' line of vision, knelt down beside his face and smiled at him. He took a revolver in his hand, reversed it so that the barrel was in his clenched fist, raised the butt, and crushed that proud, proud head to pulp.

Emily struggled in the arms of her captors, but she knew there was no escape, no clemency. 'Let me go to my husband,' she pleaded.

Young Jane, holding the baby George, said, 'Emily, I shall go with you and stay by your side. I will live or die with you.'

The two women and the infant were taken out to where the unrecognisable body of Major Biggs was lying. Emily could only look upon him with silent tears. The nurse, Jane, began to scream and, at the sound, she, Emily and the infant were killed. Attired in their nightdresses, the bodies fell like white angels to the ground.

4.20 A.M.
Hoera Whakamiha awoke from a troubled sleep. He went to the door of his home and saw the stars in the clear sky. He saw a comet flaring in the heavens, a horseman riding by and, before he could think again, a bullet ripped his brain apart.

4.40 A.M.
The war party appeared in the front yard of the home of Captain James Wilson, 32, his wife, Alice, 30, and four children. Captain

Wilson's manservant, Private John Moran, 60, also lived on the property in a whare about fifty yards from the house.

The dogs began to bark furiously. There was a gently knocking at the back door. Captain Wilson got up from beside his Alice and their sleeping infant.

'Who's there?' he asked.

'I have a message from Hirini Te Kani. For you, Captain Wilson.'

'Push it under the door,' Captain Wilson said.

'No, you must come outside to receive it.' Te Kooti's voice was taunting, amused.

Captain Wilson walked to the window and pulled the blind aside. He saw the raiders in the dim light. He knew the house was surrounded. So what to do? What to do? Quickly he shouted to his manservant. 'Moran, Moran, can you hear me? The devils are here.' Instead of escaping, Moran thought of his captain's wife and the four children. Watching his chance, he rushed to the house. A warrior leapt at him as he neared the doorway. Captain Wilson fired his rifle. Moran managed to fling his assailant off and get through the door.

The two men shook hands in the bond of friendship. Captain Wilson gave his rifle to Moran and told him to guard the front doorway. 'I have a revolver and will guard the back entrance,' he said.

'What is happening?' Alice Wilson asked.

'It is Te Kooti,' her husband replied.

'The children,' Alice Wilson said. She took the infant upstairs and reassured her other three children, Alice, Edwin and Jessie.

The raiders broke down the back door. It splintered open. Several volleys were fired into the house through the jagged gap.

Silence.

The children were weeping softly. 'Hush, hush,' Alice Wilson said.

Silence.

Captain Wilson heard raiders sliding under the house. He saw wisps of smoke curling through the floorboards.

'The devils,' he said to Moran. 'They have us.'

He leapt upstairs and brought Alice and the children down. They watched the flames flickering, and the smoke blossoming. Captain Wilson knew what he had to do.

'Come,' he said. He led the family and Moran onto the verandah. 'Have mercy on my wife and children,' he called. Unbelievably, he heard a voice reply, 'No further harm.'

The raiders approached the family and led them away into the dark. Alice carried Jessie in her arms. The child, Alice, and Jimmy flanked their mother. Jimmy's father took off his greatcoat, put it on his son, and then lifted Jimmy onto his back.

Moran, the manservant, was carrying Edwin on his back when he was bayoneted and fell down dead. Captain Wilson put Jimmy down and went to protect his wife.

'Run, Jimmy,' Alice Wilson said.

While Jimmy Wilson made his escape, his father and the other children were killed. Alice Wilson was bayoneted several times and left for dead.

5.10 A.M.

Trooper John McCulloch, 28, was in the fields bringing the cows in to be milked. He heard cracking sounds in the distance and noticed the flickering of flames from the Wilson home. All of a sudden, he saw black-jacketed raiders urging their horses towards him.

'Jane! Jane!' he yelled to his twenty-five-year-old wife. He knew she was in the kitchen preparing his breakfast. 'Jane!' Where was she? Would she not look out the window?

The war party was closing in on him. They were silent, purposeful.

Jane looked out the window. She saw the raiders fanning out and around her husband like a fatal net. She screamed, ran to the bedroom, and began to pull her brother, Sam Tarr, 11, from bed. She tried to rouse her niece, Mary McDonald, 7, and, in the end, slapped her awake. Mary began to cry.

'Listen to me,' Jane said grimly. 'We must escape with the baby into the scrub. Out the front now and don't look behind. Run away as fast as you can.' Her lips began to quiver.

Sam raced ahead to the door.

'Save yourself, Sam,' Jane called.

'Please hurry,' he cried.

Jane gathered the baby in her arms and pulled Mary with her

through the kitchen. She heard her husband calling. 'Jane!' She looked out through the kitchen window.

Trooper John McCulloch was shot dead while he was getting over his stockyard rails.

'Hurry, sister, hurry,' Sam called. He reached the scrub and pushed himself into it. He looked back.

Jane, Mary and the infant, in Jane's arms, came bursting out of the house. They were running towards the scrub when the raiders appeared. A volley rang out and little black holes, scorched around the sides, puffed in the blouses of the two women and the infant.

5.17 A.M.
Maria Goldsmith, 16, and her brother, Albert Edward Goldsmith, 4, were also out getting the cows in. Both were beautiful half-caste children and Maria was of an age to begin stirring the blood of the young men of Gisborne.

Maria was riding a horse and had just let her brother down so that he could open a gate for the cows. 'Come on,' she laughed. He was having difficulty so she rode to the gate and unlatched it for him.

The cows began to pass through the gateway. That is when Maria heard the thrumming of horses' hooves on the roadway. She looked up and saw the shapes of riders approaching. At first she thought that they were members of the militia.

The horsemen stopped.

Maria beckoned her brother close to her.

'What is your name?' a raider asked.

She hesitated a moment. She saw fires in the distance. She heard cracking sounds. Her lips quivered. Oh Daddy, where are you?

'Goldsmith,' she said.

She was shot dead from her horse. Her brother was also killed. Afterwards, Maria Goldsmith and her brother had their heads cut off.

5.20 A.M.
Mrs James woke with a start from her sleep. She lived in a barn near C.G. Goldsmith's home. Her husband was on a carpentering job

near Kaiteratahi. Yes, there it was again, that sound . . . like . . . muskets. Oh, it must be Te Kooti.

She woke her eight young children.

'We must be quick and quiet, my sweets, because we are in great danger. We must not make any noise and, if ever we see anyone approaching, no matter whom, we must hide. Those are my instructions. I am counting on you all to obey them. If you don't then we may all die. All of us.'

'Where do we go, mother?'

'We shall make for the Waipaoa River.'

Mrs James led her family out of the barn.

'Mother, what is that over there?'

Mrs James saw the bodies of Maria Goldsmith and her brother. The blood was dark, already congealed, and blowflies were being attracted by the smell.

'Keep your eyes ahead,' she said in a controlled manner.

The family got to the river and, for more than a mile, crept along the riverbank until they reached a point where the scrub was denser.

'Oh, mother.'

Mrs James' heart stopped when she saw a shape looming out of the scrub.

'Help me,' a voice said. It was Sam Tarr, also heading for Gisborne.

5.25 A.M.

Hoera Kapuaroa had escaped from Patutahi pa. He went down to the river ford near Patutahi and there met up with Meri Taiapu. 'We must warn the settlers, all the settlers Maori and Pakeha on the Gisborne flats.'

'But the river is swollen,' Hoera said. 'I cannot cross it on my horse.'

'I shall have to swim it.' Meri Taiapu prayed and entered the swift-running waters. The river was cold and yellow with silt. Her body was grazed with logs as they rushed by in the swollen water. She waved to Hoera when she reached the other side. Then she ran along the road, seeking help. She met Constable Firmin. Far off he could hear the sounds of the war at Matawhero.

5.30 A.M.

The war party began to fan out from Matawhero. One of the assault teams came across the home of Trooper John Cadle, 28, the local partner in the storekeeping business of Cadle and Blair. John Cadle was already up and readying for another day at the store. He was very happy because he had become engaged to be married only a few days earlier.

'E hoa, Cadle,' he heard someone call to him.

In a drowsy, warm mood, he stepped out of his home. He saw a Maori on a horse waving what appeared to be a letter. Perhaps it was from her, the one he loved. Smiling, he stepped over to the Maori, hands outstretched. As he did so his faithful retriever barked furiously.

He heard a rustling in the bushes. There was an explosion of leaves as several raiders rushed out. One of them had a revolver, pressed it against John Cadle's head and shot him through the brain.

5.31 A.M.

Charlie James had made good his escape from Major Biggs' home and was on his way to warn his mother about Te Kooti's attack. He saw Tom Finucane and told him what was happening. Immediately Finucane ran to the house where Mrs Bloomfield and her family, together with her sister and two guests, were staying.

'We must hurry,' he told Mrs Bloomfield. 'Te Kooti is only twenty chains away.'

The women threw cloaks and shawls over their nightgowns and, gathering up the children, made off towards Awapuni, and thence along the beach to Gisborne. One of the guests, Minnie Parker, said, 'Oh, we must take milk for the baby.' Quickly, she did so, and carried the baby for much of the perilous journey.

5.40 A.M.

A wing of the raiders penetrated through Matawhero to Makaraka. They attacked the home of Trooper John Mann, 29, his wife Emma, 23, and infant. The home stood on a sledge among some flax near the fork of the road to Gisborne.

John Mann opened the door. He recognised the Maori standing there.

'Te Kooti,' he breathed.

He was a burly fellow, John Mann, and he leapt at the prophet, threw him to the ground and began to wrestle him to death. He felt other raiders trying to prevent him from killing Te Kooti, hitting him with axes and raining blows on him from their rifle butts. He knew that they were too afraid to shoot.

He got his fingers around the prophet's throat and began to squeeze. He felt the veins distend.

'I have you now,' John Mann said.

He heard shots from inside the house. 'No, not the baby,' Emma cried. There was another volley of shots.

Trooper Mann swivelled towards his family. That was when he was shot to death.

5.45 A.M.

Tom Goldsmith was riding past Trooper Mann's house. He saw the raiders in the distance. They were tossing the body of a baby in the air, catching it on their bayonets, and tossing it up again.

5.50 A.M.

The news of the retaliation was spreading throughout Gisborne flats. Refugees of the war began to head towards the settlement of Gisborne.

6.00 A.M.

The first news about the war on Matawhero finally reached Gisborne. Archdeacon W.L. Williams, who lived in Kaiti, heard a sharp rapping at his door. It was the quality of the sound that frightened him most.

Archdeacon Williams opened the door to a Maori parishioner. 'Yes, what is it?'

It was the day of the Te Kooti Retaliation. It was Black Tuesday, 10 November 1868. The killings were not over yet. Trooper Robert Newnham, 60, his wife Jane, 45, and an adopted European child; Trooper Finlay Ferguson, 28, William Wyllie, 14, Benjamin Mackey, 14, David Kiniha, all lived at Opou. Then there were the Maori killed at Waitaruia, Tutere Kapai and Eriapa Kapai; at Oweta, 10, but the names of five only are known, Paratene Turangi, Ihimaera Hokopu, Renata Whakaari, Iraia Riki, and Te Hira Hokopu; one other known to have died was Rawiri Taiau. Finally, there were the Maori hostages who were taken at Pukepuke: Himiona Katipa, Paora Te Wharau, Ratana Tukurangi, Rangi Whaitiri and Riki Aata.

All dead, and to what purpose? To serve the vanities of man or God? And who among you is ready to cast the first stone and to say, Te Kooti is to blame? All religious wars have been marked with similar killings, whether they be during the Crusades, the Spanish Inquisition, Iraq–Iran wars, and the Arab–Israeli struggle, so don't protest to me about the Te Kooti Retaliation.

Do I hear you protest at the detailed descriptions of death? Again, your protests fall on deaf ears. Death is not pretty, and the people who were killed during the retaliation did not die pretty deaths. They died in pain. They died in agony. At least let us recognise that this is the way of all wars.

The Te Kooti Retaliation. Tuesday, 10 November 1868. On that day the sun rose at 4.48 a.m.

Eight days later, on 18 November 1868, the Gisborne flats were considered safe enough for a large armed party to be sent out to Matawhero to bury the victims. The bodies lay clear of the debris of the burnt-out homes. Some of them had, during their exposure on the ground, been mutilated by pigs.

⸮

'Kororia ki To Ingoa Tapu,' the matriarch said.

Her voice drifted into the darkness, drifting like a canoe which was lost in a storm. Her upraised hand slowly descended to caress the child across the openings of his body. His eyes. His ears. His mouth. His penis. His anus. Each touch was gentle, loving. Holy.

And it seemed as if the house of healing was also giving the child benediction after benediction. One of the pillars on the left side of the meeting house began to glow. On it was painted the Tree of Life, a beautiful painting of a tree with different branches of flowers known for their healing properties. Red, yellow, purple, white, the blossoms began to unfold.

Then as quickly as it had begun, the glowing ended. The painted Rongopai fell back into darkness. There was only the sound of the breathing of the matriarch and the child. Outside, the world continued to swirl and to thunder to a rhythm of its own choosing.

'E mokopuna, so it is ended, the song of Te Kooti. Ah yes, his name was Te Kooti Arikirangi Te Turuki and Jehovah chose him at birth to lead the Children of Israel out of the bondage of Egypt. He was exiled to Wharekauri, and there the spirit of God came to him and instructed him to build the church, the Ringatu religion; that was the beginning of the growth of the Hebrew nation in Egypt. He captured the *Rifleman* and landed his people back in Aotearoa at a bay called Whareongaonga; that was the Passover. Then came the years of flight through the wilderness when the people were pursued by their nemesis, Pharaoh. But Jehovah protected the prophet and the people and a pardon was given unto him. When the Government granted the people land at Wainui, Ohiwa, that was the settlement in the land of Canaan.

'Glory to Your Holy Name. And after the prophet ascended into Heaven, the people continued his works. They were the works of peace and not of war; that is why I have tried to teach you how to hate and then how to forgive. But oh, e mokopuna, it is still so hard to remember the ways of peace for Pharaoh is still without and we remain in the land of Egypt. Nevertheless, we must always endeavour to fulfil the prophet's vision, which is to bring the Word of God to His people as did David, the prophets and the apostles. On the twelfth of each month is the church's hui of the Tekaumarua. When you hear the bell being rung, it is the summons to you to come to the worship, prayer and to the thanksgiving, for this is the celebration of the Passover.

And learn the Maori Bible, child, Te Paipera Tapu. Memorise the scriptures, the chants and the hymns. They hold within them the word of the prophet, which is also the word of Jehovah. Remember, also, that it was of you, this younger generation, that the prophet said, "Mine enemies will never see me again, but their children's children will."

'Kororia ki To Ingoa Tapu. Wherefore, in this place of healing, in this house which was built for the prophet, I bless you, e mokopuna, and seal you unto God's purpose, just as I was blessed and sealed to this purpose by my great-uncle. I do this with the knowledge of the sign which attended your birth and which was also attendant at mine, that your path will be difficult and full of travail, and that it will be in the valley between goodness and evil, Satan and the Lord.

'For this reason we pray, "O God, look Thou down on me dwelling in misery. Here I am invoking Thy name from my bed, because Thy Angel has preserved me in life, by him I have been magnified. And what, indeed, is my own goodness? Thy Servant is altogether evil: my sins are great, they cannot be counted. Alas, O Lord! Succour me, in my wanderings, and in my bed; and I will praise Thy Holy Name from day to day. For this we give glory to Thy Holy Name. Kororia ki To Ingoa Tapu. Ake, Ake, Ake. Amine."'

The curtain was coming down but the show was not yet over. You, Pakeha, required a public sacrifice to be made, a symbolic killing through which your feelings of horror about Te Kooti's war at Matawhero could be transmuted into self-satisfaction. You didn't have Te Kooti himself but, ah, you had caught one of his followers, hadn't you? At the fall of Ngatapa:

What was his name? Ah yes, Hamiora Pere.

You transported him to Wellington to be tried for high treason in September 1869. Your chief witness was a woman whose testimony was surely suspect—she was Maata Te Owai, who said that Te Kooti had seduced her on the Chatham Islands and had married her. It was she who, knowing Hamiora had been transported to the Islands, then drew the conclusions for the Crown that Hamiora had been one of the participants at Matawhero.

Poor, poor Hamiora, you were judged guilty even before the sentence was pronounced. You were guilty by association. You were guilty because you had been on the Chathams. You were guilty because Te Kooti's wife said you were. You were guilty because the Pakeha wanted you to be. You were guilty because you were a Maori. So in that dark September 1869, after a retirement of only fifteen minutes, the jury returned with a verdict of guilty. Your judge, Mr Justice Johnston, upon sentencing you to death, congratulated you on the fact that the practice of drawing and quartering after hanging had been abolished.

Sweet, sweet Hamiora, you were held in prison for two long months before the day of your hanging on 16 November 1869. The official reports say that you wept bitterly and had to be assisted to ascend the scaffold. Pakeha psychologists would no doubt consider that you were fearful for your life and that your actions showed a lack of courage; from a Maori point of view your tangi and your tears would not have been for yourself but for your people, your iwi, your whanau, and the loneliness of that longest walk into Te Po. Perhaps you heard our prayers, Hamiora, coming to you from your people— 'Kia kaha, kia manawanui'—for it is written in the records that all traces of nervousness left you. Standing up erect you repeated, in a loud, clear voice, the prayers that were being said on your behalf.

The hangman placed the noose around your neck. The trapdoor opened beneath your feet. You felt the quick sensation of falling. It was then that your neck, your sweet neck, snapped. Haere, e Hamiora Pere, haere ki te Po, haere, haere, haere. Farewell, e Hamiora, go forth into the night, go forth to join the hundreds and thousands who have gone before you, go forth to the great tribe who await us all.

Oh yes, lest we forget, where was the Pakeha law when Gisborne settlers began to seek out Maori who were suspected of having been involved in Te Kooti's retaliation at Matawhero? Where was the law when some former followers of Te Kooti, mostly women and children, were held overnight at Patutahi in March 1869? Defenceless, they waited for the morning to come, and among them were Hemi Te Ihoariki and Nikora. During that dark night, three Pakeha settlers by name of William Benson, Captain Hardy and William Brown arrived. They called out, 'Nikora and Te Ihoariki, come out to us.' When the two Maori appeared, it was the settler called Benson who shot Te Ihoariki dead. Nikora was only slightly wounded and quickly slipped away into the night.

You ask, 'Was Benson ever called to account for the crime and for the taking of the law into his own hands?' No. Instead, he was told that he was required to serve on the jury at Te Ihoariki's inquest. This enabled the jury to make an intelligent, impartial and speedy verdict: Hemi Te Ihoariki had been 'Shot by some person unknown and served him right.' The local press, reporting the finding, commented, 'And with this verdict not a single Pakeha resident of Poverty Bay disagreed.'

The killing of innocents, Pakeha. The blood is on your hands.

Perhaps the testimony that should matter most is that of the man and the prophet, Te Kooti Arikirangi Te Turuki himself. This is best contained in the letter which he wrote to Governor Grey from Hauwai on 8 May 1879. You may judge for yourself just who was the guilty party in the matter of the Matawhero Retaliation.

'To Governor Grey, To the Governor of New Zealand, To his Colleagues, To Hon. Mr Sheehan, To Mr Grace and all their friends, May you long live—

'February First second month, 1867. This is the month when fighting between the Hauhaus and the Government commenced. I would not accept the Hauhau God, we fought and the Hauhau were defeated. Next morning I was arrested by the Government party, Maori and European, and I was put in gaol. I asked those in command what is the reason that I am arrested by you? They would not answer me. When the fighting was over the Government forces returned. After they retired I was left in the house, subsequently I was released, and I returned to my home. Not long after this, I was again arrested and taken to the Barracks of the Soldiers. At that time I was always asking that I should have a trial, I also asked the Officers to tell me what wrong I had done. They would not tell me. What they told me was that the matter was in Mr McLean's hands. After this I was removed to Napier. I stayed at the House of the Government. There were Hauhau prisoners there. For three days I went to the courthouse. (I was not requested to attend but I did so of my own accord.) My heart urged that I should have a trial. The first day I entered the courthouse I asked the interpreter of that court, Edward Hamlin by name, "Where is Mr McLean?" He replied, "Why do you ask for him?" I answered him, "I wish to be tried, so that the crime that I have committed may be made clear." He thereupon told me, "You return at eight o'clock, for he will be here at that time." At eight o'clock I went to the house, I again asked him, "Where is Mr McLean?" He replied, "He is busy; but you come back tomorrow at eight o'clock of the day." I again returned. I again asked him, "Where is Mr McLean?" He again replied, "He has not come; he is unwell." Hereupon I said to him, "You tell him tomorrow I will return again in order that my crime may be investigated, so that the reason I stay in prison may be clear." But he made no word of reply. In the morning at eight o'clock I again returned to that house, and I again asked him, "Where is Mr McLean?" Then he said to me, "Friend, you must cease coming here." I then said to him, "I thought this was a house in which crime is investigated. Why is [the theft of] a pen judged, but in my case no investigation is held?" I thereupon went outside the house, at the same time grieving because I could not get a trial. Then I saw Mr Wilson. That person was an officer over us when we were fighting against the Hauhau at Waerenga a Hika. I said to him, "Friend, let us both go to Mr McLean so as to obtain me a trial." He said to me, "I'm afraid of Mr McLean." He had just finished speaking when we heard Mr McLean's voice. He was angry at me. His first word was, "Stand aside, go away. It is not good that you should come to the town. Go back to your [koutou] house [the house of you and others]."

'That was sufficient, I then knew I would not be tried. I then was removed to Chatham Islands with the Hauhaus. I was a true

Government man. I was not a Hauhau in any sense of the word. My people begged of me strongly that I should turn to their idol but I would not agree. Whilst I was at the Chatham Islands I commenced to teach my people to rest quietly, and to put their trust in faith. They all heard of the day when we should soon return. I told my people not to steal nor assault any person but let us take our keepers into the house there to remain. My second word too was—we will take the guns lest our keepers shoot us. Hereupon a European took an axe and threw it at one of the Hauhau and struck him on the forehead— for this reason the axe was taken and that European was killed. His name was "Poui". That Hauhau who killed him was Tamihana. We the people did not see that European put to death. I caused lots to be drawn, and the lot fell to my parent. For this reason my uncle was thrown into the sea and by this means we reached this Island—for had this not been done we would all have perished in the ocean. We landed at Whareongaonga. The men of the Government came and demanded our guns, they also said that we would be arrested and put in gaol. My word to them was—friends I will not agree to the guns being given to you, and I will also not agree to be put in gaol a second time. I returned to the land and to you also. They would not agree to this and were two days persisting that the guns should be given up and that we should be taken back. I would not agree because I had not been tried by Mr McLean when I was arrested. On the third day I was attacked by the Govt [forces]. [This commenced the war.] I was not willing to fight, but the Government would fight, though I did not wish it. For this reason I said to my people, let us go to the king. They found us out, and they fought with us. After this fight, I wrote a letter to the Government that they should not destroy me, as I was not desirous of fighting. I am going to the king. I was again followed by the Govt [forces] and we fought again. After this fighting I again wrote a letter that we should not be killed—but it was not listened to, we were followed up into the bush and fought again. This was the third time we were pursued. I then thought the Govt were very bad—on this account I sent a notice to Govt Maoris and Europeans also. "Friends I agree that we fight, for I have been followed up by you three times"—then—"November is the month in which we will fight". Those are my words. "Trouble will arise." I was then called a murderer by the Government.

'This is sufficient, there is much more to be told, but I will stop here for these are the roots of the trouble.

'That is all there is still more to be said.

'[Signed] From Te Kooti Te Turuki.'

The Matawhero Retaliation was Te Kooti's first positive act of war. It was not a random attack, for Matawhero was the home of the Resident Magistrate. It took place in the early morning of 10 November 1868 and was followed by isolated killings on 11 and 12 November 1868.

Te Kooti's troops killed twenty-nine Pakeha, of whom thirteen were adult males, seven adult females and nine children; four half-castes of whom three were male and one female, and approximately thirty natives, making a grand total of sixty-three killed.

But this was not the 'worst horror since Cawnpore', as it was touted to the press. This was war, and Te Kooti had given due warning to both Pakeha and Maori loyalists. An analysis of the death roll shows that all of the thirteen European male victims were attached to the Defence Forces. They, their families and loyalist Maori were specific victims of the war, 10–12 November 1868.

~

Yes, Pakeha, you remember Matawhero. Let me remind you of the murders at Ngatapa.

I picture it this way, the killing of the Te Kooti followers by the colonial forces at Ngatapa on the morning of 5 January 1869. It is a cold grey day and the mist is steaming across the pa. The dead, brought low by the heavy mortar of the night before, lie in the position of their striking down—with eyes open and limbs dismembered by the shrapnel. At the back of the pa, the flax ladders, by which the main force of Te Kooti followers have escaped, sway in the wind. Far, far below the flimsy lifelines, is the thick bush.

The prisoners have been lined up along the edge of the cliff where the ladders sway and toss. They can feel the wind as it strikes the cliff face and curls over the lip of the bluff into the pa. There are forty in the first line, and they know that they are to be executed. Fatalism is written on the faces of the older warriors, but the younger ones are pumping their hearts to bursting with the adrenalin of defiance. The women are weeping, not for themselves, but for the children who are to die this day. Two of the women have already turned their sons away from the firing squad, facing them towards the open space of sky and the valley below, saying, 'Look to the west, for our prophet and our people have gone that way and there they pray for us who have been left behind.' Another mother has her hands ready to put across the eyes of her child and to clasp him to her when the shots ring out.

They knew that they would not be spared, even though they had been promised safe custody by some of the forces. When the news spread through the forces that every rebel head would be paid for £20, yes, they could see their fate. Nothing could save them, nothing at all. They began to prepare for death, praying as the prophet had taught them and singing the songs of Jehovah. Some of them had been together at Wharekauri, and they remembered the harshness and privation of that time in exile. Better to die in the homeland than in the prison of Pharaoh.

The time is nigh. The firing squad raise their rifles. The sun glints on the long barrels. The women begin crying and the children, not knowing why their mothers are crying, begin to scream. Some of the men, wishing to die in the stance of the warrior, begin to haka, a final act of challenge. They edge closer to the cliff's edge so that they will fall; better to fall than to have your head taken from your body and given unto Pharaoh.

The shots ring out. The sound is shocking, echoing and echoing across the valley. The prisoners jerk and dance to the obscene song of the bullets, and the blood sprays and gouts from bodies and limbs and heads ripped through by the lethal lead.

They begin to fall, pitching over the side of the cliff, 120 men, women and children, crowding the air in the long slow dive into death.

10

Te Kooti was pardoned in February 1883, fourteen years after the executions at Ngatapa pa. The prophet would have been in his early sixties, having established his church and lived close to God's presence for twenty years. He had been living in peace in Canaan for two decades. He was pardoned for a totally practical reason: the Hall Government was anxious to obtain railway access through the King Country and it needed King Tawhiao's goodwill. What better way to obtain this than by placing on the statute book a measure enabling it to grant amnesty to those who had committed crimes during the Land Wars?

The prophet was saved by that good old iron horse, the train.

As for a triumphant return to Gisborne, that was another matter.

Te Kooti was in Auckland in 1889. The Native Minister, the Hon. E. Mitchelson, called upon him at his hotel and arranged to have him driven around the city in a ministerial carriage to see the sights. 'Reprehensible,' the *New Zealand Herald* said of the minister's action. The carriage, bearing the ministerial insignia, was drawn through Queen Street by four fine horses. Te Kooti sat inside the carriage with the Native Minister.

'Such a lovely day,' Mr Mitchelson said. 'There is no doubt that Auckland on a summer's day is truly beautiful.'

Te Kooti nodded. Then he said, 'E hoa, Minita, I am preparing to return to Turanga.'

Mr Mitchelson was taken aback. 'Oh?' he asked. 'Do you think that is wise? People have long memories, you know, and it has not been long since—'

'It has been twenty years since the war was ended,' Te Kooti answered. 'I have forgiven your people for what they did to the Maori nation.'

'Now, see here—' Mr Mitcheson tried to remonstrate.

'I am preparing to return. I have lived in exile too long.'

The day, for Mr Mitchelson, did not appear lovely any longer. He listened to the clip-clop of the horses' hooves and was reminded of the days of the Land Wars. Damn the man for wishing to stir up old wounds! Mr Mitchelson tried persuasion.

'You know, of course, that should you enter Poverty Bay, the settlers may decide to take justice into their own hands. The Government would not be able to guarantee you your personal safety.'

'Ae,' Te Kooti said. 'But I will return in peace, e Minita.' He reached into his jacket and produced a pistol. 'Here, I shall give you my gun as a token of good faith.'

'Surely you realise what you are doing,' Mr Mitchelson protested.

'I am preparing to return. That is my last word on this matter. I yearn to be reunited with my kinsmen.'

Mr Mitchelson sighed. 'Very well. It appears that your mind is made up. I will try the best I can to protect you.'

Te Kooti smiled. 'My people, the faithful servants of the Lord, already await me. They have built new meeting houses, including a cathedral of the Ringatu faith. It is called Te Rongopai, the Gospel. It is at Waituhi.'

The horses clip-clopped along Queen Street. The sun shone through the trees near the Old Government Buildings. The citizenry of Auckland promenaded in the gardens.

Rongopai, O sacred house, I greet you and once, twice, thrice, I acclaim you.

You were for many years so tapu that people were afraid to enter you. So it was that from the road in front you appeared to be just another meeting house in just another Maori village, decaying in the wind and rain. But for me you were the centre of my universe, the place of the heart, and my breath always stopped whenever I reached the bend in the road and saw you there, sheltering in the lee of the foothills. Your roof, sloping up to the painted koruru at the apex, still holds up my sky, e Rongopai. Your arms, extending from the koruru, still encircle my life, wherever I am. You are the meeting house of my tupuna, my ancestors. You are my past, present and future and, thus, again I greet you and once, twice, thrice, I acclaim you.

This is how Rongopai, the painted meeting house, was built.

Following his pardon, the prophet settled at Te Tokangamutu, near the present town of Te Kuiti, as a guest of the Ngati Maniapoto tribe and of Tawhiao, the Maori King. He devoted his energies to developing the Ringatu faith, fusing Christianity and Maoritanga in a complementary relationship. He used the church to preserve and encourage Maori arts, especially carving, tukutuku and kowhaiwhai, and to restore pride in the Maori way of doing things. Instead of building churches, his people adopted the carved meeting house as the centre of worship and, as the church itself flourished, so too did the building of new meeting houses to worship in. Te Whai a te Motu was erected at Ruatahuna in the mountains of the Urewera. Its name meant 'Flight across the Island' and it celebrated Te Kooti's successful evasion of government forces. It was begun in 1870 and finished in 1888, and today it is the main meeting house of the Tuhoe people, the Children of the Mist. Te Tokanganui a Noho was another meeting house, built in 1872 near Te Kuiti. The name meant 'the Large Basket of the Stay-at-Home' and derived from a local proverb. In 1882, Ruataupare was built at Te Teko as Te Kooti's expression of gratitude to a people who had supported him during his conflict with the Government.

Nobody knows when the building of Rongopai was begun, but

it was probably in 1886. At that time, the prophet's followers in Poverty Bay and on the East Coast had increased their numbers and their faith, and after his pardon they prepared joyously for the prophet's return to his own land. Because of the Matawhero Retaliation, however, he was warned never to set foot in Turanga. The impassioned and eloquent cry of the chant, Pine Pine Te Kura, in which Te Kooti pleaded the putting aside of enmity and warfare, fell upon angry ears which would not listen. Pharaoh may have forgiven Te Kooti but the Egyptians still held the land. The prophet's words were as follows:

'Here, then, are tidings of peace, Welcome. Let us go together to Turanga, so that there I may lay down before you the machinery, the arms, the murderous weapons of the Pakeha. Arise! Let us ascend to the whirlwind path of Enoch.

'Even in being shaped by the mouth, the law is twisted, yet it touches all, Standing above even the Queen's power, even over the covenant made by our ancestor David.

'Search for the bridge, o people, the shedding of light, revealing how men can live in grace in this world.

'O people, seek that good word. It is you alone who hate. From the porch, I look across the sea and see the mist rising. My people, I tell you that your kinsman yearns to return to you, to provide you sustenance, but your banquet was of the bullets of Paparatu.

'Dig the wax from your ears and listen; although it was I who warned you not to strike me, I alone am banished. This is a false truce.

'You never were satisfied with victory at Waerenga a Hika. My people you imprisoned. Myself you exiled to the Chathams, yet I returned to you across the sea, landing at Whareongaonga. Then was to be heard the cry of the Government: "O people, here is food! Drag him to the shore! Kill him! Cook his heart! Eat it!"

'Your power was brought against me by mistake—and now the bitter taste can not be drowned in strong drink. Your animosity feeds on shame and jealousy. O my people! Leave such evil things behind!'

Despite the growing public resentment in Turanga, the prophet's followers pressed on with their plans to welcome Te Kooti home. After all, he had been born at Te Arai, or Manutuke, and he should therefore return. So it was that four disciples from Gisborne journeyed to see him in his adoptive land of the Ngati Maniapoto to persuade him not only to return to Te Arai, but also to attend a religious hui—a Hurae or Hanuere celebratory mass—at Waituhi. They must have visited him in 1886, proposing that the hui should take place in 1888. After some debate Te Kooti answered the elders, 'All right, go home and build the Gospel on charity and love.'

The disciples interpreted their prophet's word literally. On their return they each took it upon themselves to build meeting houses. The first, at Rangatira, was built by one of the Haronga family who named it Te Whakahau, meaning 'to start something up'. The second meeting house, built by Moanaroa Pere at Waituhi, was named Te Rongopai, the Gospel. The third was built by one of the Peneha family at Mangatu and it was called Te Ngawari, meaning Charity. The fourth was built by Matengaro Ruru at Tapuihikitia and was called Te Aroha, meaning Love. The four meeting houses were intended to be triumphant "stations of the cross" for the prophet on his progression back to Te Arai. He would stay at Te Ngawari first, move on to Te Aroha, then to Whakahau, then to Te Rongopai for the hui, and finally be received at Te Arai, the place of his birth.

Thus it was that over a thousand people came to Waituhi to erect Te Rongopai, the Gospel; the house was also variously known as Te Pao and Te Iri o Peta, meaning the Baptism of Peter the Apostle of Jesus Christ. The meaning of Waituhi underwent a transformation to signify 'the waters upon which God wrote His Commandments'.

The disciple who gave the instruction to build Rongopai was Wi Pere: on 9 February 1887 the *Poverty Bay Herald* reported that 'for a long time past the natives of Poverty Bay have been feverishly erecting a building at Waituhi to welcome Te Kooti back home to Gisborne. The Hon. Wi Pere, Native Minister for the East Coast, who is the ostensible head, has been building a large house wherein to receive Te Kooti on a portion of the block known as Repongaere.' It was Wi Pere's tribute to Te Kooti's struggle to retain Maori identity during the years of conflict. Rongopai became the gateway to the

Wi Pere estate and the fulfilment of the family has been in seeing Rongopai restored to its full glory.

Nine months later, in the edition of 24 October 1887, the *Poverty Bay Herald* noted that Te Rongopai had been completed and arrangements were being made for a welcome and a great feast to be given on the occasion of Te Kooti's visit. The promoters were known to be among the leading men of the district, the paper said. There was no attempt to disguise the celebrations or the purpose of the hui which, so the paper considered, might be to embarrass the Government. 'The above may be the primary objective. There is not the slightest use in appealing to the natives who are taking a hand in honouring Te Kooti. They are utterly beyond any influence of civilisation save that of the strong arm of the law. There is little doubt that the place selected for the gathering has been chosen for the purpose of showing contempt for and in defiance of the opinion of the English settlers.'

The building of the meeting house took, therefore, at least nine months to complete, perhaps longer. Wi Pere's son, Moanaroa Pere, was the architect; Pa Ruru was the priest.

Riripeti once asked me, 'Can you imagine how it must have been, e mokopuna, to have over a thousand people here at Waituhi? Here, on our land, were camped the young people of the tribe and helpers of the Ringatu religion. The smoke from the cooking fires curled like great signs in the sky, announcing that building was under way. The people themselves had prayers every morning and throughout the day, because the work was a religious mission. Ae, and our Leonardo da Vinci was named Moanaroa Pere, and he supervised the construction of the pa.

'Oh, it was quite a spectacle, e mokopuna, for there was not much time for the building of the house. The men had to travel far and wide to gather the tree trunks that would make up the framework of Rongopai. The pillars were sunk straight into the earth. The long beam within, that was of kahikatea, a tall white pine, which was originally standing in the place called Purapura Kapeti on flat ground near the Waipaoa River. Just above this ground and quite close to the main road going to Whatatutu is a place known as Whakahinu. This was the specific location of the kahikatea. It was felled, trimmed and floated down the river by many men, supervising its journey from canoes accompanying the tree. They were aided, of course, by the religious presence of Pa Ruru himself, because everything during that time was sacred and tapu. Karakia, prayers, were recited constantly during the voyage of the kahikatea down the Waipaoa. There were so many bends to negotiate and, at times, the kahikatea had to be carried manually over some parts of the river. It was quite a journey, the kahikatea under escort, like some proud ship surrounded by smaller yachts, and, when the procession was nearing Waituhi, people gathered to watch it floating downstream. Then it reached the place known as Pa Whakarau, the Place Struck by Whakarau, which, by virtue of its genealogical and spiritual connections, was an appropriate location to have the kahikatea landed. The log was lifted from the river and thus began the final stage of its journey to its resting place, Te Rongopai.

'Mokopuna, the story is told that, until this time, the kahikatea was as light as if it had been a feather. This was because of the many blessings that had been said over it. But within a quarter of a mile of its destination, while still on the flat ground, the log suddenly became immovable. Try as they might, the team of men who had been handling the log could not shift it. Pa Ruru began to karakia and to pray and, after the prayers had been completed he said, "Let us try again to move the kahikatea." This was attempted, but again it failed. Then Pe Ruru said to the men, "Someone in the group has transgressed the law of tapu; this is a very tapu log, and the tapu has been broken. Whoever has done this thing, and they will know it themselves, must leave the group immediately." Straight away, two of the men left the group. The specific tapu they had broken was this: they had slept with their wives during the night and had therefore been rendered noa. In other words, they had lost the sacredness with which the kahikatea had to be handled. When they left the group, the rest of the men then picked up the kahikatea and, as it had been earlier, it was again as light as if it had been a feather. They carried the log up a rise one hundred feet high and completed their journey without any more problems.'

When I was a boy the story of the journey of the kahikatea was told and retold and it still has its magic and power. In many ways it was quite medieval, bringing with it echoes of the great Anglo-Saxon poem 'The Dream of the Rood' in which the Cross of Christ narrated its own intimate story of how it was carried by its Lord and later, during the Crucifixion, was jewelled by His blood. The rood was raised on a hill just outside Jerusalem; the kahikatea was raised to be the long beam of the house called Rongopai, just outside Turanga. When the beam was in its place, it was seen that the house would be very large, eighty-five feet in length and thirty-five feet in width. The young people then set about decorating the house and this they did during the space of three months.

They made the house into a likeness unto themselves, the iwi, and their dreams of fulfillment as a sovereign Maori nation.

~

Te Kooti is coming.

The prophet is coming home.

The word spread like wildfire across the Gisborne plain. The police in the districts through which the prophet and his retinue were to pass received instructions to arrest any person, Pakeha or Maori, whose conduct was likely to lead to a disturbance. On the face of it, these instructions would appear to be supportive of the prophet. Instead, they were used to have him arrested.

18 FEBRUARY 1889

A public meeting assembled at Makaraka attracted 500 people to protest the prophet's return. Sympathisers said that Te Kooti and his followers had not been seen with any arms for at least two years. Others said that after all his own people wanted him to return.

The decision of the meeting? A vigilance committee was set up and a Poverty Bay defence fund was established. Steps were proposed to stop for all time the terrorism arising from Te Kooti's threatened visits; the Government was to be asked to send 300 stands of arms and the cooperation of the Ngati Porou against Te Kooti was invited.

20 FEBRUARY 1889

The prophet and 200 followers approached Whakatane.

Intelligence reports stated that no signs of arms had been seen among his party, which was to be augmented with further followers at the township. The newspapers were requested to bring pressure on the Government to take responsibility for keeping Te Kooti out of Poverty Bay. Should the Government not do so, the settlers would necessarily have to compromise themselves by forcibly opposing the visit.

21 FEBRUARY 1889

The prophet's band had swelled to 250, and the reports became hysterical with charges that all were mounted and many armed, and that most were 'native scum, full of bounce'. That evening in Gisborne another meeting was held, attracting 800 people to repeat their protestations about the prophet's visit. A Ngati Porou contingent arrived to hearten the residents. Te Kooti himself was approaching Waioeka, just outside the Poverty Bay district.

22 FEBRUARY 1889

Of all things, the Premier, Sir Harry Atkinson, arrived in Gisborne. He attempted to defuse the situation among the settlers by disbanding the Vigilance Committee. The Premier also transferred a government official to Christchurch when he said that if Te Kooti came on to Poverty Bay, he would shoot him down in the main street.

The transfer was a promotion.

23 FEBRUARY 1889

The farce continued when forty Auckland navals, fifteen police and twenty-nine volunteers were landed from Auckland at Ohiwa. Ninety members of the Permanent Artillery and a few members of the Torpedo Corps, together with a number of police, reached Gisborne from Wellington. Twenty Permanent Artillerymen, thirty volunteers and thirty members of the Armed Corps were sent on by sea from Gisborne to Opotiki, and a batch of police was posted at Motu Bridge.

Premier Atkinson inspected a muster of sixty-seven members of the fully armed Permanent Artillery, sixty-five members of the East Coast Hussars and their carbine weapons, ten members of the Armed Corps with revolvers and batons, and thirty-five Ngati Porou soldiers.

26 FEBRUARY 1889

The troops moved off en route for Opotiki, to the tune of sarcasm and ridicule from some of the local press. After all, Te Kooti had been pardoned, surely? His band was unarmed. So why all the military fuss? The *Evening Post* in Wellington said that 'the best thing that can be done is to explain to the silly and excited settlers of Poverty Bay that . . . condign punishment will follow any illegal or violent action.' The *New Zealand Times*, also in Wellington, said that the settlers should realise their legal position, to wit, that 'If anybody kills Te Kooti he will be arrested for murder, tried in a place where there will be an impartial jury and, if convicted, he will be hanged without mercy.'

The troops arrived at Waioeka Pa, to find its occupants to be mainly women and children. They then went to Waiotahi Pa and there saw Te Kooti, resting with his people under some trees. There was no sign of arms. At that stage, a squad of police was called to action. A warrant for the prophet's arrest was read, charging 'that together with diverse persons to the number of 250 or more he [Te Kooti] unlawfully did assemble to disturb the public peace to the terror and alarm of Her Majesty's subjects residing in Whakatane County of Whakatane.'

So what happened? Why, the innocent prophet was bound over to keep the peace for six months, to the tune of £500 and two sureties of £500 each. This was a lot of money for any Maori to carry around and of course the prophet did not take that sort of cash with him when travelling. The result was that he was taken to Auckland and incarcerated in Mount Eden gaol until his followers were able to arrange the required funds. In the Supreme Court, on appeal, Mr

Justice Connelly held that the conviction was not legally justified. Te Kooti then threatened to sue the Crown for £20,000 damages on the grounds that he had been unlawfully imprisoned. However the Court of Appeal, in turn, reversed Mr Justice Connelly's decision. 'The Governor's pardon cannot change a man's character,' Mr Justice Richmond said, 'nor can it efface recollections of the past. Te Kooti's reappearance on the scene of the Massacre, even in peaceful guise, at the head of a large body of men could not be regarded otherwise than as endangering lives and properties.'

According to official sources, the prophet tried once more to visit the Gisborne district. This occurred two years later, in 1891, when Te Kooti told the Native Minister that he hoped no obstacle would now be set up to prevent him from making a visit to Poverty Bay.

'Under the law,' the Native Minister said, 'you are as free as anybody to move about the country. Personally, I do not fear that you would break the law, but I do fear that if you enter Poverty Bay some Europeans might do so.'

Oh, the irony. The prophet was now called to account for the possible crimes of the Pakeha. Perhaps this was why he was reported to have said, 'I will now give up all thought of going to Gisborne out of respect for the wishes of the Government.'

Thus it was that the prophet never returned to Gisborne and never saw Rongopai. Nevertheless he gave his blessing to his people, saying, 'Do not despair that I cannot come to Rongopai in the flesh for I am already there in the spirit and you, my followers, will see me there.' And when the Ringpatu faithful, not knowing how the house was decorated, saw the painting of the Scotch thistle on one of the interior panels, they realised that the prophet was indeed within the walls of the house both in the spirit and the flesh.

And again the prophet said of the painted house, which he had never seen, that the painting of two men in a boxing match was not appropriate for such a cathedral: 'The shedding of blood is already over, and now is the time of peace.'

And it was also told that many wished to visit the painted house with the prophet. Among this number was a woman who was with child. Te Kooti immediately turned round to her and said to Mrs

Tupara, 'Ko tena tamaiti ko Te Rerenga ki muri.'

Some people say that the prophet was destined in fact never to enter the house because of its decorations. And there are some who look on Wi Pere, the man who instigated the building of the meeting house, with disfavour because of the way his good will to the prophet appeared to contradict his attitude when he was a younger man. People say that the boxing match is a symbol of the family's inner turmoil. They say that the reason we fight each other is all because of that drawing in Rongopai of the boxing match. Some even say that it is the drawing itself which prevented the prophet from visiting Rongopai.

~

Come with me, now, to Rongopai. Do not be afraid. Come. Take my hand. I will tell you something of it, not all, for I do not know all there is to know about the house. But I will try to convey something of its beauty and its sense of spirituality. It is a house of religion. It is reputed to have healing powers.

First I must tell you something about the structure of a whare nui. Stand here on the marae with me, facing the building, and I will explain about the meeting house of the iwi Maori. Both the size of the whare nui and the way it is decorated tell you a lot about the history and strength of the iwi who built it and who belong to it. The house has a head, backbone, ribcage and limbs. It is built in the shape of a person and is usually named after an ancestor of the tribe. The front of the house has at the apex of the gable a large carved head which we call the koruru. Running from the head and along the length of the house is the backbone or tahuhu. As you look at the koruru, you will see the sloping bargeboards like an inverted V, one on either side of the head. These are the arms or maihi. Within the house are rafters which represent the ribs. So, when you go into the house, you enter into the ancestor, or, if you like, you are taken into the body of the people.

Let us go onto the porch. As you know, Rongopai was for many years deserted; it was too tapu for use in the normal ways that whare nui were used. During this time it became quite neglected and it has only been recently that attempts were made to renovate the building. The porch, for instance, had taken a fair battering from the elements and many of the paintings on the walls had faded, so badly in some cases that you didn't really know what the original pattern or colour had been. Look at it now, so beautiful. This was the work of the younger generation of the Whanau a Kai. The porch was also extended, and a concrete floor put right through the building. The floor has changed the character of the house a little, but not too much. When you open the door, the interior still looks like a huge enchanted forest full of magical and mystical images. But let me tell you how it used to look when I was a child.

Open the door. Now.

The interior was always dark and had the smell of eternity about it. You entered, and were suddenly aware of a change of atmospherics: increased pressure against your eardrums, for instance, and a damping of the acoustics so that there was no echo to any accidental sound. Words uttered seemed to become substantial enough to stand on the edge of the air. The temperature rose and if your feet were bare you felt the warmth of the dirt floor like a carpet of heat. Finally, there was a decrease in the light's intensity so that when you looked around you, all you could see were white and painted shapes looming out of the darkness. You were separated from the world. You were in another world, the interior of Rongopai, in itself complete and self-sustaining, its own world without end, its own time-lock.

From the threshold of the world of Rongopai, you began to understand why the more traditional elders of Te Whanau a Kai had prophesied that Te Kooti would never set foot inside the pa. The walls and ceiling enclosed you in a strange dream world quite obviously different from those of other whare nui. In this meeting house, the wall panels were like tall mirrors receding into the darkness, to your left and to your right, an avenue of mirrors within which were held the fantasies of the young painters. In the way of the young, the glorious colours and the exuberance had been applied with little reference to tradition, an obvious break with the past. But

I have always liked to think that the prophet would have approved, for just as he had blended the Chrisian faith with Maori culture to speak for the people in the new world, so also had the young people attempted to show the blending of the old ways with the new and the world of the Maori in the lands of the Pharaoh.

The paintings were beautiful, so stunning because they were out of context with the traditional arts and, at the same time, intriguing because they seemed to have a primitive quality which was both whimsical and cynical. Taken as a whole, they were schizophrenic, a virtual kaleidoscope of colour and form, which began from a traditional premise and then were embellished with the appogiaturi of the oppressed. The gravity and reverence for the past were evident on all rafters, painted in the typical designs of the kowhaiwhai: bold red, white and black curvilinear designs in the shapes of the unfolding fern, the double spiral, the hammerhead shark, the flower of the kaka beak and the red lips of the ngutukura. The same reverence was also evident in the reed work which featured between the roof rafters and the wooden panels of the walls. Here were seen the plaited dragon's teeth, the series of small triangles known as the little teeth, the double mouth, the armpit weave, the white crosses of the star seeds, the roimata or tears, the flatfish pattern, and the poutama, the stairway to the Heavens. The basic concept of the interior illustrations, whether carved, painted or woven, conformed to the outlines of tradition. But it was the filling in that made it different. In this respect, Rongopai was like a strange Rorschach Test, unveiling the subconscious of the Maori, the persona, in highly romantic and yet realistic terms. It revealed a world out of kilter, spinning off its axis and out of its own orbit around the sun that Maui had tamed, ripping other galaxies apart and, in the process, severely damaging its own. But, ah, it was not hopelessness that the young painters showed; rather, faith, like the Children of Israel in bondage and yet being uplifted by their prophet, faith in God and in the Canaan of their dreams. Rongopai was painted in the dream's likeness and in the likeness of the people of Te Whanau a Kai.

The dream was of a new, brave world, an Eden where the kowhaiwhai was embellished with fresh colours; painted spirals and floral patterns provided a panacea for war and a prayer for peace. It was the kind of dream that people associate with psychedelia; it placed the Maori in the position of centrality but gave him the moko of the Pakeha.

There, the dreams, painted on the pillars of pukatea wood and the rafters. There, the healing powers of the house, symbolised in the profusion of elaborate trees and vines, twining and climbing in a painted Eden: reds and browns, brilliant flowers and pods popping out from large Victorian vases; oranges and yellows, sunbursting fruits defying botanical reality; the glorious purple of the Scotch thistle, personal symbol of the prophet; greens and creams of seeds winging their way through the poutama and the roimata; the fabulous Tree of Life, with its twelve separate herbal flowers sprouting from the central trunk.

Nor was this an Eden unpopulated by man, serpent, bird, fish or beast, for there they all were, inhabitants of the illuminated world. The birds, such as were dreamed of in paradise, flew among the jewelled branches, darting like sparkling avian encrustations amid the painted foliage. The fabulous monsters of the deep emerald oceans, the manaia and marakihau, the beaked bird-man, the lizard, the seahorse, the semi-human sea monster with the long tubular tongue capable of sucking in both fish and man, all slithered within the universe of Rongopai.

Finally, there were the people of Te Whanau a Kai. There, Kahungunu painted on one pillar, handsome and wearing only a garment around his thighs to hide the sight of his fabled loins. There, Tauhei, the daughter of Kahungunu, painted in the outlines of pride and etched with dignity. There, more figures painted in the traditional style, flourishing the taiaha and mere weapons, but with blue eyes and short hair parted in the European way. The woman, Kohakirirangi, was forever captured wearing a European dress with the hint of a bustle, raising a red rose to her lips. On another panel, a male ancestor wore in his hair not the royal huia feather but a Scotch thistle, again, the symbol of the prophet. Others climbed about the branches of Eden, or were shown chopping them down. Some were depicted sparring in a boxing match, or racing horses neck and neck in a never-ending hunt, or hunting with gun dogs for game in the forest. And there was Wi Pere himself, in the formal attire of the black jacket, grey trousers, bowler hat and spurs on his heels. The figure of his mother, Riria Mauaranui, was shown perched on his shoulder, indicating her substantial influence on his life and her significance as the source of his authority. (Many years later, at a Young Maori Leaders' Conference in Auckland, Mira Szazy brought the memory of Riria back with her blistering challenge to Maori male leadership to recognise the supreme role of women in forcing the pace of change. 'It is women who are coming to the front,' she said. 'They are the ones who are bringing up the children in the ghettoes of our cities. You, the men, must therefore allow us the rights to be leaders. You, the men, must provide partici-pation for us at this conference or else our solution is simple. We will leave you to your devices,' she said with withering authority. 'We will move elsewhere and hold our own conference.') And the face of Wi Pere was with tattoo when the man himself was without tattoo.

Ah yes, Rongopai was a fantasy as well as a real world. It acknowl-edged that life was holistic, a place where the spirit and the flesh were integrated and creatures of light and creatures of darkness lived coincidentally with man in the one, single universe. There were no barriers between the past and the present, the living and the dead, the spirit and the flesh, for all were contained in that eternal continuum known as the Creation. Rongopai itself was the healing place, the joining place for the Maori people, the place where the fingers interlocked in prayer and supplication as well as in union. Amid the profusion of plants, fabled creatures, men and exotic trees were the small symbols of the interlocking—the moko patterns of the young painters, the astrological signs, the nautical inscriptions, the whimsical patterns of playing cards. They were signs of vivacity, of life rather than death, of renewal rather than recession.

In the Maori nation's darkest hour Rongopai shone as one of the our most beauteous triumphs. This was its aria, Wi Pere's song of Rongopai:

'E hine tangi kino, kati ra te hakari. Whakarongo a tai ka rongo na tuau, he toro taua ra, he whakahakari ana nga waho i, e ngarue ra. I rite pea koe, te rere a te kahu i whano, a, i whakatopa ki te uru, ki te rangi te taumata ra. Koe pure i hau-ariki, ko te puke i noho ai nga manu o tane. E kore pea koe, e manakohia mai. Ka mimiti nga tai, ka ngaro te tangata noho kau ake nei. Taua, e hine, te pure ki Turanga, ki te ara o te riri, te minenga o te iwi. Kei to whaea ra he whakahoro koe, te horo o Houmea no whea a homai. Tenei to ingoa ko Wahine-ata koe, e moe i to moenga kei piki koe, te paepae tapu i te kaha o Tu. Kauaka, e hine, e tipu whakatane, e taea e koe te pehinga hau, kia aronui mai, he mate te whakamau. To pae ki Turanga kei raro i te iho, te whare o Wi Pere, kia uhia koe ki te kupu o te tikanga a koro kia tutuki, kati ra hoki mai.'

This was how Rongopai was to me when I was a child. A tapu was placed on it from the time of its completion. It was because of this tapu that the meeting house remained very much in its original condition. Although the paintings in the porch were damaged by weather, the interior was preserved. Innocent and unknowing, I often went to play in Rongopai. Riripeti told me many stories about the mystical happenings there—of flames flickering where there were no embers or fires, of miraculous healings, of men speaking in the tongues of angels, of women visited by the Holy Ghost, but always of healings, of the things of goodness rather than of evil.

Today some people speak of Rongopai as still remaining under a Tuhoe tapu, but the local tapu was eventually removed. This occurred at a special ceremony conducted by the Ringatu Church: it was then that the younger members of the present Maori nation began to resurrect the beauty of the building, and their own faith in themselves, by renovating Rongopai in the modern image, They were not always Maori, nor were they always Ringatu. They came from throughout Aotearoa, the flower of the nation, from the faiths of the Anglican, the Roman Catholic, the Mormon; they represented the local people, like Martin, Norma, Puku, Jim, Kiki, Hapi, Bill, Mahanga, Tote, Toroa and many others; they sought the guidance of local and national art authorities, both Maori and Pakeha; they were young men and women of the new generation who, while they may have transgressed some sacred laws ('Well, Dad,' Erina said to him in defence, 'it was you who told me to hop up on the ladder and start painting the ceiling. How was I supposed to know that women weren't allowed up there?'), they nonetheless had faith. They had faith in Rongopai as a symbol of their Maoritanga at a time when this was being slowly snuffed out by the way of the Pakeha. They dreamt dreams of pride in self and in the iwi. Rongopai was their political statement. This is us. This is our mana.

It was Aunt Norma who told me that the young people had come and worked on Rongopai. Many had not held a paintbrush in their hands, and some did not know the first thing about Maori language and culture. A few had never been on a marae before. Quite a few were street kids, the unemployed driftwood in the teeming sea of humanity. Many had been in pain; Rongopai healed them. Some had been junkies, high on morphine, heroin, delaudid, eukodal, diocodid, opium, palfium, polophine, demerol, diosane; they, too, were healed of the soul. Almost a century had passed since the house had been built. Yet the suffering of the Maori nation still persisted. The suffering was among the children's children of the generation of Te Kooti. The new urban Maori, removed from his rural roots, bereft of his land and his mana. The new Maori woman, fighting for the rights of the dispossessed. The new Maori warrior, protesting for his dignity and saying, 'Give me back myself.'

I like to think, for those who worked on Rongopai, on the cathedral at Waituhi, that the power for goodness was laid upon their heads and that the very real and black holes of their souls were healed of anger and confirmed with forgiveness. And, out of that forgiveness, I pray that the strength to recreate the Maori nation has come again.

Rongopai, it is still true: you still hold up the sky so that we may live on this earth and within this cleft of air and light.

We still live. We still breathe. We are still Maori.

The prophet Te Kooti Arikirangi Te Turuki died at Wainui, fifteen kilometres west of Opotiki, adjacent to Ohiwa Harbour, on 17 April 1893. This property had been placed at his disposal by the Crown. He had been on a visit to Ruatoki, and his ope had decided to camp at Maraetotara. Te Kooti felt unwell, wrapped himself in a rug and lay down. Some dogs began to fight. They collided with, and set in motion, a dray which had been left, without a wheel being chained, on a slope above where he was resting. A wheel passed over him, crushing his chest. The manner of his death was as he himself had predicted.

Various stories went into circulation concerning the prophet's burial. In May 1902, Hamiora Aparoa told the *Opotiki Herald* only he and two other members of the Ringatu Church knew the exact burial spot, and that it had been agreed, upon the death of any of the trio, the survivors should select a successor to him, to guard the burial place; this procedure was to continue forever. In August 1938, Rikirangi Hohepa told the *Poverty Bay Herald* that he was the sole survivor of a party of four which carried out the burial, and that the grave had never been disturbed. In April 1949, there was talk of removing the remains and returning them to Poverty Bay where the prophet had been born.

Nobody knows how old Te Kooti Arikirangi Te Turuki was when he met his death. The memorial erected by members of the Ringatu Church mentions the age of seventy-nine. The inscription, in Maori, goes on to say, '. . . he was a chief and a hero. He displayed great gallantry in great battles fought in Aotearoa. The Government made peace with him and gave him and his people some land; and also confirmed his religion known as the Ringatu. These matters were settled and fully confirmed in the presence of the Native Minister in the year 1883.'

This was the final message of Te Kooti, his challenge to the people of Gisborne who would not let him return, his prophecy for the future:

'He turanga tangata e kore e kitea e au; He turanga whenua ka au. Mine enemies will never see me again; but their children's children will.'

'With the end of the Hauhau war,' wrote Sir Apirana Ngata, 'we reach the last landmark in the historical past of the Maori race. Te Kooti is the last and greatest representative of the worst side of the Maori character—its subtlety, cunning and treachery; its cruelty and love of bloodshed; and its immorality and fanaticism. His character had no relieving trait; no anecdotes of liberality or magnanimity extenuate the horror we must feel for him. It was not to be wondered at; he was not a chief. In all his schemes and undertakings there is lacking the kindly liberality, the magnanimity, the true dignity of the Maori chief.'

~

Riripeti pressed the palms of her hands to her heart. '*Padre pieta, pieta.*' She was watching the night sky with the child. There was a haze covering the moon, gradually obscuring the three luminous circlets which surrounded it.

'I must live forever,' she cried, her voice echoing away, away, away. She stood looking at the sky, unwilling to accept the prophetic signs. Below lay Waituhi, the dark hills, and flames flickering.

'Grandmother,' the child began.

She hushed him, pointing at the moon. He saw a comet with a tail of fire rushing from the blackness behind the moon and falling towards the earth. She began to sing, her voice a thread of sound, to the universe itself, '*Presago il core della tua condanna*, my heart forewarned me of your condemnation.' They were strange words to sing, words of suffocation, of darkness coming with the sealing of a stone crypt, of being buried alive away from air and light.

The comet kept falling, falling, falling. The matriarch's mood changed, became fatalistic. She pointed at the falling star. '*Vedi? Di morte l'angelo radiante a noi s'appressa.*' The comet consumed the air as it fell, glowing like a fiery angel. 'Do you see? Death's radiant angel messenger hastens towards us, and carries us to eternal joy upon his golden wings. Already I see heaven opening . . .'

'No,' the child cried. 'No!'

The comet fell like a sun dying in the sky, falling into the embrace of the cold earth. The matriarch opened her arms to receive it. '*O terra addio, addio valli di piante, sogno di gaudio che in dolor svani.*'

The child cried out again, 'No!'

The comet burst into a thousand pieces, showering the night with a cascade of brilliant embers. The matriarch continued to sing, reaching through the blinding light with her voice.

'*Ah! si schiude il ciel,*' the words losing breath like a long indrawn sigh.

At the last moment, a red star began to glow in the blackness.

act three

11

Va, pensiero, sull'ali dorate; va, ti posa sui clivi, sui colli . . . Go, my thought, on golden wings; go, alight upon the slopes, the hills, where, soft and warm, the sweet breezes of our native land are fragrant . . . *Del Giordano le rive saluta* . . . Greet the banks of the Jordan and Zion's razed towers . . .

Wellington, October, 1975.

Ani Thomas and I were getting drunk in the 1860 Tavern on Lambton Quay. Ani had just flown in from Whakatane to await the great Maori Land March and its arrival at Parliament Grounds to present yet another petition for the return of Maori land. The march was being led by Dame Whina Cooper. It had begun at Te Hapua on Monday 13 October and reached Wellington, 1000 kilometres away, in only thirty days. Over 200 elders representing every tribe in Aotearoa had signed the Memorial of Rights and another 60,000 people agreed to the petition.

The sight of the march making its way down the backbone of the Fish of Maui was unforgettable. Although there had been some resistance and anger, the march had gained in strength and mana.

Ani's son, Hemi, was with the marchers. After it was over, he planned to move across the Tasman to Australia. Like many other Kiwis, Hemi was fleeing the country in search of the megabuck lifestyle of Oz. Ani was terribly sad, almost bereaved to see him go.

'Of course Hemi will be a great success,' she said. 'I knew it from the moment he was born. There were certain signs, prophetic signs, which happened just as he sucked in his first breath. I knew then that he was marked by the gods.'

Ani laughed. She was wearing a silk turban around her head and a black caftan that coiled from her shoulders. Her laughter was lost in the sound, the hubbub of the habitués at the bar.

Ani and I had known each other since childhood; she was from Tuhoe and there had been some tribal expectation that, when we grew older, we would marry. We talked a little longer about the vagaries of existence and the times we had shared together before I had gone to university and met Regan. Then we pondered the ironies and little tricks life had played on us and which, at the snap of the fingers or blink of an eye, had rendered her divorced and me married.

'I guess we just weren't made to be together,' Ani said. 'I tried hard enough, but Regan must have tried harder. All our Maori men marrying Pakeha women, aue. It's a matter of fate. You believe in the stars, don't you?'

'Yes,' I answered. 'I've seen too much in my life not to accept destiny.'

She looked at me strangely. Then quite suddenly she thrust a question at me like a silver spear. 'Tell me,' she said, 'what signs were there at your birth?' The question plunged deep, deeper still, and I remembered a psychic in Paris reading my palm and refusing to tell me what she had seen there, for 'there is so much darkness, so much of it, suffocating' and Ashok Raman in London also refusing to tell me what he had seen in his trance because 'darkness cannot light, and where there is no light I cannot see'.

I think Ani had hoped I would be taken off balance and would answer without really reflecting. There was too much calculation in her voice to make the question casual.

'I don't know,' I said.

The spear, deflected, broken into silver shards. Ani put her hands up as if to protect herself. There was something witch-like about the movement. She knew, she knew, that I had lied about the signs.

The sounds of the tavern surrounded us. Ani laughed. She reached over and kissed me. Then she took a sip of her Bloody Mary.

'You should ask your mother one day,' she mocked.

Ask Tiana?

Throughout the rest of the day Ani's question disturbed me, setting up a dissonance that was difficult to dispel. My mother's personal history was so mysterious, with the explicit sense of the violence that surrounded it. After all, wasn't that what psychologists said about a parent who did violence to their children—that they had at some point also been the subject of violence and were only repeating the pattern? To ask Tiana about anything in her life would be to compel her perhaps to acknowledge that history, a history that she had placed in denial. It would also force me to confront myself with the truth about her. We were estranged yes, but she was still my mother. Did I really want to know any more about her? If I did I could risk the last shred of love that I had for her. The possibility was too frightening for me to contemplate. After all, I had been born of her womb.

For instance, I knew that she was from Ngati Porou; but even that assumption was shrouded in uncertainty. Born just before the great flu epidemic of 1918, she had been an orphan when the priest Huirangi, around 1920, adopted her and brought her up on his marae at Rawheoro. Although she claimed ancestry through him, what had she been before and where had she lived? And I know that, when Huirangi died, as a teenager she worked on a number of Maori farms on the East Coast. One of those belonged to her Uncle Whiro and his wife, known as Old Sally. I understand that he loved her deeply. Even so, when Old Sally died, Tiana ran away from the farm. Why?

I know that she worked in the orchards of Hastings until my father met her and fell in love with her. 'Don't ask your mother about her girlhood,' Te Ariki once said to me. 'It's better not to know.'

But there was one question I was compelled to ask him. 'Had Tiana ever met Riripeti before the night you came back from Hastings and Grandmother was waiting for you at the Gisborne railway station?'

'Is that what Tiana told you?' Te Ariki answered, surprised. 'I don't know. Riripeti was so well known throughout Gisborne, Poverty Bay and the East Coast. It's not unlikely that Tiana knew of her. During 1918, for instance, Riripeti was doing a lot of work among the people when the flu epidemic hit us. Many Maori adults died. Riripeti built a temporary hospital at Waituhi, Te Waka o Te Atua, the Ship of God, for the survivors. She also took in orphaned children. Tiana may have been one of them.'

But in Ani's question, 'You should ask your mother one day,' had been the implication of some deeper spiritual, psychic identity to the woman I knew as Tiana, my mother. Certainly, although some people regarded her as a woman of no account, there was no question that she had strong mana of her own. But where did it come from? In answering this question I would have to acknowledge that in the origins of my mother was a world that didn't make sense. It was like the rest of the Maori world, without the boundaries between the real and the unreal, the past and the present, the rational and the irrational, myth and reality, the Christian and the pagan. After all, why should the Maori world be the same as the Pakeha world? The indigenous world the same as the civilised? Did the Maori dynamic have to conform to the same dictates of order and reason? If I was to argue for that, I would have to cease believing in a valley in which the human and natural worlds were in partnership—where a woman with pearls in her hair could call on spiders to aid her, or to stop the sun from spinning across the sky. I would have to stop considering all possibility of the supernatural and stop believing in a world where the gods still communed with man and his destiny. Let the Pakeha choose to put up his boundaries if he wished, and to believe in those things that could only be proven; our world was a continuum in which all things possible and impossible could bind together.

So where did Tiana's mana come from?

I know now that it came from a marae even older than Rawheoro.

For my mother's true hearth was on Hikurangi mountain, the place that Maui's hook had snared when he fished Aotearoa from the sea. When Hikurangi breached the surface it became the first location on our earth to be struck by sunlight, sending out a flare into the universe; so it has ever been from that original morning. And as the rest of Aotearoa was heaved up from the sea by Maui, his canoe was reputed to have lodged there, the water streaming away from the sloping land.

It was to Hikurangi mountain that Tiana's ancestors came. They called their marae Te Tira Maka, establishing it at the very place where Maui's canoe had rested; they did this far before the arrival of later canoe settlers from Hawaiki. Te Tira Maka, therefore, was Tiana's ancient birthground. The people from whom she was descended were known as the kaiuru moemoea, the dream swimmers. My mother inherited their striking appearance and strong, almost masculine, grace. She was always lifting her face to the light, her eyes wide, dark and staring, as if ascending to take her first breath from a sea of swirling dreams. Like her ancient ancestors, my mother was never afraid to engage anybody in battle—even my grandmother Riripeti, the matriarch.

Her sign was regarded by the Maori with great awe and reverence. It was the red star known as Poututerangi. Its European name was Altair.

And like Riripeti, who could call upon spiders to help her, Tiana had a mermaid ancestress who came whenever she was commanded.

Her name was Hine Te Ariki, and she had a connection with Waituhi because she was the wife of Tumokonui, the first to settle in the valley. He knew that she was of the uri taniwha, the people whose homes lay within the deep pools and caverns of the Waipaoa.

Hine Te Ariki's first children by Tumokonui were twins, both of whom were taken away by spirits at birth. Some time later Hine Te Ariki gave birth to another set of twins, who were also abducted by the spirits. She conceived again, and her third set of twins were removed from her. What must it be like for a mother to have her six children taken away in this manner?

Grieving, Hine Te Ariki decided to consult her uri taniwha people. She waded into the river, took the water into her lungs, plunged deep, and began to swim through the emerald depths, from river to river, stroking her way up into the mountains. She loved the liquid feel of the water and she commanded the eels to accompany her. Sometimes other mermen and mermaids joined her for a short time, swimming through the sunlight patterning of the water.

Her father embraced her. She told him of her sorrows. Her father said, 'Aue, my daughter, this is happening because you are married to a common person. You, my darling, are descended from taniwha, and your ancestors are hidden in the clouds. It is they who take your children from you. Should you wish to keep any child of your marriage to Tumokonui you must remain with the child whenever you see the clouds descending. Protect the child until the mist has lifted again.'

So it was that Hine Te Ariki gave birth again, to a daughter, Tonoa ki Aua. She saw the mists gathering, and the spirits of her ancestors coming to take the child away. She stayed with Tonoa ki Aua until the mists lifted. The mists came and went, came and went. But Hine Te Ariki wanted this daughter, and she would cry out, 'This child is mine. Leave her to me.' The spirits were magnanimous. They left Hine Te Ariki to bring up her daughter.

(And once, when my daughter Miranda was drowning, I cried out, 'Hine Te Ariki.' We were swimming in the Waipaoa River. She was about three years old and she had waded away from where my sisters and I were diving. She had been lost for at least ten minutes and, oh, my heart was bursting with grief. The surface of the water began to swirl in a strange way. I thought the motion was caused by eels. I saw Miranda coming to me from the depths. Her head broke the surface. The water rushed from her mouth and she took her first breath of air again and screamed. She did not want to come back to the world of air. But, firmly, she was propelled towards me and into my arms.

For a brief moment after cradling Miranda I saw my ancestress, the uri taniwha Hine Te Ariki. Her eyes were looking up at me through the clear water. They were dark green. She brushed the long tresses of her hair away from her face and smiled. Perhaps she remembered her own daughter, taken away by her uri taniwha ancestors. Miranda reached for her, but Hine Te Ariki shook her head and blew a kiss. She did, however, leave my daughter with a fabulous gift. From that time onwards, Miranda was able to swim like her uri taniwha ancestors and I have seen her gambolling in the depths of the rivers at home, laughing with ecstasy, while shadowy mermen and mermaids swim around her like dreams. Thank you, Hine Te Ariki, for giving my daughter back to me. Protect her and her elder sister Bianca, always.)

After Tumokonui died, Hine Te Ariki returned to the river from where she had come. Her daughter, Tonoa ki Aua, married Whakauika. She had two daughters, Pikihoro and Hineuru. She wanted a son, and consulted her mermaid ancestors, who instructed her not to wade or cross rivers, not to wash or bathe in them, nor even to drink water out of them but to quench her thirst from a special well and bathe in a special pool. Her son, when he was born, was named Tamaiuia. He became the warrior chief who safeguarded his people from the Whakatohea in the north, Rongowhakaata in the south, Ngati Porou in the east and the Tuhoe in the west. He was highly respected by his enemies and greatly loved by his friends. The tribe from whom I was descended, occupied the land marked on its western side by the rock named Puhinui at Waikohu, near Tahora. It was in this land that I grew to become a man.

Knowing that Hine Te Ariki was such a protector of her own children, perhaps it is not to be wondered at that Tiana, also, was such a protectress.

In my case, however, it went further.

12

The next day I joined Ani, my cousin Whai and local Maori at Parliament Grounds in welcoming the Land Marchers.

Te matakite, te matakite. 'The march promises be one of the most significant events of the decade,' Dame Whina Cooper said, 'and to the Maori people, it will be the climax of 150 years of frustration and anger over the continuing alienation of our land. Land means much more to the Maori people than it does to any other New Zealander. To us it has a deep spiritual value. You can realise our frustration over the first 150 years as we've seen our lands gradually fall out of our hands. Before the arrival of European settlers, the Maori had 66 million acres of land; today we have less than three million. Matakite is deeply concerned as we see more acts brought in by Parliament which continue this process of alienation. These acts include the Town and Country Planning Act, the Public Works Act, the Rating Act and the Counties Amendment Act. Matakite wants to press for the abolition of monocultural laws pertaining to Maori land, and to establish new laws for Maori land based on our own cultural values. Matakite wants to establish communal ownership of land within the tribe as a legitimate title equal in status to the individual title.'

This was the kawa, the protocol of the march: every morning the marchers woke to prayer, assembling on the road and facing southwards. Whina would talk to them, saying, 'This is a tapu task that we are embarked upon. Remember always the sacredness and do not let it be demeaned by violence provoked in you by evil bystanders. Because it is tapu, remember that there will be no alcohol. Always pray to the Lord to bless us all on this march, for we do not march for ourselves but for the sake of our land, Aotearoa.'

Carrying the pouwhenua in front of them, the marchers began the day's journey. They forced themselves to attain at least 25 kilometres for, oh, the trip might be a long one but the time that was available was as short as the shadows upon the hills. They sweated their way through the hot sun and some of them, to feel the land, walked barefoot on it. Sometimes the way was made painful by broken glass strewn upon the verges by those who were hostile to the march. The marchers watched the sun rise to its apex in the sky and race its sunlight over the land.

When darkness fell, the marchers made for a friendly marae, there to be formally welcomed by the tangata whenua of the land. 'Haere mai ki te hikoi tapu e, haere mai, haere mai, haere mai . . .' the old women would wail. The elders of the marae would make speeches recalling other sacred occasions of the past when the Maori were in conflict with the Pakeha. After the welcomes, the marchers were fed and rested from their day's tribulations. They massaged their sore limbs and applied medication to wounds received from the stones and glass of the road. They stood under the showers or went down to the nearby rivers to let the liquor of the land caress them.

In the evenings, the marchers met with the tangata whenua in the meeting house to debate the purpose of the march and the need for the Maori to be as one people, unified against the Pakeha in the fight for the land.

'We lose our turangawaewae,' Whina would say, 'and we lose everything. We become like performers in a zoo, doing our haka for tourists, with Pakeha collecting the money. Far better for us to do our haka on our own land. Far better than to die on land that the

Pakeha has taken from us. We must fight, fight, fight, for not only do we lose everything if we lose our land. We also become nothing.'

Reaffirmed, the marchers would then sleep after each evening hui. But the mornings always came too soon, and the road was always there, and sometimes it was difficult to find the strength. 'Oh Lord, help us in our hour of need. And bless this march, oh Lord, for it is sacred to your purpose and that of your children of Israel.'

They were doing it for the land. 'We are stroking, caressing the spine of the land,' Hone Tuwhare wrote. 'We are massaging the ricked wracked back of the land with our sore but ever-loving feet.' It was all for aroha, and it was all in sadness. And as had been commanded, not once did the pouwhenua touch the ground that it was carried over.

When thousands of supporters crossed the Auckland Harbour Bridge, television coverage beamed that awesome event to every home in New Zealand. The bridge swayed ominously during the crossing and police and traffic officials watched anxiously as the wave of supporters swelled and poured up Queen Street.

Again, television and the new media were there to witness the approach of the Land March upon Wellington. They made an impressive four-lane-wide column down Ngauranga Gorge, along the Hutt motorway and up to the gates of Parliament.

Five thousand people arrived chanting, singing the Matakite song, calling 'Make way, make way'. The waiting crowds burst into applause at the sight and sound of the magnificent assembly.

It began to rain, an appropriate sign of aroha bestowed by the gods.

In silence, the Memorial of Rights was unravelled in the forecourt of the Paremata of the Pakeha.

'You will find that your march is not in vain,' the Prime Minister said.

I could not help remembering the time, in 1949, when my grandmother, Riripeti, had also brought her petition before the Prime Minister. Over twenty-five years had passed and had the Maori been successful? No.

Both Ani and Whai knew what I was remembering.

'If it doesn't work this time,' Whai said to me, 'you know what your destiny is, don't you, Beloved of Riripeti.'

ᕒ

The land, always the land.

The Maori people possessed it, but the white man has always lusted for it. From the very beginning of Pakeha colonisation in 1840, many Maori tribes opposed the sale of land. Let's admit it: the Land Wars began when the Maori lost the upper hand in Aotearoa, and particularly around 1858 when the census revealed that in a small space of thirty years there were already more white settlers than indigenous dwellers. The views of Maori and Pakeha about the future of the country were absolutely incompatible. The Government attempted to buy more and more land, urgently needed by the Pakeha settlers; the Maori people considered these attempts to be against their express wish to retain it. So the long wearying war began, which the Maori people appropriately called 'the white man's quarrel'.

The Land Wars lasted from 1860 to 1881. They were mainly a series of pitched battles in which each tribe made a final, desperate stand on its tribal domain: Atiawa at Waitara, Waikato at Rangiriri, Ngati Maniapoto at Orakau, and Ngai Te Rangi at Gate Pa. In such circumstances defeat and perhaps death were honourable. No Maori patriot hesitated to fight to the last for tribal land. But the war was lost, the war over the body of Papatuanuku, and the Maori throughout the land tasted bitterness. We had to endure confiscation and become no more than a black slave in the new antipodean white South. Altogether, 3,215,172 acres of Maori land was confiscated in the Waikato, Taranaki and the Bay of Plenty to pay for Maori insurgency. (The slave handler's whip cracks above their heads, 'Get back, niggahs, back into line, and keep them little nigrah piccaninnies from a-cryin' afore they feel the massah's lash.') Of this area 1,341,362 acres were subsequently purchased or returned, mainly to loyalist Maori. The rest—and the best—was retained by the Government for European settlement. The European victory was final. Time and numbers were on their side. They were like a plague of locusts in the land of Egypt.

And the manner of the confiscations? Oh, how superbly inept this was, for little heed was taken of the degree of 'guilt' of the 'rebels'. Some tribes, like Maniapoto, lost no land, though equally involved in the conflict as Waikato, who lost almost all their land. Ngati Haua, who fought at Rangiriri, lost very little; and Ngai Te Rangi, the defenders of Gate Pa, had most of their land returned.

The white man's peace was worse than the white man's war for, after the war, the struggle for land entered a new and in some respects more dangerous phase. Under the Native Lands Acts of 1862 and 1865 the Crown's right of pre-emption was abolished, a Maori Land Court was established to individualise Maori land titles, and European settlers were permitted to purchase land directly from the individuals named in the court's orders.

Oh, it could make you weep, but the Pakeha foisted this one on the Maori by claiming that individualisation of land title benefited Maori also by giving them the same rights and privileges of European citizens, including representation in Parliament. But individualisation had most disastrous results for the Maori who became involved. Transactions were swift and shady, the land speeding from beneath the toes of the Maori; they caused tremendous friction between Maori and Pakeha and, tragically, Maori and Maori. Maori agricultural production declined as Maori lived off the proceeds of land sales; tribes were divided as individuals defied chiefs to sell land and, prompted by interested Europeans, carried their disputes into the new arena of the Maori Land Court. A wave of demoralisation swept over the districts concerned.

In New Zealand, only one horseman of the Apocalypse was needed to bring destruction to the Maori. He was white and he carried a carpetbag into the new South. As he rode the country, he scooped the Maori and his land up with his scythe and, opening his carpetbag, put them both in it. This is how he rode into Poverty Bay and the East Coast: he sent his scythe to pursue Te Kooti through the Urewera and, into his carpetbag, he began to gather the lands of the nationalists—those sections of the East Coast, Poverty Bay and

Wairoa tribes who had gone into open rebellion in 1865.

Oh, but the muddle! Confiscation began with the deceptively simple proposition that the Crown should be ceded all land between Lottin Point and Lake Waikaremoana, on the understanding that it should keep the land of the rebels and return by way of a Crown grant that of non-rebels. The deed of cession supposed that it was possible to identify these two groups and that useful tracts of land could be taken from rebels only. This was still the unreal theory when the Crown introduced the East Coast Lands Titles Investigation Act, 1866, under which it was proposed that only those land interests of the rebels would be taken and given to the friendly natives who had fought against the rebels or, optionally, some military settlers. In 1867 it was a matter of 'change lobsters and dance' as it soon became apparent that it would take many years to separate the land interests of the disloyalists from those of the loyalists. Instead, it was proposed that the loyal chiefs should magnanimously and voluntarily hand over blocks of land in Poverty Bay, Wairoa and on the East Coast as representing the land interests of the rebels; in turn, the Crown would waive any claim to rebel interests outside of the blocks so ceded.

What a military two-step! What a quadrille! The Maori who had fought for the Crown were confronted with the humiliation of handing over to the Crown tribal land as the fine for the rebels whom they, the loyalists, had fought against. The Pakeha certainly moved in a very mysterious way! The Wairoa chiefs ate crow and handed over a substantial area at Marumaru; it was promptly turned into a military settlement. The poor Ngati Porou in October 1868 were told, rather unfeelingly in view of their part in the 1865 fighting, that the area which they offered was too small. What a to do, what a performance! The Poverty Bay chiefs kept their lips tight and their lands close to them but, aue, the Crown had made a promise to members of the Hawke's Bay Defence Corps who had fought in the Hauhau War that it would find lands upon which to settle them. Thus it was that the Native Minister, J.C. Richmond, proposed towards the end of 1868 that the loyal chiefs of Te Whanau a Kai, Te Aitanga a Mahaki and Rongowhakaata be required to cede the whole of their tribal lands to the Crown on the condition that those portions which were found by the Native Land Court to be the property of friendly natives would be returned; this was the way in which the Pakeha rewarded their Maori supporters. The deed of cession was signed on 18 December 1868.

But change partners and waltz, folks, for this arrangement fell through and all that was left was a simple agreement in 1869, registered by the Poverty Bay Crown Grants Commission, that three Poverty Bay blocks were to be given up to the Crown: 5000 acres at Ormond, 57,000 acres at Patutahi, and 735 acres at Manutuke. The fun started with the carving up of the land among those who had been pro-Government. It was decided that the ceded blocks should be divided into three portions: one for the loyal Ngati Porou, another for the loyal Ngati Kahungunu, and the third for the Crown. It was also agreed that the European soldier settlers should receive their land at Ormond, that the Ngati Porou should get theirs out of Patutahi, and that the Ngati Kahungunu should be provided for out of the Te Arai lands.

Four years later, the bickering about the carve-up was still carrying on about who should get what; and on 7 December 1872, Wi Pere and others were urging that Patutahi should be returned to the rightful owners and not given to Ngati Kahungunu or Ngati Porou or military settlers. It was a ridiculous situation because with the confiscation many rebels outside the blocks confiscated were not affected and many loyalists within the blocks taken away were therefore discriminated against. As a punishment this confiscation was a piece of folly and a source of ill-feeling between Maori and Maori, and between Maori and Pakeha. It was on this ill-feeling that the city of Gisborne was established—on land either purchased for a couple of blankets and some pretty ribbons or confiscated by the Crown.

You, the Crown, listen: you have the distinction of being at once both ineffective and vicious. While individual settlers can be charged with haste, their land dealings were certainly more effective and just. Oh, Poverty Bay, the settlers began to roll in and make great inroads into Maori lands. They advanced across the flood-plain of the Waipaoa River. They claimed the rolling country adjacent to it and along the coast north and south of Poverty Bay. By direct sale or by leasehold the settlers began to take the lands radiating out from Poverty Bay, along the coastline in either direction and inland along the river—Kaiti, Pouawa, Whangara, Whataupoko, Maraetaha and Pakowai, Te Arai, Repongaere, Ngakaroa, Ruangarehu and Pukepapa; and Okahuatui, Waikohu, Rangatira, Whatatutu and Mangataikapua.

More legislation was devised to control the passage of land from Maori to European, a multitude of enactments which can have few equals for ineptitude in the history of colonisation. First, there were the acts of 1862 and 1865 setting up the Native Land Court and defining the procedures by which land could pass from Maori to European. Amendments of 1867 and 1869 and an act of 1870 attempted to protect Maori both from buyers and from themselves. Next, in 1873, a further amendment radically altered the whole alienation procedure by attempting totally to individualise Maori land ownership.

Maori people everywhere attempted to hold back the flood of land to the Pakeha in power.

On 15 August 1873, the first sitting of the Native Land Commission in Gisborne was the scene of disorder of a magnitude that had never before been witnessed in any court in New Zealand. Maori activists who held that all transfers of Maori land to the Crown should be repudiated arrived to protest the Commission's deliberations. When the first case was being read, the protest began until the judge proposed that the court be cleared of all natives except those directly concerned with the business of the Commission.

A journalist at the sitting later wrote of the protest, 'On a preconceived signal given by someone in the crowd the natives rose en masse and, amid cries of "Korero parau!" (false evidence!) and "Kokori! Kokori!" (Rush! rush!) effectively putting an end to all hope of further business being transacted. Captain Richardson and his small force were active in their efforts to eject the more prominent among the rioters and they got a little rough usage in the scuffle. Sergeant Shirley's head came into contact with a square of glass and the noise when it broke added to the tumult outside, giving rise to a suspicion that the Maoris really intended to carry out their threat (pretty freely expressed) to attack the courthouse and destroy the maps and other property of the commissioners. Captain Porter rendered good service, and, eventually, the court was cleared and the doors locked. Outside, however, the excitement became intense, and it was certainly only due to the fact that business had been entirely suspended that open hostilities did not break out.'

Sounds familiar, doesn't it? Like court cases involving Maori protests in the 1970s and 1980s? And just as is the case today, the Pakeha in power didn't like the protest at all ('Back in line you nigrahs, back I say.') It was the settlers who said to the Government, 'You must be firm with the natives. If you let them have an inch they will take a mile.' There ensued the quite farcical situation of the Government making a military and naval demonstration to show the natives just who was the boss. No sirree, no native was going to boo the Crown and get away with it!

First the Government instructed the judges to adjourn the sittings of the Native Land Commission until November 1873 when, hopefully, the unrest among the natives might have subsided. But just in case, HMS *Basilisk* (Captain Moresby, after whom Port Moresby in Papua New Guinea is named, was at the wheel) steamed onto the horizon and anchored in Poverty Bay. A fancy mock military manoeuvre then took place in which the district's defence forces were called upon to repel efforts of the marines from HMS *Basilisk* to land on the shores of the Turanganui River. At 10.30 a.m. the marines entered the river mouth under cover of the warship's guns, the guns booming, booming, booming their imposing power in loud echoing thunder across the township. The watching townsfolk applauded daintily and twirled their canes or umbrellas at the sight of the pretty sailors in their pretend assault. Perhaps it was a wee bit too realistic for the ladies though, especially when a cannon was discharged opposite Read's wharf and caused some of the mounted men to be thrown off their startled horses. Nevertheless it was a jolly good show, what with the local boys keeping up a smart fire against the marines.

Oh yes, bravo, pretty sight. But wasn't it a pity that the natives didn't even bother to turn up to witness the display! What a cheek. After all, it was mounted for them. Just to warn them to pull in their heads. Hmmmph!

The irony of it all was that when the Commission finally held its sittings, the Crown told the natives that all lands taken from them would be returned except for Te Muhunga, Patutahi and Te Arai. The quadrille had been danced ineffectively and the lobsters had thoroughly confused themselves in a mass of heads and tails and threshing feelers, falling about in the middle of the dance floor.

But the fight to retain land in Maori control was far from over. Indeed, it had only just started. Sure, at least Maori weren't forced onto reservations like the Red Indian nation of America when they were defeated; but who is to say that we might not have been better off in maintaining this kind of physical exclusivity? And yes, the Crown could have pre-empted Maori land entirely in the white supremacist manner but they knew that if they did then we would surely have risen up this time, as a nation, to defeat them.

Nor did the people of the land taken at Te Muhunga, Patutahi and Te Arai just lie there and enjoy being raped of their heritage. Over the years following the 1873 decision they persisted in accusing the Crown of having received more land in compensation for rebel activities than it was entitled to: a total area of 56,161 acres in the three blocks that were ceded.

The protests took a long time to bear fruit and it wasn't until the Royal Commission of 1920, presided over by Chief Judge Jones, that the injustice was recognised. The Commission held that the Crown should not have received, in the aggregate, more than 30,000 acres; it therefore reckoned that there was a surplus of 26,161 acres to be returned to the Maori people.

Twenty-nine years elapsed and the people of those blocks continued to feel the land coursing in their blood. They tried all ways and means of getting it back. It was their soul. It was their body. It was their spirit.

In 1949, the people heard that a hui about Maori land issues was to be held in Wellington. The Prime Minister would be there.

It was then that the matriarch decided to take an ope to the hui and demand that the Government finally settle the account and return the land to its rightful owners.

Tama tu, tama ora; tama noho, tama mate.

If you stand, you live. If you lie down, you die.

13

A week after the Land March, a storm came rolling up from Antarctica. There was only one way to describe the relentless wind and freezing cold: inescapable. It was as if both the wind and the cold had agreed to come not only from the south but also from every other compass point and flail the city with wave after wave of icy spears. 'Let us in, let us in, oh let us in.'

'I think we'll move north,' I said to Regan. 'Like the ducks.' We were in bed, listening to the storm as it howled about us. I thought of the small group of protestors still at Parliament Grounds; when the marchers dispersed they stayed on, wanting to be a reminder to the Prime Minister to give us back the land.

'Don't expect any sympathy from me,' she answered. She was referring to the fact that I had only recently returned from a conference on indigenous cultures in Hawai'i. She presumed that I had spent a lot of time soaking up the sun (true) on the beach at Waikiki (it was boring), so how could I possibly complain about the cold when I had missed the worst of the weather? 'And keep your cold feet on your side of the bed,' she said.

But I knew she didn't mean it, so I huddled in even closer.

'You're pushing your luck,' she said.

It was then that the telephone rang downstairs. Half-past eleven. I leapt out of bed and moved quickly downstairs to the living-room. The phone kept ringing, ringing. As I picked it up, I could see the full moon being shredded by swift-moving clouds.

'Is that you, son?'

It was my father, Te Ariki. I tried to keep myself calm, but the moon suddenly shattered and the clouds obliterated its light.

(Telephone calls late at night always bother me. My mother Tiana, of all those in my family, knows my anxieties, and no matter if it's day or night, never calls unless it's really important. Most times it's to say, 'Be careful this week, son. Are the girls all right? How's your health? Oh yes, if you're driving tomorrow, don't speed. If you go over three potholes as you are driving along, stop.' All mothers have an empathy to some degree with their sons and daughters— that special sight into ominous happenings which lingers long after the birth cord has been severed—but in Tiana, it's something inexplicable, frightening. In 1973 I was attending a conference of Pacific nations in Canberra, Australia, when I had to be rushed to hospital with acute peritonitis. I was able to ring Regan in New Zealand just before the operation, and I said to her, 'Don't tell Tiana.' It was only after the abscessed appendix had been successfully removed that I telephoned her. She lashed out at me, 'I've known for weeks that one of my sons was in danger, but I thought it was Mana. I kept seeing his face in a dream and I said to him every day, "You be careful, Mana." You and Mana are so alike. I should have realised it was you. When are you going to let me back into your life?' Her voice was smouldering with anger.)

'Tena koe, Dad,' I replied. 'Is everything alright at home?'

'I'm not ringing from Waituhi. I'm down here in Wellington. I just blew in with the wind.'

The moon came back again. Te Ariki, in Wellington? I wondered why Teria, Erina or Vanessa hadn't let me know. Te Ariki was such a wanderer, always dropping in on one of us at the most inopportune times, that we had organised an 'early warning call' system. If ever he was on his way to Wellington, Teria would ring Erina in Napier and Vanessa in Palmerston North. 'Batten down your hatches,' she would say. 'Prepare to repel all boarders. Your father is on his way down. And don't forget to act surprised to see him.'

When I had been a student, and before Regan was in my life, I had relied on Teria's calls to enable me to get rid of the previous night's 'guest', tidy the evidence of lustful activity, and to be at the door, the very picture of clean-living youth, to say, 'Oh, Dad. What a lovely surprise.'

'I'm here with your grandfather,' Te Ariki explained. 'He's dead set on getting to America.'

There are times when my family just don't make sense. They come out with statements in the form of conclusions, without providing the necessary explanations. Apparently Grandfather Ihaka hoped to join a Maori concert party which was to tour the western seaboard of the United States—Los Angeles, Las Vegas and other entertainment capitals. He had in fact put money into the enterprise on the assumption that that would assist his selection. (The trip would have been, I might add, his second to America, his first being to Utah two years earlier. So much for the assumption that Maori don't travel abroad!) It was all turning out to be an expensive flop: the money that Grandfather had put into the venture was to help finance it, but not enough had so far been raised. So he'd come down to offer more cash—with the proviso that he be a member of the group.

'You know what your grandfather is like,' Te Ariki said. 'He's been making himself a nuisance wanting to go on the trip. I told him I wasn't going to let him. He's too old and too sick, and he would only get in the way. He's been at Floria's place all winter. He wanted her to drive him here, but she wasn't having that on. Then he rang Hiraina to bring him, and I think he was expecting her to melt like in the old days. But she said, "No way." She really went at him, saying, "Why don't you act your age, Dad, instead of travelling to the other side of the world?" So he rang me then and said, "Son, I want you to take me down to Wellington." Of course I said no too. Next minute, Floria is on the phone saying I'd better come over there as he was getting out of bed, getting dressed and threatening to drive himself all this way. Well, if his mind was made up and if he was that determined, what could I do?'

'You were obedient to him,' I said sarcastically. Grandfather Ihaka always got his way. As arrogant as ever.

Te Ariki paused. 'I ask you again, son,' he said, 'what could I do? When I got to Floria's he was already dressed and waiting for me in the kitchen. He had on his red bandanna and a hat over it. And his coat. He looked like a shrunken old man, and my heart just went out to him.'

Oh yes, I could just picture Grandfather, milking every ounce of pity from the situation, wizened, old, purposefully appearing fragile and pitiful, and playing on the emotions of the family. If arrogance won't work then try sentiment, that's the strategy, isn't it Ihaka? Nice one, old man.

'Well, Floria was still arguing against his trip,' Dad continued, 'and he was just sitting there, leaning on his walking stick, breathing heavily. She asked him, "Who's going to give you your injections when you're down in Wellington, eh? And when you are in America? And who's going to look after you? Those air hostesses won't want to wipe your bum for you and those Americans won't want to clean up after you and those people in that concert party will be too busy enjoying themselves to be able to look after you." She was going on about what the doctor had said about his blood pressure, his sugar diabetes and his heart, and it was all news to me. She was crying and carrying on and I told her to stop it. She turned on me and said, "And what do you know about this, Te Ariki? You know nothing. I've been looking after the old man for six years now, me and Hiraina, and the only time we ever see you, brother, is when you feel like turning up here. I don't want the old man to go down to Wellington. I don't want him to go to America."'

Te Ariki's voice was strong and proud. It was as if he was building himself up into being the good, fine son, come to rescue an old man, his father, from the clutches of conniving daughters. 'I had both of them at my throat,' he laughed. 'My two sisters, boy oh boy, can they talk. Hiraina was so wild-looking, saying, "Look here, Dad, I've just got back from Tangihanga and what do I hear? You want to go to

America, how stupid! You're not going anywhere, not in your present state of health. You're sick, Dad, sick."' Te Ariki paused again. 'And you know, son, all the time they were talking, your grandfather was just sitting there, staring into nothing. Then he looked at me and said, "Well, Te Ariki, are you going to take me or not?" And I said, "No." So he said, "Will you give me the keys to your car?" And your Auntie Floria said, "You haven't got a licence, Dad." I shook my head and told him no. And Hiraina said, "You know that the doctor told you it would endanger your health to travel. You could die." Then the old man really broke down and began to cry. He looked at each one of us in turn and asked, "Am I your father, Te Ariki? Am I your father, Floria? Am I your father, Hiraina? If I am then you should cleave to me as it says in the Bible: 'Love thy mother and thy father.'" By that time Floria was really sobbing her heart out. And Dad heaved himself out of the chair and said, "Well, it sounds like you fellas have already dug my grave for me, right here in this house. If you won't let me out of here I might as well go to the bedroom and die right now." With that, Hiraina let out a long cry. I just shrugged my shoulders. 'Okay, Dad," I said, "I'll take you to Wellington."'

'You should never have brought him.'

'It's too late to think about that now,' Te Ariki replied. 'We're already here. Floria came with us. She wasn't going to let Dad come down without her. All the way she was saying, "If Dad dies, Te Ariki, it will be you who is responsible."'

'And so it will be,' I said.

'Well he hasn't,' Te Ariki answered, his tone hardening. 'And at least I've made him happy bringing him. Better to make him happy than to have him staring at four walls waiting to die. Better to have him hoping for a trip to America than just sitting in Floria's house. But the trip's been a waste of time. The organisers of the America tour don't want your grandfather's money—not if he is to go with them. They've turned him down. When they said, "No", he took it very hard.'

I closed my eyes. My foolish father, Te Ariki. Building up the hopes of an old man, knowing that they would be dashed.

'Anyway,' Te Ariki added, 'your grandfather wants to see you and

Regan before we go back to Waituhi. We're at your Uncle Alexis's place.'

'It's almost midnight,' I answered, evasive.

'Tamatea,' Te Ariki began firmly. 'I know things are still bad between you and your grandfather. I know you've never gotten on. But remember your whakapapa, your genealogy. He's the eldest son. I'm his eldest son. You're my eldest son. He wants to see you, the one who will have his mantle when he dies.'

My anger flared. 'Me? I'm the last person Grandfather Ihaka has ever wanted to inherit the cloak of leadership.'

'Give him another chance, Tamatea. It will mean a lot to him. It will mean a lot to me. I would like you and him to have a reconciliation. Will you come? Will you bring Regan? You've hardly seen him over the last few years. He might want to give you both a blessing. You know how proud he is of your accomplishments. He's always talking about you.'

Lies, Te Ariki, lies. I closed my eyes. I could feel my soul trembling as if it was ready to burst apart and unleash a cauldron, volcanic, white-hot and burning with insanity.

'Blood matters, son.'

Outside, the clouds were broiling in the heavens, conjuring up old remembered shadows like dark wings being cast over a boy and his grandfather, shadows bearing pain, anger and unforgiveness. The light was being squeezed out between earth and sky.

'It is your duty.'

The wind came up. I had a vision of my father and Aunt Floria, driving through storm clouds, bearing Grandfather Ihaka down to the windswept city of Wellington on a golden chariot. He was a splendid emperor, autocratic, triumphant, having achieved his way.

'Don't leave it too late,' Te Ariki said. 'The trip down here has tired him out. It's so cold too, and I think he's feeing the chill. He's having a sleep at the moment. Then we'll have kai when he wakes up. You know, he only eats the old Maori kai now, takes it everywhere with him, especially the kao, the dried kumara.'

My anger began to subside. 'All right, Dad,' I answered. Yes, blood did matter. And I knew my duty.

'Good. I love you, son. I know your grandfather does too.'

I put the receiver down. Regan came to stand by me and to calm me down. She nestled gently against me. 'There, there,' she said. 'There, there.'

'Dad's brought Ihaka down to Wellington. Grandfather says he wants to see me and you.'

'So we're going,' Regan said.

'I could do without it.'

'You know that you have to go. You might never see your grandfather again. You might regret that for the rest of your life.'

'No, I'll have no regrets. But, yes, we will go to see him.'

Regan hid her face in my shoulders. When she looked up at me her eyes were gleaming with tears. 'Sometimes you frighten me,' she said. 'Sometimes you can be so unforgiving.'

She walked away to the bedroom. The house grew silent.

Blood matters. It is your duty. I know your grandfather loves you. He wants to see you. You are the one who will have his mantle when he dies. You might never see your grandfather again. You might regret that for the rest of your life. Mantle. Loves you. Blood. Duty. Matters. Dies. Regret. Blood.

Blood.

⁓

The active leadership of the tribe, the iwi, was generally a male prerogative. An ariki was born into his protected office and from birth was set apart and guarded by the people. He was looked upon as a divine person and he had rights and attributes all his own. He ate only certain sacred offerings. He settled all ecclesiastical affairs such as those relating to tapu. To him were brought the first fruits of the cultivations and of birds and of fishes. He was the curator of all the sacred relics and historical weapons and heirlooms of the iwi. Though he might lose his temporal power he could never lose his sovereign rights. He was essentially holy and an absolute necessity to the people. Such ceremonies as the blessing of the crops, the freeing of a war party from tapu and preparing it for battle, were incumbent on his presence. His life was even held sacred by an attacking war party, and if necessary safe conduct was allowed to him and his guardians. Many are the stories, too, that are told of the powers in magic and wizardry held by such ariki. The ariki-god-descended-one therefore bore a proud lineage from noble ancestors and wielded powers of regal dimensions even passing the temporal sway of kings. With absolute power of governing the people, he controlled their lives and property and could dispose of either at will.

Sometimes, however, it happened that the first-born of the senior rangatira line was not a male but rather a woman. She was then made a priestess and accorded the greatest respect as a wahine ariki. Not being taught in the whare wananga, which no woman was allowed to enter, she would not have the profound knowledge of an ariki. Nevertheless she held a high position among the iwi, though the degree to which such a one wielded power varied markedly from tribe to tribe. The East Coast tribes revered such high-born women and allowed them to speak in council on the marae. On rare occasions, a female ariki became in fact as well as in name the chief of her people. Among the descendants of Kahungunu were several such women: Hine Matioro, the grandmother of Te Kani a Takirau, of Whangara; Hine e koia, of Te Aitanga a Mahaki; Hine i rukuhia, the grandmother of Paora Te Apatu of Wairoa; Mere Karaka, the grandmother of Te Hata Tipoki, also of Wairoa; and Mahinarangi, the ancestress of the Maori King of the Waikato. These women attained special honour, occupying the position of temporal queens, and as such their lives were carefully guarded by their people, the iwi.

Riripeti Artemis Mahana was one such woman, a wahine ariki. Hers was a blinding presence, imperious and commanding, bidding me forever forward to battle with the world of the Pakeha.

My grandmother, the matriarch, has always been on the topmost poutama of my life. From the very beginning, my birth, she was present, waiting for me as I reached up and out of Tiana's womb and in triumph claimed the world of light.

It happened like this: my mother carried me for seven months, felt the birth pangs beginning two months earlier than expected, got dressed, and walked to the hospital. There, without any fuss or bother, she checked herself in and, nine hours later, I was born.

That's all there was to it. Nothing dramatic. No signs in the sky to appease Ani Thomas's expectations of something arcane. Te Ariki was 'off somewhere', Tiana said, and that in its way fits her story because he was never around to witness the important occurrences in the lives of the family. I understand that at the time he was scrubcutting on contract with Grandfather Ihaka somewhere up country in the Bay of Plenty. 'How was I to know that you would arrive early?' he asked. 'Too early, too late, you've never been on time. Not like your brothers and sisters.'

The doctor who attended my birth was Ivan King. He has gone into Te Po now, but I remember how tyrannical he was once to Tiana, threatening her because of some medical problem diagnosed in my younger brother, Matiu, who died when he was three. I do not know what the altercation was about; it remains one of those enigmatic incidents viewed through the mist of childhood recollection. The doctor's surgery smelt of antiseptic. Doctor King stood over Tiana, gesticulating at her angrily and pointing at me. Although my mother was stricken with grief about the second son doomed to die she lifted her face to the light and picked up a silver scalpel, forcing Doctor King to step back from her—and from me too.

Much later, when I was an adult, I visited the nurse who had helped at my birth. She lived in Auckland. It was from her that I learnt that Riripeti had been present when I was born.

'Oh yes, your grandmother was there all right, dear. I mean, not outside in the waiting room or outside the door but, you know, right there. Yes, inside the delivery room, my word. Heaven knows how she got in! Why, I can remember seeing this empty chair and then, next time I looked, there she was. It gave us all a shock to see her, just like the Queen of Sheba, my word. Doctor King was ever such a grouch and he shouted at us nurses, gave us a real telling off, and said we had to remove her. Oh, but everything was happening at the same time and, I don't know, I don't think she stayed all that long, but certainly it was right up until you were born.

'What was that, dear? Oh. Well, she was a most striking lady, very beautiful in a Roman sort of way. Not that you could see much of her. She had this black veil on and, from my recollection, I swear that she was wearing some diamonds—no, pearls they were—in her hair. Even if you couldn't see her face, you just knew that she was a striking woman. Oh yes, she had a walking stick in her hand. When you were being born, she stood up and came to stand in front of your mother to observe the birth. Not that your mother would have known. I mean, there were complications and we had to give her chloroform, the poor dear. So I don't think your mother knew at all about your grandmother being there.

'No, I can't remember much else. Goodness me, it was almost thirty years ago, after all. Anyway, why does a nice healthy lad like you want to know the gory details for, dear me! Best not to know dear, best not to know. What I do remember clearly, though, is that your grandmother began to chant. It was such a powerful sound, authoritative, and as she was chanting she was making actions with her walking stick, almost as if she was trying to help you to be born. You were the wrong way in the birth canal, dear, and your umbilical cord was twisted around your neck. And as she was chanting, you were struggling out of your mother. Your grandmother took a long look at you. Oh my, she became so still. Then she started to laugh and lifted you to the light, joyous. She kissed your head, breathed into you and held you in such a loving embrace. One thing did strike me as being rather strange—after all, she was your mother's mother-in-law—not once did she touch your mother.'

⌒

There are very few photographs of the matriarch. She was disturbed by the camera and once explained with a smile, 'It might see things that I won't like it to see.' Nobody who knew her can deny her beauty but not one of the witnesses to her appearance can quite define why she was so beautiful. It was more than a matter of bone structure. It had to do with presence. With charisma. With the feeling that here was a woman who was out of the ordinary.

'Yes, that's Artemis,' people will say when you show them the one photograph you have of her with the child, 'but there's something missing. It's her, yes, but it's not really her, either.' The photograph shows the matriarch standing in the middle of her people at Wellington in 1949. She is dressed entirely in a flowing black gown. Her veil sweeps half across her face but you can glimpse just enough to realise how breathtakingly stunning she must have been. Her features appear finely chiselled and her eyes seem very large in the broad high planes of her face. She has a large mouth and, below it, her moko curls like a green swirling stream. The pearls in her hair are like tears framing her face. She is beautiful beyond beauty itself, and it is a beauty which has been crafted from a deep sense of intelligence and wisdom.

In the photograph, she has a slight smile like a madonna. In front of her is the child. Her arms are circled around him.

It was my father, Te Ariki, who told me that Riripeti had wanted to adopt me, from the moment I was born, in the Maori tradition. 'Your grandmother wanted you as her own. It's the Maori way for the firstborn grandson to be raised by the grandparents. So your grandmother wanted you. She loved you, son. And it was our tradition, because I was brought up by my grandmother also. Your mother, however, didn't want to give you up. Not at all, I don't know why not. When you were born, you know, she had a hard time with you. She didn't regain consciousness for six hours. She said to me that the first thing she saw when she opened her eyes was this huge black bird flying out of the mist. She thought it was a hawk coming out of the sky to take away a lamb. She'd been lambing at Joe Middleton's farm. But it wasn't a hawk at all, only your grandmother. She said to Tiana, "Give my grandson to me, e Tiana." But your mother said, "No." She was a new breed of woman. She wanted you for herself. She didn't want you to be taken from her.'

Indeed, Tiana must have had a lot of courage to reject Riripeti's request. My grandmother was not a woman accustomed to being denied what she wanted. Her beauty was a mere decoration of the person she really was. She was an ariki. She was a chieftainess of the Te Whanau a Kai, Rongowhakaata and Te Aitangi a Mahaki tribes of lowland Gisborne. She claimed her mana, her status and prestige by virtue of her whakapapa and her genealogy. Her descent lines bound her with the rangatira of the Maori people, joining her to the ariki lines of other canoe settlers, taking her backward in time to the first dawning when the gods communed with man. Beside her whakapapa, that of my mother Tiana proclaimed her as being a mere woman, a person of little account. Yet my mother said 'No' to the matriarch, despite Riripeti's clear right to take me as the tipuna wahine, the paternal grandmother.

At the time I first drew breath, the matriarch was in her fifty-eighth year. She lived with Grandfather Ihaka and most of my uncles and aunts at the old homestead at Waituhi. There, supported by her priest Tamati Kota and surrounded by the iwi and her faithful Ringatu worshippers, she ruled the valley and was the valley's provider of all things profane and sacred. I do not know when she married Ihaka, but it must have been around 1912. They had ten children, but just after the Second World War only four uncles— Uncle Alexis, who helped Tamati Kota in the religious Ringatu services, Uncle Pita and Uncle Manaaki, who were responsible for the valley's economic welfare and Uncle Danny, a gentle man filled with ineffable sweetness—were supporting Grandmother's duties. My two aunts, Floria and Hiraina, served the matriarch until my grandmother's eldest daughter, Amiria Circe Anderson, undertook secretarial services at the homestead; that is, until some dispute happened between them in the early 1950s. The two youngest sons, Cairo and Te Huirangi, were children.

My father, Te Ariki, had never lived at the homestead in Waituhi. He, like his elder sister Amiria and his two brothers Danny and Cairo, were adopted out. But in Te Ariki's case there was some other reason also. The matriarch had a purpose for him, it seemed, just as she did for all of her children. What it was I do not know, but once I caught him unawares and he said, 'Mum sent me to live in the Tuhoe. She wanted me to marry a girl from Ruatoki. But it never worked out. Mum was very angry.' I remembered then that the matriarch had told me of 'taumau' marriages, arranged between one tribe and another to seal political allegiances, the one iwi with the other.

Te Ariki was raised at Mangatu with his paternal grandmother, Kataraina, and for two years he lived in Gisborne itself. He has never talked about Kataraina, but I am led to believe that he loved her deeply. She certainly loved him because according to my aunts he had been spoilt rotten; he never wanted for anything. However, while he was still a teenager, Kataraina died. It was then that Riripeti claimed him back. She arranged for him to go to Nelson College to be educated and, when he had concluded his studies, she sent him to the Waikato. She wanted him to be an emissary between her people and the Kingitanga movement. To marry there, perhaps.

The trouble was that he met Tiana.

Te Ariki never elaborated on the arguments that must have occurred between the two women when I was born. 'Your grandmother was furious with Tiana,' he said. 'She really wanted to raise you, son, in the old Maori way. And when your mother wouldn't let you go—we were living at Crawford Road in Gisborne—she tried hard to convince us to live out at Waituhi so that, at least, you could be nearer to her. But your mother wouldn't budge an inch. She wanted us to remain in town, and that was that.'

Eventually they came to an agreement. My grandmother kept on visiting Tiana, saying, 'Give my grandson to me, e Tiana.' I don't think my mother gave in to Riripeti, but she finally accepted that, yes, Riripeti could take me to the homestead every weekend. So arrangements were made for me to be driven by car, every Friday evening, to Waituhi.

My grandfather most often came to collect me, although sometimes it was Tamati Kota, the tohunga to Riripeti, her priest and adviser.

'But that first night,' Te Ariki remembered, 'it was your grandmother herself. She arrived in the Lagonda, in the early evening, and she had dressed specially for the occasion. The moon was coming out and as she approached the house she began to karanga to you. Your grandmother always had a beautiful voice. Your mother met her at the doorstep. Tiana was holding you but I don't think your grandmother saw her at all. She never saw any of us, really. Only you, and you were such an ugly little thing. Scrawny. No flesh. You know what she said to Tiana? She reached up for you, stretching out her hands to you, and she said, "Give my grandson to me, e Tiana." Just like that. And as soon as you were in her arms, she took out this vial and sprinkled your head with it as if she was baptising you. Then without looking at me or your mother, she turned and took you away.'

'I used to feel sorry for Tiana, son. But what could she do? At least this was halfway to fulfilling her obligation to your grandmother. She came to dread those Friday evenings. You know how she is. All that day, if I was around, I could see her steeling herself for the evening. She would bathe you in the early afternoon and play with you and then bathe you again. You were her first baby; I suppose that must have been the reason. Then she would dress you in your long baby robes, pack a small bag with your food and milk, and wait. It wasn't too bad if your grandfather or Tamati Kota came. But if it was your grandmother, your mother could be so remote. Riripeti didn't make things any easier. "Give my grandson to me, e Tiana," she would say. And it was not a request but a command.'

'Once you were gone, a terrible stillness would descend on your mother. Her eyes wide and staring. Hardly breathing, as if she would never breathe again until you were back. She would lift her head to the light and dress herself in her long white nightdress and lie down. And she would say, "No matter what happens, don't wake me, Te Ariki, do you hear?" Then her feet would begin to paddle, as if she was swimming.'

'Of course life goes on, and when your mother had other babies to worry about—your sisters Teria, Erina and Vanessa—your absences became easier for her. That is, until you started to have the nightmares. Do you remember?'

The nightmares, the dreams, ah yes. They began, when I was five, to possess me whenever I was at Grandmother's homestead. Not even Tiana could banish them as I lay screaming through the night.

How could she? After all, she was the cause of them. Pursuing me, her feet paddling, dream swimming to me in my dreams.

'You will always be mine, Tamatea. Always.'

14

I nescapable was the rain, the roaring wind, the duty, as I drove again to the house of my Uncle Alexis. The night was like a desolate sea, howling in darkness, and the houses of Roseneath were like flotsam and jetsam tossed about upon its waves.

'Here we are,' I said to Regan. She nodded, bundling Bianca and Miranda in blankets and prepared to make a dash towards the door of Uncle's house. There it was, against the skyline, lighted windows like a ship receding away, away, away. I stepped out of the car and opened the door for Regan. The rain pierced us with its coldness as we ran through the night, past the flax bushes and into the shelter of the entrance. Aunt Roha's figure shimmered against the glass door as she opened it.

'Quick,' she said. 'Come inside.'

She averted her face from me so that I could not kiss her cheek. Perhaps it was merely accidental. Before I could ponder this, Te Ariki came striding down the hallway in that easy, attractive manner of his, a wide boyish grin on his face. He hugged his granddaughters in his arms and kissed Miranda so hard that she began to cry.

Then he looked at me and imprisoned me with his love. I reached for him and we embraced with passion. 'We never have much time together, do we my son?' he asked. 'But it is always good to see you.' I was puzzled at his meaning until he explained, 'No sooner do we get here than your grandfather wants to go back to Waituhi. After you've been in to him, ka hoki matou ki te wa kainga.'

'Tonight? In this rain?'

'The car's already packed, son. We'll be all right. Don't you worry. He wants to see Regan and the girls first. Then you after that.'

I nodded to Regan to go in to Ihaka with Bianca and Miranda; Aunt Floria accompanied her. I turned to my father, 'Let me be clear, Te Ariki,' I said, 'Regan and I came only out of duty.'

He smiled. Beneath the effervescent emotions I could sense his tiredness and strain. I regretted being so irritated with him on the telephone.

'Thank you, Tamatea,' he said. 'While Regan's seeing Dad, come and say hello to your Uncle Alexis.'

My Aunt Roha was sitting on a chair next to the pillows, holding Uncle's hands in hers. I kissed her and felt the salt tears upon her cheeks. My father sat himself on another chair and without speaking indicated that I should greet my uncle. In that moment, I realised how similar they were, the two brothers. The same patrician features, the wavy black hair, that look of Cesar Romero or Tyrone Power. What must it be like for one brother, Te Ariki, to look upon another and to know that some day, he also might be so helplessly bedridden?

'Uncle Alexis,' I said.

'Yes, I know you're here, boy,' Uncle responded. 'Welcome to the house of the blind.' He smiled reflectively. 'And the old.' He jerked his head down the hallway to the bedroom where my grandfather was talking to Regan and seeing the girls.

'Don't talk like that, Alex,' Aunt Roha said. 'You never used to give up so easily. Why, I remember when you were young—'

'We were never young,' Uncle Alexis answered. 'Or if we were, we were other people then. Not like now. Grown old and of no use to anybody.' He whispered to me in a guttural voice. Obscene words. 'Boy, you should have shot me. I'll up my price. Twenty thousand bucks if you do it. Shoot me in the temples. Right in the middle. Here. Here.' Then he laughed and turning to Te Ariki said, 'You remember that bull, don't you brother?'

'That's enough,' Aunt Roha cried. She looked at me. 'Your uncle should go back to Gisborne,' she said. 'He should go back with your father and Floria when they take your grandfather home tonight. Perhaps he can be healed in Rongopai. Tamatea, you tell him. Order him.'

'What's the hurry?' Uncle interrupted. 'I'll be there soon enough. In my coffin.'

That set Aunt Roha crying again and, at the sound, Uncle Alexis became a little gentler. 'Don't worry,' he said. 'And don't you worry, Tama. You know it's been so good to have my father here, and my brother and sister. The family is so important, boy. Remember that. We've been having a great time talking about the old days.'

The zigzag of emotions. 'That's the way,' Te Ariki said. 'That's the way to talk.'

'I've been asking your father,' Uncle said, 'about the land at Waituhi. You know, down by the river. It used to have willows on it. Remember? Oh how I remember those willows. Lying under them. Watching their branches drifting in the river . . .' His voice faded into reverie. Then he grabbed my arm, feeling the strong flesh, and I could sense the demons possessing him again. His eyes were staring up at me. They were wide and filmed with white. Ugly. 'I want to talk to you, Tamatea, about that land. I have a question to ask you. Have the spiders returned to it?'

The Place of the Willows? I looked at Te Ariki. His face was calm and impassive. I knew that look. Dismissive. Imperial.

Then Regan with Bianca and Miranda came out of Grandfather's room. Regan's face was like a pale star in the dark hallway.

'You'd better go in to see him now,' Aunt Floria said. 'Don't take too long. He's tired enough as it is and we have a long journey back to Gisborne tonight. Your grandfather thinks he can live forever.'

A dash of rain and wind shook the house. I got up and walked towards the room where Ihaka lay waiting.

Every person has an image of himself, more flattering in the conception than in the reality. It is only when you hear your voice on the tape-recorder or look at a photograph taken unawares that you realise how much idolatry lies in your self-perception.

In Grandfather's case, his self-image went beyond idolatry into the realm of deception. He always saw himself, as he does now, as a leader of one of the tribes of Israel.

He lies, aged and ill, in this small house, in a windswept street of a dark city settling into sleep. He is Ihaka, head of the Mahana clan. He is Isaac, as in the book of Genesis, and this night he wishes to assign succession and to place his mantle upon my shoulders. But in this, his own deception, he still fails to acknowledge that he has always lacked the charisma, the intelligence or even the sexuality of tribal leadership. He pretends not to recognise this fact—that his leadership is one of default. He simply survived the matriarch, his wife, by twenty years and on that has rested his own assumption of power, not on any innate qualities he ever possessed.

Picture him now, in this room. Propped up by pillows, he sits staring into a fire which has been lit in an antique fireplace to keep him warm. His body is a mere husk of what it used to be; there is nothing to it to explain why the matriarch chose him for her husband and for her bed. Eighty years old, his eyes are vacant of any natural wisdom; he is the one who should have died, not her. Beside her, this man is merely mortal and, yet, he has attempted foolish immortal games and has tampered with immortal concerns beyond his capabilities or cunning to complete.

The aging process has not been kind to him. The virility which one associates with a tribal leader has gone from him. The physical presence? That he never had. He is like a small wizened tuatara, unblinking and unsleeping, peering into the fire. Perhaps he is afraid to sleep for fear that death will come and snatch him away. Or, aware that death is the longest sleep of all, perhaps he wishes to spend every moment remaining to him awake. His eyes are black holes staring out of that impassive, coarse grey face. Look elsewhere for the patrician features of the family; look not here. Look elsewhere for the burning and perceptive intelligence; do not expect to find it in this man. See only an old man, swathed in blankets, eyes staring straight ahead and making no sign or acknowledgement of your presence as you enter the bedroom. The draught from the open door fans the fire to blaze a little higher. At least the burning theatricals lend some aura to the man who had always envisaged himself as patriarch. This is he, Ihaka Mahana, consort to Riripeti and adored by the Mahana clan.

Finally. 'Tena koe, Tamatea,' Grandfather said.

I approached the bed, leant down to him, and our noses pressed in the formal acknowledgement of the hongi, 'Tena ra koe, Grandfather.' I held the hongi for a few seconds and then, resisting Grandfather's wish to maintain the greeting, went and took a chair at the end of the bed. His face showed no sign of regret. We both knew that aroha was non-existent between us. Even so, we were able to show respect for each other and some measure of obligation to our blood relationship.

He was looking straight ahead and not at me. 'So. You've come. I was wondering whether you would or not.'

'It was Te Ariki's wish.'

'You've always done exactly what you wanted to do. I could never do anything with you, boy.'

'We've all done exactly as we have wanted, Ihaka. Look to your own actions for proof of that.'

'But you have never given me obedience. Or respect.'

The firelight flickered in his eyes. He fell silent. He went to say something, no doubt caustic, but changed his mind. It was then that he looked at me; in his eyes I seemed to see him as a young man.

'Your daughters are beautiful,' he resumed, attempting to reach out to me. 'He mokopuna ataahua. I am a very blessed man. My own loins were fruitful. My children's children have been fruitful. I have many fair and delightful grandchildren.'

'Yes, Bianca and Miranda are lovely girls.'

'And your wife, Regan. We had a good talk. She needs to understand more about the Maori ways. If she is ever at fault with our customs, you are the one to blame for not teaching her. Bring her back to Waituhi, Tama, so that she can learn. And why are you still here in Wellington? And why do you still travel all over the world? What can the world give you? Your duty lies in the valley.'

'When you took over from Grandmother,' I answered, 'you cut the umbilical cord connecting me to Waituhi. You exiled me, Grandfather. There was nowhere else to go except into the Pakeha world.'

'Yes,' Ihaka responded. 'Where you married a Pakeha, too, eh. But you should have married a Maori, Tama. And where is your son for the succession after you die? Daughters are all very fine—'

'My grandmother,' I reminded him, 'succeeded to chieftainship. And she was a woman.'

'But—'

'Do not be dismissive about my daughters, Grandfather. Or my wife.'

'You should have married Ani. She was our choice for you. She had the right genealogy and the appropriate tribal linkages back to us. Now even that alliance is at risk. Your grandmother married me to keep the tribal alliance. But you broke the arrangements between us when you didn't take Ani to wife.'

The fires were leaping dangerously. 'Ani was your choice, Grandfather, but not mine. I do my own choosing.'

'Yes,' he responded mockingly. 'You have always done exactly as you have wished.'

My knuckles showed white as I gripped the arms of the chair. Grandfather lapsed into silence. He kept looking at me, waiting for me to speak, but I was determined not to make things easy for him. The rain slashed at the windows, and the memories shrieked around us with the wind.

'You still play the piano?' he asked suddenly.

The piano? Oh, yes, Riripeti had given me a piano when I was a boy. 'Whenever I get the chance. Sometimes. Not often.'

'It was an extravagance, giving you that piano,' Grandfather said. 'I was against it from the start but your grandmother wanted to get it for you. And all because you had asked. I told her it would be a waste of money. I knew I was right—'

'I was only a child, Grandfather. When the piano came, I thought Te Ariki had bought it for me, he and Tiana. I did not—'

'—but she was always giving you things. Only you. None of the others ever got treated like you did. None of your other cousins—'

'—know it was Grandmother until I was older. But I gave recitals, Grandfather, and I played for her. I could have been a concert pianist but that was not to be the pattern—'

'—were loved as you were. And you might have played for her, but did you ever play for me? No, never—'

'—because she died. She died, Grandfather. And you still live.'

'—in all that time did you play for me. You never did.'

The old memories spilled out and across between us, inflicting pain. The piano symbolic of the gulf between us. Such a small memory, surely of little account, to cause such animosity.

But I was not going to give in to him, this old man trying to impose his will and misrepresentation of the facts upon my life and my grandmother. I would not capitulate. No. No. No.

I got up from the chair and went to the fire, stirred the embers to flame and watched the manuka log crackle and flare in the grate. The silence fell again between Grandfather and myself, but I could hear his breath whistling in and whistling out.

'Yes, Tamatea,' he whispered. 'Yes, I still live. And that is something that you cannot forgive me for, is it. Is it.'

'There's more than that, Grandfather. You know there's more.'

'You hate me, don't you, Grandson.'

'No.'

'I know you do.'

'I don't hate you, Grandfather. I just don't trust you. Grandmother always told me never to trust you—'

'She would never have said that, boy—'

'She told me, "Take care about your grandfather, Tamatea." Because she knew what you would try to do—'

'Your grandmother loved me, Tamatea—'

'Love? You never loved her like I did. It was because of you that she was made a cripple and had to use a walking stick. She warned me. She said you would try to take my mana from me—'

'She was crippled by accident, boy. It was not my fault. I warn you—'

'And she was right.'

'You might have loved your grandmother. But she was my wife.'

It was all so mindless. The arguing, always the arguing. I had once foolishly told my cousin Sammy that Grandmother didn't trust Ihaka, and Sammy asked my Uncle Pita if this was true. My uncle came to me and said, 'You know nothing, boy. Nothing.' Uncle Pita was like Grandfather also; misinterpreting the past.

The reflection from the fire gleamed on the rain-splattered window. Fire and water. Grandfather and I sat staring at the flames, consumed by our own passions. What was the use.

Grandfather tried again. 'I understand you just got back from Hawai'i.'

'Yes.'

And again he spoke, 'You didn't join the Land March?'

'No.'

'Your Aunt Hiraina went up north to join it. But it should have been you representing Te Whanau a Kai, not her. You're the one who should have done it. Not her.'

I sighed. I looked at my grandfather and instantly I felt ashamed. He was so small and vulnerable in that bed. 'Oh, Grandfather,' I said, 'what is the point? Why tell me what I should have done when you are the very person who has always stood in the way of my destiny? Let's admit that fact.'

His eyes grew wide. Tears tracked down his cheeks, and he began to sob, filling the room with that shocking sound.

'You are Te Ariki's son, that's the point. He is my son, that's the point. You are the eldest son of an eldest son, that's the point.'

'So you admit that now, Ihaka?'

His face crumpled with grief. 'I wish to give you my blessing before I die,' he said. 'I wish to give you the mantle of my mana. It was your grandmother's wish. It is now mine.'

Grandfather Ihaka opened his arms to me. I went towards him, in a world of fire and water, to receive the mantle of Riripeti.

And I heard voices chanting in the dark.

At long last, although the blessing had been denied me by my grandfather, I was now receiving it. The voices surrounded me in a cocoon of love, carrying me into some celestial sphere far from the earth, spinning me and spiralling me away.

But I felt myself going too far, spiralling too deeply into the pit of the night, spinning beyond all aid, and I became mightily afraid. I was falling back through Te Po, and the Twelve Changings of the Night, until I was surrounded by utter and complete darkness. So dark it was that I felt as if I had no form or shape at all. So black it was that I could sense it streaming through me, the terrible blackness. And even the blackness became more intense, more chilling, until I knew that I was in Te Kore, the Void.

'Kia kaha, kia manawanui,' the voices whispered.

I do not know how long I was in the Void. It could have been a second, or a year, or a hundred years, or a millennium. I thought I was going to die. I thought, this was what death must be like. I could not cry because I had no tears to weep. I could not call out in fear because I had no voice. I could not reach out because I had no form. In the Void, the Nothingness, I also was negated. Nothing.

But I formed a thought in the Void, a whimper of helplessness, 'Help me. Please, help me.' The thought circled outward in ever widening circles. 'Help me,' whimpering in the black jet of the forever night. It could have been just a second, or a year, or a hundred years, or a millennium. 'Help me. Help me.'

And I heard the voices chanting again, softly chanting in the pit of blackness. The voices seemed to comfort me, to tell me, 'Kia kaha, kia manawanui.' They reached down, down, down, through the blackness until they touched me. They surrounded me again with silver filaments of sound and, gently, I felt myself being lifted out of the nothingness.

I ascended out of the Void. I knew that I was journeying back through the Twelve Changings of the Night. The chanting grew stronger and louder as I voyaged in that timeless time.

Suddenly, I saw creation. I felt the first ray of light. I became part of the cauldron of energy which laid the foundations of the universe—of the earth and sky and waters, of the depths and heights, of the expanse of the skies and borders of the seas. I saw the gods. I saw the creation of woman. I saw legendary canoes glittering in emerald seas and escorted by fabulous creatures of awesome power. I saw a huge fish being pulled out of the sea by a magic hook, transforming itself into a cloud-steaming land.

The chanting became a karanga, calling me to come forward, to return, and the sound overwhelmed me with its glory. So I hastened, eager to be further embraced by the karanga. Then I felt many hands caressing me, fluttering over and across me. Anointing me. Bathing my gleaming body. Loving me. Whispering to me. Creatures of light filled the air with their songs and their laughter. I was ferried forward, ever forward, through benediction after benediction.

I felt myself returning through tribes and tribes of man, generation after generation, and gentle tears began falling like soft rain.

And a woman, with a madonna smile and teardrops in her hair, gently whispered to me, 'Nau mai, haere mai, e tama. Haere mai ki te Ao o Tane.'

'Welcome, come. Welcome to the world of Man and take your rightful place in it.'

～

The wind roared like a banshee around the house. It sucked all the air from the room, forcing Ihaka to open his mouth so widely that his face seemed to crack with the terror of needing to breathe. I was holding him in my arms as his body whiplashed forward and backward. Such a small, painfully wasted body, with its old heart fluttering like a dying bird within its skeletal cage.

'There, there,' I whispered. 'There, there.' I cradled his head against my chest. His spittle stained my shirt. It was pink with the presence of blood.

The fire in the grate burst into savage heat. In silence, Grandfather and I watched the burning wood, like white bones in the fine powdered ash. Ash to ash, dust to dust. We had been in the presence of ghosts. We had been making invocations to the past. We had cast runes among the embers. Now, exhausted, the old recriminations had been voiced between us. We had passed beyond that gateway called duty, beyond the politeness that should exist between grandfather and grandson, beyond even rage and tears, into that dark place of inevitable acceptance that neither blood nor duty would ever bring us to any emotional communion. Yet, he had wished to give his mantle to me and, oh, I had won, I had finally won.

'So it is done,' I said.

Grandfather was beyond answering. It was as if the decision to give me the mantle of Riripeti had required a price to be paid:

The price of Ihaka's life.

His face was gaunt. His body was a mere shell from which his eyes burnt brightly. I felt that I could snap him in two by exerting slight pressure on his chest.

I do not know how long we sat there, watching the flames. I think it was the closest we had ever come to one another, and I was grateful for that. For a brief moment I felt so sorry for him, oh so sorry.

I heard my Aunt Floria knocking on the door. 'Tamatea,' she called. 'Tamatea.' Her voice echoed in the room.

'One moment,' I responded. I took Grandfather's chin in both hands, cupping it so that he was looking into my eyes. 'Be at peace, old man,' I whispered. 'Find it, if you can.' Then I kissed him on both cheeks, first brushing the left cheek with my lips and, second, tracing my lips across his right cheek. His skin felt so hot. I left and walked to the door. In all that time, Ihaka did not look at me. When I glanced back at him he was staring into the fire. The flames in the dark room reached out to consume him.

'You were in with him long enough,' Aunt Floria complained.

'There was a lot that we needed to discuss,' I said.

I did not look backward again; I could not for fear that I might relent, might weaken, for in my mind's eye I could already see the single tear dropping like a pearl down his face, taking the colour of blood from the fire's reflection. But I did wonder whether Ihaka and I would ever see each other beyond this moment.

My soul softened with regret. It was then that I thought that

Judas had probably kissed Jesus in the same manner as Grandfather and I had done in our parting.

Te Ariki was waiting alone in the drawing room, staring out at the stormy nightscape. He looked so old and tired, so uncharacteristically vulnerable sitting there that I thought, 'Oh Te Ariki, one day my children will come to you for their blessing from your hands, and I will be waiting as you are now for them to return from bidding you farewell.' I knelt down beside him and he put his arms around me. His tenderness was profound, and I knew that he was reflecting on the time of his own succession when his grandfather had placed the mantle of leadership upon his shoulders.

But when he spoke, it was not about that at all. 'That elder granddaughter of mine, Bianca, is beautiful. She is just how your grandfather wanted his mokopuna to be. Fair and delightsome.' His eyes twinkled. 'She sure didn't get her beauty from you, that's for sure. Regan must have seen you in the dark.' He laughed at the joke.

'Hold me, Te Ariki. Hold me.' He understood my turmoil, letting the strength of his sympathy flow into me.

'So now all is complete,' he said.

'Yes. I suppose it is.'

'It is never easy, And you may not see your grandfather again, you know that? Perhaps I shouldn't have brought him down. Dad's not well, really, but I could never refuse him, I could never—'

Suddenly, in that world of fire and water, Te Ariki began to sob brokenly. And it was I who then was needed and my comfort was required, and I gave it as openly to him as he had done to me. I thought, 'I guess it must always be like this, the emotional whirlwind which heralds the approach of death and comes when the succession has been given.' And I listened to him, this man of strength, as he told me of Grandfather Ihaka and how wonderful a father he had been. It was a long journey through the territory of the heart, but one that I could not understand because my own relationship with Grandfather was inhibited by hostility. Even so, I could appreciate that there had been tender moments between my grandfather and his son, Te Ariki.

But Te Ariki misunderstood. 'I am so glad,' he said to me, 'that you and your grandfather have made peace with each other.'

Before I could answer, Aunt Floria came out of Grandfather's room. She looked across at Te Ariki. 'Well, he wants to get going now, back home to Gisborne. I don't know why we can't wait until morning.' Then she trapped me in her gaze. 'I don't know what happened between you and your grandfather, Tamatea. Whatever it was, may God forgive you.'

There were still a few more suitcases to be packed into the car—and blankets and pillows and boxes of tinned food that Uncle Alexis wanted Te Ariki to take back to the family in Turanga—so I helped my father take them down to the street and load them into the boot.

'Get your cousins to give you a hand,' Uncle Alexis shouted from the bedroom. 'Tell them to get out of bed. Roha, get the boys to give Te Ariki and Tama a hand. In bed all day and all night.'

But when Aunt Roha came out of the bedroom, Te Ariki said to her, 'Don't bother to wake them up. No use all of us getting wet.' So, together he and I hefted the suitcases and other belongings down the path. The rain lashed us like a thousand whips. The wind seemed to wrap itself around us and to take away our body heat. In spite of the chill, I had to grin to myself, for this was so typical of Maori to carry everything with them whenever they travelled away from home—blankets, pillows, mattresses, clothes, kai, television—not to mention the sacks of kumara or maize or pumpkins or marrows that would be brought down to their city relations. ('You don't need blankets when you come to see us,' Regan had once said to my sister Teria. 'Don't worry about it,' Teria answered. 'We're used to our own blankets, and yours are too nice.') And I remembered once how I had persuaded Aunt Hiraina and Uncle Hepi to book into a motel. They stayed one night and it was 'all right', but the next night they were back to sleeping with relatives, unpacking the mattress and the blankets and laying them on the floor for 'a good night's sleep with our whanau in our own bed'. They carried their lives with them, my whanau, wherever they went, and packing and unpacking and packing again was an accepted pattern of the journeys they had made across the years.

'Well,' Te Ariki yelled. 'All packed and ready to go.' He was completely wet, right through to the bone.

'Not quite,' I yelled back. 'The kitchen sink hasn't been packed yet.'

He laughed and we began to tussle in the rain. Then he felt how wet and cold we both were and he motioned that we should return to the house.

'Everything all set?' Aunt Floria asked.

'Yes,' I answered. 'But you and Dad better lose some weight if you want to fit in the car as well.'

Aunt Floria gave a smile. 'Trust your Uncle Alexis to want us to take all that tinned food back.' But I could see that she was pleased that he had done this and had been able to maintain our custom of sharing kai. 'Well, you two better have a shower and get into some warm clothes. Tamatea, your Aunt Roha has put some of your uncle's old clothes out for you. They might be too big, but better to be dry.'

I was already shivering. I went to the bathroom and turned the shower on. I was halfway out of my clothes when Te Ariki came in. 'Can't I even have a shower by myself?' I asked.

He gave a snort as he shucked his shirt off, 'I've seen it all before.'

I answered, 'But there isn't room for the two of us.'

He looked down at my nakedness, paused, and then said, 'Well, if you bend that thing of yours to the right, maybe we'll just make it.'

Then it was time for our prayers. We all assembled in Uncle Alexis's bedroom—Aunt Roha, Aunt Floria, Te Ariki, Regan, Bianca and Miranda and I, and my cousins whom Aunt Roha had awakened. Aunt Floria had the Bible in her hands, the Paipera Tapu, the Holy Word of God. We were all silent, waiting for Grandfather to join us. I was feeling warm now, in Uncle Alexis's clothes. I had felt quite a shock putting them on. When I had looked in the mirror the family resemblance was so striking, and it was almost as if I was seeing my uncle and aunt, on their wedding day—my uncle was so handsome and sensual—standing there on the church steps while the roses showered upon them. The clothes fitted so well, and when I walked into the bedroom my Aunt Roha's eyes had become veiled with tears. For here was I, masculine and vital, and there was Uncle Alexis, wasting away.

The door opened and Grandfather Ihaka was there, supporting himself on two walking sticks. I had not realised, not at all, how ill he was until that moment. It was as if the thumb of death's dark angel was already pressing him into the ground. Aunt Floria went to help him. She seated him in a chair next to Uncle Alexis. She put the Bible in his hands. He looked at none of us. He closed his eyes and, at that signal, we too shut ourselves in the darkness of our own contemplation and turned our thoughts to God.

'Kua tae mai te wa kua timata ta tatou karakia,' Ihaka intoned. 'The time has arrived when we must begin our prayers. Hei inoi tatou.'

Prayers, prayers, always prayers. For as long as I could remember there had always been prayers. Prayers in the morning, prayers in the evening. Prayers when we had come together as a family and prayers when, as now, we were departing from each other's company. Prayers when we were sick, prayers when we needed forgiveness, prayers for the dead. And in the beginning they had been taken by Grandmother Riripeti, but now that she had gone, they were led by Grandfather Ihaka.

She had told me, 'Do not trust your grandfather. Be on your guard.'

Soon after her death Grandfather had been converted to a new religion, and such was the power of his grip on the family that he had persuaded them all to turn away from the Ringatu faith to the new faith. And the new faith dressed them all in white and led them down to the Waipaoa, where they were baptised by immersion like doves drowning in the water. All had been forgiven him, Grandfather, but that I could not yet forgive him. Even though the new religion was still as much a force of spiritual strength to the family as the old religion had been, it was not Ringatu, the religion of Te Kooti and Riripeti.

After the prayers were completed, Grandfather motioned to Te Ariki to come to him. Together, they laid their hands on Uncle Alexis's head and blessed him, for they had the priesthood of that religion.

The wind, the rain, the blood, the duty, the prayers, the priest-hood. And now it was time for farewell in that world of fire and water. Why are farewells always so shattering? My aunts wept together. My Uncle Alexis reached up from his bed to clasp his old father to him, crying, 'Dad, Dad, Dad,' over and over again. He did not want to let Grandfather Ihaka leave, perhaps realising that they would never meet again in this life.

I looked at Te Ariki, trying so hard to maintain his own calm but I knew, also, that he realised that this, his dearest brother, would soon be gone into Te Po. Finally, Aunt Roha had to wrench Uncle's arms away from Ihaka, and the agony of that physical separation made him arch in pain.

'Oh, go now,' she cried, 'oh, oh.'

So we left him, Uncle Alexis, and he was yelling,' Shoot me now, Tamatea.' And my cousins came to quieten him.

Aunt Roha attended us, coming down the path to kiss us all. Then I took Regan, Bianca and Miranda to the car and, returning, helped Grandfather Ihaka into Te Ariki's Holden. His face was filled with distress. 'Oh my son, Alexis, Alexis.'

I kissed Aunt Floria. 'You had better be Te Ariki's eyes and ears tonight. It is so dark and the road will be dangerous.'

'I will not sleep until we get to Turanga,' she promised.

I turned to Te Ariki. 'Regan and I will lead in our car,' I said. 'We'll take you out to the motorway.'

He nodded. I went back to Regan. Tears stained her face. I told her what we were going to do and she nodded.

I started the car. I watched in the rear vision mirror as Te Ariki switched on the headlights and followed. We ascended the street swiftly into the realm of storm and sky, and the square of light that was Uncle Alexis's bedroom slowly slipped away like a lantern on a bounding sea.

We hardly spoke, Regan and I, on that drive out of the city. But once, in the lights of an oncoming car, I saw her profile etched in grief.

'What's wrong, honey?'

'Nothing, Tamatea. Nothing. It was not easy. My time with your grandfather.'

I nodded. We fell into silence again.

I led my father out as far as the lookout to Kapiti. Then I stopped the car and waited for him. I saw the headlights of the Holden approaching and waved him down. I looked in the rear window. Aunt Floria motioned me over and said, 'E noho ra, Tamatea. Don't forget to look up your Aunt Hiraina. She's down here in Wellington with Hepi trying to find your cousin Raina.'

Te Ariki got out of the car and we embraced in the rain. 'I love you Dad.'

'Ma te Atua koe e manaaki,' he answered.

Then I saw Grandfather Ihaka tapping at the window. He was motioning to Aunt Floria to open it so that he could talk to me.

'Tamatea,' he began. 'I know you will never forgive me for what I did to you. But forgive the people, eh? It's time for the *mate* to be lifted. You can do it, Tamatea. You.'

Then they were gone. Te Ariki stepped into the car and I watched as they turned onto the motorway and streamed away with the darkness. I felt my heart going with them and the emptiness invading me with the acidity of longing and loneliness.

We were in the realm of fire and water. Regan and I were driving back towards the city. Suddenly her voice drifted like broken wings out of the darkness.

'I am so sorry, Tamatea,' she said, 'that I have not given you a son.'

The great Mother of the Underworld is Hine Nui Te Po.

Her father, Tane, one of the sons of Earth and Sky, fashioned Hine's mother out of the red earth. This was because all the children of Earth and Sky were males and Tane wished to have a wife. It was Papatuanuku who told him to make a woman from her own body. Tane did so, and breathed life into the woman and called her Hineahuone. By her he had a daughter, Hinetitama, the Dawn Maid. And it has already been written here that this was the first incest, when he took his daughter to wife.

It was Hinetitama who became Hine Nui Te Po. Overwhelmed with shame she left Te Ao, the world of light, and fled to Rarohenga. She reached the guardhouse of Poutererangi and sought entry from Te Kuwatawata, the guardian of the gateway. But before entering, she looked back and saw Tane following and weeping as he came. Unlike Eurydice in the Greek myth, she did not attempt to return with Tane. Instead she called to him, 'Haere atu, Tane. Hapai i a tatou tamariki i te Ao. Goodbye, Tane. Raise our children in the light. I shall stay here to gather them to me in death.'

She entered Rarohenga and became the Great Mother. It is she who awaits the neverending march of mortals to her domain.

When his time comes, Grandfather Ihaka will go to her.

15

A few weeks after Grandfather Ihaka had been in Wellington I arrived home from a difficult day at Foreign Affairs. I was one of only four Maori career officers and we were having huge difficulties in trying to create a Maori perspective on New Zealand's relationships internationally. I had been called in by the secretary and given a roasting for what he considered personal political interference: another Maori colleague, Atareta Poananga and I had published our views on the failure of Government to support decolonisation in French Polynesia.

Regan met me at the door. 'There's a parcel for you from Switzerland,' she said. 'I think it must be from Rhys.'

Rhys! That's right: I had written to him asking if he could help locate a family by the name of di Marchesi who may have offered hospitality to Riripeti during the time she lived in Venice. The parcel was somewhat ripped at the edges and my address was scrawled in the large and lazy letters only Rhys Rickard would have written. A book, a video and two manuscripts fell out. There was also a hasty note, virtually indecipherable, addressed to me:

Dear T,

This is not the long-promised letter with joy and beauty and light. Margaret and I are just too tired these days for flights of fancy and feel quite pedestrian despite our fabulous surroundings. There has been no let up at work this year and our August holidays were fascinating (Canary Islands with my sister's family; Marrakesh and Madrid) but exhausting. Perhaps that is why we are oblivious to the irritations encountered by the longer-term residents—the unreality of UN fraternising and the frustrations of never moving anything along perceptibly; plus the surprise when one finally gets to grips with Switzerland, that its economy is based heavily on hot money, immigrant labour and a fair dash of puritan hypocrisy. Still we soldier on and attempt to shift the issues of the day as quickly as we can during the week, thereby hoping for less strain and more effective use of weekends. Do hope you and Regan are well. All the very best. As they say in Aotearoa, Arohanui.

Rhys.

p.s.

Could you please forward the enclosed two manuscripts to Dr John Cranston. You can read them if you like. You've probably forgotten that my special interest is in whaling ships which visited New Zealand 1750 to 1900. The manuscripts are not 'real' books, just research.

p.p.s.

Apropos your grandmother. I must say that the possibility that she lived in Venice for a time sounds most interesting and intriguing. At first I thought that you were putting me on but, I suppose, QueeQueeg of *Moby Dick* fame wasn't the only Maori to sail the open seas. In fact, perusing the passenger lists on ships returning from New Zealand to American ports and Europe I am surprised to find Maori names appearing with some frequency. They were probably stowaways, or cooks or deckhands (joke) but, after all, didn't Hongi have an audience with Queen Victoria? And didn't she actually adopt a young Maori child? Then there's the mystery of Maata, Katherine Mansfield's friend, who reportedly visited the

Continent. I propose to go to Italy late next year. I will see what I can dredge up from the black lagoons of the floating city. Paolo di Marchesi shouldn't be too hard to find, if he exists or ever existed, that is. Meantime, you might find the book (enclosed) will help you while away the time until I next write.

I didn't read the manuscripts. I had previously phoned Dr Cranston on an earlier errand for Rhys, and I knew what the theses would be about—whether a particular whaling ship had left Boston on 23 or 24 April 1846. Academics were all the same.

'Well?' Regan began, 'what does Rhys say?'

'Nothing much. He's yet to go to Italy.'

'What's in the parcel?'

'Manuscripts for his friend, Dr Cranston. About an American whaling ship and whether it left on one day or another.'

Regan glared at me as well as her unlensed eyes would permit. 'That,' she sniffed in her pedantic way, 'is just as important as whether there is an "r" in borogoves or not. And there isn't.'

'Isn't what?'

'An "r", silly.'

I opened the book Rhys had sent me. It was about the *Risorgimento*. I was initially puzzled as to why he had sent it. Ostensibly, it concerned the nineteenth-century movement for Italian unification that culminated in the establishment of the Kingdom of Italy in 1861. Up until that time, Italy comprised a number of independent states under the domination of Austria.

Then the parallels between this history of Italy and the Maori fight for sovereignty during the Land Wars—they had begun just as the *Risorgimento* ended—hit me like a thunderbolt. Was this why Wi Pere had taken Riripeti to Venice? Had he been inspired by the *Risorgimento* to believe that she would be better educated there in political activism in the Venetian Republic, one of the last to be added to the Kingdom of Italy?

I read on, and the parallels became even clearer, particularly between the great patriot Garibaldi and the stirring epic accounts of his army, called 'I Mille', the Thousand, and Te Kooti, the 'Maori'

Garibaldi. Between Giuseppe Mazzini, the nationalist propagandist and Wi Pere Halbert, who tried to lead the Maori toward the same goal of unification against the Pakeha.

I played the video. It was called *Senso*, a film made by Luchino Visconti in 1954 and starring Alida Valli and Farley Granger. The action took place during the Austrian occupation of Venice, with Alida Valli playing a beautiful noblewoman falling in love with an Austrian officer. Everything about Alida Valli—her beauty, her grace and her emotional dilemma—reminded me of Riripeti. As I watched the film, I could almost see Riripeti herself, gliding through those sumptuous Visconti sets, and attending Verdi's *Il Trovatore* at La Fenice—for Verdi's music, too, was inseparable from the spirit of the *Risorgimento*.

Inseparable also from the story of the Maori, with its texts of a people looking for liberation in Aotearoa, and from my own story of growing up with a woman who was so much like a diva herself.

Riripeti, the woman who wore pearls in her hair and who, when she was born, had her hands around her own throat as if attempting to strangle herself.

ᶜ

The land, the whenua.

There came a time, just after I had turned five, when staying with Riripeti only on the weekends was not sufficient. Indeed, Grandmother formally claimed me at a Ringatu gathering at Rongopai and, when she did that, Tiana was powerless to stop her. From that moment began my education at the hand of the matriarch.

'My grandson, I have shown you the land of your ancestors. Now that you know the place of the heart, here in the Waituhi Valley, and have walked the proud land, that part of your journey is completed. E mokopuna, now begins your journey from Waituhi throughout the confederation and, then, to the pillars of the sky.'

('Is that what you remember?' Te Ariki once asked me, amused.

'Tiana still fought against Riripeti of course, but after all, she was the mother of three more children by then. I think what happened was that after your illness the doctor recommended a long recuperation. Riripeti suggested that you stay at the homestead and he supported her. And Tiana felt in the end that having you off her hands would leave her with time to concentrate on the others, eh!

'But I don't think your mother and I anticipated that you would stay out there at Waituhi for two years. I expect that your mother missed you, son. But in the end she accepted the situation. Perhaps she felt that two years was small payment, small concession, to your grandmother after having refused to give you up to her at your birth.

'Yes, I did hear that you were taken everywhere with the old lady in the Lagonda. Why did she do this? I don't really know, son. She loved you, that's all. She wanted you with her wherever she went. You certainly have a good memory. Are you sure it wasn't all a dream?'

Looking back, I remember mornings when Riripeti bent and kissed me awake, saying, 'E mokopuna, wake. It is time to go.' The pearls would be shivering in her hair, and the charms tinkled at her wrists. So many, many mornings were begun like this, before the two windows, Te Awatea and Hine titama, were blocked in by the dawn. I looked up into her face and she would smile down at me, curling a finger through my hair. There was such tenderness and, sometimes, a tinge of sadness in her glance; the Italians would define it as *morbidezza*. But it would be fleeting, like a bird's wing, before she became firm with me, saying, 'Come now. Kua tae mai te wa kua timata ta tatou haere.' Then she would sweep away from me, her long black veils folding around the darkness and taking it with her. Quickly I would dress and, as I slipped into my clothes, I would hear Riripeti calling to Uncle Alexis to bring the Lagonda round to the side of the homestead. Sometimes, looking out the window, I saw Grandmother there, with Tamati Kota beside her, and sometimes Grandfather, saying prayers in the dawn.

Then I would join them and after prayers were completed Uncle

Alexis would start the car and point it like an arrow at the dawn. ('A Lagonda V12?' a friend asked incredulously. 'What a beautiful and classical car. And you say that your grandmother owned a Lagonda V12? She must have had it shipped here just after World War II.') Riripeti and Tamati Kota sat in the back and, because Grandmother preferred me to sit with her, I was placed in the middle. How I loved that car! And how I loved listening to Grandmother and Tamati Kota discussing some issue or other, or going over financial matters or legal papers. 'Aue,' Grandmother said once, 'I need a secretary to handle all this.' Tamati Kota suggested that my aunt Amiria Circe Anderson, who then lived in Auckland, should be called to do the work. Riripeti smiled at me and thoughtfully said, 'One day, e mokopuna, this will be your task. You must grasp the tools of the Pakeha and understand them. Particularly, you must understand the words of the white man, not only what he says but what he really means.'

She began to involve me in the discussions. Sometimes they were about religion or about some legal problem but, most often, they were about land—litigation to have land returned, litigation to prevent land from being taken, or litigation to simply hold onto the land. 'We must be alert, always alert, grandson. We have to fight the Pakeha in his courts. Even his Parliament, if it is necessary.'

Speeding through the dawn in the Lagonda. Such a stunning car for a Maori woman to own, as dark and mysterious as she was herself. ('You could always tell if the Matua was at a hui,' one of her contemporaries told me before his death. 'There was always that great big black thing out there where everybody could see it. The rest of us came on horses or in dirty rundown decrepit trucks, but not Riripeti. She'd come sweeping silently down the road and, boy, that Lagonda of hers was always impeccable. Your uncle was sure good on the spit and polish.')

Sometimes Riripeti told me about the business of the day or of some controversy or other which was threatening the iwi. Always she would patiently repeat the whakapapa, the history of the people.

'The Maori are the tangata whenua of this land, e mokopuna, always remember that. Our tribal histories tell us of the arrival of seven canoes to this Land of the Long White Cloud. Remember? The *Tainui*, captained by Hoturoa, landed near Cape Runaway. It coasted northward and rested finally at Maketu, spreading its people inland from Tamaki in the north to Mokau and Taumarunui in the south. The people of *Te Arawa*, led by Tamatekapua and Ngatoroirangi, landed near Cape Runaway also and travelled widely in the Bay of Plenty and inland to Tongariro, naming and claiming the land as they went. The people of *Aotea*, sailed by Turi, finally settled in Patea. The *Tokomaru* began its voyage to Aotearoa in turmoil, made its landfall in the South Island and then, in its voyage northward, settled the north Taranaki coast from Mokau to New Plymouth. The *Kurahaupo* scattered its settlers mainly along the western coast of the North Island. The *Horouta* landed at Ohiwa and peopled the Ngati Porou area from Cape Runaway to Whangara. The *Mataatua*, commanded by Toroa, is the canoe from which the Ngapuhi, the Rarawa, the Ngati Awa, the Whakatohea and the Ngai Tuhoe people are descended. Remember them all, e mokopuna. Fix the history in your memory.

'Pay special attention to the *Takitimu*. This was a very sacred canoe, captained by Tamatea ariki nui. It brought the gods from Hawaiki to Aotearoa. Without them the land would not have been able to be made sacred.'

Listening to Grandmother in the hush and warmth of the Lagonda, season after season. Looking out upon the land as it rose and fell like a plunging fish in and out of the sea's emerald depths. Traversing the land from the sea to the pillars of the sky. Visiting marae after marae. Attending one hui after another. And the people became accustomed to seeing the matriarch with the child at the major gatherings throughout the land.

('You must remember,' John Lawrence said, 'that the post-war period in which Riripeti lived was a time of great turmoil for the people. Not only here in Gisborne, but throughout the land, many meetings were held to discuss the plight of a population who were becoming landless in their own country. Also, New Zealand after the Second World War was a different society. It was te ao hou, the new world, an industrialised world. So the landlessness of the people combined with the power of the Pakeha coin to attract Maori to the cities in great numbers.

'Your grandmother was one of the old people who could see what was happening. She realised that it was important to try to bring the land back into Maori hands because otherwise the young would continue to leave it. Your father and mother, for instance, were prime examples. I don't think that Te Ariki ever wanted to leave Waituhi, but your mother most certainly never liked it out there. As it happened, they only migrated as far as Gisborne. But that was, in fact, far enough, because it drove the wedge between the old and the new. How can the old generation teach the new generation if they are not there to listen? This is how the discontinuity developed between the old and the young. It was a great faultline, right across the population.

'That's why the period is noted for the many hui that were called. I can quite understand why your grandmother went to most of them. She was a leader after all. It was her duty. You were very lucky to have been taken with her.')

I remember travelling fast in the Lagonda. Watching the sun rise on meeting after meeting. Dust swirling against the glass windows. The names of the villages like magical runes: Mangatu Bartletts Te Karaka Makauri Hangaroa Ngatapa Matawhero Whatatutu Wainui Waerengaokuri Manutuke Ormond Hexton Muriwai Otoko Waingake. Hearing the karanga on the marae, and the old men bidding us, 'Piki mai, kake mai, haere mai'. Windscreen wipers slashing at the rain. The Lagonda like a black bullet traversing the winding Waioeka Gorge. The many marae of the people: Te Mana o Turanga Poho o Rawiri Tapuihikitia Takipu. Dozing on the long journeys. The carved sentinels above the meeting houses. The debates on the marae. The long returning journeys in the Lagonda. The matriarch's face, gleaming in the interior light of the car.

And always spiralling back to the centre.

To Waituhi.

There came an afternoon when Riripeti took me to the pillars of the sky.

This was the highest point overlooking the Waituhi Valley, a mountain with three vertical cliffs like a corona. It was here that Riripeti gave me my last blessing and consecrated me to my task. The sun was setting. The sky was blood red.

'Grandson, I have taken you from Maunga Haumia to the river of Paoa, across the length and breadth of the confederation to which you belong. I have also taken you beyond the mountains to other tribes; in future years, you will learn of them, your relationship by descent or historical association with them, and the various allegiances and treaties that we have contracted with each other.

'E mokopuna, what I have shown you is the seen world but there is also the unseen world. Here, I join you to the spiritual realm that is also yours. The spiritual and the physical are one and the same, Grandson, and when you walk the land you are in the company of gods. Tamati Kota and I have been teaching you for three years now but, ara, in your awakening you can receive more of the food of knowledge. Aue, how much more can we give you in this time of waning, when our own powers have diminished? How can we prepare you when even our houses of learning have long ago been destroyed by the Pakeha, and our religious precepts made mockery of by the crooked cross? Yet, try we must. There is a dimension beyond the physical world which you must understand. Then, and only then, will you truly be a person who will love the land. And once you are that person, you will fight for the land with your last breath, as I have done, and all my forebears in the centuries past.'

Then she uncovered the diamond of Te Kooti, a gem of fabulous dimension and colour that was only whispered about among the faithful Ringatu. The diamond bathed us both with holy light.

And I looked out, and I saw the kowhaiwhai swirling patterns of calm among the clouds. And the matriarch was with me, looking across the greenstone land.

'Be calm,' she whispered. 'Kia kaha. Kia manawanui.'

Her voice struck the reverberating drum of the land, and the sound boomed out, loud and long, and it seemed to open a crystal gate, lifting the portcullis between ourselves and the past, and we were in some otherworld. A world where gods and men communed. Where timelessness began and there was no separation of past and present. A world energised with glowing forces and creatures of light fading in and out of the landscape.

'Ara, ara,' the matriarch said. 'Behold.'

And her voice sounded a deeper drum. It splintered the physical landscape so that I was able to see into the essence of things. I saw the gleaming sap ascending the trees, and the sap and the dark red blood coursing in my transparent body were one and the same. I saw into the geological structures of the earth, and the diamond sparkling structure of the mountains, Maunga Pohatu, Maunga Haumia and of Paparatu, was one and the same with the cellular structure of my body. I saw the movement of light and wind and cloud, and they were one and the same with my own life force. The whole landscape was alive, and there were creatures of light and creatures of darkness moving upon it. Their shapes defied description, but some were giant birds with human torsos and others were serpents with faces of men. And among them, humanity lived in holy communion. The earth was in the form of a goddess, Papatuanuku, and I was one of her children.

The matriarch spoke a third time, and she filled the air with ageless music.

'E mokopuna, this is your inheritance. The land still lives, still breathes, and it has a life which must be protected or it will die. And if it dies, we die also.'

It was then that the final barrier lifted, and I looked into the faces of the gods and I was not blinded.

'And so I begin your journey, e mokopuna, at the time of your awakening, by pushing you out into the universe. This the people did in Hawaiki, when the *Takitimu* voyaged to this land. And this is what the mother of Moses did when she placed her sacred son into a tiny woven vessel and consigned him to the Nile so that he would escape the fury of Pharaoh. And the child was guided to the daughter of Pharaoh and lived in Pharaoh's palace and from there, he grew into manhood until the time came when he said unto Pharaoh, "E hoa, let my people go." And in our own country, these were the words said by your ancestors also. By Te Kooti on the rebel side, and by Wi Pere in the parliament of the Pakeha. And these were the words which have come down to me, and which I now pass on to you.

'My grandson, these instructions are like the sacred kumara which Pourangahua carried from Hawaiki to this country. Your ancestor had to do this because the precious seed had been discharged overboard when the *Horouta* canoe, accompanied by *Takitimu*, was partly wrecked at the mouth of the Ohiwa. Many kete of the seed kumara were thrown overboard and it was because of this that Pourangahua returned to Hawaiki. There he landed at Parinuitera, where he went to see his uncle, Ruakapanga. "Uncle," he said, "I have come to take the kumara to my land to the south." So his uncle provided Pourangahua with the kumara. Then Pourangahua said, "Uncle, now that I have the kumara I must return quickly to Aotearoa for, when I left there, the kowhai trees were already beginning to bud, and the planting season is near."

'Ruakapanga allowed Pourangahua to return to Aotearoa, across the sea of Kiwa, on the backs of his two pet giant birds. Their names were Hora Ngarangi and Teu Ngarangi, and Ruakapanga loved them very much. He told Pourangahua that he could fly back on the birds, but only on condition that they were not flown anywhere near Mount Hikurangi, because a taniwha dwelt there; he was also not to touch or pull their feathers, and they were to be fed and given water before he sent them on their way back to Hawaiki. Pourangahua agreed and, astride the two birds, he set off. In one hand he held the kumara seeds, in two baskets named Houtakerenuku and Houtakererangi; in the other hand he held two digging sticks named Mamaerangi and Mamaenuku.

'Aue, he forgot his promises to Ruakapanga and, first, flew right over Hikurangi. The taniwha attacked him and the giant birds and there was a battle from which the birds suffered a great deal. Then, as he was approaching his homeland, the two birds began to circle and circle because they were looking for a place to land. Impatient to feel the earth, Pourangahua plucked a feather from each bird to hasten their descent. One of the feathers floated down into the sea and sank onto a reef in the bay called Tokapuhuruhuru, becoming a makauri tree which grew and bloomed under the sea.

'Naturally, the people rejoiced at Pourangahua's return, and they celebrated the bringing of the kumara seed, and made ready to plant the seed. But for the two giant birds, there were no rejoicing celebrations. Pourangahua forgot to feed them and give them water, so that in the morning, they wept with one another. They were tired from the journey, from the battle with the taniwha at Hikurangi, and from the loss of their feathers. They knew that they would not have the strength to return to their master, Ruakapanga, waiting in their homeland of Hawaiki. It is said that their tears formed a pattern which was so beautiful that it became used in the tukutuku work, the weavings, in the whare nui throughout Aotearoa. The name of the pattern, roimata toroa, or the tears of the albatross, commemorates the grief of the birds.

'And indeed, tired and hungry, they flew too close to Hikurangi and were devoured by the taniwha. Ara, and all this, and the story of the eventual planting of the kumara between two rivers near Manutuke, Manawauru and Araiteuru, is remembered in this chant. E mokopuna, listen to the chant and let it be the first of the blessings as you go forth on that unending journey called life.

'Po! Po! E tangi ana tama ki te kai mana! Waiho, me tiki ake ki te Pou-a-hao-kai, hei a mai te pakake ki uta ra, hei waiu mo tama; kia homai e to tupuna e Uenuku. Whakarongo! Ko te kumara ko Parinui-te-ra. Ka hikimata te tapuae o Tangaroa, ka whaimata te tapuae o Tangaroa, Tangaroa! Ka haruru!

'Ka noho Uru ka noho i a Ngangana; puta mai ki waho ra ko Te Aotu, ko Te Aohore, ko Hinetuahoanga, ko Tangaroa! Ko Te Whatu o Poutini, e!

'Kei te kukunetanga mai, i Hawaiki ko te ahua ia, ko Maui-wharekino ka noho i a Pani, ka kawea ki te wai o Monariki. Ma Onehunga, ma Onerere, ma te piere, ma te matata! Te pia tangi wharau, ka hoake, ki runga ra, te Pipiwharauroa. Na Whena koe, e Waho e! Tuatahi e Waho e!

'Tuarua, ko topea i reira! Ko te Whatanui, ko te Whataroa, ko te ti-haere, na Kohuru, na Paeaki, na Turiwhatu, na Rakaiora! Ko

Waiho anake te tangata i rere noa, i te ahi rara a Rongomaraeroa, ko te kakahu no Tu, ko te Rangikaupapa, ko te tatua i riro mai, i a Kanoa, i a Matuatonga! Tenei te manawa ka puritia, tenei te manawa ka tawhia; kia haramai tona hokowhitu i te ara! Ka kiia Ruatapu e Uenuku ki te tama meamea.

'Ka tahiri i te Huripureiata! Ka whakakau tama i a ia. Whakarere iho ana te kakau o te hoe! Ko Maninitua ko Maniniaro! Ka tangi te kura, ka tangi wiwini! Ka tangi te kura, ka tangi te wawana! Ko Hakirirangi ka u kei uta, te kowhai ka ngaora ka ringitia te kete!

'Ko Manawaru, ko Araiteuru! Ko kitea e te tini, e te mano! Ko Makauri anake i mahue atu, i waho i Toka-ahuru! Ko te peka i rere mai ki uta ra, hei kura mo Mahaki! Ko Mangamoteo, ko Uetanguru, ko te koiwi ko Rongorapua, waiho me tiki ake, ki te kumara i a Rangi! Ko Pekehawani ka noho i a Rehua! Ko Ruhiterangi ka tau kei raro, te ngahuru tikotikoiere!

'Ko Poututerangi te matahi o te tau, te putunga o te hinu, e tama!'

Ah yes, clever indeed was the matriarch. She set me on a luminous voyage. She took me through the land. First, the land of my birth, Te Whanau a Kai. Second, the tribal confederation of Te Whanau a Kai, Rongowhakaata and Te Aitangi a Mahaki, that world within another world. Third, the spiritual world which encompassed both the land of my birthing and the tribal confederation. She told me how we came to this land, on the *Takitimu*. Now, she prepared to launch me on my final voyage.

'E mokopuna, you will need all of the intellect, the spirit, the heart and the memory to guide you on your journey. You will need to be at one with your world, for this is a world made by gods and man, and there are forces of both which may aid you. Learn about them, and understand them, so that when your sails unfurl you will ride with the winds and be supported by the electric currents of the universe. Let no baleful forces prevent you from reaching the unending destination which awaits us all.

'E mokopuna, I now consign you to the longest journey. For what use is the sacred kumara if the land is gone and there is no soil to plant it in? Go into the world of the white man. Say to him, as

Moses did, "Let my people go." Say to him again, "Take no more of our land, and let us go into our own land of Canaan.'"

She was standing at the pillars of the sky. Her face was luminous with grief and anger. She conjured up the creatures of light and creatures of darkness to attend her words, a maelstrom of light and dark, swirling around the diamond of Te Kooti.

'This is your land,' she said, 'and your task. You have heard the groans of the Maori. Listen to the way in which the land and the people suffer under the Pharaoh. Come now.'

I was five years old. The year was 1949.

'Pass into life.'

~

Parliament Grounds, 1949.

A flash of black light struck Riripeti like a spear of obsidian.

'Uh,' she gasped. Her luminosity flickered like a dynamo giving out an irregular current. The pearls in her hair began to splinter, to crack, to flake away.

She was swaying imperceptibly, her eyes closed tightly. The veil had fallen over her face, but the child could see pain there. Still within the whiplash of the forces of the marae, she battled for possession of herself.

'Give me your strength,' she said.

It was as if a tattooed creature of darkness had passed by and, while acknowledging her accomplishment, had at the last moment brushed Riripeti with a touch of its power. The creature of darkness curled above her head and struck. Quite without warning, Riripeti's face began to vein with blood. Blood trickled from the orbs of her eyes. From her nose. Seeping from between her lips.

'Grandmother?' he asked.

'It is a warning. Just a warning,' she told him. 'It will pass.'

Riripeti opened her eyes, and they were as one eye swimming in blood.

'Give me your hand,' she said.

Shocked, the child put his hands into hers and felt how cold she was and how weak. She pressed him close to her, and it was as if she was drawing his energy into herself, some restorative force which would repair her dark wound.

'Grandmother, I am afraid.'

She shook her head. 'It will pass,' she said again. The shadow of the taniwha receded, the body swirling away. And as it did so, the pain drained from Riripeti's face. The bleeding, the moko placed there by the taniwha, slowly faded until where once had been bleeding there was now no blood.

'E mokopuna,' Riripeti breathed. 'It is a warning. It is my price.'

She knelt down to hug him close and the crowd roared in further acclamation.

'Remember this day,' she said.

He looked into those green eyes. No bleeding, no blood. The pearls, gleaming in the light, seemed to surge with radiance.

'We did it then, didn't we, Grandmother,' the child said.

'Yes,' Riripeti nodded. 'And now nobody will dare not to receive us.'

Her voice was strong and challenging. It seemed to ring out and across the marae, filling the air with its authority and its arrogance.

The crowd continued to applaud. With a dramatic gesture, Riripeti stood, climbing into the sky, to receive the acknowledgement of her mana. The child saw Tiana watching like a dark star.

'Come,' Riripeti said to him. 'This acknowledgement is for you too, e mokopuna. Receive it as your due.'

('Oh, it was quite a show,' the journalist said. 'There's no doubt in my mind whatsoever that Artemis was an actress of the first magnitude. She had us all eating out of her hand. All, I should say, except the elders in the paepae. They were sitting there, grimfaced. All around them, people were either laughing at Artemis's boldness or arguing loudly at the claim that you had made for credentials from the gods. Really, you and your grandmother were quite audacious. But you had brought it off, that's the point. And seeing you both standing there hand in hand, nobody, but nobody, could feel anything but admiration for the guts and the gall you both must have had.

'Anyway, I asked the Maori chap standing next to me, "What happens now, sir?" I had the feeling that anything, after all this, would be an anticlimax. But he disagreed. "Oh no," he said. "This is just the beginning. Now that the Matua has established her right to be here, she needs to be welcomed in the hongi. After the hongi will come the real fireworks. This old lady hasn't come all this way for nothing. Although this is the last day of the hui, she will probably demand the right to speak about her lands of Te Whanau a Kai. That is what all this is about—the land."')

'Be alert,' Riripeti said to the ope. She inclined her head in the direction of the paepae. The elders were in consultation with the Prime Minister, and there was much shaking of heads and serious discussion.

'They wouldn't dare not invite us to the hongi,' Aunt Hiraina said.

'Well, it look like they're having a difficult time making a decision,' Uncle Manaaki added.

Bernard Scott joined the discussion. Riripeti watched him keenly. Grandfather Ihaka came to her side.

'You shouldn't have done it,' he said.

Riripeti's eyes flashed in anger. The pearls in her hair glowed crimson. 'We had the right,' she answered.

'It was a gamble,' Grandfather said.

Two of the elders, Timoti and Whai, began to argue with Bernard Scott. The private secretary made a dismissive gesture. Then he looked across to where Riripeti was standing and smiled.

'—Which it appears we have won,' Riripeti said with finality.

She inclined her head to Bernard Scott. Timoti took a few steps from the paepae. For a moment, his face appeared very close. His face was threatening. It was terrible in its anger.

'Yes, Timoti,' Riripeti whispered to herself. 'We meet again, and this time one of us will not survive.'

Timoti called to Riripeti and the ope to come to the hongi, to press and shake hands. It was a challenge which sent an arrow of fear through the child's heart. 'Haere mai koutou ki te ruru,' he beckoned. 'Haere mai, Haere mai. Haere mai.'

Riripeti turned to the ope and said, 'Kia tupato. We go now into the Paremata o te Pakeha. As many Maori delegations have done before us, we enter the House of the European. It is a house of slaughter. We have come so far and the gods have been with us. But do not let your guard down. Our task has only just begun.'

Then she looked at the child. 'E mokopuna, be alert and stay by my side always. Take care for the butcher lest he plunge a knife into your heart.'

She led the ope to the place of the hongi.

('I had always understood,' the journalist said, 'that the hongi is rather like the sealing together of the tangata whenua and the manuhiri. Is this not so? The pressing of noses, the firm touching of forehead against forehead, the shedding of tears, are all acts of aroha. Yet, on this occasion, although all tapu had been lifted, I could not help but sense that there was still tension in the proceedings. There was no doubt where it was coming from. The elders called Timoti, Maui, Henare and Whai, and the paepae of chiefs.')

The elders of the paepae were readying themselves, forming a line in front of the carved meeting house. 'Haere mai koutou,' came the call. 'Haere mai, haere mai, haere mai.' Others of the local people came to join the line, smiling and laughing and eager to welcome the matua. A young girl with a baby in her arms pointed out at the ope; she was of Rongowhakaata blood and wished to embrace the people from whom she had been so long separated.

'E ma,' Uncle Manaaki quipped, 'we had better begin. Otherwise, instead of the steamer going to the wharf, the wharf might come to the steamer.'

Members of the ope began to laugh. They were relaxing, now that the ordeal of the mihimihi was over.

'Ae,' the matriarch breathed. 'Kua tae mai te wa.' Her eyes were already locked with Timoti's. His face still seemed so very close.

The distance closed between the tangata whenua and manuhiri. The shadows of the two peoples met and became one shadow. Amid the hubbub, the hongi began.

('At this stage,' the journalist said, 'I decided to get closer to the action. I pushed my way through the crowd and, by surprise, I found myself in front, right in the line of people who were waiting to hongi with the visitors. Naturally I tried to turn back, but there was an old woman next to me and she said, "Oh no you don't, once you're here, you're here." That caused some laughter, I can tell you.

'So there I was, standing there, in the reception line, as it were. The only Pakeha except for the Prime Minister and Bernard Scott. I must say it was quite an experience. I watched as your ope began to hongi. The old people shook hands and pressed noses two or three times with everyone they met. Very soon I too was involved in the ceremony. I don't think your people liked my sharp nose, though. Now I know why we Pakeha must kiss, rather than press noses.

'All the while, I was keeping an eye on Artemis. She had pulled her veil away from her face. Her profile was extraordinary. Her complexion was so glorious that the pearls were almost outshone by her own radiance. She was about ten people away, moving towards me. My heart began to thunder.')

Riripeti moved down the line, greeting the tangata whenua. When she came to old and dearly beloved friends, she kept her nose firmly against theirs and let her tears mingle with their own. The pearls in her hair darkened like greenstone. She moved with dignity and great beauty.

She came across the young blond journalist. She paused, and a smile played across her lips. She looked at his nose, cupped his chin in her hands, and angled his face so that her own nose pressed just above his left nostril.

'You could do damage with that,' she said. 'Tena koe, e Pakeha.'

He felt her breath upon him, softly warming his skin.

('That was probably one of the most erotic experiences I have ever had,' the journalist said. 'I was quite unprepared for it. The warm caress of a person breathing on one's face. Tantalising. Sensual. I had to close my eyes because of the thrill of it and, when I opened them, I could see that she was watching me with some amusement. Her eyes were green, with hazel flecks in them. They surprised me. Her nose was aquiline and her mouth was full and generous. She was, at once, the most patrician and earthy woman—and the most beautiful—I had ever met.

'Artemis moved on from me, away down the line. I couldn't help it, I had to keep her in my sight. So I pushed along the line also, watching her across the shoulders of the tangata whenua. Then she reached the Prime Minister and his private secretary.')

'Tena ra koe, e te rangatira,' Riripeti said.

The wind stirred her black veil and made it drift across her face like a shadow. The bracelets at her wrists tinkled.

The Prime Minister smiled at her, but it was a smile without emotion and cautiously applied to the face.

'Sir,' Bernard Scott said. 'May I introduce you to Artemis Riripeti Mahana.'

The Prime Minister observed her with coolness. 'I understand you already know my private secretary?'

'Yes,' Riripeti nodded. 'We have met.'

'Artemis?' the Prime Minister asked. 'An unusual name.'

'For a Maori?' Riripeti countered, amused. 'It is the name of a Greek goddess who, in earlier times, was regarded as the Great Mother. That was before the world turned to patriarchy.'

The Prime Minister's eyebrows lifted. He extended a hand to her, expecting her to take it in a handshake of greeting.

Riripeti inclined her head. 'No,' she said. 'Let our prior acknowl-edgement of each other suffice.'

There was a gasp from those nearest to the Prime Minister. Riripeti moved away from him.

('Well,' the journalist said, 'that little incident caused a stir! The Prime Minister went crimson. He muttered something to Bernard Scott. As for the rest of us, we were trying to suppress our laughter. It is not often that a Prime Minister is snubbed in public.

'Then she reached the elders of the paepae.')

Riripeti said to the child, 'Stay close to me. Kia tupato. Now you meet with your peers. Their mana and ours are equal. They must be accorded the respect that is due their rank.' She bent down and, giggling, whispered in his ear. 'Even if they are such foolish and pompous men.'

Rising, Riripeti adjusted her veil. Eyes downcast, and face grave with dignity, she greeted Whai. 'Tena koe, my brother chief,' she said.

Tears of humiliation ran down his cheeks as he felt Riripeti's warmth against his. She caressed him with kindness. She introduced the child. Then she moved on.

'E Henare,' she said, 'tena koe, e te rangatira.'

He would not look at her. His face was impassive as Riripeti faced him and put her nose to his.

'And you, Maui, tena koe also,' Riripeti said.

He shrugged his shoulders. He kissed her in a perfunctory way. 'My sister,' he said, 'you should have saved yourself the bother of coming. The meeting is already over. You are too late.'

'Oh, is it now?' she murmured in his left ear.

Then Timoti was before her.

('Naturally, I was fascinated,' the journalist said. 'The politeness, the ritual, appeared to be quite contrary to the way in which the elders of the paepae were really feeling. They were absolutely enraged with Artemis, yet they were able to contain their anger. All, that is, except Timoti.')

'Tena ra koe, my brother, Timoti.'

''You, a woman!'

Riripeti looked into his eyes. The child felt her grasp tighten on his shoulders. 'My brother, tena koe,' she repeated.

'How dare you. A woman. You!' His face was chalk white. He was beyond anger.

'My brother,' Riripeti repeated. Her voice was level. Her manner was calm.

And Timoti put a hand around her waist. 'Homai koe ki te hongi,' he hissed. 'Homai koe.'

('That's when the strangest exchange of all occurred. The man, Timoti, began to draw Artemis to him. He was whispering to her. Whispering. And his words were like a whirlwind.')

'Yes, come to the hongi, my sister. And let me, by virtue of my descent from Tane, take back the breath of life which he gave to Hineahuone when he fashioned her from the red earth. He gave her the breath of life, from his nostrils into hers, in the first hongi. In Tane's name, let me take the breath of life from you.

'Let this be your last breath, my sister.'

His nose was almost touching hers. Almost.

('Then Riripeti spoke to him. It was unearthly. Dangerous.')

'My brother, be warned,' she began.

('Her voice came from the depths of the earth. From the pits of hell. Like the arrival of death.')

'Be warned, lest the evil in your words and intentions be returned to you. For although Tane breathed life into Hineahuone, and mated with her, it was their daughter, Hinetitama, who became Hine Nui Te Po. And in her name I, a woman, can claim my right to take your breath, my brother.'

Within her eyes Timoti saw a shape. It was her spirit shape, that of her kaitiaki from the Place of the Willows. He cried out and began to loosen his grasp on the matriarch.

But it was too late. Riripeti no longer stood before him.

'Come to the hongi,' she said, 'if you dare.'

It was the time of the spider.

16

Oh, mia patria si bella e perduta! Oh, membranza si cara e fatal! Oh, my country so lovely and lost! Oh, remembrance so dear and ill-fated! *Arpa d'or dei fatidici vati* . . . Golden harp, why do you hang mute on the willows? Rekindle the memories of our breasts, speak to us of times of old . . .

I must tell you now of the holy ark of the iwi Maori, the *Takitimu*, and the two taniwha who escorted the sacred canoe from Hawaiki to Aotearoa. I will tell it as it was told to me by Riripeti when we were standing at the pillars of the sky. *Takitimu* is gone to rest in the well of the world, forever protected and sealed from the evil of man. But to understand all, you must know all, from the very beginning of *Takitimu's* making. So draw near and listen to the story of the holy ark.

It was the late Te Kani Te Ua who said that while the Maori people might be called a barbaric and savage race, their knowledge and conception of the spirit world show a high plane of thought, similar to the philosophical speculations of the earliest Greek philosophers—Empedocles, Anaximander and others. For instance, the myth of the separation of Rangi and Papa by their offspring reminds us of the Greek myth of Uranus and Gaea. The god Tutakangaahau cut the sinews which united Papa and Rangi, and Tanemahuta wrenched them apart and kept them eternally separated. In the Hesiodic fable, Cronus separated the heavenly pair by mutilating his oppressive father Uranus. Remember this context as I tell you about *Takitimu*.

The story begins in faraway Hawaiki at the settlement of Pikopiko i Tawhiti. The people saw a strange waka, larger than any canoe that they knew, approaching the island. The strange thing was that its navigator appeared to know the entrance to the lagoon for, without fear, the waka plunged through the tidal rip to cross from the open sea into the calmer water.

'Who is the navigator who steers the waka with such confidence?' they wondered.

They peered into the face of the sailor and recognised him. 'Is this you, Hoaki? Who left us a few years ago to see if all the stories about a great and beautiful land far to the south were true?'

It was indeed Hoaki. Now he had returned in triumph to verify the existence of the southern land. Why, his canoe itself, *Te Ara Tawhao*, was made from the driftwood of the strange land. Not only that, the crew had all been born there. And why had he returned? To tell all in Hawaiki of the bounty of the new land.

The days went by, and Hoaki's stories filled the people with excitement. From the way he talked about it, it was a paradise waiting to receive the moko of Hawaiki, a place to escape to, away from the quarrels and bitterness of Hawaiki's overcrowded estate. As the romance of the new land flooded the imagination of the people, they called upon their chiefs to consider an exodus across the Pacific. The chiefs agreed and, eventually, at least seven wondrous waka were built. The *Takitimu* was one of them.

It was Tamatea ariki nui who gave the order to his iwi, 'Let a giant waka be made and be called *Takitimu*. Let us journey on it to this southern land of which we have been told. But let the waka have a special mission. Let it be a holy ark to carry the gods of Hawaiki to

Aotearoa so that that land may be blessed and made sacred.'

When he made his proclamation the people acclaimed it. 'Yes! Let it be so.'

'Therefore,' Tamatea ariki nui continued, 'let it carry no common man, nor woman, nor children, nor cooked foods. Instead let only priests and selected chiefs embark on the waka, taking with them the sacred gods—and the ancient lore of Hawaiki—to render to the new land.'

From the very beginning, therefore, sacredness attended the saga of the *Takitimu*. The making of the canoe was placed in the hands of Ruawharo, Tupai and Te Rongo Putahi, all of whom were priest-craftsmen. The tribes under Tamatea ariki nui's leadership—the Ngati Hukamoana, Ngati Hakuturi and Ngati Tutaka hinahina— were all consecrated to the building of the ark. 'All my people, living in the villages of Whangara, Pakarae, and Rehuroa, attend to my command,' he said, and the people did so because of the profound purpose of the voyage.

Selecting the tree from which *Takitimu* was carved was the first holy task. Which tree should it be? The three priest-craftsmen performed the selection themselves. We might imagine them standing in a forest, with mist streaming from the greenery like wraiths. There is magic in the clearing where they stand, a gathering of supernatural forces. The priests have been saying prayers for many weeks, searching for guidance, asking the gods, 'E nga atua, show us the way and the place of the tree already hallowed for *Takitimu*.' Their prayers have led them here, to the dark forest near the hill known as Titirangi. Here they await the sun's arising, and with them they have their sacred adzes, living artefacts with names of their own: Te Awhiorangi, Te Whironui, Hui te rangiora, Rakuraku o Tawhaki and Matangirei. Te Awhiorangi was a greenstone adze of such power that it was used only ritually, in a ceremonial and religious manner. During the voyage of the *Takitimu*, it was the adze that cut a passage through the high seas. Hui te rangiora was also credited with mystic and miraculous powers, having been given to Ruawharo by the renowned priest Timuwhakairia.

The dawn came up. The first light of the sun struck the trunk of the tree ordained to be the ark. At the same time, Te Awhiorangi began to pulsate with fascinating patterns of light until it was glorious with dazzling brilliance. Only a true priest was able to hold it and not die. To confirm the choice, the sun sent a bolt of light to weave through the forest, a blazing messenger, which circled like a flame around the girth of a giant tree, announcing, 'Here, here.'

The three priest-craftsmen clasped Te Awhiorangi as it bucked within their hands. Their prayers soared through the opening sky, the mist breaking away so as to leave a clear space for the tree's fall. Far above, a golden halo revealed that the gods themselves were in attendance to ensure that the deed was done according to proper ritual. The forest filled with the sound of trilling birds and the clattering of tree bark and leaf, a wondrous symphony of praise for the tree itself, singing, 'You have stood so long with us. You have been companion. You have been friend. This is not your ending but, rather, this is your beginning. Go forward. Pass into life.'

As the singing reached its climax, there was a whirlwind around the tree. The three priests struggled within the wind's grasp. Slowly but surely they brought the cutting edge of the adze to that massive trunk. It was a symbolic stroke, not touching the bark at all, yet the tree was seared as if by laser, the line of the cut moving swiftly and cleanly through the wood.

In absolute ecstasy, the tree relinquished its links with earth and began to fall. The forest bowed in homage to it, and birds spiralled in a living feathered wreath about its limbs.

Whano, whano, haramai te toki, haumi e, hui e, taiki e.

Once the tree was felled more karakia were said as it lay there in the forest. Then began the second task, the initial shaping. The three priest-craftsmen placed a tapu on the area. Only those men who had been chosen to work on the tree dared to enter. They and their tools were all specifically blessed. They worked many days. While they were working, they observed the absolute commandments of their priest-craftsmen because the penalty was death if they did not do so, just as surely as it had been death in biblical times for any person who touched the Ark of the Covenant. All the chips from the tree were gathered and burnt. This was done in deference to the great lord of the forest, Tane mahuta, and because the debris was far too sacred to be used for any common purpose such as cooking or to be left as litter. Once they had completed the task of shaping the log, they took their tools and proceeded to the nearest river. There, they stood in a row in the water and were completely submerged as the three priests chanted more prayers to release the tapu.

The log was hauled on sacred rollers to Whangara, the residence of Tamatea ariki nui. Here, the canoe was built in an enclosure into which no women or common people were permitted to enter. Again the same rules of tapu applied, rules observed with severity. A priest under heavy tapu did not touch food with his hands; he was fed by others. He said karakia constantly to maintain the holiness of the work. Any error, any falling from grace, and he was deserted by the gods. He was therefore rendered open to attack both physically and spiritually, as defenceless as the matriarch was when she chose to confront the powers of the marae in Wellington. All his power and knowledge deserted him. Like a dead tree, he existed only as heartwood with all the sapwood and sap-bearing bark rotted away. He was a kohiwi, a skeleton, powerless to defend himself against the shafts of black light, damaging his body and soul unto death. His retribution was less kind than that of the Christian: the Christian was punished in an afterlife; the Maori was punished here and now in this world.

Thus there were always karakia during the building of *Takitimu*. They were said during the adding of the topsides, the rauawa, and the fore and after pieces, the haumi. They were chanted when the taumanu or thwarts were finished and fastened by the tokokia; the kauhuahua or stringboard which supported the flooring was then put in. They were recited when the rahoraho, the decking, was placed in position, the raising of the figurehead and sternposts, the making of parts of the awning frame, the weaving of the masts, the carving of the two kinds of paddles, and the stitching together of the puhi, the ornaments of feathers. These feathers decorated the taurapa or sternpost. This was the special place where the gods of the skies rested and was called the Puhi kaiariki. Another trailer of feathers, called the Puhi kaimoana, was attached to the taurapa and this touched the water.

There were more prayers when six ornamental and special paddles were made for *Takitimu*—Rapanga i te ati nuku, Rapanga i te ati rangi, Maninikura, Maniniaro, Tangiwiwini and Tangiwawana. The first two paddles were used by Tamatea ariki nui when steering the ark. The remaining four paddles were also used for steering, but by the two priests Ruawharo and Tupai, whenever spiritual assistance was required to combat the malevolence of the seas.

Karakia were also said when two bailers were made, named Tipua horo nuku and Tipua horo rangi. A very special ceremonial was enacted to make sacred the compartment at the bow of the canoe immediately in front of the seat of the high priest Ruawharo. It was here that the ark containing the gods was placed during the voyage. Ah yes, Ruawharo, high priest, you were made guardian of the gods of the earth and of the heavens. And you, Tupai, high priest, your role was to guard the gods of the whare wananga. I salute you, my ancestors, guardians of the gods brought by *Takitimu* to this land of Aotearoa. And I pay homage, also, to the sacred roller, Manutawhiorangi, upon which the waka was heaved through the place of two cliffs on that long land voyage from the hill of Titirangi down to the trial of seaworthiness in the lagoon called Pikopikowai.

So we come to the launching of the *Takitimu*. The people gathered on the shores of the lagoon. Tamatea ariki nui took his place at the stern. Ruawharo the High Priest was at the bow and the other tohunga stood along the strakes. Holding the paddle Rapanga i te ati nuku in his right hand, Tamatea ariki nui invoked spiritual blessing and power upon the sacred ark, investing the waka with psychic force. It became glowingly alive, breathing deeply and wishing to feel the emerald water, wishing to plunge its carved beauty through the green depths. A calabash of water was splashed over the bow of the waka. Four rollers named Te Tahuri, Mounukuhia and Mouhapainga and the sacred Manutawhiorangi eased the waka into the water.

The trial of seaworthiness began. It was soon obvious that *Takitimu* was swift and fleet, travelling so fast that the people exclaimed 'Horouta', meaning 'The land swiftly past'. The waka was surely of a kind that the world had never before seen. With great euphoria, the vessel was taken to the place Te Whetu Mataurau where the final blessings and karakia were sealed upon it.

Hail *Takitimu*. Hail. Hail. Hail.

⌒

The elder, Timoti, cried out.

He staggered back, recoiling from the matriarch's ahua, the spirit shape of the black spider with the red moko which she had invoked in the face of his own threat to her.

'Foolish man to try to overcome me,' Riripeti said. 'You have only imperilled yourself.'

The voice she spoke with was not her own. Her body was not her own, possessed now by her kaitiaki. No matter how hard Timoti struggled, Riripeti only enfolded him more tightly in the web of her dark gown. When he looked into her face, she was no longer Riripeti.

Timoti fell back. Aggressive, the spider which had once been Riripeti reared and then fell upon him. With quick, sickening movements, it made ready to paralyse him. The spider's fangs were hollow but already the venom was flooding into them, ready to be injected.

'Riripeti, no,' Tiana said.

('I was standing right there,' the journalist said, 'when Timoti fell. It happened so quickly that nobody quite knew what to do. Your grandmother bent down and her black veil obscured him completely. I imagine that she was ministering to Timoti and endeavouring to assist him. I had the fanciful thought that at that moment she looked like a spider feasting on its victim. It was a fleeting impression, nothing more than that.')

'No, Riripeti,' Tiana repeated. She reached forward to pull Riripeti away from Timoti.

At her touch Riripeti became taut and still. Slowly the spider turned to Tiana. And Tiana looked into the face of the spider. 'You too, e Tiana, would come to your death?'

'Riripeti, your power has taken you too far, over the border of the human world into the natural world. Override your transgression. Return quickly to the world of humankind, before it is too late. And let this old and foolish man live.'

'Foolish?' Riripeti asked. 'Yes, foolish indeed he was to challenge me in this game of life and death.' Riripeti made a sudden spiderlike movement toward Tiana, rearing above her. 'And foolish are you, also, to intercede on his behalf. Be careful that your justification is well argued, e Tiana, for if it is not then you, like he, must come to your death.'

Unafraid, Tiana stood her ground. 'It was Tane who made woman,' she reasoned, 'and I, on his behalf, make plea for the life of this man. It is utu.'

Riripeti paused, considering. 'That is not enough, Tiana, for although man made woman, woman makes man at birth. The utu, the payment, has therefore already been rendered many times since the time of the gods, many times.'

'Then I make my plea as Hinetitama, the dawn maiden, who brings light and life to each day. Let this be this foolish man's dawning. Let him live.'

Again the spider paused. 'You are a mere child to the intellectual debate, Tiana. Yes, the dawn always comes, but there is a goddess greater than her in whose name you must invoke mercy. And this greater goddess favours neither man nor woman and both are reaped unto her and unto the endless night.'

Riripeti turned back to Timoti. She plunged her fangs into him.

Timoti cried out. His eyes were wide with terror as he looked at Tiana.

'Please, help me.' His breathing became erratic, his heartbeat elevated. The toxicity was building up throughout his abdomen, chest, neck and head.

Tiana restrained the spider again. Further venom could be lethal to the old man. 'Wait! Advance on him no further, Riripeti. You have been the mother of sons, and you know the power of the male line. In the name of love, grant clemency to this foolish man.'

'You invoke love now, Tiana?' Riripeti asked. 'The merciless do not know that emotion. They know only the power of death over life and the implacability of fate. You have lost the debate. You are mine. Come to my hongi.'

The pearls trembled in Riripeti's hair. The veils, fluttering in the wind, flattened themselves against the spider's face as she advanced.

'Grandmother, no,' the child said.

⌒

We come now to the journeying of the holy ark.

There was an atmosphere of excitement throughout the island as the time of departure drew near. The High Priests had not yet divined the most propitious hour. Only then, and not until then, would the waka be pointed through the lagoon and towards Te Moana nui a Kiwa. And it is said that other legendary canoes were ready for the exodus at the same appointed hour and that, when the tide was at its fullest and making deep the channel between lagoon and open sea, *Takitimu* was joined by them: *Tainui*, *Te Arawa*, *Mataatua*, *Kurahaupo* and *Tokomaru*.

The high priests continued to consult the heavens, the various conjunctions of the stars, and all augured well. The days drifted past, too slowly for the priests and ariki who were departing, but much too fast for their loved ones. This was a time of sweetness but also of pain as families took leave of the exalted ones who were journeying upon *Takitimu*. It was a time of festivity, of drum dances, of joy, of incredible upward spirals of delight—but also of sadness.

But for the very holy among the voyagers there was little festivity. The chanting in the whare wananga was incessant, day and night, as the sacred ones memorised and rechecked the whakapapa, the lore, the tenets, the tapu teachings which were to be taken to Aotearoa. There must be no mistakes in transmission. There must only be accuracy. Once they left there would be no return to Hawaiki to fill a forgetful memory or a space in the whakapapa that should never have been omitted.

Then Ruawharo, the high priest, climbed the highest mountain in Hawaiki, stepping out onto a giant stone slab and, lo, he saw a dark hole appearing in the constellated sky. The stars moved towards that black space and showered into it, a spectacular stellar waterfall. He knew the time had come.

He returned back to the whare wananga. As he approached the doorway, the chanting inside the house stopped. The other tohunga made way for him as he strode to the back of the house. There, in front of the sacred altar, he lifted his hands. The altar began to shimmer, becoming transparent with light.

Swimming in phosphorescence were the awesome cargo of Atua: the gods of Hawaiki.

The Maori word for the cargo is 'mauri'—talismanic objects holding sample life forces, genetic material, if you like—that were representative of the gods of Hawaiki and could be replanted or reanimated in the new world. More mundane minds have imagined the mauri as being mere carvings of wood and stone, relics representing the children of Ranginui, the Sky Father, and Papatuanuku, the Earth Mother. I like to visualise them as talismans holding creatures of light and of darkness, gods of the pantheon of Hawaiki, covering all that life itself was dependent upon. Here they are, within the crystalline altar, ready to be transported, gifts to bring sacredness to the new land: Tawhirimatea, god of the elements, like a swirling cloud of wind, thunder and lightning shimmering in the altar; the glowing crystal of sparkling greens of all hues, that is Tane nui a rangi, spinning the song of trees, forests and birds; Tangaroa, god of the sea and all fish and deep sea creatures, a spectacular creature of light, spiralling sinuous and blinding coils; the pyramidal illumination, tumbling in the phosphorescence and scattering triangular rainbows, is Rongo marae roa, god of peace and agriculture, and all cultivated foods in particular; Haumia, god of uncultivated food, such as the rhizomes of the common bracken fern, is like a pulsating orb of brilliance; last, but certainly not least, is Tu matauenga, the supreme god of war, to whom all male children are consecrated. He is the creature of darkness, of black light beyond imagining.

But there were more mauri representing other gods: Maru, Uenuku, Rangomai, Kahukura, Te Po tua tini, Tunui a te ika, Moko, and a host of others. And perhaps, the very phosphorescence itself was the Supreme Deity, parentless, eternal, the Creator known as Io.

Such was the psychic power of the altar and cargo of gods therein, that when it was lifted by the priests, there was an instant gathering to Hawaiki of all the tipua, the unseen escorts, the great beasts of earth and sky and sea. The progress of the altar from the whare wananga was marked by a tremendous earthquake; the whare wananga disintegrated and collapsed into the earth. Lightning blazed a trail through the forest for the bearers, cleansing the rude earth with burning ash. Above, in the dark sky, fiery birds appeared, hovering and protecting the altar with their burning wings. On either side of the trail, many taniwha assembled, to make an avenue of tall, rearing, awesome beauty: serpents having the faces of women, men with the bodies of serpents, bowing in homage to the gods of their creation. Waiting just outside the lagoon were the monsters of the sea led by the fabled Ruamano and Arai te uru.

The stars continued to shower through the fabric of heaven. Conch shells brayed in the night. It was a time of fear and dread.

As the bearers of the altar approached *Takitimu*, one of them slipped. A young man put out his hand to steady the altar, and he was of common descent, and was struck to stone. Another, who looked too boldly upon the gods, was immediately blinded by a bolt of lightning flashing blackly from the altar.

Yet there was no slowing of the progression of the altar to its special compartment in the bow of the waka. When it had slid silently to rest in that holy place there was a moment of absolute quiet, as if time itself had stopped.

The quiet was broken by an ululation of land, sea and earth, a shrilling sound, high-pitched and eerie, coming from the throats of the tipua of the island as they swayed their long serpentine coils across the earth; the ululation announced the farewell of the gods from Hawaiki. They charged the tipua of the seas to protect the gods and the ark that carried them.

Far out to sea, the acknowledgement was returned by the fabled creatures of the deep. It came as a whirlwind made by the threshing tentacles of many squid and a deep dull booming caused by the sound of a thousand diving whales.

And as Tamatea ariki nui had ordained, only those of noble rank were permitted to travel as custodians of the gods and culture of Hawaiki. Apart from Tupai and Ruawharo and Tamatea ariki nui himself, were Nukuroa, Hautahi, Rongopatahi, Matuaiti, Matuatonga and other tohunga and ariki.

Then Tamatea ariki nui looked into the sky and saw that the black hole had closed. The tipua of the deep awaited the waka. He looked at his people. 'The time has come to depart this place,' he said.

A blazing comet fell, plunging into the lagoon, burning the coral reef so that a wider underwater pass might be made for the *Takitimu*. The water seethed and boiled. On the shore, the people sang hymns of praise and of glory as was appropriate, for this was no ordinary departure from Hawaiki.

The *Takitimu* quickly sped across the lagoon, disappearing into the tumult.

Listen now to the saga of the voyage of the *Takitimu*. Provisioned by dried kumara, dried fish and a supply of water, the waka left Hawaiki at dawn. According to Percy Smith, it had an outrigger, on each side an enclosed cabin and twenty-six thwarts. Each of the thwarts and its adjacent space was allotted to a special family, the name of which was given to each thwart. There were four topsides built up on the solid bottom; the upper edges were lashed fore and aft with closely woven popoki, inclining inwards, to keep off the splash of the sea. Each of the crew was provided with two paddles, with special paddles at the bow and for steering in the stern. There were two bailing places and four bailers of the usual ornamental kind. Of the two anchors one was a korewa used to cast over the bows in heavy weather, thus allowing the waka to ride with the head to the sea.

The first three days of sailing were without problem. After

all, the gods were travelling and therefore the elements were in abeyance. As well, the priests were master astronomers, divining the weather and the sea and the moods of the elements with superb precision. The fabulous Ruamano led the way for the waka, plunging through the waves and making a smooth path for the *Takitimu*. The equally awesome Arai te uru kept protective custody over the holy ark from behind. On either side and below the waka were four whales, Hine korito, Hine kotea, Hine makehu, and Hine huruhuru, sheltering the *Takitimu* from marauding sea monsters. Other taniwha also accompanied the holy ark on its journey south, including Te Wehenga kauika, Rua riki and Maurea; and Tunui a te Ika, Te Po tuatini and Moko. Every now and then, the high priest, Ruawharo, called to them all, 'Attend to your places. Keep safe the gods. Protect the sacred cargo of mauri for you will surely perish should you not be mindful of your task.' The flying fish caught his words in their wings and took them to the many tipua. Ruamano threshed at the pain of the reprimand.

Then, land was seen, a green diamond jutting out of the sea. This was the island of Rarotonga where other legendary canoes had already landed. Some were still there, the voyagers resting, but they could see the glory surrounding the holy ark. '*Takitimu* approaches.' What a wondrous sight it must have been to see a waka arriving in such holy splendour!

At Rarotonga Tamatea ariki nui took on board further and final provisions. Although the other legendary canoes began to leave before *Takitimu*, to be harbingers for the coming of the holy ark, *Takitimu*, being swift, overhauled them like a silver spear streaking through the emerald water.

But this time the voyage was not tranquil and the journey, estimated to take nine days, instead took eleven. The voyagers and their faith were being sorely tested by the gods. Would they turn homeward instead? No. They forged onward.

The tipua escorting *Takitimu* were hard-pressed to maintain a calm passage for the holy ark. Close to exhaustion, they fought the mounting seas. Winds from the south brought snowstorms to dash against the waka. 'What wizardry is this?' Tamatea ariki nui asked;

the priests had never seen snow before. Ruamano tried to bear the brunt by rearing high like a wall in front of *Takitimu*. The four whales joined him to form a spearhead against the towering waves.

But it was no use. 'You have done well,' Ruawharo declared. 'The time has come for the sacred axes to be used.'

Te Awhiorangi and Te Whironui were brought forward from the sacred compartment, Ruawharo took Te Awhiorangi up in his hands. He motioned the tipua to stand off from the waka and, for a long moment, the holy ark was caught up in the raging tumult until all on board felt that they would perish. He raised the axe aloft until it began to gleam with supernatural power. With both hands he brought the cutting edge down onto the sea. At that symbolic stroke, there was a fire burning on the water, the line of the cut moving swiftly and cleanly away, away in a direction to the south.

However, there were more perils to confront, for after the ice and the snow came banks of mists, pouring across the ocean and flooding the sky so that the priests could not see the heavens and therefore could not chart the course southward. The mist penetrated the ocean, also, so that the tipua themselves were bewildered.

This time Ruawharo called upon the aid of the gods themselves. From one talisman, he entreated, 'E Kahukura, come forth, and light our way by day.' So it was that the rainbow, which could arch over the mist, became the beacon for the holy ark to follow. And from another godly talisman, Ruawharo prayed a lunar halo to come forth. Thus the *Takitimu* continued its voyage south, lit by a rainbow during the day and by a lunar halo at night, following the path which had been chopped for it through the towering seas.

The journey came to the ninth day, and the food had run out. The voyagers were becalmed in their misery. But Ruawharo said, 'Fear not, for I will invoke the aid of Tangaroa, the ruler of the ocean. And I will also ask Tane, the ruler of the birds, to send us food.' He raised the mauri of both the gods and even as he began to speak, a shoal of fish like a rain of diamonds, and sweet birds fell upon the thwarts. And again, it was said that when the people were hungering a second time, Tangaroa made the ocean seethe with iridescent paua, which rose from the depths and attached themselves to the waka.

Two days later, the mighty Ruamano stopped its forward swimming. Slowly, it rose on its tail to look beyond the rim of the horizon. The four whales spouted spumes of excitement. Far off, Tamatea ariki nui could hear the sighing of the sea reaching a strange land. He looked back at the high priests. In the compartment in front of Ruawharo, the gods were glowing with anticipation.

'The great southern land is ahead,' he said. 'It awaits its blessing.'

In supreme majesty, the monster Ruamano led the holy ark and its cargo of gods to Aotearoa. Anyone looking from the land would have seen an illuminated cloud attended by elemental creatures and, arcing over both, the most wondrous rainbow ever known to man.

～

The spider swivelled its head to look at the child. As it hovered over him he saw the matriarch imprisoned in its multifaceted eyes. She appeared to be in a trance, unseeing and immobilised by the power she had unleashed.

'So you, also, would come to your death?' Riripeti asked. She heaved herself away from the old man. As she turned, her body dealt a massive blow to Tiana. Tiana fell, clasping her side in pain.

'Save yourself, my son!' she cried. She attempted to restrain Riripeti but was flicked away with a contemptuous gesture.

The spider's shadow fell upon the child, fangs ready to puncture his skin. He stepped to one side, but not quick enough. Even so, as soon as Riripeti grazed his skin, she set up a huge wail of agony. The dark crystals of the spider's eyes shattered and fell like mirror shards.

With a sob, she collapsed. The spider convulsed once, twice, thrice, and fell, becoming still.

('It is interesting to conjecture,' the journalist said, 'what actually happened in that short space of time. I saw your mother approaching Artemis and speaking to her. I couldn't understand what she was saying but urgency has a tone all its own. Most of all, however, is that I could feel the presence of danger and of death. Yes, the spider image is appropriate, but there was something else more horrifying about the perception. I don't think I was alone in feeling that we were all in the grip of a powerful and unexpected force. It was as if there had been a sudden surge of psychic energy which boosted reality beyond the norm. Artemis, your mother and you were caught up in it, enacting a struggle that none of us could possibly comprehend.')

When Riripeti recovered, she hugged the child closely. Beneath the veil, her face was pale with exhaustion.

'I would never have hurt you, Grandson,' she said. 'My kaitiaki is your kaitiaki. No spider with the red moko would harm you, for you are as one of its own children. As soon as it touched you, it knew—'

Even so, Riripeti's voice was fearful and disturbed. 'My invocation took me too far,' she murmured. 'I must take care or it will go beyond my control.'

She bent to Timoti. The pearls shivered in her hair. 'Be at peace,' she whispered. He shrank from her, but with firmness she pressed her nose to his in the conciliatory gesture of the hongi. 'Kia tupato,' she said. 'It profits neither of us to take our enmity with each other from this world into another.'

But Timoti was raging. 'There are other ways of getting at you,' he seethed. 'The next time I will be the victor.' He moved away from Riripeti, returning to the other elders of the paepae.

The child watched him. 'He will try again,' he said.

'No,' Riripeti answered. 'It is only an idle threat.'

The child knew it wasn't.

('It was at that point,' the journalist said, 'that I took a photograph of the gathering at the hui. Really, you know, the opportunity was too good to miss. This was the first time that so many chiefs, representing all the tribes of New Zealand, had gathered for many, many years. The Prime Minister's presence, naturally, made the event more newsworthy. And, to be truthful, I wanted to take a photograph of that marvellous and unbelievably beautiful face of Artemis.

'I yelled out to a fellow scribbler, Bob Grant, and asked him if he could help me to assemble everyone in front of the steps of Parliament before everyone dispersed to have dinner.')

Riripeti heard laughter coming from the iwi. She looked across at them and saw the blond Pakeha with the sharp nose remonstrating with them, miming with his camera. Some of them were pretending not to understand. Others were making out that they were too bashful, hiding their faces in their hands, but all the time making sure that their best sides were to the camera. Some of the men were already sucking in their chests so that their pot bellies wouldn't show. A few of the women were dying to be photographed, posing like ugly swans and fluttering their eyelids like Ginger Rogers.

'Aue,' Riripeti sighed. 'The Pakeha only has to dangle a toy in front of our people and we want to dance to his drum.' She turned swiftly to the child. 'Remember the spider,' she said. 'Make sure that when you invoke the power of the natural world, you do not walk too far into it. The next time it might not be possible to return.'

The sounds of gaiety and hilarity which the Pakeha stimulated was a welcome back to normality. It was obvious he was getting nowhere in his attempts to get the group together. Nor did it help that some of the women were competing for his attention. 'Don't put Heni in your picture,' one woman was saying. 'She'll only spoil it with that huckery face of hers.'

'Better to have a huckery face than to be black,' Heni answered. 'At least I'm fair enough to be seen in this Pakeha's picture. You'll just come out a shadow.'

'Maata could never be a shadow,' a third woman interjected. 'Not with a beautiful big figure like hers.' There were gales of hilarity at that one. Maata winked and sashayed around, showing off her ample bosom and bum. 'Laugh all you like,' she scoffed. 'My husband got two for the price of one. And he sure knows when I'm in bed.'

'If he can fit,' someone interjected.

'And if he likes the bumpy rides,' Heni rejoined.

Riripeti smiled. It was good to hear the ope relaxing. Best to let them laugh for a while because the rest of the evening was not going to be a laughing matter. She winked at the child. 'We'd better rescue that Pakeha before he gets eaten,' she said.

But before she could do so, the matriarch saw Bernard Scott approaching the photographer. The private secretary listened to the journalist, laughed, and nodded reassuringly. His laugh was clean and infectious and as he threw his head back, his iron grey curls gleamed like spears. Nodding, he went to explain to the Prime Minister what the journalist wanted. The Prime Minister listened carefully and shrugged his shoulders, 'Why not?'

Smiling, the private secretary spoke to Timoti, Whai and other elders of the paepae. They turned to their respective tribal groups and began to yell at them and arrange them in ranks. Then the private secretary looked across at the matriarch. There was a strange yearning in the gaze.

('I must admit,' the journalist said, 'that I was grateful for Bernard Scott's help. I was getting such an awful ribbing from your people. They were making fun of me and nobody was taking me seriously.')

Bernard Scott strode purposefully across to where the matriarch was standing with the child. He was a handsome man with a strong profile, but there was a weakness in the very cavalier manner of his bearing. It was as if his strength came only from his position, his power from the office he held; take that away and he would be an empty husk.

Even so, the child sensed some unhappy relationship between the man and the matriarch. Whatever it was, Bernard Scott tried to gloss over it, speaking to the matriarch even before he reached her, as if fearful that she would turn from him.

'Well Artemis,' he began affably, 'will you come to be photographed with the Prime Minister, you and your iwi?'

Her face clouded, and her look made the private secretary falter in his steps. 'I do not like strangers to address me by my first name. How dare you be so familiar.'

('Although Artemis denied knowing Bernard Scott,' the journalist said, 'I found out later that they had once been very close friends. It's strange, really. I was looking into the camera when Scott walked over to her. I felt compelled to keep watching, through the lens. It was almost like eavesdropping. I knew that whatever they had meant to one another had long been ended.')

Oh, Artemis was so good at reopening old wounds and old memories. She could reach back into the past and grasp the memory like a bloodied head and ask, 'Remember this?'

'This is not the way to treat an old friend,' Bernard Scott said.

'Yes, we were friends once,' she answered. 'I trusted you and gave you my friendship. But you found a new master, and you no longer have the right.'

His eyes became haunted and tragic. 'Even after all these years, you are still unforgiving?'

('I saw Scott's face,' the journalist said. 'I felt so sorry for him. She turned her back on him, you know. But he would not move. I will never forget the words, like poison, which she confronted him with when she faced him again.')

With a swift movement Riripeti looked into his eyes. Her voice was low and guttural. Her lips curled in contempt. 'You are now dismissed.' She indicated the Prime Minister. 'Return to your master.'

و

And the holy ark came to land.

Landfall was at Awanui, on the west coast of the North Island, Te Ika a Maui, at the western end of Ninety Mile Beach. Here began the first landing of the gods from Hawaiki, the implanting of the mauri, the life-giving forces, into the body of Aotearoa. Sacred fires were lit, locations for shrines where whare wananga would become the ultimate repositories of the history, tribal lore, genealogy and tradition which had been brought on the *Takitimu*. Out to sea, Ruamano and Arai te Uru, the great monsters which had accompanied the waka, plunged deep into underwater caverns, surfacing only now and then into the light of the burgeoning centuries to guard the progress of the people in this new land, now possessed of godliness.

The first gods were implanted at Kaitaia, a little inland from Awanui; some of the priests decided to stay among the people already at that location. The remainder, after resting there, rejoined *Takitimu* and proceeded north, intending to round North Cape and voyage down the eastern side of the North Island. In taking this course of action they were heeding the instructions of earlier voyagers, who had advised them that the eastern side of the island possessed beautiful landlocked harbours, while the western side had few harbours and many treacherous river mouths.

The *Takitimu*, after rounding North Cape, resumed its southward journey down the eastern side until it reached Tauranga. Here, more gods, ceremonial mauri, were implanted and Tamatea ariki nui decided to remain, saying, 'This is the place of my destiny.' It was Tamatea ariki nui who also planted the sacred flax called Te Manga Tawa and took a wife from the people of Toi; in this new land, he became known as Tamatea mai tawhiti, Tamatea who has come to us from a distant land. A son was born to him and the boy's name was Rongokako.

In a brief ceremony, Tamatea ariki nui bequeathed the holy ark to the command of Tahu, the younger brother of Porourangi. 'Tahu,' he said. 'promise me that you will continue to voyage south. Find the place of the pounamu, the greenstone from which the sacred axe, Te Awhiorangi, was made.'

So Tahu ventured further south and, as the *Takitimu* cruised the coast, more of the cargo of gods, more mauri and more of the priests and ariki were offloaded. Placenames were given to landmarks which resembled those in Hawaiki—to the mountain, Hikurangi, the first mountain in the southern hemisphere to ever see the sun, to the bay, Whangara, and the nearby river, Pakarae, and to the hill, Titirangi, on the mouth of the Turanganui River. Titirangi in the new land was so like the hill in Hawaiki on which the *Takitimu* had initially been shaped; indeed, it was a prophetic name-giving, for the hill became the cradle of the powerful people of Te Whanau a Kai, Te Aitanga a Mahaki and Rongowhakaata.

And it is said that ceremonial fires were built throughout the Gisborne district and many mauri were implanted in the land. One of them became the location of a whare wananga called Tokitoki, having an altar dedicated to Ruamano. The house was blessed to be 'Tokitoki whakaonge tangata, whakaonge atua': the sacred house where one is taught to overcome men and gods. The blessing was so powerful that the house itself became feared by any priests outside Turanga having hidden or evil designs on the people of the district.

When Christianity came to Aotearoa, the last priest of Tokitoki, whose name was Tupai whakarongo tarawhare, took council with his chiefs, saying, 'We must remove the altar from Tokitoki, for this is as the god of the altar, Ruamano, so wishes.' The due ceremonies were undertaken and the altar was carried downriver from Tokitoki. Mermen and merwomen of the Waipaoa attended it, and so too did other tipua who still lived in the land. The altar was reinstalled in a branch house of Tokitoki at Waerenga a Hika Irirangi. The house was called Maraehinahina and the altar was removed just in time for, when Tupai died, Tokitoki was destroyed by the Christians; but Ruamano prevailed. When the chiefs of Te Whanau a Kai and Te Aitanga a Mahaki made invocation to him, saying, 'Come, reside in your new house,' they saw his appearance in the form of a lizard swimming within a rush of water which flowed into the building during the ceremonial.

Maraehinahina was significant because it was there that three tohunga, Ruka Te Kohu, Ruka Ruru and Ruka Mokaituatine, instructed the matriarch's great-uncle, Wi Pere, in the ancient arts of the gods. And it was from Wi Pere that Riripeti received the life force brought from Hawaiki, a life force truly come down to her from the gods.

Another sacred fire was lit when the *Takitimu* arrived at Nukutaurua, Mahia, at a place called Te Papa. As well as the gods, the priest Ruawharo himself decided to take leave of the holy ark. During his lifetime he proceeded to plant the mauri of the whales and the fish of the sea, and also built his pa at Oraka. When the whales became numerous in that location, bearing witness to the fruitfulness of the mauri, he settled at Tirotiro kauika, meaning 'The place where you can watch the progress of the school of whales'. There he continued to extend and establish the feeding grounds of whales and of other kinds of fish. His mission was so purposeful that he took his three children in his canoe and planted them along the coast as mauri. He placed the first child, Matiu, near the harbour of Waikokopu, saying, 'Stand here, my son, guard the ocean and make it flourish.' Proceeding further south, Ruawharo reached Aropaoa nui and left his second child, Makaro, saying, 'Oh my child, the guardianship I was given of the gods of the earth and the ocean, must be bequeathed to you and my other children. Stand here, and protect all the creatures of Te Moana nui a Kiwa.' Then, Ruawharo paddled on with his last child, Moko tu a raro, until he came to the mouth of the Ngaru roro River. He set his son on the shore, turning him to look towards the sea, and his heart wept, for his lastborn was so young, so young to the task. 'My dearest son,' Ruawharo said to him, 'I would wish that you might have been born to some other parent for then your life would have been fulfilled. Instead it is cut off even before it has begun. You and my other children are all sacrifices unto Aotearoa. Watch the sea, like your other brothers. Be brave.' Each leavetaking was sad for Ruawharo; even while giving his instructions to his children, they were already becoming petrified, turning slowly into rock sentinels of the sea.

And so Ruawharo honoured his guardianship of the gods of the earth and the ocean and both became fruitful. He even placed some sand which he had brought from Hawaiki at Mahia, at Wairoa, at Whakamahia Beach called Tahuna mai Hawaiki, saying, 'Let these be the principal burial grounds of the iwi. Though they be descendants from a people far from the ancestral place of their ancestors, let them be buried in the soil of Hawaiki.' The people, praising him, named a meeting house after him at Opoutama. It was because of Ruawharo that whales became so plentiful around the Coast. Alas, those days are gone, along with the diving of legendary beasts to their last resting places at the bottom of the sea.

Now under the command of Tahu, *Takitimu* sailed around Mahia Peninsula and visited the island known as Waikawa because the water was so bitter. Here ceremonial fire was made for a whare wananga named Ngaheru mai tawhiti. It was said that this house of learning was the origin of the mauri which controlled the whole of the East Coast. The fire was made by Tupai; of the three greatest men on the *Takitimu*, only he remained.

The next alighting of gods was at Te Wairoa. The *Takitimu* rode the waves over the bar of the Wairoa River. It sailed four miles inland before landing at Makeakea. Here one of the skids fell by accident into the water, plunging down into the dark green depths. When it surfaced the skid had become transformed into a fabulous taniwha which, from then on, lived on the riverbank. A portion of another skid was cut off and fashioned into a tiki which later decorated the house named Takitimu built at Te Hatepe. This house was thereby made extremely sacred. It was removed and rebuilt at Waihirere where it stood for over thirty years, the tiki like a huge seeing eye upon the great changes of the iwi. When it was grown extremely de-cayed, the house was destroyed by fire. The tapu in the land still lived on and it was for this reason that the present house, again named Takitimu, was built in the place of the sacred ashes of the old.

Tahu then returned the *Takitimu* to the open sea and pointed its prow again southward. As the canoe neared the mouth of the Waihare River, the voyagers saw a high mountain range inland. Tupai threw a piece of wood with a carved likeness of birds on it, a mauri named a papauma, into the air. When the papauma arrived above the mountain range, it received life and the birds from it flew to the top of the range. It was said that the mountain, in gratitude, gave forth a rumbling sound. For this reason it was named Maunga haruru.

It was at the Wairarapa that Tupai, the last of the three chief men of the holy ark, departed from *Takitimu*. It could not have been an easy farewell, for Tupai would have known that with his going, the special mana which had preserved the waka of the gods would also go with him. But his destiny lay in delivering more mauri unto the land. Yet, was it his imagination or was the *Takitimu* beginning to labour into the wind where once it had struck through all storms like an arrow? And was it lying less easily in the waves? He shed tears at his departure, for the waka was a tangible reminder of Hawaiki; never again would he see his homeland.

I like to think of him standing on a rocky outcrop, watching the *Takitimu* coursing ever southward. He had grown old. His boyhood memories were going with the holy ark. Perhaps he recalled the time when the tree from which the canoe was fashioned was chopped down. He remembered the tipua, coming to form an avenue for the altar of Hawaiki. He thought about the long voyage to Rarotonga and thence to Aotearoa, and the many fabulous beasts which accompanied the holy ark to protect it. As these thoughts raced through his mind, he called out to the disappearing craft, 'Speed on, *Takitimu*, speed southward to the home of the greenstone. Like that treasured stone, find your place of rest, holy ark. Rest well there, for you have acquitted your task with honour and acclamation. Farewell, great waka, farewell, farewell, farewell.'

Some scholars say that the *Takitimu* then became a common or polluted waka. The name for this state is paraheahea. I like to think that the holy ark still retained enough of its sacredness and majesty to continue on its voyage, marvellous to look upon. I imagine it as a Viking ship breasting into the sunset. Or the dark barge upon which King Arthur was placed when, in death, he journeyed to Avalon. I see it as a living thing, a vessel which has grown lonely and old, but yet knows that its destiny is not over. It must still attend to its duty.

Tahu potiki continued to the South Island, Te Wai Pounamu. His destination was the Arahura River, on the West Coast, a river famous for its greenstone. There, the final disembarkation of the gods and all others who remained with the holy ark occurred. The tribe which arose in that place called themselves the Kai Tahu after their final commander.

Then, and only then, could the holy ark come to its rest. It had made its journey and fulfilled its destiny. Its people had brought the gods of Hawaiki and implanted the mauri, the life force the homeland—and they themselves had begun to mingle their blood with that of the tangata whenua.

Who was there on that day when *Takitimu* came to its final resting place? Perhaps Arai te uru and Ruamano were, watching as Tahu potiki and the last men of the waka navigated and pulled the holy ark up the Arahura. Perhaps it was Ruamano who came to assist by pushing from behind with its snout. Tipua of the river, fish of all kinds, might have made a living cushion upon which the waka might slide to its place of burial. Did Tahu potiki ask the birds to take hold of the flax ropes and to help in the hauling of the holy ark whenever this was necessary? I like to imagine the sky filled with flashing wings, beating the air with their turbulence so strong as to bend the trees of the forest. I see some of the trees uprooting themselves to fall before *Takitimu*, becoming rollers for it on this, its last journey. Until *Takitimu* is there. In a gorge far from Hawaiki.

Tahu potiki leads the final rites of sacredness. But even he is unprepared for what occurs. Ah yes, the holy ark was chopped down by the greenstone adze, Te Awhiorangi. This was the same adze which had chopped a way for the *Takitimu* through the southern seas; it was only appropriate that Te Awhiorangi should be present at this, the end of the *Takitimu*.

Tahu potiki notices that the wind has come up. It is blowing fiercely through the gorge. Only he and a few others still remain with the sacred ark. The rest of the people have been sent away so as not to know where the final resting place of the waka is located.

The farewell rites do not come easily to Tahu potiki or his men. In many ways they consider themselves to be inappropriate to the task. Why is it that the high priests have left *Takitimu* to their care? The question is beyond their understanding. In utter loneliness, Tahu potiki completes the prayers for *Takitimu*.

The final words are said. The waka creaks in the wind. Tahu potiki signs for the priests to follow him and to leave the holy ark. They turn to go.

Suddenly, Tahu potiki sees the holy ark beginning to buck in the river. The ripples have become waves, mounting higher and higher, as if some giant tidal current is coming upstream. Tahu potiki urges his men to climb higher, away from the river. Something warns him to shout to his men, 'Don't look back. Keep your eyes closed. Nobody must see where the *Takitimu* is taken.'

But one of the men cannot resist. The wind tears at his eyes, ripping them from their sockets. In a blur, he sees a huge wave bearing a greenstone adze, Te Awhiorangi, gleaming and glorious. The adze places its cutting edge against a wall of the gorge and instantly the wall is split open, a shimmering casket of dazzling greenstone. The river, swelling higher and higher, swirls the holy ark into the greenstone altar.

Te Awhiorangi strikes the gorge again and, lo, the altar is sealed. The greenstone adze topples back into the river and begins to swim in undulating movements back to the place of its origin. Swimming, swimming, swimming.

The wind lessens. The river becomes calm. Above, a rainbow appears. Below, a rock sentinel stands where once had been a man. The *Takitimu*, the fabulous holy ark, is gone from the world of man forever.

E *Takitimu*, rest in peace, rest till world's end, rest in the well of the world, rest, rest, rest. Takoto, e waka tapu, takoto, takoto, takoto.

Not long after the Great War, and a few years after the death of the fabulous sea creature known as Ruamano, the Maori prophet Tahupotiki Wiremu Ratana was on a tour of the South Island. He was in the vicinity of the Arahura River, on the West Coast, when he felt the presence of some great energy force, like a long-hidden dynamo, thrumming beneath his feet. The prophet asked his guide, 'E hoa, there is something here, something of great power. Do you know what it is?'

The guide told the prophet, 'The mountains around here are called Takitimu. They are tapu because there is a tradition that this is the final resting place of the canoe known as *Takitimu*. It is said that the waka rests somewhere in the wooded foothills below the great Southern Alps.'

The guide pointed to the lee of the towering mountains. The Alps were capped with gleaming coronets of ice and snow.

'Somewhere below these mountains,' the guide continued, 'there is a deep gorge. In that gorge, miles inland from the sea, the *Takitimu* is said to rest. Apparently, the timbers lie petrified to a papa ledge in the stream.'

Ratana lapsed into a thoughtful mood. His feet were still tingling from the energy of the region. 'Notwithstanding the tapu,' he said. 'I should like to go to this gorge where the *Takitimu* is said to be sleeping.'

The next morning, the prophet set out for the gorge with a number of his followers. There was a forbidding chill and calm in the air. When all but three miles of his journey had been completed, the prophet called his contingent to a halt. Before him, he could see a dense fog pouring down from the alps and filling the valley like a cauldron. He may well have seen creatures of light and creatures of darkness gleaming within the mist, and muted lightning flashing through that strange cloud. Whatever he saw, it was enough.

The prophet therefore turned to his followers. 'Even though I have the privilege of calling on holy angels to lift the fog and so allow us to proceed,' he said, 'I will instead bow to the wish of the ancient gods. We will not go further.'

The prophet took his leave of the valley of the *Takitimu*. There are some who say that the great psychic powers of the holy ark are still of such force as to petrify any who might challenge the tapu of the gods.

17

*A*rpa d'or . . . *O simile di Solima ai fati traggi un suono di crudo lamento* . . . Golden harp . . . Just as for the cruel fate of Jerusalem, intone a strain of bitter lamentation, otherwise let the Lord inspire you with a melody to give us strength to suffer . . .

ↄ

'Return to your master.'

Riripeti clutched the child tightly and he felt her fingers digging into his arms, hurting him. 'Oh, what is happening to me?' she whispered. 'There are too many cross-currents here. I am in conflict with my world rather than in communion with it. Help me, e mokopuna, to find the calm and quiet stream which flows in the time's tide.'

She bent down to him and, silently, willed him to see what others could not see, the ebb and flow of the psychic currents that bound the past with the present and future. No matter what external turmoil might prevail in the world, at the very centre of the currents was the calm river that provided the unifying force to carry all forward in harmony. Slowly the child divined the rivers swirling between earth and sky. Some of the rivers were filled with creatures of darkness. They swam, divided, united, and swam again in a dazzling *son et lumière*; they were beautiful to look at but they were often volcanic, sending shafts of light through the river itself.

The child saw a river which was the colour of greenstone, folding itself within the blinding river. 'There it is,' he said.

Riripeti followed his gaze and saw the river swirling towards them. She called to it, 'Haramai.' The river curled towards her and the child, snatched them both up, and took them away from the conflicting psychic elements that still reigned at the Paremata o te Pakeha. They were made luminous with beauty.

('The light was going quickly,' the journalist said. 'I had to take the photograph before it was too dark. I was very pleased to see Bernard Scott had convinced the gathering to pose for me. The Prime Minister, Timoti, Whai, Maui and other elders of the paepae were all in place.

'Bernard Scott came over to me. "Are we just about ready?" he asked. I nodded and said that the only one I was waiting for was Artemis. He said, "She has promised me. You can always count on Artemis to keep her promise—even if it is to despise you till the day you die." I was startled by that. You must admit, it was a strange thing to say.')

'Well,' Riripeti said, 'we'd better go and smile for the Pakeha.' She took the child by the hand. Grandfather Ihaka, Tamati Kota and Te Ariki joined them as they walked to the middle of the waiting group. Big fat Wallace, one of the hardcases of the ope, wanted to be beside Grandmother but, 'E Wallace,' she said, 'you go and stand at the back. You'll spoil the picture standing with your fat puku in front of us.'

Everybody laughed and Millie, who was almost as big as Wallace, yelled to him, 'Come and stand by me, Wallace, and make me look skinny.'

A wag, right at the edge of the crowd, joked, 'But if you two stand together the rest of us will be pushed out of the photograph.'

The child saw Tiana looking at him from afar, and he tried to wave to her but, oh, there was an expression on her face which he had never seen before and it made him think of winter.

'Mrs Mahana?' the Prime Minister asked. He motioned that she should stand beside him. She hesitated, inclined her head, but did not accept the invitation.

Grandfather Ihaka said to her, 'You are only embarrassing him.'

'I know what I am doing,' she answered. 'I cannot stand too close to Pharaoh. He may use the photograph for his own purposes and without my permission.' She turned to the child, saying, 'You must always be careful of the cunning of the Pakeha.' Instead, she saw the private secretary and gave him an impish smile. She threaded her arm in his and looked into his face. 'E Bernard, let there be peace between us.' He was too overcome to respond.

'I will count to three,' the journalist said, 'and I will take the photograph.'

'Mr Journalist,' Riripeti called. 'I cannot guarantee that your photograph will come out, but you may proceed.'

('I was a little alarmed at her remark,' the journalist said, 'but I presumed it was a jest. I was a bundle of nerves because I knew I would only get one chance at the shot. There would never be a second opportunity. I counted, "One, two . . ."')

'Just one moment, Mr Journalist,' Riripeti said.

The world stood still. A heartbeat went by.

Slowly, she lifted the black veil from her face. The sun flooded down and shone full upon her incredible beauty. The pearls blazed in her hair like a scatter of tears.

'Three,' the journalist yelled. He took the photograph. The shutter clicked. A moment passed. He let out a cry of joy. 'That's it,' he said.

Just in time. The light faded. Darkness fell.

A bell sounded. It came from far away, from the Maori marae close to the Parliament Grounds. It called all the assembly to kai in the dining hall beside the meeting house. As custom dictated, visitors to the hui had to be fed. Once the kai was over, the last session of the meeting of all the chiefs could begin.

'Shall we go?' Riripeti asked the child.

He gave an exaggerated bow and offered his elbow. Already, others were hastening to the dining hall. Aunt Hiraina came, grinning, towards them. She hugged the child affectionately, saying, 'Gosh I'm hungry. I could eat a horse. Couldn't you, boy?'

He grinned back and gravely said, 'Yes, a horse sounds fine, Aunt.'

She laughed and poked him in the ribs. 'Oh, you and your dutiful ways.' Then she looked at Riripeti and said, 'I'll take the boy with me, matua. He can have kai with me and Manaaki while you talk business with the chiefs.'

He saw a look of affection on Riripeti's face. She held his gaze and nodded, saying, 'Every farewell, my grandson, even if for a short time, is sad to me. Yes, go with Hiraina and Manaaki. But always be on the alert, kia tupato, and be on your guard. You understand?' She kissed him on both cheeks and he felt the cold caress of the pearls. 'And you, Hiraina, look after him.'

'Don't I always?' she said to the child. 'Come on then, slowcoach.'

She took his hand and led him through the crowd.

A shadow fell over him. He looked up. It was Tiana. Her face was calm and a smile trembled upon it. She looked beautiful at that moment, with the light slanting down on her cheekbones and illuminating her eyes. 'Hello, my son,' she breathed. But when she bent down to him the child drew back because, behind her eyes, he glimpsed a fragment from his nightmares—a woman swimming towards him and into his dreams. She held a knife in one hand, and raised it as she approached him. She was in a place of spiderwebs, slashing away at the webs as they tried to wrap around her, slashing, slashing, slashing.

'Tiana,' Hiraina interrupted. 'You know you are not to approach Tama.'

Tiana had already seen the child's fear. She stepped back and, instead, traced a finger down his cheek; it was like the slice of a razor. 'It's all right, my son,' she said. 'Don't worry. But now that you're staying out at Waituhi with your grandmother, I don't see you often. You look fine, son, just fine.' She kissed him gently. 'Is Hiraina taking you to get some kai? Don't forget to eat, will you.' She looked at Hiraina. 'You tell Riripeti that he's too thin, Hiraina, too thin.'

('I was so thankful,' the journalist said, 'that I had been able to take the photograph before the assembly was called to kai. I didn't know then, but I understand now, why food is said to be the true symbol of hospitality on the marae—the welcomes are such exhausting encounters.

'I hastened to the dining room. I saw you being hugged by someone who I now know was your mother. She looked very strong and of independent will. She said something to you, I don't know what it was. Then she turned. She ran right into me, that's how I remember her. When we collided, I don't understand, but she exhibited a most violent reaction. She raised her hand and I'm sure if there had been a knife in it she would have plunged it into my heart.

'But then my attention was drawn to Timoti, one of the elders of the paepae. He had seen Riripeti leaving your side. A thought flashed through my mind: if ever there was a moment when he could harm you, this was it, when you were alone, exposed and undefended.')

'Come on, boy,' Hiraina said again. 'Let's put some pork on your bones, build you up, and make you strong. Mmmmmn, I can smell that hangi kai from here. The kanohi wera must have been flat out cooking for this crowd.'

Indeed all week the 'red faces', as the elderly cooks were known, had been up every morning at dawn, stoking fires, boiling water, chopping meat and vegetables so that the manuhiri would be fed in true style and the honour of the marae upheld. They were going to make quite sure that the prestige of the marae would not decline because of poor kai. These visitors would be filled to bursting so that when they were asked on their return home, 'How was the food?' the answer could only be, 'Fantastic! The best we've ever had.'

The press of the manuhiri, as the crowd neared the main entrance to the dining hall, became tighter. Hiraina said to Manaaki, 'You better carry the boy,' and the child felt himself being lifted from the ground. The aroma of the kai was sweet and mouthwatering.

'I can smell the koura,' one man said.

'And the poaka,' another chimed in.

Only the best kai, the cream of the crop, the most succulent of the food was good enough for the Prime Minister and the elders, men and women, gathered here from the four winds. The men had been hunting and fishing for the kai moana prized as delicacies: crayfish, flounder, fish of all kinds and the wild pig, the poaka, from the hills. The women gathered the shellfish: the pipi, scallop, mussel, pupu, seaweed and watercress and puha from the abounding sea and earth. Local farmers had donated carcasses of beef and sheep, sacks of corn or cabbage, or money to purchase flour for the paraoa rewena, butter, golden syrup and the large quantities of tea and tinned food that would be consumed. All of this had been stockpiled for the hui.

Now, local men were working in the kauta, led by a head cook with long experience in the hangi, the earth oven. Open fires had been kept burning day and night, great metal drums or copper steamers strung above them, filled with water or meat or vegetables. It was hot work and the red faces of the cooks instantly proclaimed their importance.

'Ara!' someone in the crowd exclaimed. 'The hangi has been opened.'

The breeze brought the tantalising and unmistakable smell of food cooked in the deep earth, teasing nostrils with the scent of pork cooked in its own delicious fat, of beef chunks ready to fall from the bone, golden poultry and turkey, succulent lamb or aromatic muttonbird, and fish of all descriptions. Wire baskets overflowed with kumara and potato, watercress from the streams or puha from the fields, yellow corn and other offerings of the bountiful land. Some among the assembly, being connoisseurs, assessed the worthiness of the hangi kai by the amount of stimulation the aroma made to their already watering tastebuds. Ah, the kai was so important to the Maori, and the head cook well knew that his reputation rested on whether or not the food had been lifted out of the hangi at the right time—not too soon so that it was undercooked, and not too late so that it was overcooked—and not tainted by the smoke from the oven. This moment was always one of great suspense for the kanohi wera and, particularly, for the head cook himself. He had dug the earth oven the night before, with his men assisting, because he wanted to make sure that the dimensions and depth were right. He had even looked up into the sky and, just in case it rained overnight, placed a drain in the hangi. This morning he almost lost patience when he was told that there were complications—nobody could tell him when kai was to be served because, apparently, a new group of tribes from Te Whanau a Kai, Rongowhakaata and Te Aitanga a Mahaki had decided to come to the hui. If they was late, then the food could be overcooked, aue.

There was nothing for it but to proceed. He told his men to get the oven stones ready—they had been loosely buried in soft earth and were still warm from the previous day's cooking. While they were doing this, he made a fire with paper and kindling in the oven and piled manuka and dried brushwood upon it. He knew that this wood made little ash to taint the food. Once the fire was blazing, he said, 'Now place the oven stones into the pit.' His men quickly obeyed and silently sympathised with their boss, knowing the agonies of calculation that he must have been making about the timing of the various stages of the hangi.

An hour later, the head cook conferred with his chief. There was still no word about when the new ope might arrive at the hui, but they were led by a Ringatu priestess which would mean that they would certainly come to kai before sunset. The head cook decided: dinner would therefore be delayed one hour. Luckily, the hangi stones had been well selected so none exploded with the heat. He let them continue heating a while longer, then he signalled his men, 'Timata.' The stones were pushed aside and the ashes carefully shovelled out of the earth oven. Then the stones were rearranged in the hangi to await the kai.

First, they were covered with cabbage leaves and watercress to stop the food burning or sticking to them, and to give the kai extra flavour. Then the wire baskets of meat, fish and vegetables were carried out to the hangi and lowered into the pit. This process had to be done speedily so as to take full advantage of the heat of the stones.

'No, no, no,' the head cook said to one of his men. 'Put the food that is slowest to cook at the bottom. Be quick so that we can cover the hangi and retain its heat!' Mutton, chicken, pork, pumpkin, kumara and potato, all were layered in the hangi.

'Now the wai,' the head cook ordered. Instantly water was sprinkled on the stones to start them steaming. Leaves and flax mats were laid over the baskets and, on top of them, a wet sheet to keep the food clean. Then came wet sacks, piled one on the other, and a layer of earth to seal in the steam. Just to make sure, sheets of tarpaulin were laid on the earth for further insulation.

One of the head cook's men asked, 'How long now, before the food is cooked?'

'Two and a half hours,' the head cook answered. Oh, how he had sweated during the mihimihi. Aue, how he had silently railed against the matriarch when her ope had arrived late and prolonged the welcoming ceremonials. Ae, and he had been ready to throttle the journalist when he had asked to take a photograph of the gathering. Was that a telltale wisp of steam arising from the hangi already? Oh no. Oh yes, Oh no. Oh yes. Oh!

This had been his inner turmoil, but he had put a face of impassivity upon it. His men admired his seeming imperturbability and his impeccable timing; immediately following the call to the people to come and eat, he had turned to them and said, 'Okay, boys. Out it comes.'

Kei te pai, the head cook could tell as soon as the hangi was opened that the food was just right! The gods were therefore praised with vigour and thanksgiving. As his men carried the wire baskets into the kitchen, and carved up the meat, he allowed himself the luxury of a surreptitious 'phew'.

('We were all waiting for the dining hall doors to open,' the journalist said. 'Everyone was sniffing the air, hoping not to smell overcooked or smoked meat. And yet not one person dared to voice an opinion until one old man, bravely, averred, "Ah yes, the hangi is going to be good." With that pronouncement the whole crowd surged into the dining hall.

'You Maori must know quite a bit about psychology! A feast like a hakari is a wonderful way to get people laughing and talking and forgetting any animosities they may have had. I happened to see Artemis with Bernard Scott; the earlier differences between them had now been settled. As luck would have it, I was able to take a table near her.')

But as the journalist went to take his seat, Timoti pushed past him, making for the child.

'Get out of the way, Pakeha,' he said.

The child entered the dining hall with Hiraina and Manaaki, and he was instantly confronted with the cornucopia of the land.

'Come on,' Hiraina said to him. 'Let's sit here.'

There was a great hubbub of approval and admiration for the visual and very real feast placed on the rows and rows of tables in the room. Under the inverted V of the roof, with its painted kowhaiwhai arms opening out to welcome the visitors, had been spread a remarkable array of kai. Plates of seafood, aerated drinks, cakes, biscuits, paraoa koroua, paraoa parai, fresh fruit, sweets, dried shark, eel, jelly, fermented corn spilled throughout the dining room in glorious disarray. Bread, butter, cheese, jam, sugar, salt and pepper had been put on each table, with a cutlery setting and a bread plate for each guest. The young beauties of the local people waited gravely to serve the diners, excited by the admiration being voiced by the manuhiri. Indeed, as they had entered the dining room, some of the visitors began to waiata, and one old lady was so overwhelmed that she stood to karanga the festival appearance of the hall and the hakari.

'This is all for you, e mokopuna,' Riripeti said. Although she was far away, across the other side of the room, the child heard her voice as if she were standing next to him. The pearls in her hair shimmered and sent splinters of light through the hall.

With an explosion of colour, a long line of women, beautifully dressed in Maori costume, came singing into the hall. Each carried a kono of green flax, a plaited basket containing the hangi kai, which had just been prepared in the earth oven.

'Only for you, my dearest grandson,' Riripeti continued. Her voice was honeyed and loving, intimate and full of pride. Triumph flooded through it like a glorious cantilena, an arching sound of pure beauty soaring above the buzz of the assembly.

The women skipped like songbirds through the hall, flirting and glorifying their guests, 'Haere mai e te manuhiri, haere mai.' The congress of the tribes roared with acclamation.

'Only for—'

Riripeti's voice broke in pieces. The child felt a maelstrom of anger beyond all imagination emanating from her. Hiraina felt it too and cried out.

('I was watching Artemis,' the journalist said. 'She was glowing with such a strange light. She was smiling her madonna smile. Suddenly, she gripped the table and stood up. She was looking straight at you.')

'Kia tupato,' she called. She saw Timoti approaching the child, a kono of food in his hands. What had he said earlier? 'The next time, Riripeti, I will be the victor.'

('Oh, her look was deathly. You see, one of the elders of the paepae had come up to stand behind you. He put the plaited food basket down. He knew full well what he was doing.')

'Manaaki! Hiraina! Guard the child,' Riripeti called.

The hubbub, the acclamation was all around the hall. Mockingly, Timoti saluted the matriarch with his right hand.

'The child.'

Slowly and with obscene deliberation, he began to lower his hand upon the child's head.

Because the male was tapu, his body was also sacred. An enemy or a woman could destroy the tapu, either wittingly or unwittingly, by a number of acts. For instance, if a woman stepped over a man her noa qualities could cancel out his sacredness; such an act, whether accidental or not, could only be punished by death. Again, in times of war, the victor could obtain the sacredness of his victim, thereby increasing his own tapu, by consuming his flesh. As a final example, if the victor wished to ensure that all knew his triumph, he would sever the victim's head and place it on a stake so that nobody could doubt that the tapu of the victim was his.

Of all parts of the body the head, the upoko, was the most sacred. In the old days there was a trade in Maori preserved heads, which still occasionally surface at auctions. ('And what are we bid on this beautiful Maori head with its fabulous Maori moko? Ladies and gentlemen, do I hear £5000?') Modern Maori abhor this practice, and still grieve at the continuing retention in museums around the world of preserved heads and so-called 'mummies', or bodies stolen from Maori burial grounds, for display in their ghoul-glass cases.

All an enemy needed to do was to touch the head of the male against whom he wished ill. Just a touch was enough to take away the tapu.

Thus, when the new Christian religions of the Pakeha came to Aotearoa they took away much more than the old religions of the Maori. They also took away the tapu of the male in baptism and, by the laying on of hands in the conferring of priesthood, made the Maori noa, without sacredness.

Similarly, Grandfather Ihaka had wished to give me his blessing. I saw the palms of his hands reaching out to enclose my skull. He had wanted to give me a gift, the mantle of Artemis and his own. But he could also have taken away my tapu. For Riripeti had warned me, 'Kia tupato, mokopuna. Be careful. Do not trust your grandfather.'

It could all happen in a second. The giving of mana or the taking away of it.

All in the simple act of the laying on of hands.

⌐

The reports are conflicting, so it is difficult to piece together what actually happened in the dining hall that day. You must remember that all this occurred in 1949 and that time has dimmed the reality and added to the legend that has grown around the incident itself.

Even so, I have tried to divine the truth from the pattern, the facts from the flawed recollections. If I could but reconstruct the physical stage for the incident, that might help to pinpoint the truth; alas, the dining hall no longer exists, having been burnt to the ground in 1953.

But this is the setting: imagine a long hall, medieval in appearance, with a timbered ceiling supported by massive kauri beams. The timbers have been roughly adzed and some bear rudimentary carvings in the shapes of manaia and other mythical creatures. Others have been painted in kowhaiwhai colours, but the smoke and soot of many feasts have discoloured the panels. The whole ceiling area is vaulted with darkness, like another world. The sunlight never reaches there, nor the wind.

Perhaps this is why the curtains of spider webs have reached such beautiful dimensions, like cathedrals spun with silver, delicate suspensions spun with air.

Beneath that timbered ceiling, far, far below, the people have gathered for the feast. The dining hall is lit by twenty electric bulbs hanging from the apex of the ceiling. There are seven long tables running the length of the hall, with one at each end running across.

Riripeti is seated at one of the end tables, in the place reserved for the main guests to the hui. Although she is talking to Bernard Scott, her eyes are seeking out a child where he sits with his uncle and aunt.

'All this is just for you, e mokopuna, only for you.'

The kitchen doors open. Young women, bearing food in their hands, are singing as they distribute their kono to the guests. There is a roar of approval at the blaze of colour and the burst of song, for it is not often now, in these days of the Pakeha, that such pageantry is seen.

But quickly now! Look there. It is Timoti, the elder of the paepae. He is a dark presence moving amid the young men and women. It is he who precipitates the drama of the piece and the appearance of nga pungawerewere.

Oh, if only Uncle Manaaki was still living, for his testimony would have been impeccable. He was the epitome of truth, and his view of the event in the hall would have been authoritative. But he has gone now, gone into Te Po, this uncle, brother to Te Ariki, whom we all loved and cherished.

'Manaaki, Hiraina, guard the child.'

In my uncle's absence, let me try to reconstruct his part in the drama. First, I don't think he was even aware of the presence of the elder of the paepae. Like the rest of the ope, he assumed that the danger was over, now that we had been welcomed on the marae. Second, while there is no doubt that he took his duties of guardianship seriously, he had in fact relaxed his guard—but then we all had, even Riripeti. Not one of us could possibly have foreseen Timoti's intentions. After all, he had tested the fury of the spider once; who would possibly have believed his foolhardiness in testing it again? Third, it is obvious that Uncle Manaaki was distracted by the theatricals of the occasion: the women skipping like songbirds through the hall and the responsiveness of the guests as they roared with approval. In the mêlée, he would not have seen Timoti take a plaited kono from one of the servers, make a quick authoritative gesture to her, and begin to push his way through the singing women towards me.

Only Riripeti saw it. Or perhaps she was warned of it by witnessing a brief shuddering of the webbed cathedrals above the gathering. She saw Timoti, bearing the kono in both hands, a smile of triumph on his lips.

Uncle Manaaki was seated to my right. Aunt Hiraina was at my left. I doubt if either of them heard Riripeti's voice alerting them. Certainly the instruction registered itself forcefully on those nearest the source of the delivery—those seated with the matriarch at her table.

Bernard Scott recalls her cry. 'We were chatting together and, in mid-sentence, I saw her eyes widen, and she looked away from me, stood up and started to hunt through the crowd with her eyes. Her words hurled like a thunderbolt through my head. But her lips never moved, that is the strangest part of all.'

Others at the table have verified that Riripeti did call across the space of the hall. Her call has been described variously as loud and vibrant, frightening, supernatural, otherworldly, emphatic, like lightning in the head.

One of the witnesses recalled putting both hands to her ears to protect herself from this invasion into her brain. 'I had this absurd notion,' she said, 'that someone was inside my head. It was an awful feeling, I can assure you.'

The witnesses all agree that the voice was the matua's and

that, coupled with her sudden rising from the table, it focused their attention on her. However, the participants at other tables, when questioned, do not remember hearing her voice at all. What is interesting, though, is that some of the testimony admits to an impression of unease, of premonition, a presence of darkness somewhere in those bright surroundings. The brilliance of the occasion obscured this presence to some degree and, certainly, by the time the young men had entered to perform action songs for the guests, the unease had begun to be dispelled. The men were handsome and virile as they moved towards the stage to perform waiata. One of the performers recalls Timoti, whom he almost collided with on his way to the stage.

'Hey, old one . . .' he laughed.

Timoti said to him, 'Be on your way, boy.'

The young performer joined the ranks on the stage. 'We were all having fun there, just singing for the manuhiri,' he told me. 'Well, I happened to look up and I saw a dark haze floating down from the ceiling. It looked like dust.'

Yes, I have tried to divine the truth from the pattern, the facts from the flawed recollections. It has been difficult for, once the legend was established, the recollections aligned themselves with that rather than with the reality. But the outlines are clear: there is no doubt that the matriarch called to Uncle Manaaki and Aunt Hiraina, 'guard the child' (and years later, I called in the same fashion to my daughter, Miranda, and she appeared beside me saying, 'Yes, Daddy? You wanted me?'). It is also probable that Manaaki and Hiraina did not hear the warning.

But I certainly did. I turned to look at Riripeti. She was so far away. And it seemed as if I was looking through her eyes. I saw young men moving down the aisles between the tables, singing and dancing on their way to the stage. One of the young men almost collided with an old man, bearing a plaited basket of food in his hands. The old man's face became suffused with ugliness. But he recovered his bearing and, smiling, approached me.

I knew it was Timoti.

And now, I must deal with Hiraina's testimony. Dear, sweet, silly Hiraina, she was always the one to tell stories and to make me laugh, and that is why I loved her and always will. But she had a penchant for making herself the centre of any drama, so her version of the incident is suspect, to say the least.

Well, Hiraina swears that she did hear Grandmother's voice and was aware of the danger all along. She tried to get Uncle Manaaki's attention, but he could not hear her in the hubbub. She says she saw Timoti's shadow as he stood behind me and placed the kono on the table. He gave a slight mocking bow both to me and to the matua.

Then, slowly, and with obscene deliberation, Timoti began to lower his hand upon my head. As he did so, there was stirring in the darkness of the vaulted ceiling and a cloud of fine black dust drifted down into the hall.

('It was then,' the journalist said, 'that Artemis started to chant.')

Perhaps his version of the incident, as it appeared in his newspaper, is definitive.

('The sound was soft and guttural,' the journalist said. 'It had the presence of death in it. The chant was not a long one; it was quick, rather like an incantation. An invocation.')

Someone in the crowd screamed.

('Artemis was looking up at the ceiling while she chanted,' the journalist said. 'I was wondering what she was doing. I noticed dust was falling from the beams. I saw what I had never seen before—the huge spider webs strung between the rafters.')

All eyes were looking up to the ceiling.

('The webs swayed and billowed as if the wind was disturbing them—but of course there was no wind in the dining hall. I saw small black shapes, hundreds of them, seething in the bellies of the webs.')

Riripeti stopped chanting.

She drew an unseen line between the webs and the place where Timoti was standing. His right hand was motionless, above the head of the child.

('By that time, everybody was aware of the dust and was looking up at the ceiling. There was absolute silence.')

Riripeti closed her eyes. She gave one brief nod.

The web cathedrals ripped open. Hundreds of small black spiders hung motionless, suspended on crystal threads.

Suddenly, they released themselves from their droplines and fell like a cloud upon the elder from the paepae.

act four

18

'*Tu che le vanita,*' the matriarch sang in the place of the dead at Waerenga a Hika, '*conoscesti del mondo.*' She raised her arms in supplication to he who had once been her Caesar. 'You, who knew the vanities of this world and enjoy the grave's profound repose, take my tears to the throne of the Lord.' Before the vault she stood with the child who, with her, had come to judgement. Ave, ave Caesar.

⁓

It is now time to bring in from the wings the matriarch's great-uncle, the Honourable Wi Pere Halbert. He has been chafing and fuming there for some time, because his life overlaps that of Te Kooti, and traverses the years from the Hauhau troubles to the Great War. I apologise for keeping you waiting, my ancestor. Blame it on the narrative process, which would only have been confused if you had made too early an entrance. Better still, consider that I have at least given you the stage to yourself. Quickly now, without any authorial prompting, tell it all in your own words. But one stage direction, just one—while you are telling it, think of yourself as the Maori with his own hands around his neck.

THE GISBORNE TIMES, 16 FEBRUARY 1916
'*My Goodwill Was Always Towards the Pakeha.*' There has been handed to the *Gisborne Times* for publication a remarkable document which the late Wi Pere had had prepared shortly before his death. It is a striking record of the early Native troubles in the district, the incidents in which he touches dating back to the first Maori intertribal war of the East Coast in which the combatants used muskets. Truly it is a most interesting story. The object of its compilation by Wi Pere was for the express purpose of putting before his fellow Pakeha citizens a full account of the dealings with which he was entrusted in regard to the notorious Hauhau. In this document Wi Pere seeks to remove for all time what he refers to as an unjust suspicion held by some people that he did not do all in his power to assist in crushing the Hauhau.

'I was born'—so runs Wi Pere's narrative—'in the month of March, 1837, and have lived all my life in Poverty Bay. My mother was a woman of great mana over the whole district; her name was Riria Mauaranui.

'In the year 1848 when I was only eleven years of age, war broke out between the two tribes of Rongowhakaata and Te Aitanga a Mahaki, and as both sides had become possessed of the new weapon, te pu pakeha or the musket, it looked as if the breach would result in serious slaughter. My mother sent me, in her name, to the leaders to deliver her message to them. My mother's words were, "Tell these people that no good will come of their fighting, only death and sorrow to both sides. Let Almighty God judge between both sides." I went and delivered the message to both sides and, after consultation, my mother's advice was taken and the war parties returned to their homes.

'Afterwards, at a meeting between the hostile chiefs, among whom were Raharuhi Rukupo, Paratene, Turangi, Wiremu Kingi Paea, Kemera Manutahi, Pita Ngungu and Te Waaka Marotiri, I was thanked for the part I had taken in avoiding trouble between the two tribes.

'In the year 1852 trouble again broke out between Rongowhakaata and Te Aitanga a Mahaki. The trouble arose over the ownership of a horse. I was again sent to Whenuakura, where Mr Smith's farm now stands at Patutahi, and found the Rongowhakaata under arms. I was again successful in settling the dispute and the war parties again dispersed.

'I was frequently sent to settle minor disputes which were instantly arising and I never failed to avert bloodshed.

'*The Te Kooti raids*. The trouble with Te Kooti arose in 1853. He had a strong following of Rongowhakaata among the young men of that tribe and had become a terror to the district. They took all the horses, pigs and cattle they could lay their hands on and made great hauls of grog which they took from the pakehas and would pay for with the blow of a tomahawk if anyone asked for payment. Then they raided the district and gathered in all the young women. Their only reply to the protests of angry husbands was to point to their loaded guns. The husbands invariably left without their wives.

'The people round about were very indignant with Te Kooti, but as to attack his stronghold would have meant the death of their wives and daughters, the chiefs hesitated to attack his pa.

'News of Te Kooti's doings reached me at Waerenga a Hika, and I assembled one hundred young men of the Aitanga a Mahaki and went down to Te Kooti's stronghold. We crept through the high flax and, leaving my men at some distance, I pushed on, accompanied by two others and climbing a tree, called out to Te Kooti that I wished to speak with him. I had left orders with my men that while I was engaging Te Kooti in conversation they were to rush the pa and overpower the occupants without bloodshed if possible.

'When Te Kooti heard what my mission was he was very angry, and called out to his men to shoot me. He himself was unarmed or I could have finished my career then and there. When my men heard the disturbance they sprang from their hiding places in the flax and rushed through the open gate of the pa, taking the occupants by surprise and easily overpowering them. Te Kooti, himself, however, escaped, and swimming the river where the Bridge Hotel now stands, got clean away.

'I took all the prisoners to Manutuke and handed them over to the town people.

'*The Eye-swallower.* The church committee demanded £400 from Te Kooti for the damage he had caused, but at the time he only laughed at them and sent back insolent messages so we seized all his pigs and cattle and sold them, realising thereby £1,000.

'The district still continued in a disordered state and minor quarrels were frequent, but it was not till the trouble with Kereopa Kauwhata and the Taranaki people that anything worth recording happened. Kereopa arrived here and asked permission from Hirini Te Kani to be allowed to kill Bishop Williams. We immediately posted a guard two hundred strong to protect the Bishop and his property, and called Kereopa and his following to a hui or meeting at Waerenga a Hika.

'Kereopa held the Rev. Mr Grace a prisoner at Opotiki, and we feared that if Kereopa were not handled with tact that he would murder Mr Grace out of revenge. We kept Kereopa engaged as long as possible to save time, meeting him at Tureka, near Ormond, and escorting him to the hui at Waerenga a Hika.

'There was a man-o'-war in the bay at the time, and the captain came to Waerenga a Hika, accompanied by Mr Rice and an interpreter, for the purpose of arresting Kereopa and Patara.

'We advised him to be cautious as Mr Grace's life was in jeopardy, and prevailed on him to return to his ship and to sail for Opotiki. We sent two men with him and a letter to Kereopa's people there, advising them to hand over Mr Grace to the captain of the man-o'-war and return to their homes. Mr Grace was handed over to the captain and taken to Auckland. The man-o'-war did not return to Gisborne as we thought had been arranged, and we kept Kereopa for over a month, when he grew impatient and returned to Opotiki.

'Shortly after his departure, Rutene Piwaka—one of the men sent to Opotiki on the man-o'-war—returned and told us that Mr Grace was free and in Auckland.

'*The Hauhaus.* The Hauhaus now occupied a strongly fortified pa at Waerenga a Hika, and here again I nearly lost my life in endeavouring to obtain the preserved head of a European they held as a trophy. I was subsequently successful in obtaining possession of the head and handed it over to Sir Donald McLean. About this time a prophet named Maru—who was afterwards burned to death at Makaretu— was causing a great amount of unrest, urging the Hauhau to burn all the European houses. European houses were plundered and their cattle taken and driven away and I was sent for and had an interview with the prophet when he promised to cease stirring his followers up to deeds of violence and returned twenty head of cattle which had been stolen, also twenty horses. I would have rooted this pest out from the district altogether, but had not a sufficient force, as I was afraid to leave Bishop Williams' house at Waerenga a Hika unprotected, for I knew that the Hauhau were only waiting for an opportunity to set fire to it.

'At the trouble at Waerenga a Hika Te Kooti was fighting on the side of Queen Victoria, but about that time he was sentenced to imprisonment for stealing liquor from Captain Read's store. Captain Read also accused him of supplying the Hauhaus with powder and bullets, but he was not sentenced on that account, as the charge was not proved. However, he was taken to Napier with the Hauhaus and from there he was sent with them to the Chathams. He escaped with others from there after overpowering the guard and seizing the government schooner which had been sent to the Chathams with stores. He landed at Whareongonga in 1868. At that time I was living at Matawhero. Major Biggs was in charge of the military force stationed there.

'*Te Kooti's Return.* News reached me at Ormond of Te Kooti's unexpected return, and I hastened to Muriwai to find that all the Europeans and Maoris had gone to Whareongoaonga to capture Te Kooti. Shortly afterwards two of the chiefs returned and asked me to go to Te Kooti and try and prevail on him to give himself up quietly. I replied that it was now too late for me to do any good in that direction and asked them why they did not wait for me in the first place. They said that it was the Europeans who prevailed on them to go. Shortly afterwards the Europeans came back and again asked me to go down and try and avert further trouble. I replied it was as much as my own life was worth to go to Te Kooti now, as his fanatical followers were thoroughly aroused. They prevailed on me, however, and gave me a letter to Te Kooti, offering to let bygones be bygones, and inviting Te Kooti to return and live in peace amongst them.

'Armed with this message of peace and accompanied by four natives I set out to find Te Kooti and came on him at Te Puninga and delivered my message. Te Kooti replied that he was now in the hands of Almighty God and would not return unless the Almighty so directed him.

'I told him he was foolish not to return when he had a guarantee that he would not be molested, for the people of the Queen would surely hunt him down in the end. He replied angrily that he would not listen to me, that the Almighty was directing his actions. He said, "Look at these women and children who have come from over the sea." I replied that if he had not stolen the Pakeha's ship he would still be a prisoner at the Chathams. With this he became very angry and called out that he had spoken his last word to me—"Go." Seeing that he was working himself into a great passion, and not knowing the moment he would relent having allowed me to depart, I hastened to where the Native contingent were stationed and left with them for Paparatu.

'*Military Service*. When we got there the fight was over. We spent the night burying the dead of both sides. While thus engaged, Major Gascoigne asked me to carry a letter to the troops at Te Reinga, but Paku Paraone who knew the road was subsequently chosen. He had a bottle of rum with him on his errand, which I tried to dissuade him from taking as he was on the most dangerous mission. He was captured by the Hauhaus, the letter destroyed, and he himself put to death.

'In the subsequent chase after Te Kooti I was under Major Westrupp who refused to go past Waihau as we were forty miles from Gisborne and his orders were not to go past that point. Sir George Whitmore left us and pushed on in Te Kooti's wake while we returned to Gisborne.

'Afterwards I accompanied the forces of Major Ropata to Wairoa, and now held the rank of captain. Major Ropata had four hundred men under his command. We took forty prisoners at Waikaremoana and took them on to Waiapu. My company captured Kereopa at Ruatahuna, and I addressed the Urewera Natives and prevailed on them to lay down their arms. I saw further fighting against the Hauhaus under Major Pitt and Captain (now Colonel) Porter, under the command of the last of whom I took part in the fighting at Tolaga Bay.

'Prior to Te Kooti's raid on Matawhero by my direction sentries were stationed at Te Arai, Ngatapa and Waikohu, nine men at each station but after a couple of months Major Biggs called them in and sent three men to look after these outposts, spending three days at each station. I strongly objected to this, and advised more vigilance as I was convinced that Te Kooti was only waiting for an opportunity to attack and in the meantime was strengthening his forces. Major Biggs replied that he had it on good authority that Te Kooti was leaving for Waikato. Even when Paora Para, one of the sentries, returned and reported that he had seen smoke to the east of Puketapu, Major Biggs treated the report as a "cock and bull" story, and did not take precautions against a sudden attack. I urged him to send to Wharekopae, where a good view was obtainable, but he sent his men to Te Arai.

'Te Kooti swooped down through Ngatapa on to Matawhero, and Major Biggs and Captain Wilson were taken by surprise and killed in their own houses, as also were my uncle and my brothers. I escaped to a pa called Oweta, the people of which seemed friendly disposed towards Te Kooti and refused to take any steps to check him. Seeing this I left and went on to Pakirikiri. When I got there I found there were only about twenty or thirty old people and children left, and the only arms in the pa being an old gun. I was getting these people ready to take them on to Mahia via Muriwai, when a Native called Tamati came in and told us that the Hauhaus were all around us. I escaped along the beach with the children, but was taken prisoner when nearing Manutuke. My companions were all put to death, but Te Kooti yielded to the influence of my people and spared my life.

'I was taken on to Makaretu and escaped with others during the fight there. Our party could not travel fast as we had eleven children with us—three of my own and eight belonging to my slaughtered companions. I arrived at Puha and, leaving the women and children there, went on to Mangatu to get horses. Hearing shots at Puha I knew that the Hauhaus were after us and thinking that the women and children had been slaughtered, set out for Opotiki, where Major Mair was in command, and warned him of recent events. I warned all the people of the Pas along the road against Te Kooti, and advised them to strengthen their Pas against him. The people at Whakatane, taking my advice, made ready for Te Kooti and when he attacked them they beat him off. But for the warning which I conveyed the Whakatane would have fallen into the hands of the Hauhaus.

'I was unable to return to Gisborne as to do so through Waiapu would have been almost certain death so, after some time, through Mr J.W. Preace's efforts, a steamer was sent to bring me back to Gisborne. Mr Atkinson met me on arrival and said that I must give some land in payment for the mischief my people had caused. I asked him if he had heard anything against me personally, and he replied that he had not, but on the contrary all the old people of whom he had made inquiries had assured him of my goodwill towards the pakeha and of my efforts to bring about peace.

'At that time both European and Maori were very sore over the murders committed by the Hauhaus and there were many who, while not accusing me of open complicity in the deeds of violence of these fanatics, sought to incriminate me somehow by insinuating that I was in some way in sympathy with them and did not act as I should have done to try to prevent Hauhau pillage and murder.

'I asked Mr Atkinson to hold an inquiry and to clear up the matter then and there once and for all. He assured me however that he had made all the necessary inquiries and was satisfied that I had acted as I should have done and that my conduct throughout the whole campaign was blameless.

'Few of my old officers—companions in arms—are alive today. Colonel Porter, Major Pitt, Major Gascoigne, Captain Ferris, and Captain Mair are among the number. I have no fear as to what their answer would be if questioned as to my conduct during those stirring times.

'*Signed*, Wi Pere.'

19

Riripeti was sitting with the child in the darkness of Rongopai. He was weeping to himself and the soft sounds sighed like a lonely wind in the night. Riripeti had been endeavouring to teach him the whakapapa of the people, reciting to him again and again the descent lines to which he might lay claim. But his mind was not on the task and lay blunt and useless to the remembering. Impatient and tired herself, Riripeti had lashed out at the child with her walking stick and pushed him to the earth floor. 'You must learn, Tamatea,' she said. 'By Heaven, I swear that you will memorise everything even if it kills us both in the doing.' Now, exhausted, they sat close to each other.

Suddenly, the waning light flooded through the window of the meeting house and onto one of the panels on the back wall of Rongopai.

'Yes, that's it,' Riripeti thought. She prodded the child to follow her. Together, they stood in front of the panel. Painted on it was a whimsical portrayal of a tattooed man, standing in profile, in black jacket and grey trousers. The man had spurs at his heels and wore a bowler hat.

'E mokopuna,' Riripeti began, 'The time has come to tell you about your ancestor, Wi Pere, and his mother, Riria Mauaranui the chieftainess. In many ways their relationship and ours are similar. I am your chieftainess, and you are my Wi Pere.' She laughed at the comparison, amused at the sound of it. 'This is Wi Pere,' she said, indicating the figure on the panel. 'He became Member of Parliament through the help of Riria. How did she do it? She gained the vote of Tuhoe, the people of Mataatua. This is why you must learn the whakapapa and the links between the tribes for, one day, you too might need to call upon the people of Mataatua.'

Riripeti paused. The light seemed to focus on one detail of the panel. 'This,' she said, 'is Riria Mauaranui herself.'

The child had to look very hard to see the chieftainess. She was what appeared to be a bird, perched like the owl of Pallas Athene, on Wi Pere's shoulders. When he took a closer look, he saw that it was not a bird at all but a woman.

'In this manner,' Riripeti told him, 'did Wi Pere choose to acknowledge his mother's role as the major force in his career, whispering in his ear and always guiding him in his decisions.'

ʾ

Nobody knows when Riria Mauaranui, the chieftainess, was born, but we can assume some details about her. She was, for instance, high-born—in her converged all the rangatira blood lines of Te Whanau a Kai, Te Aitanga a Mahaki and Rongowhakaata—and she was therefore a person accustomed to command. Born with mana, she did not need to justify her decisions; they were correct because she had made them.

I picture her as a dark woman, someone of the same stature as the matriarch herself. In her youth she has dark eyes like a deer but she is not startled to flight in the way of that shy animal. Perhaps this is how she became a captive of the Tuhoe people at Hauturu in 1826. She stands her ground rather than flees before the might of Tuhoe and, by doing so, becomes their prize. How she came to be released by Tuhoe is not known but, when she is returned, it is not in the way of a slave but under the escort of Tuhoe as is her right.

Riria obviously knew what changes the coming of the hairy man from the north would wreak upon her world. Did she consciously reject Maori suitors for her hand? I can quite easily hear her saying, 'What use is the taiaha against the pu Pakeha?' She would have been calculating enough to make a quick decision about whom she would want: one of equal mana to hers in his own Pakeha world and who would therefore give her a son to rule in that world as in hers. Indeed, she would have waited until the time was right before sending the message of her need quivering like an arrow to the feet of Thomas Halbert, the Pakeha with the barrel chest and ridiculous red hair.

After the birth of Wi Pere, I see Riria Mauaranui playing a game of politics on life's black and white chessboard. Like the fabled Egyptian queen who attempted to put her son on the throne of Rome as well as Alexandria, she places Wi Pere upon it, and carefully starts to manoeuvre a course for him between the Maori and the Pakeha pieces of the game of the future. Her feather cloak is like the wings of a dark bird sweeping over those who would wish to stand in the way of her or her son.

Some dates suggest that Wi Pere first drew breath in 1835, some in 1836, but he himself mentions a specific date of 7 March 1837. Perhaps he was born three times, carried to parturition over a period of three years, waiting for some conjoining of heavenly signs before finally thrusting out and into the word of light; a triple birthing would be in keeping with the magnificence of the man who became as important to the matriarch's making as the revolutionary Te Kooti. Riria the chieftainess would have watched the night sky for the blazing comet or star shower signifying a propitious birth. Only a monumental pronouncement would have been worthy of her son, only some sign such as a disturbance in a faraway galaxy would be appropriate for his coming. Perhaps she kept her son within her, waiting for such a time, and perhaps we gain our arrogance from such a woman, one who could control her natural processes in this manner. Until, ara, the stars shower into a black hole in the heavens. Quickly, she goes to a sacred place, kneels down and, with both hands, pulls him out of her.

What was Riria Mauaranui's first move on the chessboard? She knew that her son's mana, descended from her own, was intact and could not be challenged. But her Pakeha husband had another son by an earlier marriage, the boy Otene Pitau. Did Riria shift her son on the board and take from it the chess piece with Otene's name? Did she go to Thomas Halbert and say, 'Give my son your mana. Deny Otene Pitau.' When he agreed, what was the utu, the price, for the agreement? It might well have been Pouparae, which Thomas Halbert asked Riria to obtain from her people so that it could be settled on her son; but Halbert afterwards sold his piece to other Europeans. In this act lay the seeds of Wi Pere's adult strength of purpose; deprived of his birthright he could not stand by and watch the Maori nation becoming landless in their own land.

In later years, Wi Pere and his half-brother Otene Pitau became firm friends. Indeed, after Otene's marriage to Mere Jones, Otene adopted Wi Pere's daughter, Mere Tahatu, to be his own child. Otene also adopted Heta Te Kani, grandson of Rawiri Te Aho, after whom the grand Poho o Rawiri meeting house was named. There is a cycle of conciliation here at work. In this manner, despite the devisings of those who demanded the mana, the relationships between Maori iwi were sealed and the lines of genealogy tightened between families.

And now, the second move on the chessboard, as Riria shifts her son through his childhood. It was Thomas Halbert who proposed that Wi Pere should be sent to Auckland for his schooling. Riria almost assented but then, recovering, decided that he should remain close to her where she could control his destiny. Not only that, but she found out that the teacher was a Negro. 'I would rather chop my son into little bits,' she said.

With firmness, she therefore pushed Wi Pere towards a sacred education among her own people and not a profane one in the Pakeha world—time enough for that. So Wi Pere received individual tuition and training in tribal history and genealogy. He was taught in the oral literary tradition by word of mouth, by chant, by recitative. Later, when he was adept enough, he entered the whare wananga, one of the most exclusive universities in the world. Only the most brilliant young men, possessing superb powers of recall, were able to do so, and only those with mana could survive. Wi Pere the half-blood was one of those who did.

It was not until Wi Pere was proficient in his Maoritanga that Riria the chieftainess made her third and boldest move of all. She herself was a black queen on the chessboard; she removed herself and put him down in the place where she had been. His Maori powers were now secured. The time had come, not only to command those powers, but also to claim those of his father. Particularly, the time had arrived to begin the long journey to the Paremata of the Pakeha.

We do not know when Riria divined that her son should represent his people in the Pakeha parliament. It was not enough for her to bequeath him her mana; she had to push him out in front where he would receive his due acknowledgement as a leader of his iwi. Therefore, at the age of eleven, Wi Pere embarked on his first mission to prevent war between Rongowhakaata and Te Aitanga a Mahaki. The people, from then on, recognised the power in him, and began to raise him to take a place above them when the time came.

Similarly, Wi Pere began to walk among Thomas Halbert's people. He obtained some schooling at the Whakato Mission Station and, later, worked in the Maori Land Court as an interpreter. His Pakeha elders, realising his gifts as an orator, began to consider that he should have a role as a mediator between Maori and Pakeha. He was half-breed, after all, and therefore symbolic of this ideal of mediation. Best of all, despite his Maori background, he looked like a Pakeha, like one of them.

But Wi Pere was not a Pakeha. When he married, at eighteen or nineteen, he married Arapera Tautahi Matenga. Perhaps it was even arranged, a taumau marriage, by Riria herself. By Arapera Wi Pere had three children: his son Te Kani, born about 1858 when Wi Pere was twenty-one, his daughter Mere Tahatu, born about 1860, and his second son Te Moanaroa, born about 1862.

But history is never tidy. Looking out upon that chessboard of the future, Riria Mauaranui must have felt some fury that she could not control the piece which bore the crest of the Scotch thistle and was named Te Kooti. She must have divined that his life and her son's would collide at some point, and that it was beyond her powers to prevent this. They were of the same blood but they were not of the same destiny.

We can imagine her pacing back and forth on the edges of the board, muttering imprecations at the unruly actions occurring on it. With her quick eye, she would have seen that her son's and Te Kooti's moves upon the board were so alike. Te Kooti, for instance, joined the militia to fight against the Hauhau; Wi Pere, in turn, was with the native contingent at Matawhero and had attained the rank of captain at the time of Te Kooti's retaliation. Te Kooti had also been at the Whakato Mission Station and had been wrongfully accused of siding with the Hauhau; so, too, was Wi Pere suspected of siding with Te Kooti, after the Matawhero Retaliation. The point of divergence between the two men, however, was this: there were forces at work within the Pakeha world which forever cast Te Kooti on the outside; in Wi Pere's case, these same forces compelled him to confront the Pakeha from within.

Perhaps a bargain was struck between them when Te Kooti captured Wi Pere on the beach near Manutuke. 'Your companions will be put to death,' Te Kooti said,' but you and yours I will give clemency because you must follow your dark star and I mine. I have known ever since you were a boy, e Wi, that our paths would cross again and again, and so it has been. You first attacked me with a hundred warriors at my stronghold—that was even before my real troubles started. I told my men to shoot you but their bullets were deflected by some spiritual force and I knew then that you were being protected. Ae, and then you came to me at Te Puninga with the message of the Pakeha. That was after I had escaped from Wharekauri, where I had been under wrongful arrest. The message was that bygones should be bygones and that I should now live in peace with the Pakeha. But I was by then in the hands of Almighty God and you, you were in the hands of the false prophet of Pharaoh. I could have killed you that second time, but my hand was stayed by the power which protected you. Pharaoh then pursued me and you were part of that pursuit and now, after I have avenged the wrongs of Pharaoh, I have you in my hands. For the third time, I could kill you, but for the third time I cannot. You must go your way and carry my burden with you, just as I must go mine and carry yours with me. I am powerless against you, as you are against me. I make a prediction that although we will never see one another again, we will meet each other again. Our two stars will become one star, but that will not be in our time. And you will be reviled by your own people for appearing to be against me; and you will receive the same anger from the Pakeha for seeming to side with me. We ride the comet's tail, you and I. May God have pity on us both.'

Wi Pere still needed to learn one more lesson: that the white man could not be trusted. Let us therefore look at the chessboard again. There is still one further piece to be taken in the game of the future. For Wi Pere did indeed come to understand the Pakeha and to distrust him, and he learnt it when he took a white king bearing the name of his father, Thomas Halbert.

'When I was a child,' Wi Pere said, 'my European father asked my mother to obtain from her people some land, to be settled upon me. She asked for two pieces, and Pouparae was given her, which was bought by my father for me; he afterwards sold this piece to other Europeans. When Mr Bell, Commissioner, arrived here in 1859, I asked that the case of my father having sold this land should be investigated. The day the case was to be heard my father asked me to withdraw the charge because, he said, "If you press the charge I shall be in great trouble; this is a very serious charge, and I should get a long term of imprisonment: but the rule is with Europeans to bring cases of this sort forward after the death of the person who sold"; to which Mr Wyllie assented.

'In 1863 I went to the Bishop and asked that this land might be returned to me; he agreed on condition that I would refund him the money he had paid for it. I then went to Tutere and Matenga Kerekere; we mustered a hundred horses and cattle, which we intended to drive to Napier to sell in order to obtain money to pay back to the Bishop; in the meantime the Hauhau disturbance occurred. After Waerenga a Hika fell I sold my sheep and obtained

£200; Tutere had £50. We then went to take this money to the Bishop, who was living in Waikahua, at the entrance to Turanganui River; we met the Bishop descending from his house; there were three of us—Tutere, Himiona and myself. We told him we had brought £250 to pay him back for Pouparae, he replied, "That arrangement is ended, I cannot now accept the money"; and the Bishop now owns the land.'

It was a hard lesson to learn: a son could not trust his father. It was therefore not unexpected that in 1872 Wi Pere was in the forefront in urging that Patutahi should be given back to the natives; he saw that the Pakeha was coming upon the home ground and taking it away from under the feet of the Maori. Indeed, Wi Pere went further. Many Europeans held him in ill favour because, among other things, he favoured the repurchase of all properties in the hands of the Pakeha at the prices which had been given for them. One of the prophecies of Te Kooti came to pass when Captain Read, in retaliation, accused him of going away voluntarily with the prophet after the massacre, and of deserting Te Kooti only when he had suffered a defeat. His father had taken away his birthright, and now the Pakeha were attempting to discredit him.

Wi Pere realised that the Government was like a great big shark eating up the land. He began to move purposefully across the board, closing in on his goal: only by representing his people in the Paremata o te Pakeha would he be able to get the land back.

In 1883 he campaigned for the parliamentary seat for the Eastern Maori District. That was when the chieftainess went to the Tuhoe to ask them to give back Turanga into the hands of her iwi. In particular, she asked for the vote of the Mataatua. With that vote she secured Wi Pere's success.

᷇

Ecco l'orrido campo ove s'accopia al delitto la morte. The owl. The fire-eating salamander. The tomb's cry.

'Turanga was given to Tuhoe,' the chieftainess said. 'But I now wish you to return it to my son. I, who was a captive of Tuhoe and was returned to my people by Tuhoe, request this of you. E Tuhoe, give my son the vote of Mataatua.' *Perire! Ebben, quando le sorte mia il mio dover tal e, s'adempia e sia.*

Ahakoa, he aha te utu. But what was the price, chieftainess?

The land, always the land. In the year 1884, now a parliamentarian, Wi Pere arrived in the capital, Wellington. It is likely that he landed by coastal steamer from Gisborne, approaching the harbour through the Heads. Wellington must have afforded a thrilling sight for this young man who was embarked on a political career. Certainly, it wasn't too long before he himself began to attract attention from the newspapers. In one pen portrait of the new representative for the Eastern Maori District he was described as having features which 'are decidedly European—his forehead is broad and intellectual, his nose long and straight, his eyes black and piercing; his black hair is parted in the middle; his beard is abundant, black and glossy. He speaks indifferently . . . His mother fled with him into the wilds, where he lived on roots and grew up as a little savage. What a change in one man's life. The little wild root-eating savage has been transformed into a grand courteously-mannered Member of Parliament.'

'He speaks indifferently.' It wasn't too long before the papers were playing a different tune. From the very beginning, when Wi Pere first raised his voice in the Paremata of the Pakeha, his reputation for outspokenness was established. Here was no savage, no indifferent speaker. This was an orator with outstanding vocal and histrionic abilities, a man of passion, especially when debating the land.

PARLIAMENTARY HANSARD: ADDRESS IN REPLY, AUGUST 20, 1884, MR WI PERE
'Mr Speaker, Sir, I am a stranger to this House, but although I am a stranger I am inclined to say a few words. I . . . consider that great trouble has been brought upon certain people . . . and that they should be fully considered. The yoke that has been placed upon the neck of the Maori people is not a light one. For that reason I think that the present Government should have an opportunity allowed

them of developing their policy. If their policy is not a good one, disapprove of it; but, if it is a good one, uphold it. If one member of that Government is not worthy of confidence, have him replaced by a better man. If a division is called for now, I propose that myself and the other Maori members do not vote, because if we vote now we shall be voting in the dark. We have not yet been able to find out who are our friends in this House. We know that great troubles rest on the Maoris. What has been done by the late Native Minister is not right. He is like a certain person named John, who was not baptised with water—who was not baptised in proper form. I thought, in my simplicity, that, as he was called "Native" Minister, he would be a minister for the Native people, and that he would take care of the Native people—that he would lead them in the right path and teach them to acquire prosperity. The Europeans acquire prosperity without being possessors of land in large quantities. Sometimes they acquire prosperity although they may not be possessed of one or two thousand acres. But the Maoris, although they may hold a great deal of land, cannot acquire prosperity, or do not acquire it.'

(Straight away Wi Pere identified the problem. The problem was the Pakeha. He played power games with the Maori, administering 'Native' affairs and keeping prosperity—and the land—from Maori hands. He was impudent and courageous, this young parliamentarian from Turanga, even to the point of threatening a boycott by all Maori MPs.)

'I am considering our position. We are all strangers in this House, and as we are all strangers I ask for your indulgence towards us. Do not let any revengeful thoughts arise in your minds against us, but let us all meet together to do what is best for all, and perhaps you will be able to show some love to us the Maori people of these Islands. I have many thoughts which I desire to give expression to at some future time. My great desire is that you will unite in devising the best laws for the Natives. The Government have done wrong and so have Europeans. Will it not be possible to devise some good laws for administering the portion of the land now held by Natives? My desire is that the work of Europeans and of the Government in connection with Native lands be stopped. You, the Europeans, have made all the laws relating to the Natives. Let us now make our own laws, and if trouble comes from them we shall only have ourselves to blame.'

(Maori sovereignty, that was the issue, ah yes. In one bold stroke, Wi Pere made his play for independence of the Maori. We can imagine what a stir that must have set rippling in the House.)

'My desire is that land-purchasing by Government shall cease utterly. It is said that the Government possess twenty millions of acres which are not occupied. Let the Government commence to place population on those lands, and leave the Maoris to devise some means for utilising the land remaining to them, as they are the owners of the land. Let the Native Committees decide what is to be done with the land of the Natives. Let each tribe decide what is to be done with their land. We shall be able to devise some method for administering what land remains to us.

'Sir, my hope and my intention, when I came to this House, was that I should be a very humble personage amongst you, but that you would take compassion upon me and help me to do right.'

PARLIAMENTARY HANSARD: WANT OF CONFIDENCE, AUGUST 29, 1884, MR PERE
(Nine days later, Wi Pere took up the taiaha again. He derided the Government for its imperialist policies towards the Maori people. There was no doubting his fearlessness. He was not one to run in the face of the Pakeha.)

'Sir, in my opinion the present Government appear to be bankrupt. If you ask me why, I will tell you. In the year 1882 the Crown and Native Lands Rating Act was passed. Because you are not able to pay your own debts, you make this law to make the Maori people liable for it. And this law was brought in force over their ancestral lands. It was not right, because the land had been left to them by their ancestors . . . The Act I refer to is very hard; after it has been in force a few years, if the rates are not paid, then the Government will take our land in payment of those rates. I had an interview with the Hon. The Premier today and asked him if he would not make concessions with regard to that particular Act. In my opinion his appearance on that occasion was like that of "Friday", the man you read about in *Robinson Crusoe*, who was startled and frightened when Robinson Crusoe began to shoot the birds. I have come to the conclusion that the Maoris can derive no benefit if the present state of things continues.

'I consider that the Maori people should make their own laws with regard to their land; let those laws be made in accordance with Maori customs, and be brought into this House for confirmation. If The Act I speak of is allowed to remain in force, I believe that the whole of the Native lands will be taken; all the Native lands will be passed through the Native Land Courts, and the Natives will be deprived of their land. They will have to sell their land in self-defence in consequence. If they do not sell it, their land will be taken in payment for rates. With regard to Native lands, I say again, let the purchasing of these lands cease utterly. Let Native Land Courts cease also. Let us pass a better Act—another Act—through this House, and after that Act is passed there will be time enough to deal with the Native lands.'

(No wonder this 'little wild root-eating savage' began to attract such attention. His language was astonishingly direct and forceful and, while gentlemanly, had the strength of tigers in it. Growing into the part, he amplified his reputation and his ascendancy.)

'It is not right that the Native lands should be taken away. This is almost the same as the story we have heard about Daniel; it is just the same as throwing Daniel into the den of lions. A hard law is made for obtaining the Native lands. From the time that this Assembly first commenced it has always been passing laws affecting Native lands. These laws have not been good; therefore I say that the Maoris should make laws for the disposal of the balance of the land, and then we can make them justly.

'Look at all the troubles which the law passed by this House has brought upon the Natives . . . Europeans who were purchasing land went and bought shares of married women against the will of their husbands, and got the land from children during the absence of their fathers. They deceived the Natives, the whole of whose lands passed from them. I think the Europeans are greatly to blame for what they have done with regard to Native lands. They never protected the Natives with regard to them. While the Maoris were still in a state of ignorance the Europeans made laws affecting their lands. In my opinion the Natives are in a state of great destitution at the present time.

'Sir, my great desire is that every member of this House shall unite in passing laws for the benefit of the Natives. Let us combine in passing good laws respecting Native lands . . . The Native lands are like Naboth's vineyard.'

PARLIAMENTARY HANSARD: SUPPLY, SEPTEMBER 24, 1884, MR PERE
(One month later, Wi Pere rose again. He gave no quarter. If the House had any doubts about his weaknesses they were dispelled in his scorching accusations. He was a force to be reckoned with.)

'Mr Speaker, I intend to speak the opinions of my tribe. The Maoris are not an indolent race. It is on account of the stringent laws passed in this House that the Maoris are unable to attain prosperity or make use of their lands. If these stringent laws were not enforced the Natives would have had some incentive to work. I was sent here by my people to do away altogether with the rating and other taxes. I have been sent here to say that they should be stopped for the present, until some proper measure could be devised doing away with the troubles that exist at present.

'In account of the conflicting laws that have been passed affecting Native lands the Natives for a time cannot make any use of their lands. They have no encouragement to have sheep and to farm their lands, or to lease them; and the result is that their lands remain in their natural state. They are unable to make use of their common lands on account of their tribal disputes. Therefore I say that the laws which press upon the Maori lands should be repealed, and some better law be substituted. This new law I compare to the horse which I say brings in the cart.

'According to the ideas of my people, if the law relating to Native Committees is improved, it would not be more than two or three years at most before the whole of their lands would be brought into occupation and made some use of. Under the present law as many as two or three hundred people are put in the same grant. One of these three hundred people may breed sheep, while another breeds dogs, and another pigs, and another horses. The man who breeds dogs finds that his dogs eat the sheep, and the owner of the sheep gets very angry in consequence. The owner of the dogs says, "I look upon my dogs as my sheep"; and so the dogs eat the sheep, while the pigs of another man destroy the crops of one of the other men, and there is trouble through that. It is on this account that my people wish that the arrangements affecting their lands should be placed in the hands of five, ten or fifteen persons to be elected by the people to do that work. The Committee so elected should carry out all the arrangements respecting the lands. If this became law, in a short time the whole of these waste lands would be occupied by Europeans and covered with farms, and many of the Natives themselves would be able to have sheep and cattle of their own running on the land. These are the reasons why I think the rates should not be put on the Native lands at present, because this House has passed stringent laws respecting the selling of those lands.

'Now, I say the whole of the Natives are looking at us to pass more just laws regarding the land. In former years the Europeans alone passed laws affecting the Maori lands. Whenever evil has resulted from these laws and the Natives made an outcry, the law has been altered, and another law has been passed, with the same result. The intention, no doubt, in passing these laws has been that they should be of benefit to the Maoris, instead of which they brought trouble to them. This House has passed many laws during the past years, but none of them have been of any benefit to the Natives. It may be that the intention of some of those who passed those laws was not honest. They may not have had the welfare of the Natives at heart. One great desire among the Natives of my district is that they should devise some laws respecting their affairs, and that it should be brought here for confirmation. I think the whole of the Natives should act in that spirit, so that if any troubles do come over the Natives they will be of their own seeking. The law concerning the leasing of the Native lands is not just. One man has not power to lease his land, and the laws respecting the dividing of the land are not good, or are not in accordance with Maori custom. According to Native custom, the dividing of the land invariably followed the boundaries of their ancestors. The whole of their tribal lands were subdivided, and the Maoris knew who were the chiefs and the great owners of the land. According to the present system the shares are all assumed to be equal, and the result is that the slaves and inferior persons get just as much as the chief. Another evil is that, if one of the Natives sells his share to a European, the shares of the whole of the others who have not sold go to the European as well. By these means the lands of some people are taken from them unjustly.

'I think that we should have the advice of the Natives in devising measures about their lands, and I think we should not be precipitate in passing laws affecting those lands. Give them time to consider what they think best for their own districts. Do not let threats or coercion be used. Do not let us be frightened into doing anything against our will; because our land is dwindling down. There is not much left. The bulk of our land has passed from us owing to our ignorance. Our land was taken because the Natives were in a state of ignorance. The Europeans, being the superior race, superior in education, came amongst us foolish people and took advantage of our ignorance.'

(His voice, his stance, his delivery and his words were impassioned and glorious. He held every person in the sway of his rhetoric.)

'Yes, you baited the hooks with sweet bait, and we swallowed them, and the result is that our land has departed from us. Therefore I say that great trouble has been brought upon us by the Europeans; we have been brought very low, and you should now turn and raise us up. Do not let the liability which the Europeans are incurring be made a burden upon Native lands. None of the Natives have advised the Europeans to go to England to raise the money; yet you use the argument that this railway will be a great advantage to the Natives. Who asked you to bring the railways on to the Native lands? That originated with you, the Europeans; not with us Natives. A lot of land in my district is owned by the Government: let the Government make railways there on that land, if it pleases them; but do not take advantage of the Native tribes, who are ignorant.

'My fervent wish in coming to this House was that the European members would help me devise some good law for the Natives for their land. After that is done it is time to begin action upon the Native lands, because the Natives will then be in a position to make some use of these lands. Europeans should remember that they have obtained possession of these Islands quite by accident, and therefore they ought to show some consideration to the Natives.'

PARLIAMENTARY HANSARD: NATIVE LAND LAWS AMENDMENT BILL, OCTOBER 2, 1884, MR PERE

'Mr Speaker, I wish to say something in regard to the Bill now before the House. It will authorise Natives to sell their individual shares in the land: that is to say, it will take the land from under the protection given by the Act of 1873.

The Act was passed by the House for the purpose of protecting the lands and preventing their alienation. But, since the passing of that Act, the Europeans have been acting in contravention of it. And trying to purchase land the title to which is held under that Act. I think the provisions of the Act are oppressive to the Europeans, and that is why they wish these alterations to be made, and why the present measure has been brought in—so as to enable them to purchase the land from the Natives. This Bill authorises a single Native to have his share defined, and gives the Europeans the same right as the Native owners of land. Any European, under this Bill, can have the share that he has purchased defined. It is my firm belief that this provision is wrong; and if the Bill become law, in a very short time all the Natives' land will pass away from them . . .'

(And was there nothing new under the sun, for 100 years later, the same arguments were still being raised by Maori people against the selling of Maori land to the European. A march was begun from Te Hapua in the north to Wellington in the south, with banners proclaiming 'Not one more acre of Maori land.')

'I think Europeans should cease making laws affecting Native lands; that the making of future laws should be left to the Natives and the Government. Then the laws which are so devised will be brought into this House for confirmation. I say this, because the

Europeans have hitherto made all the laws affecting Native lands and the result has been that the bulk of their land has been passed away from them. That is why I should like the Native Minister to visit all the Native districts and personally inquire of them what their ideas are with regard to these matters. If the Native Minister will agree to meet the Natives in my district, I shall be glad; or if the Government will agree to call the chiefs to Wellington to discuss the question, that will be well, so as to devise some law and give the Natives some relief. One reason why I object to the Bill now before the House is that the lands belong to the Natives, and the Europeans make laws affecting them. These lands have been inherited by us from our ancestors, and it is only by leasing or selling them that the Europeans have any right to them. So the Europeans are making stringent laws so as to get the advantage, and they bring in measures quite contradictory to former laws passed by this House. I know that Europeans make their own laws. I think the Government should assist the Maoris in this matter, so that we may all work together. This House has been passing Native land laws during the last twenty years, and the results have always been some troubles with the Natives—'

PARLIAMENTARY HANSARD: NATIVE LANDS SETTLEMENT BILL, NOVEMBER 1, 1884, MR PERE

(A month later, Wi Pere again returned to the attack and by so doing established the pattern of argument he was to use consistently on behalf of his people: that they, and they only, should determine the Maori destiny. His voice was like a sword, cutting and thrusting with fervour and intelligence.)

'I will speak with regard to the measure now before the House. I wish to speak the more because it is a matter which affects the Native people very deeply. I wish to show this House the ideas the Maoris have on this subject. It is the wish of the Natives that a just law should now be passed. During past years all legislation with respect to the Natives has been carried out by Europeans only. The result of these laws has been that all Native Lands have passed away.

'The Maoris will never consent to the Government having absolute control to sell or lease Maori land without the consent of the Natives being first obtained. The Maoris will not place that power even in the hands of their own Committees. They will not consent to a Board going so far as that; but it is not for the bulk of the people, to decide whether the land is to be sold or not.

'The Government should not pass any measure that the Government alone would devise; let that be done jointly by the Government and the Natives. Let the Government consult with the Maori landowners, and devise a law which the Native Minister could bring to this House for confirmation. This House will then be able to give effect to it. Do not let this House, when that law is brought before it, alter it by various amendments, and destroy its effect; for this reason: that this will be the first time that the experiment has been made of allowing the Natives to make their own laws.

'This House should reflect that the Europeans have obtained at least thirty million acres of this country; and they ought to be satisfied with that land for the present, and leave the remainder of that land that still belongs to the Natives to be administered by the Natives; so that, if there is trouble, the trouble that results hereafter will not be the fault of the Government or of this House but it will be brought on by the Natives.

'It should be considered that the Natives in various parts of New Zealand are in great trouble. I earnestly ask and hope that all the present evil will be done away with. This is why I consider steps should be taken immediately to consider Wahanui's representations to this House. His request in coming to this House is this: He says to the Government, "Keep back your dogs from coming and killing my sheep." He means by this that the Government should restrain those Europeans who desire to go on to his country and cause trouble. Wahanui knows that he is powerless himself to prevent these Europeans from going through his country.

'Let a fence be placed round his land, and, if the gate is opened to let anyone in upon the land, let it be done by the owner of the soil: let him open the gate himself.

'According to the old Native custom, the chiefs derived all the benefit from the land: that is to say, the people paid tribute to their chiefs by giving them the fruits of the soil. The fatness of the land went to the chiefs. Now, all the fatness is taken by the Government, and it goes to the Queen. I think the Europeans should be satisfied with that, and leave to the Native Committees to say what shall be done in the way of settling the land by putting Europeans on it. If the whole of the power rested with the Government, and they could sell or lease or dispose of Native lands without consulting the Natives, the result would be that great trouble would come upon the Natives. It might be that one Government would carry out the administration of the Native lands satisfactorily, and that another might do just the reverse. When the Natives go to complain of the wrong which has been done to them, the Europeans just whistle and walk away. Now, if the Native chiefs were in authority over the land, there they would remain from their birth until their death—there would be no change; so that if any of those chiefs did wrong, such pressure would be brought to bear upon them that they would die from very shame.

'It is quite different with Europeans: they do not feel shame. They forget all about it. They are like stone images—the blush is never to be seen on their faces. Their love is all outside; but their hearts are hearts of stone. Their words are pleasant to the face; but they turn away and forget all about what they have said. They sometimes say, "We will do everything that is good for you"; and then somebody else comes to speak to them, and they forget all about it. I beg of the House to remember that they have had all the voice in the past; and what remains in the future, leave to us Maoris. If our wishes are given effect to, then prosperity will come upon us. If prosperity comes upon the Maoris I will not say it is only the Government who have caused it, but I will thank the whole of the members of the House for it, and will say that it is owing to their efforts.

'I think a great matter in this House is voting. Everything is carried by the majority, whether it is a good law or a bad law. That is quite different from the Maori ideas. That is a European institution; the Maoris do not approve if it, for it is not a good arrangement at all. But, if a good law is now passed, I will thank the House that now for the first time light has been thrown on the Maori people. Then I shall think that the efforts of this House are directed to relieving the weak and suffering. That will be like affording relief to hospitals and charitable institutions. Former laws we can only compare to the work of a doctor who performs certain operations to find out what is wrong with a patient, and causes great pain in doing so.'

(By now, of course, Parliament was beginning to sit up and take notice. This Wi Pere was someone to be watched and listened to. He was no ordinary Maori, showing his style in a rampaging speech— the third in a row that year—when he decided to take on Sir George Grey, the Premier himself. The House could only listen astonished as Wi Pere rose from his seat and began the attack.)

NZ PARLIAMENTARY DEBATES: NATIVE LAND ALIENATION RESTRICTION BILL, NOVEMBER 7, 1884, MR PERE

'My sincere desire is that the Government should accept the amendments proposed by the Upper House. The Premier has stated to the House that he will not agree to Natives having the carrying-out of the sales and leases of the land, and the result will be that the Natives will think that this Government intend to do wrong to them.

'Why should the Government desire to take away these Native Committees? Are they afraid to trust the Native people? I think the Government should have some consideration and give way in this matter. If the Government and the Natives jointly act, then great benefits will result, because this law prevents outsiders from dealing with the land. Seeing that outsiders are debarred from dealing with the land, what have the Government to fear?

'The evil doings of the Europeans in the past have stopped; but now the door is being opened again for such proceedings to be carried on again by the Government. I think that the Government and the Natives jointly should deal with the land. We, the Natives, do not think that the people who give the largest price for the land should alone deal with the lands. Europeans will not give their lands for 6d. an acre—not for two pounds, or three, or ten pounds an acre. But, because you deem the Maoris a very simple people, you offer them only 6d. an acre for their land. But, now that the Natives are becoming aware of the facts of the case, I think they should legislate upon their lands.

'The Government should not force the natives to sell their lands for only 6d. an acre because, if the Government obtains possession of the land, they will sell it at one pound, two, or three pounds an acre—for more, probably. Considering that the Natives have lost nearly the whole of their lands, I think the Government should take care of what is left for them. I believe, if the Government continue in their present course, that it must be their desire, I think, to cause trouble. And thirdly, I think that their desire must be to murder the Natives. I think that only giving a small payment for the land—I think that amounts to murder: it is tantamount to killing people.

'My desire in coming into this House was that the Government should assist the Natives, because the Natives are now only a remnant that has been spared from the action of former laws and Governments. And now this House is going to murder the Natives; but the Upper House has evinced some consideration for them. I entirely approve of the action of that Chamber, I now beg that the Premier and the Native Minister will assent to the amendments, and not return the Bill to the Upper House.

'There are only four of us Maoris in this House; and the Government should pay some attention to the prayer of the Natives who are consistently coming to this House and asking for just laws. Look at my district; look at the state of it in 1869. On that occasion the Government said to the Natives, "Give us your land and we will take care of it; the Queen will take care of your land, lest the Europeans get hold of it." After that, the Land Court was sent into the district. The lands were passed through the Court, and were awarded to the owners; but in 1872 it was found that the law under which the land passed through the Court awarded it to joint tenants. It was then found that the land could not be bequeathed by the people in the grant.

'The Natives think that the promise made to them about the Queen taking care of their land was false, and that the object of that law was that the land should eventually pass to the Government. Europeans are always casting in the face of the Natives that they are the means of increasing the value of Native lands; but I say the Native lands have not been improved by the fact of Europeans coming here. The prosperity of the Natives depends upon the present state of their lands—that is, their forests. They were in the habit of deriving very great benefit from their forest lands, from the food and the birds and the rats that they got there. But the animals introduced by the Europeans have destroyed all the rats and the birds that formerly lived in the forests. The European rat has eaten up the Maori rat, and only the people now remain, and they are now being killed in their turn. I think it is quite time that the Government should now commence to try and save the Natives.

'I am not speaking as if I wished to go down among the Europeans. I want you to listen to what I have to say. I want you to listen to me and hear me speaking of the grievances of my people. This House has for the past thirty years been passing laws respecting the Natives. I do not think that honourable members should laugh at me. I am speaking because I feel very deeply about this matter. Let the Europeans laugh within themselves, for they have always been in the habit of doing that. Do not let honourable members say, "I did not laugh; it was somebody else who laughed." How am I to know whether you are laughing or not? I do not understand the English language. My great desire now is that a great many evils shall not come upon the land and the people; because the work which has been done in this House will be known hereafter. The Government should be guided entirely by the Maoris in regard to Maori matters, and listen to the Europeans on matters which concern Europeans. My coat that I have on is my own. Therefore I have no hesitation in speaking about that coat, and I shall not feel ashamed because of the remarks that anybody makes about that coat.

'I will not be deterred from making a long speech by anything that anybody says. I came here for the purpose of making speeches. If I saw that the Government was willing to help me, my mouth would never be opened at all; I should never get up to speak. Perhaps honourable members may find fault with me for the length of my speech. I do not think that that should be the case, because the Europeans have occupied the last three months in dealing with their own affairs, and all that is left for me is to bid farewell to them, and let them go. If any one in this House has any love for the Maori people let him stand up now and show it. Do not let it be known by saying Yes or No. Do not let it be settled in this way; if any plan is proposed by which the Natives will derive benefit, to say "No" to it. Is it because they are afraid of the Premier that they all call out "No"? I think right and justice is a thing you should consider, and truth and love.

'Perhaps you think I have no better subject to talk about than this. The Hon. The Premier stated that he will not agree to the amendments proposed by the other House, and I now know the meaning of those words. The result of those words of his will be that the Natives will go to the place of departed spirits.

'My desire is that honourable members should gather around me and assist me, and not pay any attention to what the Premier says. The Premier has had his way; and I think you should help me now. I think Wahanui will make friends with the Premier and the Native Minister if they help him. My love for that chief, when he stood up in this House like a slave as it were, was very great; he was in the position of a suppliant. I hope the Premier will not be angry with what I am saying. I speak this way, because the Maoris are only a remnant that has been left. The bulk of them have been killed. The reason for our coming to this House was that we hoped to obtain relief.

'It seems to me that you are afraid of the amendments proposed by the Upper House. I take this fear of yours as a great compliment to ourselves. It shows our strength. I thought that the power rested with the Europeans—that this was a House where good and bad laws were made. But the Maori people are not in this position. They have no House wherein to make laws. But why should you, who are in possession of this House, be afraid of this amendment? I hope the Premier will consent to this amendment. If he does not, I will speak all night. I could talk for a whole week, repeating these few simple words, "Agree to my proposal"; and, if all the honourable members go away, leaving no one but the Premier and myself in possession of this House, that will not matter. I shall wait until the Premier agrees to my wish.

'I do not think the Government should have any hesitation in agreeing to my wish. I do not think that the older brothers and younger brothers should quarrel. We want to find out the causes of prosperity of the European population. The people here in Wellington have no lands, and they live in prosperity. We want to find out the causes of that prosperity. I want to find out where they hide it. This knowledge the Europeans keep from the Natives. I believe that this knowledge must be in the Committees. That is why the Government desire to prevent us from getting on the Committees. They are afraid that, if these Committees administer the land, the land will be cut up into small blocks and sold to the advantage of the Natives. Let this cause of prosperity be given to the Natives now.

'This is our request to the Government: to give me what I ask for. If I get what I want, then it will be for me to say how much land I shall give the Government, and how much I shall keep for myself. Why should the Government get everything, and I nothing? At the present time my love for the Maoris is very great. My love for the Maoris is much greater than my love for my own mother. I am justified in making this request because I am suffering from great trouble. A sick person need not be ashamed of asking for relief; for what else has he to do? I again ask that my question be answered. If the Minister of Public Works will say "Yes", I shall be satisfied; or if the Minister of Justice will show his love for me, I shall be satisfied. I hope that his love for me shall be as tall as this hat is. I hope that he will speak to me like a chief, and that he will show some consideration for me, because I am sick. The Government is the doctor.

'If the members of this House will show love for the Natives I am sure that the Native people will have no other idea than that of wishing to act jointly with the Government. I do not like this proposition that the Government shall have the power to buy land from the Natives. That is what I object to. I hope you will not curse me in your hearts; but, if you do, I cannot help it. If the Government will consent to my wish, then I will sit down. I hope you will not complain about my constant repetitions. What is a sick person to do but to repeat his request over and over again? If Her Majesty the Queen were near at hand, I should go straight to her and ask for relief. I am not urging for a speedy answer; I can afford to wait. I hope that the House and the Government will show me some consideration.'

(In that third intervention in his first year in the Paremata of the Pakeha, Wi Pere had revealed the power in him. We can all of us imagine the silence which attended upon the conclusion of his speech. It was up to Mr Moss, MP, to give the House the words which had to be said.)

'I am quite sure that the House will bear with the honourable gentleman who has just sat down. I feel myself that he is fighting for bare life. The terror of the Natives which Mr Pere and his colleagues in the Maori seats represent is not altogether without foundation. I have a feeling of sympathy with the honourable members in the corner of the chamber who are struggling, as they are, against superior numbers.'

On that day the house adjourned at ten minutes past one o'clock a.m.

20

Aue, aue, Wi Pere.

In the darkness of Rongopai, Riripeti stood with the child before the panel of the man who had been the tribe's caesar.

'Yes, e mokopuna,' she said, 'and when Wi Pere came back to the people from his first session in the Paremata of the Pakeha he was acclaimed by all. Who amongst us had spoken so boldly against the Pakeha? Who else had shown himself an equal to the white man? Who was to say, therefore, that Wi Pere was not as brave and cunning as Te Kooti? Because of this, we enthroned him, because of his mana, above us all. His star was in the ascendant, streaking its glory across the night sky. All who saw that star believed that it was twinned to that of the prophet, Te Kooti, and that the two men thus made the circle of triumph complete. So it was that the vote of Mataatua continued to support Wi Pere, aue, for the land was still disappearing into the bottomless pockets of the Pakeha, and Wi Pere was needed to fight for our lands and to stop it from moving to Pakeha possession.

'Listen: in our own Turanga district, prior to the Land Wars, the only freehold land held by the Pakeha had once been principally at

Matawhero but he also held leases at Kaiti, Whataupoko, Pouawa and Whangara, to the south Te Arai, Pakowai and Maraetaha, and directly inland Repongaere, Ruangarehu and Ngakaroa. By the 1870s, however, the Pakeha invasion had expanded and most of the leasehold land had become European freehold. The still-Maori Tangihanga block became isolated in a leasehold sea. Moving from north to south, the European began to take further leases over Mangatiakapua, Pakake o Whirikiki, Whatatutu, Rangatira, Manuwhitikitiki, Te Karaka, Waikohu and Okahautiu blocks. Again, by 1881, many of the leaseholds had become converted into European freehold. Ara, and when we looked again the land had passed from Maori to settler, government, freeholder, leaseholder and speculator—European, all.

'Wi Pere therefore became, unquestionably, the most crucial Maori statesman of the 1870s and 1880s. The people increasingly went to him for advice in disputing past transactions which had made them landless. He became a repudiationist, upholding the rights of Maori to own their own land. His way was to form a partnership with W.L. Rees and Karaitiana; the partnership brought the Repudiation movement to its full flowering against the Pakeha. Through the partnership he established the New Zealand Native Land Company which acted as trustee of 250,000 acres of Native Land in Poverty Bay.

'It was a bold move, e mokopuna. What your ancestor attempted to do was to take upon himself the title of an emperor. He established an estate in the Roman mould. He took up the triumphal wreath and said, "I am your Caesar, your destiny, and you are in my hands."

'Emboldened, he returned to the Paremata of the Pakeha.'

〜

PARLIAMENTARY HANSARD: EXTRACT FROM NATIVE LAND DISPOSITION BILL, ADJOURNED DEBATE, AUGUST 5, 1885, MR PERE

'Sir, I will first draw the attention of the House to The Native Committees Act, 1883. The Natives received no power whatever under that Act. I think that that Act was only passed to flatter and please the Maoris—to make them believe that real power was being given to them, while, as a matter of fact, no power whatever was being given to them. I think that Act ought to be called "An Act to soothe the Maoris' Susceptibilities"; but it is very well known that they cannot carry on any business under it.

'I will next refer to the Rating Act as brought into operation over Native lands—that is, lands unoccupied. The Native people object very strongly to that measure on the ground that the land affected by it does not bring in any revenue to them. They receive no rents or benefit from such land, and therefore they get nothing out of the land from which they can pay this taxation. The land is being swallowed up under this Act.

'I will now refer to the Stamp Duties Act. It is the Maori people who have to bear this tax. They have to pay ten percent on all sales and leases of land. It is true that the European pays this duty in the first instance, but eventually it falls upon the natives. The European knows very well that he will be called upon to pay this duty, and therefore he makes a corresponding deduction from the money that he pays to the Natives.

'Sir, this House passed a measure entitled the West Coast Reserves Act. In my opinion, and in the opinion of the Natives, that was a very bad measure indeed: that is to say, there are certain provisions in that Bill which are bad. No power whatever is left to the Native owners of the land. The whole authority is vested in the Commissioner, and he can do what he likes against the wishes of the Natives. The Commissioner has full power under that measure to hand over the Native lands on very low rentals, or to do whatever he pleases.

'I will now refer to the law by which not more than ten persons are allowed to have their names inserted in Crown grants. Great troubles came upon the Maori people under the provisions of that Act. It may be that the land belonged to two or three hundred people; but under that law the whole of the land passed to these ten persons. The ten grantees disposed of the land for the benefit of the people. I think the persons who devised this Bill must have had very hard hearts indeed: I think that Bill must have been devised with the expectation that the Europeans would obtain all the Native land.

'I will now refer to the Native Lands Act of 1867. I will not speak of the Native Land Act of 1873. I will now refer to the Native Land Division Act. And I will speak of the Crown Grants Act. The Natives are anxious to have committees of their own to deal with their lands without interference of law. I am convinced that if the Maoris are not allowed to have committees to administer their lands the whole of their lands will pass away from them; not an acre will be left. I think it would be a very good plan if a Royal Commission were appointed to inquire into the grievances under which the Native people have suffered in the past. Sir, I omitted to allude to a Bill which was formerly passed in this House—that is, the Lands Frauds Prevention Act. I look upon this Act as a very useful measure; but the Commissioners who had the administering of that Act did not carry it out in its integrity.

'With regards to the provisions of the present Bill to which we, the Native people, object, I would earnestly request, and do request, the Native Minister to withdraw those sections. I approve of the principle of the Bill; but it is the wish of the Maori members and of the Natives that it shall be in every respect a Maori Bill—that is, a Bill to meet the wishes of the Natives. I am the more urgent on this point when I think of the great evil that has come upon the Native people in the past in consequence of past legislation.

'Sir, I wish that all transactions in Native land should be carried on in daylight. There is no encouragement in the Bill in the direction of assisting Natives to farm and cultivate the land. The reason why I am persistent in my remarks is because of my love for the Native people. I think that Europeans are well able to take care of themselves, because they are a superior race. They are people of great possessions and great knowledge. The Maoris have no other earthly possessions than the land which they have inherited from their ancestors. I call upon the colonial-born Europeans to assist us in obtaining what we want. I also call upon those elderly gentlemen who have resided in New Zealand for a long time to help us in the same direction. What has happened in the past in regards to the legislation respecting the Natives should be considered. The laws have not been satisfactory. The Maoris are groping about in darkness under the laws passed by the Europeans. The Maoris remind me very much of the dog about which we hear, which, when crossing a bridge with a piece of meat in his mouth, saw the reflection of it in the water, and left the substance to grasp at the shadow. He saw the shadow in the water and dived after it, and left the substance, and when he got out of the water he felt that he had done a very foolish thing indeed. The Maoris are acquainted with the boundaries of their own land; but when they bring those lands under the administration of the European laws, very often they lose the substance and get the shadow only.

'Now with regard to what has been said in this House as to the dividing of the Maori lands: I ask that the purchase of land may stop absolutely until the land is divided. If the dividing of the land and the leasing and purchasing are carried on simultaneously, the Maoris will lose all, because the Maori lands are at present a source of revenue to their owners. It is on account of the past troubles that I think we may be able to obtain some relief under the provisions of the Bill now before the House. This is the first time that the Maoris have had a chance, and that is why I ask that the Maori members may be allowed to make amendments to this Bill; and I hope the members of the House will afford them every assistance. I hope we shall not be treated by the Europeans as the European rat treated the native rat, or as the bees treated the native birds—that is, killed them out. The native game has disappeared before the rats and the birds which the Europeans have introduced; and in like manner the laws which have been passed by the Europeans in this House have affected the Maori injuriously. If the rats and other creatures which have destroyed our game were capable of acting on advice I would pray them to desist.

'I need have no hesitation in appealing to the members of this House to help us in getting what we want, because honourable members know that we have now no authority left to us. The authority of our chiefs has been taken from us. Formerly the Native people used to pay tribute to their chiefs. The fruit of the forest and the fruits of the seas were given as offerings to the chiefs. The

Queen has now obtained authority over all these things. Formerly the seashore of this very harbour belonged to Wi Tako and the Natives, but it is now said to belong to the Queen; the place where the wharf stands formerly belonged to Wi Tako, but it is now said to belong to the Queen, although she never purchased it: and yet rates and tax are imposed on the Natives in spite of the Treaty of Waitangi, which assured all our possessions to us. I think it would be quite sufficient if the sovereignty of the Queen referred only to her ships and to her people who sail on the sea. I think that very likely, when the land round Wellington was purchased from the Maoris, high-water mark was the boundary of the purchase; but now the Maoris are frightened by being told that the rivers and the sea all belong to the Queen. That is why I say the authority of the Natives has disappeared, and that is why I ask that the small power we ask for may be assured to us by this Bill, so that we may be able to administer our own affairs without complaint.

'There is a Native proverb which I should like to see applied to this Bill. "You take half, and leave us half." I wish you all prosperity— the members of this House.'

PARLIAMENTARY HANSARD: ORDER OF BUSINESS, AUGUST 31, 1885, MR PERE

'Sir, I have observed very often that when matters affecting the Maoris are brought before this House some honourable members do not support them at all; they vote against them. So far, nothing has been done for the Natives—nothing during this session. Numbers of petitions protesting against rates have been presented to this House. Nothing has been done in the way of affording relief. The same remark applies to the Native land duties: nothing has been done to remove the complaints which the Maoris make against those duties. The Maoris have asked, too, that they should have additional representation. They think they are entitled to one member for every five thousand persons. In my own case I have to represent fifteen thousand people. It would be a very good thing if this House could see its way to increase the Native representation. But perhaps honourable members would be afraid to give us that, lest we should afterwards give a block vote. Great complaints have been made about the four Native members having all voted on one side. The reason we voted as we did is that we consider that measures affecting the Natives are thrown out by other members. For instance, if the Native Land Disposition Bill is brought before the House, I have no doubt honourable members, we will combine to throw that out—that is, a great many honourable members will.'

PARLIAMENTARY HANSARD: NATIVE LAND ADMINISTRATION BILL, JUNE 11, 1886, MR PERE

'Sir, I wish to make some remarks upon this Bill. I support this Bill, in order that any future dealings with Native lands may be done under the light of the law; that there may be no trouble between the Natives and the Europeans, and no cause for grumbling; and so that the land may be justly taken by the Europeans, and the money fairly paid over to the Natives.

'I will now make some remarks apart from this—I mean with reference to certain remarks which have fallen from honourable members of this House. I may say that there has been no permanent Native Committee appointed by this House which has yet had to perform any work. Those Committees which are referred to are only falsely represented as such to the Natives: they have not yet worked according to the law. There was an Act passed in 1883 giving power to Native Committees; but the Natives have not yet done any work under the conditions authorised by the Act, because such committees were not furnished with any sufficient power. I have actually heard that that Act was passed simply to appease the Native mind.

'My desire is that there should be Committees to deal with Native lands. I believe that the Europeans have derived benefit from the system of Committees. This House sitting here now is a sort of Committee, and there are other Committees dealing with the management of hospitals and other institutions. It is only now that the Europeans and the Natives have ceased to kill each other, and it in only now that the Natives have ceased to quarrel among themselves; and I now say, positively, that if this Bill is passed no European will hereafter be killed. If the law stands as it is now, it is possible that some European or some Native may suffer. Do not think that I wish to intimidate anybody by the words I now speak; but it is well known that, from the beginning, persons have been killed owing to this trouble in connection with land: and that is why it is desirable that we should find some way by which land may be dealt with in a straightforward manner, and also that some of the land may be retained by the Natives. I think therefore, that we should strive to pass some Act by which these Native lands should be dealt with.'

PARLIAMENTARY HANSARD: NATIVE LAND ADMINISTRATION BILL, JULY 6, 1886, MR PERE

'Sir, I desire to make a few remarks about this Bill. A statement has been made by an honourable member that a great deal of trouble will come upon the Native people under the provisions of this Bill. They raise no objection to it on the score that it will bring trouble to the Europeans.

'It is quite vain for honourable gentlemen to come to us and say, "Object to this Bill", because we know that if we did we should have to return to the state of things which existed in the past and has brought trouble upon us. I allude to the Native land laws, which stink in the nostrils of the Native people. These laws brought trouble upon Natives and Europeans: they estranged the two races, and stirred up fighting between them. They have caused thousands of petitions to come before this house praying for relief; but no relief has yet been given to them.

'I will not be a party to patch up the provisions of years past, particularly the pre-emptive right. I will not restore the broken clauses of the Treaty of Waitangi. I do not approve of that, because it resulted in our getting perhaps twopence or threepence an acre for our land. I also object to free trade in land, and I object to individual Natives having power to sell to Europeans; and I altogether uphold the proposal to dispose of land through the Native Committees, so that the wishes of the owners may be carried out. If the Natives wish to sell land to the Government they will be in a position to do so. All that I ask is that the power of the Europeans to purchase from individuals may cease, and that the power of Europeans to purchase from individuals may cease also, and that the magnitude of a man's interest in land may be ascertained, so that he may receive a proportionate amount of purchase-money or rent for the land.

'I say that the measure before the House gives effect to and carries out certain provisions of the Treaty of Waitangi. It confirms to the Native Chiefs and the Native people their right in the soil, and says that the Queen shall be the protector of them. I say that is the direct effect of the Bill. The Maori owners will have authority over the land. All that remains for the Government to do is to carry out the wishes of the Native people, and I think under this Bill the Queen's law will be carried out. It will also carry out the Treaty of Waitangi, by preventing private individuals from selling to Europeans. If it does not pass this year, by next year a very great quantity of the Native lands will be alienated. If the measure is put off until next session, so that it may be circulated by the time the House next meets, a great part of the Native lands will be parted with, and there will be nothing to fight about.

'I think every step should be taken to obtain for the Natives the best advantage on account of their land. I am not afraid of delay, for if there is any delay it will be in favour of the Maoris. There is an old proverb which says that if a man swallows his food with haste very likely he will be choked, but if he masticates his food carefully it will do him a great deal of good. Perhaps some honourable gentlemen are jealous—they do not wish the Native Minister to have the credit of bringing in a measure for the benefit of the Native people. There have been some thousands of petitions sent to this House praying for the rehearing of cases with regard to Native lands, but none of those have been answered.

'I think this Bill should be called "An Act to prevent Satan dealing with Native Lands". By "Satan" I mean those who have obtained our lands wrongfully. I do not think that any European members ought to object to this Bill; because his own land will not be affected by it—it only touches the lands of the Native people, and will save them from the teeth of the dragon which has been devouring them hitherto. If, however, you will not pass a Bill restricting the traffic in Native land, and object to this Bill passing, then I say that your desire is that all our lands at Taupo, in the Waikato, and elsewhere shall pass from us.'

'Sir, I am the member of the East Coast. In all my transactions as to this Bill I knew very well what I was about—at least in the little I understood it. I would like to ask which is the best law for the Natives at the present time. I think the best law would be one against buying any Native land at all. I would like this House to consent to not buying any more lands from the Natives, and to throw this Act on one side altogether. But if this Act is thrown on one side, and we go back to the old ones, the same old abuses will commence. The Natives have lost about thirty million acres, perhaps more.

'The Natives will derive great benefits from the present Act. If a block of land is sold in accordance with this Act there will be no trouble amongst the Natives. With the former laws there was nothing but trouble and lawsuits in all directions, and it was stated that the Natives were flattered and cajoled. What I like in this Act is that the owners hand the land over to a Committee to dispose of. I think the only Act the Natives should now have is one to prevent them selling any land at all. Why should not the House sympathise with the Natives and let them keep their land? Let the Government put settlers on the land they have already.

'I ask honourable members not to flatter the Natives with speeches, for I can perceive what is meant by the speeches. If I were to introduce a Bill preventing any more land being sold, I do not believe there is one European member who would sympathise with the Natives and vote for the Bill. I think they would run out of the House. As to the alligator which has such long teeth, and is devouring our land, it grieves me very much.'

Was Wi Pere really serious, one wonders, when he spoke out against the Women's Suffrage Bill? 'My opinion,' he said in the House on 11 May 1887, 'of this measure is that, if it becomes law, it will be a source of trouble that came upon Adam through his wife giving him an apple. We should bear in mind the evil that befell Samson when his locks were shorn by Delilah. We should also bear in mind the story of Naboth's vineyard—how a woman incited a man to murder another in order to obtain possession of his vineyard. I am afraid if ladies were allowed seats in this House it would distract the attention of some honourable members and they would not pay so much attention to the affairs of the colony as they would otherwise do. Although I am getting up in years I must confess I should be affected by a weakness of that sort. If the honourable gentlemen in charge of the Bill would introduce a clause providing that only plain women be allowed to come into the House, I think the source of danger would be removed; but if any beautiful ladies were sent to this House I am quite sure they would lead astray the harder hearts of some honourable gentlemen, particularly the older members of the House. I say in conclusion that if attractive ladies are allowed to come to this House I am quite certain my wife will never consent to my standing here.'

The reference to his wife, Arapera, is ironical for he was already perhaps well into his affair with the woman who later became known as his 'Wellington wife', the winsome Pakeha by the name of Annie O'Neill.

'Te Mana o Turanga. Wi Pere. Te Ihi. Te Wehi.

'E mokopuna, your ancestor's star was in the ascendant, streaking its glory across the night sky. But, aue, something went wrong. There was a disruption in the universe and it was momentous enough to break the pattern. It was like watching the hand of God suddenly catch that ascending star in mid-flight and, contemptuously, fling it down to earth.

'Watching, Riria Mauaranui, the chieftainess realised why. Ah yes, she knew the reason. Even more, she understood that she was powerless to prevent that untimely descent, that plunge into doom.'

21

By the 1890s, although the Pakeha was firmly established in New Zealand, the world of the Maori, of communion between gods and man, the fabulous with the real, still manifested itself in apparitions of immense power. So it was that in August 1891, the SS *Rotomahana* was nearing Portland Island when there was a turmoil in the dark depths and a giant shadow began to ascend from out of the sea.

'All engines stop,' the captain instructed.

The officers looked ahead at the place where the surface was boiling like a cauldron. Then it appeared, the sea serpent, the taniwha, rising out of the water to a great height, the sea streaming like fluid ribbons from its sinuous shape. The officers reported that the taniwha was about 100 feet in length, and that it had a white belly and a black back. Two ten-foot fins were spiked along the spine.

'Oh my God,' one of the officers whispered in awe as the taniwha rose in the sky.

The taniwha hovered there for a moment, a creature of such physical and psychic strength that the crew of the SS *Rotomahana* were stunned into submission by its presence. It dared the crew to believe in its existence and to open their minds to the possibilities of the unknown. Then, almost with an air of contempt, the taniwha made its slow descent back into the sea, sliding into the water from where it had arisen.

The officers of the SS *Rotomahana* reported the sighting to the authorities. As Hawke's Bay had just experienced a severe earthquake, the general opinion was that what had been seen was the trunk of a large tree wrenched from the bed of the sea. The Maori people of Turanga, however, were greatly disturbed by the report. It was a portent. It was an omen. It was Arai te Uru, one of the two taniwha which had accompanied the *Takitimu* canoe on its voyage to the fish of Maui. The sea serpent was a reminder of the past, ripping through the fabric of the real world and bringing with it the remnants of fantastic dreams.

↩

Deh! Mi reggi, m'aita, o Signor, Miserere d'un povero cor. Ah, support me, help me, oh Lord. Have mercy on my wretched heart. *Miserere, Miserere d'un povero cor Miserere di me, Signor.* Have mercy, have pity, have mercy on me. Lord.

Ae, Riria knew that she was powerless to prevent the plunging of her son's star to doom. Like Te Kooti before him, Wi Pere found himself at the mercy of the force of destiny. Power, charisma and leadership were not enough to alter that destiny. Wi Pere had the all these qualities, but not in sufficiency to maintain his ascendancy.

In the general election of 1887 he lost his seat—it was as simple as that. He lost to the redoubtable Sir James Carroll, Timi Kara, and to the power of the Ngati Kahungunu who wished the seat to return to a son of Hawke's Bay; they gained the vote of Mataatua which had earlier been Wi Pere's. From 1887 to 1894 Wi Pere the Great was unseated and the triumphal wreath was taken from him. The sound of his fall was like a cry of pain felt in the psyche of the people.

And even though in 1894, Wi Pere regained his seat, his comet was falling, falling, falling. The cynics would say that he would not have achieved this had it not been for Timi Kara's decision to seek the mandate in another electorate, the Waiapu European Electorate. Nonetheless Wi Pere kept it in spite of the hostile vote of the Arawa electors for ten years until 1905 when he was defeated by the charismatic and amazing Sir Apirana Ngata. But during this time his comet kept falling, falling, falling. An attempt to establish the New Zealand Native Land Company failed and his performance in Parliament, and within this company, became a divisive issue in East Coast politics. Wi Pere sealed his destiny when, under great financial difficulties himself, he sought assistance in 1899 from the Government. He asked that an estate, bearing his name, was established. He was in debt to the tune of £70,000; if Parliament would give him a loan, and an estate, then he would repay the loan from the operation of the estate. Parliament agreed. But to many people, this was nepotism. He was feathering his own nest. Instead of joining with the Maori who had lost their lands, he was seen to be protecting himself.

We must summon Riria Mauaranui, the chieftainess, to appear before us. We must demand her presence and her explanation for that cruel downward flaming of our ancestor's star. Let our call go echoing forth across the night. Let our meeting again take place on a landscape charged with symbolism—a lonely spot at the foot of a steep hill, where the chieftainess earlier bargained with the Tuhoe for the vote of Mataatua. Ara, and watch as she comes, upon the jagged wings of a manaia monster, slicing through the moon's light. Listen to her waiata of fear and sorrow, keening across the night sky, conjuring up the lamentations of the dead. Watch as the manaia monster descends to earth, landing swiftly and folding its webbed wings into its scaly form. Wait as the chieftainess steps down from its luminous head. As she approaches us, she covers her face with shame.

E, Riria, come forward. Tell us why the emperor's star was struck from the heavens? Justify yourself. Did he not have the vote of Mataatua? Was he not given the support of Tuhoe?

She is like a veiled shade, the chieftainess, as she stands before us. Then she whispers one word, 'Maraehinahina.' Then she continues, 'Seek your answer there, at Maraehinahina.'

Maraehinahina. She, Riria, the chieftainess, gave her son her mana. She put her feather cloak upon his shoulders. She gave him her power, but still it was required to be formalised in him. So it was that Wi Pere was taken to the whare wananga, the sacred house of learning, to understand about his powers.

That was where the reason lay. At Maraehinahina.

The whare wananga was the university of the Maori, one of the most exclusive universities in the world, erected by priests and selected members of the rangatira and ariki. No commoners took part in raising the building and the students were chosen from among the high-born. Women were not permitted as academic acolytes and entered only on pain of death. They could, however, if they wished, enter the lower school, the whare-maire, the house of necromancy, wizardry and shamanism, but their destinies would then have been ruled by the more sinister gods—by the flying star, the dog, the shag and the lizard. Other alternatives for women were the school of astrology, the whare-taiai, or in the school of recreation, the whare-matoro.

The prime directive of the whare wananga was to preserve for all time the ancient lore, the history and genealogies of the race and all incantations necessary to important karakia and sacred hui. For this reason, only the most brilliant young men, possessing superb powers of memory, were able to qualify for entry.

And what did they see in the whare wananga? They saw a place tapu like the sacred tabernacle of the Hebrew people as described in the Old Testament. The building itself would have faced east. In the mahau, the easterly complex, sacrificial offerings would have been made to the gods and all the ceremonies attending to the worship of the gods were undertaken with due respect and honour. There would have been a flax bush or tree fern growing in the centre of the mua, and a shrine to Kahukura, the rainbow god, near at hand. All human sacrifices would have been buried close to this location, the blood of the victims being offerings to Mua and the heart to Tu, in this place charged as with electricity by extremely potent tapu. Finally, there would have been the whare wananga proper, where the students were taught. Sacred fires were lit in this part of the building at the rear of which was buried the ahurewa, the stone talisman marking the most sacred place of all. It was here that the most important ceremonials were performed. A special sanctuary was reserved for the high priest of Io alone.

Once chosen, the student was faced with a full curriculum lasting five long years. The actual annual academic term lasted during the winter months but the rest of the year was committed to the other tapu tasks. Students were banned from all association with the ordinary members of the iwi and, if any had wives or families, a total separation was demanded during the period of instruction. Nor were students allowed within any place associated with cooked food. Inattention, whispering, drowsiness and restlessness were occasions for severe punishment. Serious misconduct led to expulsion.

First-year students were termed pia. As proficiency advanced, the student was awarded the degree of tauira, indicating his possession of first-level occult knowledge and the tribal traditions. Later in his five-year study he would become a tohunga and, if he was high-born, he would automatically assume the rank of ariki. Already born a holy person, an ariki was destined to be the medium between the iwi and the gods. The whare wananga was the means of his assumption of holiness and tapu appropriate for his divine intercourse with them.

The curriculum was long and difficult. The chief priest would sit on the right hand side of the whare wananga and the other teachers would sit on the left. It was the duty of the chief priest to see that no interpolations or omissions were made in the instruction. Like the laws of the Medes and Persians, the coursework of the whare wananga was constant, and, should any of the teachers vary from the constant the chief priest would interrupt him and instruct another teacher to carry on. (And I remember, yes, the matriarch taking me in the evenings to a dark place lit with shadows and flickering fires, and the frightening droning, on and on, coming from the flames. Afterwards, the matriarch wept over me, saying 'This is not the way as of old but this is the only way we have in the world of the Pakeha. O Ruamano, forgive the manner of the child's teaching, for this is his only way.')

But the reward was greatness. Every test of proficiency brought the student nearer and nearer to godly powers. So the student hurled a stone at a shrine and prayed it would not break for, if it did so, he was unfit to proceed from one year to the next and would have to remain for a further term of instruction. He uttered incantations and, behold, if he broke a stone into fragments, he had passed one of many examinations. He uttered a karakia and concentrated on killing a flying bird and, if the bird fell dead, another test was passed. If, by further prayers, he could render himself invisible, again he advanced in the university. As his powers increased, so did his abilities—to control the tempest at sea and the storm on land; to command the taniwha and whale, and also demons, to do his will; to take giant strides across the earth, fifty miles apart, like the hero Rongokako.

The thrill of obtaining the power! To control the elements. To control matter. To conjure up the solar halo or the lunar halo. To will men to do as you would wish. All this and more was taught in the whare wananga of old, and such a whare wananga called Tokitoki existed in the Gisborne district.

But it was at Maraehinahina, and not Tokitoki, where Wi Pere was taught.

The time of the Christian God had come across the land and the last priest at Tokitoki feared for the safety of the house. His name was Tupai Whakarongo Tarawhare and he took council with the neighbouring chiefs, saying, 'We must transfer the sacred altar of our gods to another place of haven.' The decision was made to remove the altar pertaining to the god Ruamano to Maraehinahina. After the removal, as Tupai had feared, Tokitoki was destroyed and desecrated by the adherents of Christianity and divested of its ancient glory; the time of the Christian cross came upon the land. Those religious tokens and sacraments which had not been removed by the tohunga were defiled by the Christians who celebrated the destruction they had wrought.

It was a time of confusion, when the people were caught between the old gods and the cross. The confusion proved fatal in Wi Pere's case. It was related that during the ceremony of instilling knowledge into him, by immersion, his people objected. The three tohunga cried out in pain, saying, 'The ceremony is interrupted and the boy will have lesser powers.' It has been said that Wi Pere, perhaps in sympathy with the family, whispered, 'Despite the interruption, the powers I have will be sufficient for my people. For if I am an ariki I do not need the wizardry of the ceremonial alone to sustain me as I make a way for my people in the world of the Pakeha.'

It was not enough after all.

⌒

The Maori king of the Waikato, King Mahuta, had been given the absolute right to govern his vast territory. After some years, however, he was persuaded to submit his sovereignty to the New Zealand Government. This was partly secured by giving the Maori monarch a seat in the Legislative Council. A cartoon was published at the time showing Sir James Carroll putting a hook in the mouth of King Mahuta. The result was that the whole of the King Country was opened for Pakeha settlement.

King Mahuta came to Wellington to attend his first session of the Legislative Council. Wi Pere looked at him intently and then smiled. There was an ironic lilt to his voice, one tinged with reflection and sadness.

He began his welcome, and the floor fell into silence. 'There was a certain owl,' he said, 'who lived in the darkness and fastnesses of the forest. While in his protected surroundings he was one day attracted by the joyful crying of the other birds outside the forest. "Oh!" thought the owl, "What a lot of good things there must be there." He flew through the trees, but on reaching the forest edge his eyes were blinded by the light and he was obliged to perch on a tree. A man saw the owl and took a firebrand in one hand and a stick in the other. As he neared the owl it prepared to fly, but the man blinded the bird with the firebrand in one hand and stunned it with the stick. He then put it in a cage and made an ornament out of it.'

The Legislative Council began to laugh. They thought that Wi Pere was telling one of his usual nonsensical jokes. He raised his hand to stop the laughter. He put out his arms to King Mahuta.

'Welcome,' Wi Pere said. 'The owl is you, and we, the Members of Parliament are the other birds. The man is the Prime Minister, the firebrand is the bundle of notes for your salary, the stick is your oath, and the cage is the House of Parliament.'

Even then, Wi Pere knew that the Maori cause may have been forever lost. All of the birds had now been blinded and stunned and there they sat, the parliamentary representatives of the Maori people, on the perches of the Pakeha. But his words were a warning to the new generation, and they were taken to heart by the woman he chose to carry on his fight—Riripeti, the matriarch.

The chieftainess, Riria Mauaranui must have been an amazing woman, as amazing as the matriarch herself. There is no doubt that she demanded and received the love and respect of her son. Nor is there any reason to question this affection between them and, certainly, if you wish to see how much influence she had on her son, look again to the panel of Wi Pere and his mother in the painted Rongopai. He who was without tattoo is shown with tattoo symbolic of his great mana, while she who aided him is perched on his shoulders, forever advising.

Once, when I was younger, I sat in Rongopai at dusk. I was alone with my ancestors. In the dimness of the interior I became aware that there were three figures on the panel, not two. The vision was only shown me for a second. I, who was only a young boy, seemed to see someone in his adulthood whom I could not recognise. Perched on the shoulders of that man were not one, but two bird-like figures. One of the figures wore pearls in her hair. The other was ill-defined, merely a ghostly image with her hands covering her face.

I know now that the other figure must have been Tiana.

And who now sings the aria, as she leaves the moonlit field and the gallows whitely shining?

'Deh! Mi reggi, m'aita, O Signor, Miserere d'un povero cor.'

Is it Riria, who goes now? *'Ah, support me, help me, Oh Lord.'* Is it Artemis?

'Miserere, Miserere d'un povero cor Miserere di me, Signor.'

Or is it Tiana herself? *'Have mercy, have pity.'*

Oh Lord, have mercy.

22

WITNESS 1: *HORI MATENE MATENGA, KAHUNGUNU. AS TOLD TO HIS SON ON 17 APRIL 1982*
'My name is Hori Matene Matenga. I am ninety-four years old, so they tell me, I don't know myself. I was born by the Wairoa River, but I been living with my mokopuna in Napier since 1961.

'You have been asking me about the year 1949. I was a young man then, sixty-one years old, just a spring chicken, still had all my teeth, my hair and good eyesight. I tell you why, because I ate Maori kai, no sugar, no butter, no beer, no hot liquids. Yes, I was at the marae, by jingo, when the people gathered there to talk about Papatuanuku, our land. What a big hui! Everybody was there. And she was there, Riripeti, whom some called Artemis. But Riripeti, that's her ingoa Maori. You wouldn't want to cross her, no fear.

'E hara, don't hurry me. You know I don't like talking into your tape machine. How do I know what you will do with my voice? What's that? You want to know about nga pungawerewere. Why do you want to know about them for? You know, there are some things that Maoris don't like to talk about. Yes, they were there all right. Put me right off my kai. I was sitting down with Heni on my right and Watene on my left, they've both gone to Te Po now, aue. I miss Heni especially.

'Well, we were sitting there. Must have been hundreds of manu-hiri at the feast. Tom Maxwell, he was the one who said the karakia for the food. Wonderful, the Maori kai in those days. I was hoeing into the kumara, and all of a sudden I noticed out of the corner of my eye that Riripeti had stood up. Well, you know, I could see her looking up at the ceiling, so I had a look too. And that's when I saw a huge cloud of black dust beginning to drift down from the ceiling. Then they came, nga pungawerewere.'

WITNESS 2: BERNARD SCOTT MVO, MAORI HILL, DUNEDIN. INTERVIEWED ON 7 MAY 1980, SHORTLY BEFORE HIS DEATH

'My MVO? Oh, I got that in 1964, old chap, in recognition of my services to the Queen during her tour of New Zealand. As you know, I have always been involved in government service. Were it not for the spot of bother I had with my heart I would probably have made Secretary of Internal Affairs but, alas, when one's doctor commands one to retire early then one must.

'But let me get straight to the point. I was Private Secretary to the Prime Minister, if memory serves me correctly, between 1947 and 1953. They were grand years for Government. New Zealand was just getting back on its feet after the Second World War and we were all involved in returning the country to normal. They were heady years and they proved to be quite a challenge, particularly in the sphere of Maori politics. You see, all these returning servicemen chappies, well, they needed to be absorbed back into the community and, New Zealand being a farming country, it was only logical that Government should consider rehabilitating them on Maori land.

'This, I recall, was the main underlying reason for the gathering of all the tribal elders in Wellington in 1949. Of course we never actually came out publicly and stated as such, but our intention was fairly well known. As you probably know, I argued against the Prime Minister but without success. I suppose that this was why Artemis was always so disappointed in me. Despite my high position I was pretty ineffectual and, even if I say so myself, this MVO was not well deserved.

'Yes, I had known Artemis well before 1949. I met her before the War and she quite surprised me with her excellent knowledge of Italian. She was an incredible beauty, also, and quite turned my head, but that's another story. We would never have been well suited. She was much too strong as a person and I would have made a fairly weak consort. But more than that she was strongly pro-Maori and I don't think she would ever have entertained the prospect of a Pakeha match.

'You should be justifiably proud of Artemis, old chap. She was a wonderful champion of Maori rights. She had charisma, charm, and not a little ruthlessness, I might add. Above all else, she had a power that can only be described as supernatural. People these days don't seem to understand that word. They tend to equate it with the fantastic, the unreal. Whatever it was, she certainly possessed it. I was sitting next to her at luncheon on the marae. This was in 1949. We were chatting together and, in mid-sentence, I saw her eyes widen and she looked away from me and started to hunt through the crowd with her eyes. She shouted in Maori, it seemed like a shout, and it was like having a thunderbolt flashing through my head. I put my hands to my ears. I happened to look up.

'I saw these beautiful webs, like fragile cathedrals, strung between the rafters. Suddenly, they ripped open. Hundreds of small black spiders, suspended from crystal threads, began to fall like a cloud.'

WITNESS 3: AGNES MEREANA WAIPARE, WELLINGTON, AS RECORDED AT TITAHI BAY, LDS CHURCH, 21 OCTOBER 1983

'I was just a young girl in 1949. I was born in Wellington, lived all my life here, married here, had my children here, and I am very happy here, thank you very much. I have a nice house in the Bay, I have my health, and I have my Church. I am a person who has been truly blessed by God.

'I don't know how you found out about me but, yes, I was the one who was serving at the table at that hui, the table where the young boy was sitting and the old man was standing behind him. My auntie told me to help out with the kai. She said, "Agnes, you and Ruta go and look after table seven." I think I must have been seventeen in 1949. Could have been younger. I don't know.

'You know, I never used to be religious. Gosh, me and Ruta used to get up to some tricks, I can tell you. But the Lord saved me that day and I have been thanking him ever since. The elders say that what happened was my deliverance from evil. They say that it was not accidental that I was there. I was chosen to be there. To suffer. And to see the light. Oh yes, and I suffered. Is that how you found me? Through the records of Porirua mental hospital? I thought so. After that day, I went a little porangi. Even now I can't stand to see nga pungawerewere. I have this phobia about them. With God's help I may be able to overcome it. After all, all insects are created of God.

'I had come out of the kitchen with two kono of food, one in each hand. This was my second trip to the table. On the first one, this old man had been in my way and I almost spilt the kai. On the second one, I could see him ahead of me, so I was very careful when I approached him. Well, the funny thing is that I heard this chanting in my head, and I came over all dizzy. It was a horrible sound, like what death must sound like. One of my problems has always been that I hear and see things; some people say it is a gift, well, I would freely give it to them. It is not a gift that I would wish anybody to have.

'I stumbled, you see, so I put the kono down quickly on the table. I was right beside the old man and this young boy. I was getting a huge dark feeling in my mind, and I couldn't see properly. Then I heard people screaming. I can remember putting my hands on the table to steady myself. My vision was all blurred.

'I saw a spider on my hand. And another. And another. And then I began to feel these soft movements in my hair and on my neck and all over me. I knew then what was happening. I opened my mouth to scream, and I felt spiders crawling between my lips.

I was in Porirua for many, many years. But it was God who saved me, and my Church, and I tell you these things in Jesus' name, Amen.'

'Well, we'll be building another hall, no doubt about that, but it certainly won't be the same as the old one. The old one was special. It was built in the old style. Tall ceiling. The beams were floated down the Wanganui and hauled overland. There were special karakia done on the beams. This was in the 1850s. The place sure lasted a long time. It is no good, this fire, or any fire, for it destroys our history.

'You know, it was the Reverend Williams, way back then, who is credited with first noticing the pungawerewere. He was on a visit to Wellington and came into the old dining hall. He saw the webs being spun way up in the rafters. Anyway, the story goes that when he pointed them out the elders wanted to get rid of them. But Mr Williams said, "No, leave them, for they do you no harm and they are in God's care." So they stayed up there and, over the years they wove beautiful webs which were glorious to look at. In the morning, the sun made them glisten like fine-spun silk. When the sun went down, the webs would change colours from crimson through to blue to dark jet black. I tell you, they were a natural wonder, and this marae became famous for them. Around here, the appearance of a spider was a good omen.

'Well, you need to know this background because of what happened in 1949. And the other thing I should mention is that what happened that year was not unique. I am told, for instance, that the webs also ripped open in 1870, 1901 and 1936. I suppose it has something to do with overpopulation of spiders, or something like that. Only, on the three other times, it didn't happen when the hall was full of people, including the Prime Minister.

'It must have been the vibrations or sounds which caused the spiders to appear in so dramatic a fashion. I know some people panicked when they began to fall. And I have heard some rumours about Artemis, that kuia from Turanga, being responsible for the appearance. But as I say, their appearance was a good omen, not a bad one. The only trouble is with people who did not understand this.

'I believe that if that old man had not raised his hand and cried out, the spiders would not have continued to fall. I think that they would probably have begun weaving another web, at a lower level, below the beams. But when he cried our like that, he angered them. That is why they did what they did.'

WITNESS 5: ALAN GORDON HITCHINGS, JOURNALIST, WELLINGTON. INTERVIEW NO. 7, TAPE 12, 7 FEBRUARY 1969
'Yes, I am aware of Mr Ellis's comments back in 1953, and of the history of the marae. In particular, I can confirm that the webs were certainly very beautiful and, without doubt, a most glorious sight. Yes, I think he is correct in suggesting that the spiders simply appeared like that to weave a further layer across the ceiling. After all, that is what they began to do, to our surprise and delight, weaving their webs backwards and forwards across the beams, a brilliant concert, put on just for us. Oh, the cries of admiration from the crowd. It was fantastic.

'But I beg to differ from him on the matter of Artemis. Now, I was right there, and I heard her begin to chant. The sound was soft and guttural. It had the presence of death in it. The chant was not a long one, but it was quick, rather like an incantation. An invocation.

'Well, most people were looking up at the spiders as they wove their web. But I saw what she did. She drew a line between the webs and the place where the elder from the paepae was standing, right behind you. The web cathedrals suddenly ripped open above the elder and you. The spiders elsewhere fell no further than a few feet at the most. But those that were right above the elder, they continued their descent. It was Artemis who caused them to do this. I swear it.'

Except in one small space, the spiders fell only a few metres. There, above the elder from the paepae, they descended quickly, dropping so fast that it was like watching a seething, living waterfall.

They fell upon the elder from the paepae so that, in a second, he was completely covered with them. There was a young girl standing next to him who was also covered.

'Manaaki, Hiraina, guard the child,' the matriarch said. The spiders were falling, falling, falling. Manaaki gathered up the child and pulled him away from the radius of the spiders' descent.

The spiders began to spin a web, enclosing the elder and the girl in a tight-webbed cocoon. The girl screamed and fought against the strands. It was Manaaki, with the help of a teenage boy, who pulled her free.

The web was so tight that, as they pulled the girl free, her skin was ripped from her face, legs and arms. Blood marked the tiny pinpricks of the fangs of the spiders. Even when she was pulled free, the spiders still clung to her, feeding on her.

The elder turned to face the child. 'Help me!' he cried.

He was disappearing beneath layers of spider silk, like a fly caught in the web.

Then he could speak no longer. Paralysed, he could only wait until the spiders had completed their work. He ceased to struggle. But his eyes lived a little longer, shining through the silk of the web.

'Help me, help me,' they pleaded.

'Have mercy upon me.'

act five

23

The Great Land March of 1975 ended in a dazed euphoria. The concourse at Parliament resounded with the hopes and joys of the marchers like circlets of gladness crowning the air. But there were some among the protesters who were not fooled. 'What has been achieved?' they asked. 'What has the Government done in response to our pleas that not one more acre of Maori land should be sold? Nothing. The Government has done nothing. All the Prime Minister has done is receive us at Parliament and promise to look at our plea. We have nothing to show for our march. All is in vain. Nothing. Nothing.'

A splinter group of young protesters decided to pitch a tent in the grounds of Parliament. 'We shall remain here,' they said, 'in the sight of the Pakeha, to remind him that we demand action. We shall not move until our plea is heard.' Tame Iti, Titewhai Harawira and her children were there, Ted Nia, the mercurial Greg Whakataka, Dun Mihaka and many wahine toa.

Nulla. Silenzio. There were others, and they were an intense, committed group, a disturbing presence in Parliament Grounds. They were vilified by their elders; in turn, they accused their elders of having sold out to the Pakeha. 'The Land March has become an empty gesture if we have not achieved our ultimate aim,' they said. 'Our land is still being taken, still being sold. The Pakeha owns us.'

We were still slaves in the Land of Pharaoh.

～

'Of course you're talking about the legend, not the person,' Aunt Hiraina said. 'You're talking about the way she appeared to be and all the stories about her, but they aren't her. People used to think that your grandmother Riripeti was some kind of witch. That she could stop the sun. Or change into a spider. Or cause nga pungawerewere to fall upon Timoti, the elder of the paepae. Rubbish. All these events were coincidental. They were freakish. And they certainly weren't caused by witchcraft. Your grandmother believed in God, Tamatea. She was a godly woman who prayed to our Atua every morning and every night. No such woman would ever have been possessed by the devil. Certainly not Mum.'

It was February 1976 and, after the Land March and the visit of Grandfather Ihaka, Foreign Affairs had sent me on a two-month secondment to the United Nations in New York to do some work with the Committee on the Elimination of Racial Discrimination. As a consequence, it wasn't until I returned to New Zealand, and was reminded by a phone call from Te Ariki to help Aunt Hiraina and Uncle Hepi, that I was able to search for them.

'The last we heard,' he told me, 'they're still down in Wellington looking for Raina. We've been expecting Hiraina back in Waituhi before now. When you see her, tell her that Dad's not very well. Perhaps your Uncle Alexis would know where she and Hepi are.'

And so I found myself climbing again those steps to Uncle Alexis's windswept house. Aunt Roha appeared, gliding towards the cut-glass doorway like a grotesque fish, to let me in. When I told her why I had come, she said, 'I should have known that me and your uncle weren't the reason. Your Aunt Hiraina? Yes, I have the address. She and Hepi are staying with Sammy at the top of Aro

Street. But you're not going straight away, are you? You'd best say hello to Alexis, otherwise he'll think I turned you away. And stay for dinner. I insist.'

The house was possessed of a terrible stillness. My cousins drifted in and out of the corner of my vision, their faces filled with a fearful expectancy. The roses had faded from my aunt's cheeks and, although she had made herself up with her usual fastidious care, she lacked animation. She seemed to be drying up inside, her sensuality draining away.

'You've got a visitor Alex,' she said to Uncle. 'Your nephew.'

My uncle grinned across at me. I was appalled by the physical alteration. He lay half propped up by pillows like a huge grey slug on the double bed. The lack of exercise and sunlight had turned him into a gross creature of the dark. His voice, when he greeted me, sounded emasculated. There was no virility there, no sense of the overwhelming maleness he had once possessed. Was this what it was like when one of your senses was taken away from you? 'Tamatea . . .?'

One of his daughters was sitting on the bed next to him. She was feeding him with a spoon. The food was trickling down the sides of his mouth. He ate mindlessly and without joy. I felt sickened by it. Perhaps I should have gotten a shotgun after all. Better that than to see him this way, eating himself to death.

'How long has he been like this?' I asked Aunt Roha. She had lurched back into the corridor and was leaning against the wall, hugging herself tightly, her left fist bunched against her mouth.

'How long? How long?' she murmured. 'Forever and ever, that's how long, I don't know. Maybe after your grandfather left here. At least this is easier to handle than the silences. You never saw him in his silences, did you? He never spoke for weeks on end. Not a word. He lay there, in that bed, not speaking. It drove me out of my mind. Going in there, seeing him, trying to reach out to him. He wouldn't reach back. Not a single word of praise or damnation. Then one day, as I was shaving him, he grabbed my hair and whispered in my ear, "If you had the choice, would you prefer me blind or dumb?" And then he laughed and laughed.'

I tried to embrace my aunt but she wrenched herself away. 'I don't know how much longer I can stand it. After the silence came his rages. He got up out of bed and went from room to room smashing all the mirrors. I tried to stop him and he slapped me. "This is a house of the blind," he said, "and the blind don't need mirrors." He belongs in psychiatric care, Tamatea. But I love him. I don't want him to go into a place like that. Why can't he be the same as he used to be? Why can't he understand that I still need him, even if he is blind? And now he's starting to eat. He begins at five o'clock every morning. Eating. All the time. Once he was so handsome, and when I saw you dressed in his clothes when you were here last I remembered how wonderful he was. I really did. But it is taking so much effort to hold the memory of the way he used to be.'

I heard my uncle calling to me from the room. 'Tamatea . . . Tamatea . . .'

I left Aunt Roha and went to him. I motioned my cousin away and took her place beside him. He was panting from the exertion of eating. His face was bathed in sweat and there was spittle dribbling from the side of his mouth.

'Tamatea . . .Your grandmother . . . Forget her . . . Kill me, Tamatea, please, pleasepleasepleaseplease . . .'

He began to moan and rock back and forth and back and forth. 'It's the *mate*, Tamatea, don't you understand? That's why I have been consigned to Te Po and its never-ending darkness. Always black, so black . . . Have mercy upon me.'

～

The next evening I went around to the address in Aro Street that Aunt Roha had given me. It was a small decaying flat halfway up a street of lost souls. The street unwound in the moonlight like a shroud spilling its undead across the city. Some places have the feel of death about them; this street and this flat were like that, damp and cold, and stinking of years of vomit and urine. It was in need of a priest to exorcise its sorrows and evils.

My cousin Sammy answered the door. For a moment he was

shocked to see me, and I him. Although we were of the same age, he looked tired, ill and old. There were valleys of darkness in his face and feverish flames in his eyes.

'You,' he said. Reluctantly, he let me in.

Aunt Hiraina was in the kitchen, heating a pot of bacon bones and puha. As soon as she saw me, she began to cry. 'You've come at last,' she said. 'Now I know that everything will be all right and that we will find Raina.'

I held her tight. After a while, she stepped out of my arms. 'Oh, look at me!' she said, upset. 'Please forgive me, Tamatea, for being dressed like this. Had I known you were coming, I would have been prepared for your visit.'

She rushed to the bathroom to wash herself and brush her hair. Sammy looked at me, cynical. 'Don't expect me to put on flash clothes,' he said. 'As far as I'm concerned, you're no better and no worse than any of us.'

'I'm not here to fight with you,' I told him.

Aunt Hiraina returned. She was looking like her old self, pretty and vivacious. I asked her about Grandmother Riripeti and the incident involving the spiders that had occurred in 1949. She dismissed the question. She was preoccupied with whatever was happening in the present, and I should have known that there was something wrong in her and Uncle Hepi's lives. The street, the flat and the setting were all too morbid for our encounter. Darkness lay behind her feverish gaiety, and something was shifting in the shadows of her eyes which I could not define because of its shapelessness. She wanted something of me.

"Where's Uncle Hepi?" I asked.

'He's still out there searching for Raina,' she answered. 'We've tracked her down to a gang headquarters. But they won't let us see her. And they won't let her go.'

She began to weep again. Sammy gave her a look of disgust. 'I don't know why you think Tamatea can help us,' he told her.

'He's the Beloved of Riripeti,' she answered. Then she looked at me and said something strange: 'You've forgiven us, haven't you?'

'I'm getting out of here,' Sammy interrupted. 'Maybe I can find

Dad. Together we might be able to do something useful.' Before he closed the door he turned to me, aggressive and unfriendly. 'This is all your fault,' he said.

'Don't talk to Tamatea like that,' Aunt Hiraina reprimanded him.

Sammy looked at me, and his eyes were dangerous. The outside light shone full upon him, but there were shadows like knives falling across his face. 'I'll talk to Tamatea any way I damn well like,' he said. His voice had hysteria in it. 'This isn't his house and I'm no slave of his. Barging in here as if he owns the place. You are the cause of all our troubles, Tamatea. Our Uncle Alexis, his *mate* is because of you. My sister, Raina, her sickness also. Why? Because that old lady, our grandmother, she gave you our souls, Tamatea, and left us prone to all illness. Aunt Circe tried to prevent it, but you got everything, Tamatea. Everything.'

Before Sammy could go any further, Aunt Hiraina looked beyond him and gave a cry. From out of the darkness Uncle Hepi appeared. He was carrying Raina.

Aunt Hiraina and Sammy rushed out to them. Uncle Hepi saw me and his eyes softened with gratefulness. 'Hello, boy,' he said.

They laid Raina on a sofa in the sitting room. I was shocked at her condition. She was emaciated. Her eyes flickered open and, when she saw me, she smiled.

'Hello cousin,' she said.

Uncle Hepi interrupted her. He looked at Aunt Hiraina. 'We have to get away from here. Tonight. The gang will be after her.'

Aunt Hiraina turned to me and said, as if finding Raina had been my doing, 'Thank you, Tamatea.' She kissed both my hands. 'Will you help us?'

'Of course,' I answered.

Uncle Hepi bundled Raina into some blankets and took her out to the car. 'Sammy,' he said to his son, 'stay with her and don't let her out of your sight for one minute.'

'How did you get her out of there?' Sammy asked him.

'Our Uncle Vance in gang liaison,' he answered. 'He managed to strike a deal. But I don't think it's going to last.'

I followed him into the house. Aunt Hiraina was busy packing their suitcases. He stopped her. 'No, dear. We haven't got time. We have to go. Now.' Although his voice was gentle, it was also firm. 'We have what we came for. Our daughter. Nothing else is important.' He turned to me. 'Could you pack everything up for us, Tamatea? And send it to us? And clean the house and give the key to the landlord?'

I nodded. I was concerned at his anxiety. I followed him as, lovingly, he shepherded a whimpering Aunt Hiraina to the car.

'Just like that?' she asked him. 'We're going just like that?'

'Yes, dear,' he said. 'The gang want Raina back.'

My dear, sweet, lost cousin Raina. She was hungry for life from the moment she first drew breath, gulping the air down in huge gasps. Her parents adored her, of course, this third child who was given to them in their late years. They called her 'Baby' and talked babytalk to her. Naturally, she responded, to their great joy. 'Raina want this, Mummy,' she would say. 'Raina be good girl.' She wanted to be loved. She wanted her parents to love her because then they would give her anything she asked. Raina wanted everything.

They gave it to her—new dolls, new books, new friends, new clothes. Nothing was good enough for their young daughter. 'Old doll broken, Mummy. Want new one.' They could never refuse her. Nor could they see what we could: this pretty, precocious little girl with ringlets who, bored with her latest 'old' doll or attracted to a new one, would calmly push its eyes out and smash its head to pieces on the concrete pavement. 'Look what happened to dolly, Daddy. She felled over and broke her head. Poor dolly. Kiss not make dolly better.'

She grew up to be a pretty teenager with a pout for a mouth. We all loved her because she was so child-like, and how can you be cross with a child? 'I hate school. I don't want to go any more,' she said to her father. 'The teachers are mean to Raina, Daddy. They don't like me, Mummy.' Because her parents did not want Raina to remain where she was not loved, they took her out of school.

She tried to get a job in Gisborne but she lacked concentration for office work, got bored with factory work and, really, didn't want to work at all. Unemployed, she started to hang out with the crowd down at the Pitstop. There, her brand of sweet innocence made for instant appeal. They called her 'Baby Blackbird.' They loved the way she tried everything. Alcohol, for a time, gave her what she wanted. But she wanted to kick higher. She discovered sex, but it still wasn't quite the stimulation she craved. Her nirvana approached when she began to smoke dope.

One night, she shacked up with an aging Aussie surfer. He stuck a hypodermic needle into his veins while they were making love; he did the same to Raina. She wrapped her legs around him with a scream and shot right over the moon and into the sun.

Aunt Hiraina and Uncle Hepi tried to understand what was happening to her. But they were looking through the eyes of love. They were blinded to the fact that they were no longer able to sustain the needs of their daughter. She wasn't a callous girl but she had no further use for them. Like everything else, she simply got bored with her parents and their attempts to stop her from having fun.

One morning Raina walked out the front door, having lifted $200 from Uncle Hepi's pay packet, met a friend from the Pitstop, and hitched down to Wellington. She was sixteen. Her nickname was shortened to 'Blackbird' and her air of country sweetness came as a breath of fresh air to the pox-ridden crowd up at the top of Cuba Street. She took a job as a waitress in a Chinese cafeteria where her fumbling little-girl helplessness made patrons remember the wonder of girlhood. 'I'm really sorry, sir,' she would squeal as she got yet another order wrong. The men loved her like a daughter; the women adored her as the young girl they had aborted from their wombs.

Around this time Raina, the country girl from the Waituhi Valley, started to lose her freshness. The fluttering of the eyelids became too emphatic. The giggle was just too breathless and arch. There was a certain foxiness in her face. 'I love you,' she would say to every new john she met. She wanted them to love her because then they would give her everything she wanted. She was new meat and popular. She screwed, oh how she screwed, and that golden charm bracelet of hers was moist and warm. All she wanted in return was a fix, some dope, a mainline now and then, another fix, another.

'I love you,' she would croon as the smack hit her brain and shot her out to the sun.

Aunt Hiraina and Uncle Hepi finally found her in Wellington. 'I don't want to go back to Gisborne,' she screamed, 'and you can't make me.' But they forced her to return. The next morning she ran away again. When they located her in Wellington the second time she was very cruel. She showed them a wedding ring. 'I'm married, I'm grown up and I want you to go back home and forget about me. It will be better for all of us if you do.'

'Blackbird is really flying high, man,' the crowd said about Raina. 'She really packing up her cares and woe and there she go swinging low. Bye bye, Blackbird.' Her husband was a junkie and she had met him in a casual encounter. He knew he was onto a good thing with Raina, and she thought he would be a good supplier. They weren't really married at all except to the syringes, the needles, the rubber tubes and the smack, which they shared with a glutton's delight.

'Yeah, that Blackbird is really flying,' the crowd said. She was on the same flight path as they were, circling around inside a big box, circling, circling, with no way out, hitting against the sides of the walls, battering her head against the ceiling, circling, circling. Fluttering. Tiring. Trailing syringes from her bloodied wings. Falling to the bottom.

Then she fell in with a Black Power gang. The gang had links with a messianistic movement, part charismatic and part Rastafarian, led by a new Te Kooti. His name was Chris Campbell.

A story began to attach to her. About how special she was, being a direct female descendant from Riripeti to Hiraina to Raina.

And the gang gave her a new name.

Mary.

24

My grandfather Ihaka, head of the Waituhi Valley and the Mahana clan, died two days after Aunt Hiraina and Uncle Hepi returned with Raina to Turanga.

It was Te Ariki who told me about the passing. My family hates telephone calls late at night. When Dad phoned at 3 o'clock in the morning, I already knew that his words were harbingers of death. I had been expecting it ever since Hiraina left; Hiraina divined the future and saw Grandfather walking towards Te Po.

'You must come home for the tangi,' Te Ariki instructed. His voice was drained of feeling, remote, coming out of the morning chill. As for me, I felt neither sadness nor elation.

Later that morning I telephoned Uncle Alexis. Aunt Roha answered my call. 'Your uncle is desolated by his father's death,' she said, 'but I don't think he'll be going to the funeral. The farewells were said between him and Ihaka when the old man was here last year.' Her voice was dark and frightened. 'I don't think that Alexis will ever leave this house, ever, Tamatea. He said to me, when I asked him if he wanted to go to the tangi, "How can a dead man travel to farewell a dead man." I don't know what to do for him,

Tamatea. I just don't know what—'

I caught the late afternoon flight to Gisborne with Regan, Bianca and Miranda. We were lucky to get seats. It was a beautiful clear night, the moon riding across endless silver clouds; the sun had plunged into darkness, down, down, down into the depths of the sea. As it did so, I could not help but recall Riripeti and her ascendancy to power in those days before her marriage to Grandfather Ihaka.

⁓

In 1886, at 2.40 a.m. on 10 June, there was a series of loud detonations which threw everyone in Poverty Bay into great panic. The ground shook and buildings creaked. Flashes of fire shot up into a dense white mass which, at first, assumed the shape of a mushroom, but later obscured the whole sky. The Maori people believed this to be a portent of some great anger or blessing. Showers of fine ash fell over Poverty Bay; the fall was most pronounced around Ormond. Beyond Anaura the hills were mantled with volcanic ash. On the Tuparoa run the pasture was hidden.

Seven hours later, at 10 a.m., it was as dark as midnight at Wai-o-matatini. People began to pray for deliverance. The *Southern Cross* ran into a dense cloud of dust off East Island and put well out to sea.

It was the date of the Tarawera eruption, when seers and diviners of the past and the future had visions of the world gone and the world to come—of phantom canoes and ghost people gliding through the veil between the dead and the living.

Nobody knows when Riripeti was born, but I like to think that it was at the time and during the turmoil of Tarawera that she drew her first breath and announced her coming.

The matriarch. Her face was alive with ecstasy as she pulled the child towards the Place of the Willows. 'See?' she said. 'I told you we would get away this time. Is there no sound of pursuit?'

The child listened in the long grass. He peered above it and down the road. Far in the distance was Waituhi and the smoke of many fires curling like wreaths in the blue sky.

'Nobody coming after us?' Riripeti asked. Her eyes danced with amusement. There were small beads of sweat on her brow and at the nape of her neck.

The child shook his head. Straight after Sunday dinner, they had slipped away from the homestead and managed to get clear away. Grandfather, Te Ariki and his uncles must still be unaware that they had gone. Tiana and the child's aunts would still be in the kitchen, cleaning up after the Sunday kai.

'Good,' Riripeti said, 'because now we will be alone.' So saying, she urged him to follow her into the sanctuary. 'But to make sure, let me call upon my spiders to weave their threads around us so that none can enter.'

Even as she said the words, the tribe of spiders with the red moko began to spin through the air, using their gossamer droplines to create a shining silver web around Riripeti and the child. When it was done, they acted as sentinels, rearing into the attack position.

Within the confines of the web, Riripeti and the child walked beside the slow-moving Waipaoa. 'T'offriama il giglio soave stel,' Riripeti sang. The sunlight cast sun-stars across the mirror surface of the water. Uri taniwha were dark shapes, keeping pace with grandmother and child, beneath the river.

'This place is very important to me,' Riripeti said. 'It was important to my great-uncle, Wi Pere, also. He gave me this piece of land to be mine and mine alone. It was the source of his power. It is the source of mine. The lands around are held in common by the tribe but this earth—' she bent down and clawed at the dirt '—is mine. When I am gone, it will be yours.'

There was the note of possession in the matriarch's voice. The child shivered at the sound of it. A kingfisher, disturbed, fled its nest in the bank of the river and sought the blue vault of sky.

'I came here often with my great-uncle,' Riripeti continued. 'He taught me games of memory like—' quickly she picked up some small pebbles '—how many have I in my hand?'

'I did not see, Grandmother.'

'Seven. And—' she picked up some twigs and threw them into the river. 'You should have counted them while they were in the air, e mokopuna,' she reproved. 'How many rakau are there?'

The child sought them in the river. 'Three,' he said. He watched them being swirled by the strong currents of the Waipaoa into midstream.

Riripeti nodded. 'You must always be observant, e mokopuna. Always quick-witted. It is not enough to calculate after the event. You must know even before the action is over. It is not enough merely to have competence. You must have excellence.' She looked at the child with kindness. 'And you must have a place which is yours alone, a place where you can be at one with the natural world.' Her voice drifted across the water.

The sun slanted golden cartwheels through the willows. 'A te le porpore, le perle e gli ostri,' Riripeti sang. Eels, attracted by the moving light, came to suck at the surface of the river. Dragonflies skimmed across sunken logs.

'I brought Keita here once,' Riripeti said. 'That was a long time ago. She was the only friend of my childhood.' She smiled at the memories. 'We grew up together, Keita and I, until my great-uncle took me away from Waituhi. I don't know where she is now. Probably dead and buried. But that won't happen to us, mokopuna, for you and I are immortal.'

Immortal. The word had mystery to it, and magic was in its syllables like stones scattered in the riverbed. The child went to ask Riripeti the meaning of the word, but voices drifting in the wind disturbed the intention. Grandfather Ihaka and his sons were approaching.

'Yes, I hear them,' Riripeti said. She turned in a rhapsody of movement to the child and her voice soared into the stillness.

'Ah, e mokopuna, the world may change but I will go on forever and ever, for how can I die when nobody knows when I was born? And this place of the willows, it too will live on and on because it is where spirits of fire and air, of water and earth, have haven. A te, te la florida messe dai grembi.'

She held her arms out to the child. Silhouetted against the

skyline Tiana watched as Riripeti embraced him in the sanctuary that only the matriarch could enter. The tapu place. The place of sacredness. The Place of the Willows. The source of the power.

The child saw his mother like a dark presence waiting at the rim of the world.

'He will never be yours,' Tiana vowed.

༈

She said to Uncle Alexis, 'I have made him into a likeness as unto me.'

Such is the statement of a person arrogant with power; but Riripeti herself was also an image as unto others. On one side was the rebel leader, Te Kooti Arikirangi Te Turuki, of whose religion she became a priestess. On the other side was her Caesar, Wi Pere Halbert. Both were present in her blood and she, caught in the midstream of their battles against the Pakeha, had to find her own way. Te Kooti on the one side and Wi Pere on the other were not warring elements. Rather, they were the crucible in which her own image was formed. She was neither greater nor lesser than they were but she was, without doubt, worthy successor to them both.

Come forth now, Artemis Riripeti Mahana. Let Te Kooti on your left acknowledge you before he exits from the stage; he never knew you well, but he left his mark like a brand on your soul knowing that you would take it up when the time was right. Stay for a while, Wi Pere, for yours was the greatest influence on she who became the matriarch of us all. But boast not, and beware of taking too much credit for the shaping of Artemis. For by making her more than equal to the Pakeha you also made her more than equal to yourself.

'It was Wi Pere who took and raised Artemis when she was just one year old,' my cousin Whai told me. 'One evening, after returning by steamer from his parliamentary duties in Wellington, he appeared in his hansom cab at the home of her parents in the Waituhi Valley and said, "This one is mine." His eyes had the look of madness and despair. His battles in the Paremata o te Pakeha were over and, to all intents and purposes, he had been defeated.

'From that time onward,' Whai continued, 'Artemis was always seen with Wi Pere the Great. He took her with him whenever he travelled throughout the length and breadth of Aotearoa. She was with him at every hui. She had no formal schooling. Instead, Wi Pere taught her himself. He passed on to her as much as he was able, the lore that had been given to him from the sacred whare wananga at Maraehinahina. In particular, he bequeathed to her the power to call upon the past, by virtue of her descent from *Takitimu*, whenever she needed that authority. He also gifted to her the mana available to her from the natural world. Her kaitiaki, her supreme protector, was the spider with the red moko.

'Wi Pere also had designs to ensure Riripeti's training within the Pakeha world, too. He hired tutors to teach her at the homestead. She was given her first stallion when she was six years old. At seven, she began learning the pianoforte and taking singing lessons. Although Maori was her first language she was also taught English, French, Italian and Russian. The education was not wasted, for Riripeti had a voracious appetite for learning and a natural aptitude which set her apart. When she was nine, she started to take lessons in the art of fencing.

'Then, in 1895, Wi Pere Halbert embarked on a steamship bound for London. Ostensibly, the purpose of the visit was to try to raise money for the New Zealand Native Land Company which he and W.L. Rees had established to assist Maori owners.

'This is where the story gets puzzling,' Whai said, 'because in that same year, Artemis disappeared. Some people say that she was sent to boarding school in Wellington; others say that Wi Pere sent her to stay with relatives in Sydney, Australia. But the story that has found most favour is that Wi Pere took her with him when he sailed for London. This is when the legend of Artemis begins. It is a legend, I should add, that has no substantiation. I myself have looked up the passenger list for that sailing, but Artemis's name does not appear, nor are there any references to Wi Pere being accompanied by a young girl.

'Wi Pere had many engagements in London. The steamer stopped at a number of ports on his return to Aotearoa. One of his calls was to Rome from whence he took the overnight train to Venice. If Riripeti was with him, as the legend says she was, he left her there in the care of a Venetian family. Why? I don't know. Perhaps it was because Italy had itself fought its battles against Austrian rule. The di Marchesi family had been instrumental in the liberation of Venice. Wi Pere may have felt that their tutelage would be the best training for her, so that when she returned to New Zealand she would be able to take up, more securely, the eternal fight with the Pakeha.

'And then there is the story of Riripeti's sword. Nobody knows where it is now, but people saw it when she was alive and, if it was here today, it would prove that she was indeed brought up in Italy.'

⸲

The matriarch stood with the child at the entrance of Rongopai. She had shown him how to fight and the legacy which he must secure for the people when he attained manhood—the land. That night she had been tormented by dreams. When she awoke she realised that she must teach the child the most bitter lesson of them all.

'E mokopuna, haere mai,' Riripeti said. She motioned him to enter the doorway. 'No,' she continued, 'bring the kete with you.' She had given him a woven basket to carry, a large woven kit; inside was an artefact wrapped in cloth.

The sunlight streamed through the doorway, darkening briefly as Riripeti and the child stepped through. Her walking stick tapped hollowly on the earth floor. Her long black dress made spider patterns.

'E noho,' she said. 'Sit.'

The child did as he was told.

'E mokopuna,' she said. 'I have taught you to be a Maori and to fight in a Maori way. But there is another lesson which you must learn, one which my own great-uncle taught me when I was a child. He sent me away from this place to another across the sea. I did not understand why, but I did when I returned.'

With the edge of her walking stick, she flipped open the cloth covering the object.

'E mokopuna, whakarongo mai. I have taught you how to fight the Pakeha. But I have forgotten that to fight the Pakeha you must learn to be like him. You must become a Pakeha, think like him, act like him and, when you know you are in his image, then turn your knowledge to his destruction.

'Titiro mai, e mokopuna, behold the Sword of Caterina.'

Riripeti saluted him with the sword. The blade gleamed. As she raised it, he glimpsed the hilt. It was unusually large and, although not decorated, had an embossed figure on the hilt. It looked like a lion, only it had wings. Then she slashed the air to ribbons and began to display her prowess. As she did so, she uttered instructions that sounded as if they came from a tutor of the taiaha.

'*Saluto! Guardo! Invito tuo! In atto di spada in armi! Misura camminando! Gioco stretto! Coda lunga e stretta! Cinghiara! Porta di ferro alta! Mandritto! Riverso! Tramazzone!*'

'You saw the sword?' Whai asked. 'Are you sure Artemis called it the Sword of Caterina?'

'Yes,' I answered.

'She didn't say Te Kooti rather than Caterina?' he parried. 'You know, don't you, that the prophet was reputed to have a sword also? People say it's buried at Matawhero. Perhaps it came down from Te Kooti to Riripeti. Perhaps they were one and the same.'

I described the sword to him. He referred me to a woman, Cecile Robinson, who had been a fencing instructor and was a specialist in the field.

'Your enquiry was most intriguing,' Mrs Robinson said as she warmly invited me into her office. 'Sadly, our records of competitive fencing in New Zealand do not go back as far as 1920, but it is well known that there were sword championships for, oh, many years before then. We weren't all that backward, you know.'

Mrs Robinson was a trim, healthy-looking woman in her mid fifties, fashionably dressed, with a Dior scarf floating around her neck. Her office was hung with photographs of herself as a young woman in various fencing poses. 'Oh, I really should take them all down! One's past successes only remind one of the passing of time and, at my age, those sorts of glories only point out how dreadfully out of fitness one has become. Yes, I did win the Women's Open three years in a row. I am proud to say that it is a record that still has to be surpassed.

'But we didn't come here to talk about me, did we?' she continued. 'Now let's see. From your description of it, I would say that your grandmother's sword was a rapier, undoubtedly, a rapier. This was a style of sword which came into being in the middle of the fifteenth century. I think it was first referred to in the French document of 1474 as *épée rapière*, but it was also termed the *espada ropera*, the Spanish for dress sword, meaning 'the sword of the robe' because it was worn with ordinary civil dress.

'The rapier, you see, was a civil weapon mainly, not a military one, although it occasionally had military purposes. It became a part of one's dress, if you were a man, of course, but some women did take it up also. Your grandmother must have had an aptitude for it, though Heaven knows where she must have received tutorship. In Italy? Venice, you say? She really does sound quite extraordinary! Now, let me show you an illustration of what I assume your grandmother's rapier looked like.'

Mrs Robinson invited me to look at a large sketch on her desk. Her perfume was Chanel, delicate and exquisitely sensuous. 'Yes,' I said to her, nodding. 'I only saw the sword once but that's what it looked like.'

'Oh, I am so pleased,' she answered. 'I only made a guess at it. You see, there were various types of rapier, though each was mounted with the same kind of "swept" hilt. It was the form of the blade, not the style of the hilt, which determined the type. Now, the blade on your grandmother's sword would have been either hexagonal or square, rarely more than 9.5 mm in width. I would say that it would also have been at least one metre long; though, because she was a woman, it might have been somewhat shorter than this. But obviously, it was a graceful, practical blade, which she could carry easily.'

'The hilt,' I observed, 'seemed larger than in the sketch.'

'Larger?' Mrs Robinson asked. 'Was it ornate?'

'No,' I answered. 'But it looked like there could have been something concealed in it.'

She nodded. 'Ah, the Venetians!' she said. 'You could never tell what their cleverness might lead to! A craftsman could have constructed a cavity for a vial of poison, perhaps, or a small stiletto. But I must admit that I am pleased you do not remember your grandmother's sword as being elaborate. That would have made me mistrust your story as something imagined, some fanciful dream. Instead you describe a fighting sword, rather than a decorative one. I suspect I would have enjoyed duelling with your grandmother! I can feel that in my bones! She must have been taught by one of the masters of the old school. The hilt of her rapier seems to have been so elegant, well proportioned, restrained and well designed. Let me explain.'

Mrs Robinson opened a glass cabinet and took out a sword similar to the one in the sketch. 'This is the kind of rapier I think your grandmother must have had. See the hilt? It is a slight variation on the basic *espada ropera* hilt with grip, pommel, knuckle guard and back guards, forward and rear quillons, a ricasso and the ring guard. This was my most favoured rapier when I was competing myself. You should have seen me then, young sir!'

She invited me to hold the sword. 'I remember a raised decoration. I think it was a winged lion.'

'A winged lion, you say?' Mrs Robinson's eyes sparkled. 'On the hilt also? Ah, then it was an aristocratic weapon. Yes, definitely Venetian. Without doubt. How superb! Young man, you do not realise how much you have lifted my day! There is so much romance in the sword. You know, of course, that the rapier could thrust much further than the conventional cutting sword. How do you tell the difference? Why, if you feel that you could cut off a man's arm with it, then it is a sword. If not, it is a rapier. It is all in the blade. If a blade is needed to thrust, it must be narrow, rigid and of thick section. Thus, one might thrust like this. And this. And this. Ah yes, strike!'

⌐

The year: 1911. The place: Gisborne. It is well documented that Wi Pere visited the Post and Telegraph station at Gladstone Road near the Kaiti Bridge. He instructed the telegraph operator to send a communication to Italy. At the time, Wi Pere was ailing and the shadow of death was upon him. The operator shrugged when he read the text; it was in Maori and not understood by him. He asked a casual question as to its meaning and was told, 'It is not your place to question. Simply send the message.'

Wi Pere asked the operator when a reply might be received. The operator told him, perhaps, a week at minimum. Accordingly, Wi Pere booked a room at the Masonic Hotel and began a long wait. He stirred from the room only to take a morning and evening constitutional walk, and to check at the P & T office.

Finally, the awaited reply arrived. The operator could not understand this one either. It was in Italian, so its meaning was lost to all except Wi Pere himself.

Two months later Wi Pere took a coastal vessel from Gisborne to the port of Auckland. He was in his best dress coat and he appeared to be in a mood of calm anticipation. His trunk was filled with his best finery. On arrival in Auckland he took an adjoining suite in the Royal Hotel, Symonds Street. His housemaid was requested to take meticulous care in ironing his dress shirts. When he signed the register on 17 July 1911, his usually bold stroke betrayed an inner trepidation. During the following five days he visited friends and old colleagues from the times when he had been a parliamentarian.

On 23 July, the *New Zealand Herald* lists the arrival of a packet steamer from San Francisco: the *American Queen*. The steamer was very small and did not carry many passengers. Among them is listed a 'Miss A.R. di Marchesi, accompanied by her maid, Signora Ana di Stasio'. One might have been mistaken for assuming that these were two women in some travelling theatrical company, but this would be incorrect. All doubts would have been swept away if one had read the report of the social columnist for the *Herald* who was, by chance, at the landing:

'A touching scene was enacted when the retired Minister, the Hon Wi Pere, met young Italian heiress Miss Marchesi, just off the *American Queen*. Miss Marchesi was dressed in beautiful gold silk and was wearing a cape of the richest green fabric. When she first appeared on the gangplank her face and hair were hidden by the hood of the cape, but when she saw the Hon. Wi Pere, her joy made her run towards him and, in that motion, the hood fell from her head. Miss Marchesi must assuredly be one of the loveliest young women that this reporter has been privileged to see and I understand that she turned many heads on the *Queen*. Her hair was dressed in the Italian style with pearls at the nape of her neck. Her complexion was olive from the Mediterranean sun. Suffice to say, however, that she surprised all, when Wi Pere responded to her, by calling in Maori to him. Her voice possessed the most limpid tones. Without a look either to left or right, she ran along the dock to where he was standing and flung herself into the arms of the said Hon. Wi Pere. There was not a dry eye among the bystanders witnessing the welcome.'

The hotel register of 25 July 1911 bears in beautiful script the first-ever record of the matriarch's handwriting: Miss Riripeti Artemis Pere. Just below is another signature: Signora Ana di Stasio. That evening Hon. Wi Pere dined privately with the two women.

On 29 July 1911 Wi Pere returned from Auckland to Gisborne on the regular coastal vessel. With him were two women, one of unsurpassing beauty, who spent most of the voyage watching the coast. The log of that journey reports sights of some amazing phenomena: schools of dolphins and whales escorting the vessel, *aurorae australis* in the evenings and, on the approach to Gisborne, a rainbow. It is told that when she who became the matriarch was alighting from the coastal vessel one of the pearls which was threaded in her hair fell into the mud. When she bent to retrieve it, bystanders saw that her face was clustered with pearls which were, in fact, tears. In an affecting gesture she touched her fingers to her lips and transferred a kiss to the ground.

～

The world was changing; the juggernaut of progress was rumbling across land, seas and skies, with an inevitability that threatened the realms of dragon or sea serpent, mermaid or siren, giant or ogre, winged horse or unicorn, phoenix or other legendary beast. The cities spread across the lands where once had been enchanted forests and fabulous kingdoms. Aeroplanes and dirigible airships droned the skies, scattering the winged horses with their metal blades and thrusting through the clouds which once had known dragonflight. The mermaids and sirens sought deeper caverns where the clipper ships and submersibles could not disturb them.

But every now and then there were sightings in the more isolated places of the world. In New Zealand, the last of the fantastic sea serpents made its appearance in a proud gesture which was both a homage to the past and an acknowledgement of the passing of the time of man's communion with the creatures which had shared his existence since the world's creation. The appearance took place in July 1913. The officers of the SS *Mokoia* reported that they tracked a taniwha off the East Coast. It was described as being between 60 feet and 80 feet in length, sinuous and square-headed, and equipped with three large fins along its back. There was a large growth, like a cock's comb, where the head joined the body. And its appearance was as portrayed in the painted house Rongopai.

Too fanciful, perhaps? Listen: the crew and officers of the SS *Rosamund* also reported sighting the same sea monster, this time between Tolaga Bay and Gisborne, where it appeared to be heading. A school of porpoises was said to be in attendance upon it.

From Young Nick's Head, tohunga who had received their training from whare wananga established by the *Takitimu* canoe, awaited the taniwha's arrival. The monster appeared, swimming towards them, half obscured by the tumult of its coming. All that could be seen of it were its huge square head and the large shining eyes looking up from beneath the sea. It trailed phosphorescence in its churning wake and, when it reached the appointed place of its destination, the lights in the water clothed it with dazzling glitter.

For a moment, all was calm except for the dancing of the taniwha's heralds, the porpoises, around the fabled creature of light.

Then, as if in tune to some inhuman orchestration, the porpoises withdrew from a large circle around the taniwha, to stand on their fins in the calm ocean.

The head of the taniwha began to arise from the water, and it was seen to be covered in a large cancerous growth, so deeply rooted into the brain that it must have been causing incredible pain to the beast. The water streamed away, across the large paua-shaped eyes, the left one of which had been terribly gashed, as if by the propellers of some huge battleship. As the body of the taniwha lifted itself from the water, the priests could see the wounds of the ages upon it. They saw that the tongue had been sliced half away so that it was no longer able to eat. Two fingers of its right hand were missing, and the remaining finger was crippled beyond use. The scaly covering was blotched and discoloured from the pollution of the waters, and raw flesh showed through on the left breast where the scales had been dissolved away in some encounter with lethal acid seas. Some attempts had been made to apply seaweed covering to the wounds of the beast.

The taniwha climbed into the sky. It stood on its tail and its body shimmered with the effort, pulsating with exhaustion, its coils thrashing the seas. This was the remnant of the taniwha which had led *Takitimu* to Aotearoa. Eighty feet tall, it hovered above the holy men, bidding them, 'Look upon me, for you will never see my like again. I am Ruamano, the mighty, who with Arai te uru, my companion, brought you here to this place. And he who came after me has now gone before me along the path that all must travel. My time is ended here.' The monster shimmered in the daylight.

The priests knew the taniwha had come to seek their permission to die. They agreed, ministering to it and uttering many karakia. They praised it in its death throes.

When the ceremonials were completed the taniwha, with great gladness, turned on its tail, facing first east, then south, then west, then north, saluting each compass point once, twice, thrice. Saluting life. Saluting death. Saluting heaven. Saluting earth. Saluting man. Saluting the gods.

Once this was done, there was one last communion of its soul with those gathered with it. Then, in silence, it slid back into the sea. The porpoises which had so long attended it waited until the last long out-breathed sigh had trembled through the taniwha's body. They churned the water into thunder, pushing the dead beast out to the open sea and accompanying it down, down, down to some dark underwater cavern where it could never be found.

The next year was 1914. It was the year of the beginning of the Great War. The long-held communion between man and the gods was coming to an end. From that year we can date the beginning of the world of man and his ascendancy over the natural world.

25

Te Ariki met the flight at Gisborne Airport. It was dark and I could not see him as Regan and I disembarked with the children, but his presence was palpable even before we had landed.

'Kia ora Regan,' Te Ariki greeted her.

She kissed him on both cheeks. 'Hello, Te Ariki,' she said. 'I'm so sorry about Ihaka.'

Bianca and Miranda reached for him. 'Papa,' they said.

He kissed them and then turned to me. 'Your mother, sisters and brothers are waiting for us at home,' he said. 'I asked them not to come to the airport because I wanted this time alone with you. You are my eldest son, just as I am of Ihaka, and as he was of his father Emmanuel.'

Te Ariki was without tact, for Regan was within hearing and I saw her grief as she gathered our daughters in her arms. 'We'll wait for you at the car,' she said.

'The male link with Ihaka's generation has gone,' Dad said, 'and it is only me and you now.' He looked at me, searching my face for some sign that I understood. I suppose he felt that I would be affected by the disruption by death of the genealogy that had bound three generations together.

'I'm sorry about Grandfather,' I said. In a rush of emotion I hugged him, oh I hugged him so tightly because one of these days I would be farewelling him to death's embrace and I felt the cold breath of mortality on him. Beneath the fedora, his eyes burned like stones.

'It means a lot to me that you are here,' he said. 'Thank you, son.' He waited with me while our luggage was unloaded. 'How long will you stay?' he asked.

'Until after the tangi,' I said. The aircraft, silhouetted against the darkness, looked like a weary gannet. 'When did Grandfather die?'

'This morning,' he answered. 'At your Aunt Floria's place. In his sleep.' Slipping away, away, with the dawn.

'And where is his body?'

'He's resting at the chapel until tomorrow night. Then the tangi is to begin at Poho o Rawiri in town. On the final day, we are taking him to Rongopai to lie in state. He will be buried in the family graveyard on the third day.'

I hefted the suitcases into the stationwagon. Regan was sitting with Bianca and Miranda in the back seat. 'Dad didn't mean to offend you,' I told her.

'I know,' she nodded. 'But sometimes, Tama, it's so hard for me, a Pakeha, to be married to you.'

I stepped into the driver's seat. We drove to Palliser Street, and every now and then Te Ariki's profile was etched with the light from street lamps.

Tiana and my sisters, Teria, Erina, Vanessa and Meri, were waiting like a Greek chorus, silent and eternal. My sisters had been crying; we hugged each other.

'So you've finally arrived,' Teria said.

Behind her, my brothers-in-law and younger brothers Hamuera and Mana waited also.

Tiana's face, like mine, was without tears. Pale with light it shone like a star. Sometimes my mother has the power to pounce on a moment and take it into a realm beyond reality, beyond the mundane or expected. She did so now, her words like arrows piercing my armour to the heart beneath. 'Your grandfather came to you in Wellington to ask your forgiveness. Ihaka also came to me. Now that

he is gone I bear him no ill will. Have you forgiven him, Tamatea?'
Her fingers gripped me like talons.

We drove through Gisborne to the chapel. Regan, the girls and
I went with Te Ariki and Tiana in the stationwagon. My sisters and
brothers followed in their own cars, a caravan of mourning making
slow procession through the deserted streets. It is said that time is
relative; although the procession must have only taken about five
or six minutes, it seemed as if we were on our way to the end of
forever.

Then, there it was, the chapel, our destination, like a lost planet
in the black centre of eternity. This was where my grandfather's life
had come to, this point on the map of his personal geography, lying
beneath the tall spired dome of a house of the Christian God.

The lights were on in the entranceway. Beyond the glass doors
I could see dark shapes materialising out of the brilliant phosphorescence; the Mahana family awaiting my arrival—the return of the
eldest grandson. All of a sudden, I felt a sense of claustrophobia, the
suffocation of being in this huge family, stretching from one end of
time to the next. It was as if I was in a crystal coffin, falling through
the various changes of Te Po, the night, and I was beating against its
sides and crying, 'Let me out, let me out.' Around me wraiths were
gathering, ferrying me forward, pulling off the lid, and I wanted
to change my mind then, and to hide away. But Riripeti was there
also, in the coffin with me, and the flesh had rotted from her bones
and the pearls had fallen from her hair, but she was still alive. She
clasped me tightly to her, saying, 'I have made you into a likeness
as unto me, you are mine,' and the crystal coffin kept on falling and
falling out of the darkness.

Te Ariki stopped the stationwagon at the entrance; I could see
my uncles and aunts. He stepped out, and I followed him. Tiana and
the rest of the family arranged themselves behind us.

'You stand with us,' Teria said to Regan. 'Tama and Dad will lead
us in.'

The glass doors swung apart, and there was another door swinging
apart behind the first, and another and another and another. I had
to close my eyes to regain my sense of equilibrium.

'Do you wish to speak when we are in the chapel?' Te Ariki asked. 'You know that the family will expect you to pay homage to your grandfather in the Maori way.'

I swayed with indecision. Beyond the phosphorescence, on the other side of the glass doors opening and opening, I could see Ihaka, lying in the open casket, lying there in the light.

(The hardest word in the English language, a friend told me, is the word 'No'. It is a very powerful word. People who possess the ability to use it have tremendous power.)

'No,' I answered Te Ariki. 'You are here and, by so being, you represent me also. You are the head of the family and my head as well. There is therefore no need for me to speak.'

No. No. No. Never.

Aunt Hiraina began to call in the karanga, 'Haere mai ki o tatou mate e. Haere mai. Haere mai.'

'Come to our dead.'

The call came to us where I was standing at the entrance to the chapel. Te Ariki bowed his head, but I refused to bow mine. I watched Tiana swathe her face in her scarf; only her eyes could be seen, those strange eyes so large, dream swimmer eyes that could see their way through dreams; my sisters and Regan followed suit, tying the knots of their scarves tightly against the caprice of the night wind. Tiana had always been largely unsentimental about death (when Artemis had died Tiana said, 'There will be no photographs of your grandmother in the house. Let the dead rest . . .'), but she always observed the customs and rituals of the tangihanga. On this, the first night, we the family would be the main mourners but, come the dawn, the full grief of the tangi would be upon us.

'You will not change your mind and speak when we are inside?' Te Ariki asked again. 'Your uncles and aunts might still expect it. They may wish you to speak on behalf of this generation, for the sake of your grandfather's many mokopuna. No? Then let us enter.'

'The family already know my feelings about Grandfather,' I answered. 'Isn't it enough that I come to farewell him?'

Teria came to my side and held my hand tightly. Tiana led the way in, returning the call. 'Karanga mai, karanga mai, karanga mai . . .' she responded, 'we come to our dead and we lament with the mournful wind which brings notice of his departing. Aue . . . aue . . .' The words were ancient and profound. I had not heard Tiana perform the karanga before and I was surprised at the authority which she vested in the delivery. In profile, her face lifted as if to drink the light.

We approached the glass doors of the chapel. The light in the foyer was harsh. The doors opened and we were ushered inside. 'Haere mai, nau mai, kua tae mai nei.'

Te Ariki and Tiana bowed their heads and made ritual acknowledgement to Ihaka. I know that I should also have done so but I chose not to. I lifted my head so that all could see that I, Tamatea, was here. I saw the family at a glance: six of Grandmother and Grandfather's surviving children. Aunt Floria and Aunt Hiraina were sitting beside Grandfather Ihaka's casket. Uncle Pita, Uncle Danny, Uncle Cairo and Uncle Te Huirangi were standing to one side of it. Like a diadem in their crown was the body of Ihaka.

Suddenly the wind swept through the doors, scattering petals from the brilliant flower wreaths, and I smelt the perfume of death.

'Aue, e Tamatea, aue. The bloom of the rata is shed. Kua horo nga puawai o te rata,' Aunt Hiraina sobbed.

All around me I could hear weeping, and I heard Aunt Floria addressing me and entreating me to come forward. 'Haere mai ki to tatou papa. Aue. Haere mai. Nau mai.'

The light was blinding in the chapel. I saw that apart from the family there were many other close relatives and the iwi present. I nodded to them, acknowledging their presence. Ihaka's death had caused so many people to gather on this first night.

Te Ariki signalled that Tiana, my sisters, Regan and I should take our seats opposite where Grandfather lay. In the ceremonial of welcome the formal speechmaking had to be made before we could join the mourners. The first speech would take place in the space between ourselves and Ihaka and, because I had indicated that I would not speak, Te Ariki would respond on our behalf.

I watched as Abraham, a local elder, stood up to welcome our family. As long as I had been involved in Maori protocol, I had always found the mihimihi an exhausting emotional, mental and physical process; no more so than now because I could feel the tensions of the relationships between myself and the clan. In many respects the welcoming mihimihi was designed to sublimate the tensions and release them, so that the spirit of the community, of family, would prevail. We would all become one in the flesh and in the mourning of our grandfather, Ihaka.

'Na reira, e Tamatea,' Abraham concluded his welcome, 'hoki mai. Hoki mai ki te wa kainga. Therefore, Tamatea, return, return to your home, and to the grandfather of us all. Hoki mai.' He sat down. 'Ka huri,' he said, indicating it was time for our reply.

Te Ariki looked at me again. 'No,' I said for the third time. I knew he was bewildered by my continuing intransigence. He began the whaikorero.

'Tihei mauri ora . . . I sneeze and it is life . . .'

Te Ariki was always a careful speaker, lacking the usual histrionics of marae declamation, but I was thrilled at his authoritative bearing and manner. 'Join the descent line, join the genealogy, join, join, join.' His invocation rose from his throat, calling the past to intertwine with the present, the gods with the mortal, and the family one with another. Ah yes, he did not need the grand gesture or melodramatic flourish; his impact came more from the fact of his mana. Nor did it matter that you had to lean in on his words to hear them; by virtue of his prestige, they had natural magic in them. So it was that I looked upon the clan, feeling such pride that he was my father.

But I still could not forgive Ihaka. After all, Riripeti loved me and I loved her.

She had never loved Ihaka. Indeed, when she returned from Venice, Wi Pere had forced her to marry him.

⌒

Marriage among all high-ranking women, writes Berys Heuer in *Maori Women*, was predominantly political. Great importance was placed on the matching of equivalent rank to retain the mana of the individuals and their offspring. Where women were married out of the tribe they became primarily symbols of the whole tribe. 'He taura taonga e mutu, he taura tangata e kore e mutu; a gift connection may be severed, a human link cannot.' The marriages were arranged by chiefs of both tribes. Sometimes the betrothal was made in infancy.

These primarily political alliances were motivated by several factors, including the hope of establishing or reinforcing ties between tribal groups, of ensuring assistance from a powerful neighbour in case of emergency, with specific interest in acquiring material possessions in the form of land, fishing rights, greenstone weapons and carved ornaments, or to end fighting between groups and cement peace.

In Wi Pere's case, he may well have made the taumau arrangement between Riripeti and Ihaka for another purpose: bereft of the Tuhoe vote of the Mataatua subdivision he tried to manipulate its return, at some later stage, to his chosen successor, Riripeti herself. Her marriage to Grandfather Ihaka was the price which had to be paid for that earlier vote and his time of ascendancy; it was also an account, which she could render at a later point whenever or if ever she needed Mataatua support.

The child stirred in his sleep. Somewhere in the darkness of his dreams he could hear the rustling of giant wings like some giant manaia monster flying closer and closer. With a cry he awoke in time to hear the Lagonda whirring in through the gateway at the homestead.

A car door slammed. The child sat up. He was in Riripeti's bed, and he remembered that his grandmother had carried him there saying, 'Haere ki te moe, e mokopuna, go to sleep. There is a hui which I must attend, but I shall be back soon. Rest well. God keep you safe.' She had kissed him on the forehead and caressed his face with her hands. '*Buona notte*.' The bracelets on her wrists had tinkled like charms in the wind.

Now Riripeti had returned. Eagerly the child awaited her. He reached upward towards the bedside cabinet and increased the flame in the old-fashioned oil lamp. The flame cast an amber glow throughout the room.

Riripeti's bedroom was like a small chapel. It was painted with frescoes, similar to the Adam and Eve panel in Rongopai. The colours were rich and the hues were bold aquamarine, vermilion and topaz extracted from the clays of Papatuanuku. The frescoes themselves depicted scenes from Maori life: women drawing water from the Waipaoa River, men harvesting in the fields, children spinning tops, and other pastoral idylls. The mood was peaceful and calm; there were no scenes of war or animosity to disturb the sanctuary.

To the right of the room was an alcove hidden by red damask curtains. Recessed into the alcove was the doorway to the bedroom. The child heard footsteps approaching the door. There was a click as the ornate doorknob was turned. A draught of wind eddied the curtains.

But there were voices raised in argument: Grandfather's and Riripeti's.

'Come to me,' Grandfather was saying, 'I need you.'

'No, I am tired from the hui,' Grandmother answered. 'Goodnight, Ihaka.'

Grandfather must have touched her because she gasped. 'I will make you forget your tiredness,' he said in a voice hoarse with mystery, 'Come to me.'

There were sounds of a struggle. 'No, Riripeti said, 'the boy . . .'

Finally, through the silence, came Grandfather's voice. 'Always the boy first and me second. Night after night, Riripeti, I will not stand for it. I'll thrash the living daylights out of him, one day, you mark me, kui.'

'You touch him, Ihaka,' Riripeti answered, 'and you will pay for it.'

Grandfather turned away, but his voice still echoed in the deep well of the night, 'Go to him, your man-child, but remember this Riripeti, if we fight, he and I, in future times, I will give him no quarter. It will be his mana against mine. You'd better be there to protect him. He has taken you away from me, he whose boy-cock is a match for that of a full-grown man. You'll come begging me for it, Riripeti, one of these nights, ah yes, one of these—'

Then she was there, in the bedroom, closing the door quickly. For a moment she did not see that the child was awake and, in that moment, she was unguarded. For the very first time, the child saw her vulnerability. Her body, taut like a fully-stretched bow, was arching in the grip of passion. Her face, reaching as if to drink from a high-held pitcher, was suffused with desire. Her hands raked at her long black gown.

'Grandmother?' the child called.

She saw him, sitting up on the bed, and she was vulnerable no longer.

'You still awake, e mokopuna?' she whispered.

She came towards him. In the candlelight, her beauty was breathtaking. She sat beside him on the bed and imprisoned him in her arms. She was as soft as silk, her skin brushing against him with its distinctive scent of musk. Her embrace seemed to last an eternity. She shifted to a more comfortable position and cradled him with his head under her chin. Slowly, she began to rock back and forth, her veils swaying with the movement. Then she started to sing in that clear dramatic soprano voice; he could feel the sound vibrating in her throat and the way in which her breath floated the sound so that it was like a seamless silk.

'*Mio superbo guerrier,*' she sang, '*quanti tormenti, quanti mesti sospiri e quanta ci cindusse ai soavi abbraciamenti . . .*'

'I don't understand, Grandmother,' the child said.

'You don't need to understand,' Riripeti responded. '*Oh com'e dolce il mormorar insieme*, all you need to do is listen and feel the emotion, *te ne rammenti?*'

Without knowing why, the child nodded in acknowledgement.

Riripeti laughed and hugged him. 'See? You do remember!'

The child was carried away in the flood of her approval. 'I love you, Grandmother,' he said.

Riripeti looked at him, amused. 'I know,' she answered. Her face became shadowed. 'You will love me forever and ever,' she seemed to be remembering the embrace of Ihaka, 'and you will obey me.'

Her tone was vicious. 'Say it.'

'Yes. I promise.'

The silence grew between them. The child could feel his heart thundering in his chest as if it wanted to break out. The thundering threatened to put the light out with its intensity.

Riripeti got up from the bed and went behind a screen and began to undress. '*Poi mi guidavi ai fulgidi deserti,*' she sang. The screen bore frescoes also, but they were of a patrician city suspended in the sea, shimmering in blue and gold beauty, and guarded by winged lions. '*All'arse arene, al tuo materno suol.*' She reappeared. She was wearing a long nightgown and her hair cascaded like a burnished river around her shoulders. 'Move over,' she smiled as she raised the coverlet and slipped into bed.

Then she did to him as was her custom. She began stroking the child's limbs, kneading them, massaging them.

'You're a bony child,' she said. 'Never mind, I will build you up into a strong man and teach you how to be desirable to both women and men.'

The child was puzzled, and Riripeti knew that he did not understand. All he wished to do was to give himself over to the languorous liquid in her stroking and to push himself into her warmth.

'In sex is power, e mokopuna,' Riripeti said. 'Knowing when to give pleasure and when to take, to be ruthless, are lessons that you must learn. When to be active and when to be passive. These too you must learn, as I have done. Most of all, you must know when and how to overrule the passions of your body as necessary.' She began to sing again. '*Disperda il ciel gli affanni e amor non muti col mutar degli anni.*' When she began talking again, her voice was like a dream hardly disturbing the air. 'When I was younger and living with the di Marchesi family I almost succumbed to the passion of love. My lover's name was Paolo. He almost ruled me rather than I him. When my great-uncle called me back to Aotearoa, I did not want to come. As the ship was leaving port I saw Paolo, dived into the ocean and swam back into his arms. But he deceived me.'

'Deceived?' the child asked.

Riripeti looked into the child's eyes. '*Disperda il ciel gli affanni.* I did not miss the next sailing. I returned here where my great-uncle had arranged my marriage to—

'Never trust your grandfather,' she said. 'Never.' The room whistled with the flutes of premonition, and age-old runes were cast across glowing embers.

'Then she reached over and snuffed out the lamplight with her fingers. Her voice was deep with desire and longing. 'But you will never deceive me, e mokopuna.' She embraced him totally in the darkness. *Tarda e la notte.*'

Vien . . . Venere splende.

My grandmother was twenty-seven in 1913 when she was somewhat brutally introduced to Ihaka by Wi Pere with the words, 'Riripeti, this boy is to be your husband.'

'I found the suggestion quite unbelievable,' she told me when I was a child. 'Your grandfather was only fifteen. Nor did I feel physically attracted to him. He was shorter than I was, squat, and there was an air of ruthlessness about him which he never lost.'

About their first meeting at least the family would agree.

'Oh, she hated him on first sight,' Uncle Pita said. 'Disliked him intensely. And don't forget that he, on his part, felt a laughing stock among his friends for having to marry someone much older than he was. But they had no option but to go through with it. After all, it was a taumau marriage. It had already been arranged with Ihaka's parents even before he was born.'

Knowing that the marriage was arranged makes it a little easier to understand the angry attitude that my grandmother took to Te Ariki's marriage to Tiana. Although she bent to her grandfather's will and married Ihaka, Te Ariki disobeyed her when he ran away from Gisborne and married my mother. What was worse was that Riripeti had promised Te Ariki in marriage to a woman from Tuhoe, a political union which would have secured the link in his generation to the Mataatua confederation. But it was Tiana, rather than Te Ariki, who incurred Riripeti's wrath.

'Te Ariki knew all along that he had to marry Awhina,' Uncle Pita told me. 'They were well matched, really. About the same age and same temperament. But, even if he is my brother, I have to admit that Te Ariki was a bit of a ram and liked to play around. He had a lot of girlfriends and, boy did he treat them like dirt. Here today, gone tomorrow. Then he met your mother in Hastings and she wouldn't allow him to trample all over her. You know what Tiana's like; she can be tough when she wants to be. I can still remember when he came back from Hastings, after she had spurned him. He had this huge black eye. He was too proud to tell us that a woman had given it to him. But we knew, we knew.

'Of course, if you were to ask your father now,' Uncle Pita continued, 'he would deny his past relationships with women. As people get older they get more moral. They like to pretend that they were as white as the driven snow. Don't you believe it! When we were young we were all as white as soot, so when you hear your other uncles going crook about their kids' misbehaviour, you remember to remind them about the times they used to sneak out the window. Me, well, I was the exception to the rule. I didn't know anything in those days, true.'

It was Riripeti who contacted Tiana's parents and told them about her marriage to Te Ariki. Naturally they were aware of the mana of the matriarch, her chiefly status, and that is why, when the train arrived at the Gisborne railway station on that night in 1943, both sets of parents were there to separate the two lovers. What they had not realised was that Tiana was pregnant. My arrival left my grandmother no option but to reunite Te Ariki and Tiana after I had been born. After all, I would be the first grandchild of her eldest son.

And who was Awhina? If I sift back through my memory my mind hesitates over an incident which happened when I was a child. Riripeti had taken me to a hui in Ruatoki, in Tuhoe country. I remember dark handsome people and an aristocratic elder with a young woman beside him. Grandfather Ihaka went to greet them, and the woman fell upon his shoulders and wept copious tears. My grandfather beckoned me to join him and, when I did, he gripped me savagely by my shoulders and, pointing at the woman, shouted in an accusing tone at me. The veins in his neck looked like they would burst, and his face was crimson with rage. I think he would have struck me had the woman not pushed herself in front of him. She bent down to my level and took a long look at me. It must have been raining at the time because her hair was matted and her cloak was wet. Rivulets of rain tracked down her face. I would not say that she was beautiful, but I can remember feeling the aura of authority tempered with kindness. The reason why I remember her is because she wore long greenstone earrings and had a huge tiki against her breast. Her inner sadness seemed to reflect itself in the dark depths of the greenstone ornaments.

The woman looked at me so hard that I felt at any moment I would fall into the orbits of her eyes. Then, slowly, her head began to turn and I was compelled to follow their gaze. Across her shoulders, and in the distance, some children were playing—except for one who stood apart from the rest. He was about my age, but he was taller and more strongly built than I was. His fists kept on clenching and unclenching. Grandfather Ihaka's face was impassive as he nodded at the boy and he, catching Grandfather's movement, bowed his head in return.

Then Riripeti arrived. I don't know what it was that she had in her hand—perhaps it was her walking stick—but she struck Ihaka across the face and, with its point, pushed the young woman to the ground. She gave a cry of pain and, at the sound, the young boy began to run towards her. The woman tried to motion him not to do so, but it was too late. Even before he was halfway to us Grandmother had raised her hands before her and was making a squeezing motion in the air.

He began to reel and sway and to clutch at his throat.

I must have yelled, 'Grandmother, no,' because she stopped the motion.

The boy fell to the ground.

But Riripeti was still in a dangerous mood. The pearls in her hair were ablaze with fury. She looked at the Tuhoe elder, Grandfather Ihaka, the young woman and the boy in turn, and to each she uttered a warning. I had the feeling that the warning to the boy was the most potent of all.

'I have made my choice. Tamatea is my beloved. Abide by it.'

At that, the young woman backed away. I wanted to reach out to her. I was sure that she would not, at any time, wish me any harm.

I am sure, now, that she was Awhina.

⁓

The dying of the taniwha, Ruamano, in 1913 coincided with the beginning of great changes for the iwi Maori. The Pakeha had proved the victor and the Maori had been vanquished. The disillusionment of defeat was like a cancer in the blood.

Perhaps this was why there were so many illnesses in the people. From the beginning of Pakeha settlement grave epidemics had already become endemic among the Maori. Influenza and typhoid fever raged regularly through Poverty Bay and the East Coast. In 1854 measles had been carried to Wairoa by some Bay of Plenty visitors to the tangihanga of the chief Apatu, who had drowned the previous year. The malady quickly spread to Poverty Bay and the East Coast. It was followed by an equally grave epidemic of dysentery. Influenza raged both in 1855 and 1860, and there was also an epidemic of typhoid in the latter year. In 1875 measles killed a large number of the Ngati Kahungunu in Wairoa. It was between June and October 1891 that the resistance of the Maori to Pakeha diseases was severely tested. In that year, typhoid broke out on the East Coast, causing scores of deaths. There were seventy-two fatal cases in Waiapu alone. Typhoid again broke out in the Waiapu in March 1911 and, in 1917, sixty cases of diphtheria were reported in Poverty Bay.

However, the greatest test to the iwi Maori came four years after the last sighting of the taniwha. It was known as the flu epidemic of 1918, and it was brought back to New Zealand by soldiers returning from the battlefields of Europe. This was the time just after the Great War ended. It was the year in which unmarked graves were seen to disturb the body of Papatuanuku the Mother Earth.

The number of deaths registered in Aotearoa was 5959. In Gisborne and the East Coast all steamer services to and from the township and small settlements were stopped. All municipal buildings—except churches—in which large numbers of people were accustomed to congregate, were closed. The banks did not open for ten days. Business premises were closed at 3 p.m. Food for invalids was distributed by voluntary drivers. Tangi were prohibited.

A Vigilance Committee at Wairoa advised that callers there would be required to be disinfected and medically examined, and that suspects would be quarantined for five days. Visitors were also warned that no accommodation would be made available to them, and they were on no account to approach a garage for petrol.

It is said that in Maori villages throughout Gisborne and the East Coast the wailing was unceasing and that fires lit to burn the dead continued day and night. Because here's the revelation: nobody really knows the total number of deaths that occurred among Maori. Whatever the number, it was devastating. The evidence is in the whakapapa, the genealogical records kept by tohunga from the beginning of Time. If you look at them in the year 1918, what do you see?

A major discontinuity, like a fault line running right across life. A sudden erasure of complete villages and families—men, women and children—gone during the months November 1918 through to February 1919. No signs of life afterward. The Pakeha disease reaped a rich Maori harvest.

It is at this time of death that the ascendancy of the matriarch, she who was also known as Riripeti, really began. By this time her consort, Ihaka from the Tuhoe iwi, stood by her side. She had the power and the mana but she needed some special purpose to activate it. The Paheka war, in another hemisphere, and the stench of death in her own, resolved the problem.

Because here's another revelation. In some parts of Aotearoa, Maori were denied hospital and medical support. In Turanga, when rural Maori tried to get help they were turned back at the crossroads at Matawhero, Te Karaka and Manutuke.

This was why Riripeti said, 'Then I will build my own hospital for the iwi. And it will be a place that all Maori can come to when they are denied Pakeha medical services.'

And so the word spread among the people. 'Go to Waituhi. There, you will find succour.' When they arrived they saw that huge white tents with canvas flaps had been erected on the hillside overlooking the meeting house, Rongopai. Had not the meeting house always been associated with healing?

Waituhi became a centre of the rehabilitation of the iwi, a place of life in the midst of death; when that was achieved Riripeti, like Te Kooti, decreed war on the Pakeha.

The hospital became known as Te Waka o Te Atua. The Ship of God.

And Riripeti ascended unto her greatness as the Matua, the Matriarch.

～

Parliament Grounds, 1949.

I had reached the inner depths of Te Kore, the Void. I do not know how long I rested there but I began to be afraid. I formed a thought in the blackness, calling for someone to help me. Gently, I felt myself moving out of the dark, falling from the Void into Te Po, the Night. Ahead, I could see the many gradations of light, and I knew that I was approaching Te Awatea, the Light.

Suddenly, spiders were descending in silken strands through the universe. The spiders were weaving a web between the Darkness and the Light, closing out the dawn. The web drifted around me, brushing me as I sped forward. I saw in that realm of spiders, an old man.

It was Timoti, the elder of the paepae, and spiders were at his throat and his mouth. They were binding him tightly into a silken cocoon, but I could hear him screaming.

Then a woman swam towards me and, as she did so, a red star began to glow in the night. She ripped herself through the spider webs with a knife and the spiders, sensing her presence, turned to attack her. Unheeding, she tried to set the old man free.

The woman was Tiana.

Spider webs drifted across his dreams and the child cried out.

He ripped his dream apart and, when he revived, he saw Riripeti looking down at him.

'Did Timoti touch you?' she asked. Her face was grim, her eyes like meteors flaming through the night. 'Did he touch your head?' She had thrown her veil aside from her face and the child could see the mark of mortality upon her. In that moment she looked less of a goddess and more human.

The child could not comprehend for a moment. Behind, he could hear his Aunt Hiraina sobbing.

'Be quiet, Hiraina,' Riripeti said.

The child gave a look of comfort to his aunt and Uncle Manaaki; both of them were standing shamefacedly near the bed.

'Did Timoti touch you, Tamatea?' Riripeti asked again. 'Did he?'

The child remembered. 'The spiders,' he cried. 'The spiders.'

Riripeti calmed him with a soft kiss. 'You have just had a dream, e mokopuna. A very bad dream.' She began to stroke his forehead, smoothing away his anxieties. 'Be at peace now. But I need to know. Did the old man touch you?'

The child thought for a moment and then shook his head. 'No.'

A look of relief passed like a shadow across Riripeti's face. She raised both hands to her lips and closed her eyes as if offering a prayer of gratitude.

Then, Tiana was there and with a cry the child reached out to her. 'E ma,' he said.

Her face was sphinx-like, showing no emotion, but when she tilted her face to the light there were signs of tenderness. 'Kia kaha son,' she said. 'None of this is your fault or of your making. The price is not yours to pay.'

At her words Riripeti ceased her karakia. When she removed her hands from her face the child sensed, briefly, a splintering and cracking of that glorious beauty as if it was a cliff flaking away.

('You had been taken to a tent near the meeting house,' the journalist explained. 'I think you were unconscious for quite some time. I was there when your mother entered. I thought her words were very strange. There was more meaning to them than I would ever know.

'Whatever the case, there was certainly tension. Your grand-mother, Artemis, and your mother exchanged some quick words in Maori; I couldn't understand of course. Then the tension eased when one of your elders came in. From your description it must have been Tamati Kota. He reported on Timoti, the elder of the paepae, I don't know what it was, but it was the last reference I heard that day to him. The memory of all that had happened was being sealed away as if the occasion had never existed. Perhaps it didn't; I don't know any longer. All truth is fiction really, for the teller tells it as he sees it, and it might be different from some other teller. This is why histories often vary, depending on whether you are the conqueror or not.')

'Kua tae mai te wa kua timata ta tatou hui mo te whenua,' Tamati Kota said. 'The time has come to begin the meeting about our land, our Mother Earth, Papatuanuku. Everybody is beginning to assemble in the whare nui.'

Riripeti made a swift, imperious gesture. 'Let them go in,' she said. 'They will not start without us.' Her expression was weary. Her vitality still needed to replenish itself.

'Kei te pehea ta tatou tamariki?' Tamati Kota asked. 'How is the boy?'

She breathed a sigh. 'He is all right. Kei te pai.'

'Perhaps he should stay here, resting,' Tamati Kota said. 'Tiana will look after him.'

Riripeti turned to Tamati Kota. 'No,' she said, and the pearls in her hair shimmered dangerously. 'I need him to help me, to give me his strength.'

'But the others,' Tamati Kota began, 'the Prime Minister, the other tribes, the rangatira, the iwi—'

'They will wait,' the matriarch said. 'Meantime, gather our ope together, our people from Te Whanau a Kai, Rongowhakaata and Te Aitanga a Mahaki so that all will therefore be ready to enter the whare runanga. Go now, quickly. Manaaki, Hiraina, you go also. Make sure that everyone is here, prepared to move when the boy and I are fully recovered.'

Like a warrior queen, Riripeti instructed her forces to deploy themselves in readiness for the coming combat. She gripped the child's hands in hers; he felt the force of her dynamism flowing into him. Equally, she felt his energy flowing into her.

('She was a charismatic leader,' the journalist said. 'The force of her instructions made me leave too. It was dark and, outside, the scene appeared rather chaotic, but I shall try to describe it as best I can. There were hundreds of people milling around the whare runanga. Many of them were entering the meeting house in groups. Dotted in the darkness were flaming torches, burning small holes in the night.

'The whare runanga itself was like a huge hulking presence, a hostile warrior crouching in the dark. The interior was flooded with bright light, and some of the light issued from the building like rays. Smoke was drifting in the wind. People were talking and laughing. The hubbub was immense. There was a sense of great expectancy about the occasion. One had the impression that the course of history in Aotearoa was going to be changed that night. A giant door was opening and, when we were inside, the future for all of us would alter.')

'Haere mai, haere mai, haere mai,' a kuia called in the night. Silhouetted in the doorway of the whare runanga, she beckoned people to come, enter and take part in the hui. She noted, with some unease, that some of the visitors were standing to one side, waiting by the small tent at the side of the whare runanga. 'Haere mai koutou,' she called to them. 'Come.'

Inside the tent, Riripeti heard the call of the kuia.

'E mokopuna,' she breathed. 'It is the time of the hui. We have passed many tests. There are still great challenges ahead but with God's help we will be victorious.'

She knelt beside the child and began to pray. The ope, waiting outside, saw their two shadows blending in an embrace of God. 'We are the Children of Israel,' Riripeti began. 'Deliver us, oh God, from Pharaoh.'

('I had gone on into the meeting house,' the journalist said, 'but we knew, all of us, that Artemis and her ope were absent. Indeed, I was standing near Bernard Scott, and apparently he was anxious to make sure that all the people were assembled in the whare runanga before the Prime Minister himself entered. "Why the delay?" he asked Maui. "Artemis is at prayer," Maui answered. "But the Prime Minister will be here soon," Bernard said. "Cannot anything be done?" Maui shrugged his shoulders. He conferred with a colleague and, after a while, said, "We shall send a messenger."')

Outside, the ope from Te Whanau a Kai, Rongowhakaata and Te Aitanga a Mahaki waited in the darkness.

'The old lady's taking her time,' Uncle Manaaki said. 'They'll be getting furious in the meeting house.'

Big fat Wallace started to complain about the cold.

'You, cold?' Uncle Manaaki laughed. 'E Wallace, there must be a crack in your fat letting the wind in.'

It was then that the messenger arrived. 'He aha te aitua?' he asked. 'What's the trouble? We want you people inside before the Prime Minister comes in.'

'This is a Maori hui,' Tamati Kota answered, 'not a Pakeha one. Why should we have to conform to the Pakeha kawa?'

'Ka tika, ka tika,' people called. 'That's right. Let the Prime Minister be seated. Let him wait for us.'

'You people are trampling on the protocol of our marae,' the messenger continued. 'You must come now.'

'Then you,' Tamati Kota said, 'you interrupt our kui's prayer to God, for I certainly will not.'

('The messenger returned,' the journalist said, 'and he told Maui what was happening. His words were heard by those sitting next to me and, very soon, the whole assembly knew about the delay. Some, I think, were cross. But others took Tamati Kota's point of view about Pakeha kawa and there was a ripple of amusement. Maui, however, was extremely angry. "Send out the call once more and, if the Matua and her people do not come in, then we shall greet the Prime Minister. And we shall shut the door."')

'Haere mai, haere mai e kui. Haere mai,' the old woman called as she stood at the threshold of the whare runanga. 'Come, come Riripeti, enter.'

The messenger delivered the ultimatum. 'Once the Prime

Minister is inside the doors will be closed to all—including you.'

'Then it is Pakeha kawa,' Tamati Kota said. 'I say again to you, e hoa, you be the one to interrupt the karakia of Riripeti to our Atua.'

('Well,' the journalist said, 'the messenger again reported the outcome to Maui. He conferred only a moment with the other elders of the paepae. They reached consensus. "Let us proceed," they said. "Welcome the Prime Minister into our midst and, after he is here, let the door be closed."')

Riripeti opened her eyes, 'Amine.' They were green like a dark river, and flecked with gold. She saw that the child had fully revived. 'Let us go now, e mokopuna,' she said, 'and take the groans of our people so that they are heard by all.'

She took the child by the hand, lifted the flap of the tent, and the light of a thousand torches made her look like a golden goddess. Together, the people approached the meeting house. At that moment, however, another ope went through the doorway. The figure of the Prime Minister and his entourage passed across the threshold of the meeting house. From within came a burst of greeting.

'It is too late,' Grandfather Ihaka said. 'For the mere sake of the boy you have jeopardised all opportunity to make our plea for the return of the land.' His face was purple with rage. 'Why do you do this, kui? Why always bend to the boy?'

('The Prime Minister entered the door. He was smiling and affable. He was shown to the position of honour. I don't think he knew what was going on. I was horrified. "The door is not really going to be closed, is it?" I asked. That was the question on everyone's lips. Then Maui issued the instruction.')

'Tutakina te tatau,' Maui said. The door began to be closed. The people inside fell into a silence so deep that it could have been an eternal well.

Outside, Riripeti saw the door closing. The shadow of the whare runanga embraced her and within that darkness the door was like a diminishing prism closing out the light completely. 'How can they do this?' she asked. 'This is how it happened also at Ruapekapeka when the people were at prayer. That was when the Pakeha made his attack. And because I was at karakia, the attack is being made again.'

The door closing, closing. Riripeti lifted her hands to that closing prism of light. Her fingers were long and beautifully sculpted. It was as if she was trying to use them to widen the gap. Her voice was guttural, determined.

'Homai te toka ki ahau,' she said.

The door closing, closing.

'Bring me the axe.'

26

'Haere mai ki o tatou mate e, haere mai.'

Grandfather Ihaka lay in state at the chapel. He would remain there overnight but, tomorrow afternoon, his body would be taken to Poho o Rawiri marae in Gisborne. There, the tangihanga would begin.

Meanwhile, after I'd kissed, hugged and shaken hands with my aunts and uncles and spent some time renewing our family kinship ties, I took Regan, Bianca and Miranda back to Palliser Street to sleep. They would need the rest. The next few days would be emotional and, for Regan, who had never experienced the tangihanga before, arduous. As we sped away from the chapel, the family came out to watch me. I felt uneasy. They seemed to be expectant. Waiting.

When we arrived at Palliser Street, I bathed the girls. They loved splashing each other and, when I wasn't looking, splashing me as well. Tiana looked in at them and smiled.

'They're water babies, aren't they!' she said. 'They must get their love of the water from my kaitiaki, Hine Te Ariki.' It was a lovely, unexpected thing for her to say. Whenever she let down her guard, Tiana could be almost loving.

Regan and I dried the girls and put them to bed. We spent some time with Teria, Meri and Vanessa before they went home with their husbands. I had a few beers with Te Ariki and my two brothers Hamuera and Mana.

'Well, we better get some sleep now,' Te Ariki said. He knelt on the floor and we followed, closing our eyes as he began to intone the last prayer of the day, 'Kororia ki To Ingoa Tapu. Glory be to Your Holy Name.'

By that time it was after midnight. I wanted to make love but Regan was diffident. 'Your parents are sleeping in the next room,' she explained. Instead, we lay in each other's arms, talking softly about the day. 'What happens to the tribe and the family now that your grandfather has died?' she asked.

'Dad will take over from him,' I answered. 'He'll become the head of the tribe and the family.'

'Didn't your grandfather give you his mantle? The mantle of leadership?'

'Yes. In due course, my time may come.'

'You sound unsure, Tama.'

Regan's reply bothered me. 'I don't know if I am the one, now,' I began, 'to fulfil Riripeti's great dream of liberating the iwi. When she died, something went wrong. I don't know what it was.'

Riripeti's spiders, Tamatea, nobody's seen them since she died.

'But everybody in the family still believes in you,' Regan said. 'You can tell they do. This might sound fanciful, but they seem to be waiting for you to wake from a deep sleep. Don't you sense it?'

'Yes, but I don't believe any more that I can carry on the dream, Regan. The umbilical cord has been cut between me and what I supposed was to be my destiny. That's if you believe in destiny. I'm never too sure what I believe in any more.' I tried to make light of it. 'But destiny will right itself,' I continued. 'Someone else will come along, born in the same manner as I was. As Riripeti was. With our hands around our neck. And our left eye swimming in blood.'

'Don't joke about it,' Regan answered. 'That's the same question that Tiana asked me when the girls were born.' All of a sudden, she pulled my arms around her. Tight. Tighter. 'You do love us, Tama, don't you?'

'You know I do,' I answered.

'Even though I haven't given you a son? And although you have daughters?'

'Yes,' I answered again.

I should have known that Regan would not let the matter rest. Once she was on the track of something, she never let it go—like, for instance, whether there was an 'r' in borogoves. 'Maybe that's why there is a *mate*,' she said. 'Since Riripeti died everything's gone wrong. You didn't take over the leadership; your grandfather and father did. And what was supposed to happen got diverted. Subsequently, everyone is being punished.'

'Some people, like my cousin Sammy, think it's because Riripeti gave me everything and they were left with nothing.'

'That doesn't fit,' Regan persisted, 'because now that you have nothing they should have everything. No, it's something more complex.' She gave a gasp of realisation. 'I always told you that your family was so Italian, so Sicilian, didn't I? Well, it's also very Greek. It's like the *Orestaia*. You know the Greek myth don't you?' Regan had the bit between her teeth now. 'It's long and convoluted but there's a character named Orestes, son of Clytemnestra and Agamemnon, in the story. He has two sisters, Electra and Chrystothemis. Anyway, Clytemnestra takes a lover, Aegisthus, and together they murder Agamemnon. They hold Orestes' sisters with them but banish Orestes, who is really the heir to the throne, from the country. The *Orestaia* tells us that from that point the whole world falls apart. Famine and plague make the once prosperous kingdom a wasteland. The House of Atreus descends into dissolution. Guilt starts to gnaw at Clytemnestra and Aegisthus. Electra goes insane, and she and her sister are treated like animals in the court, chained up like dogs. There are signs and portents in the sky because the ordained destiny of the House of Atreus has been stalled. Order will not be restored until Orestes returns to rescue his sisters and—'

'And?'

Regan's voice drifted in the night.

'He kills his mother.'

Kills his mother?

I tossed and turned in that fitful zone between sleep and wakefulness, pondering Regan's words. Without comprehending it all, I knew in my heart of hearts that at some point I would have to confront Tiana, for she, as much as anybody else, was implicated in the *mate* that had come upon the family and the iwi. But how? Why? And to what purpose?

Bothered, I got up and left Regan sleeping. I checked on Bianca and Miranda, made a cup of tea and took it out to the back porch. Without any bidding my thoughts went back to the summer of 1973 when Regan and I were in Europe, two years ago before we returned to New Zealand. I had a few weeks' holiday from my diplomatic secondment to the Commonwealth Office and decided on the spur of the moment that we should visit Venice.

'Your mother won't like it,' Regan said. 'Didn't she tell you to go anywhere in Europe but not to Venice? I thought you promised you wouldn't.'

'What Tiana doesn't know won't hurt her,' I answered. 'Anyway, how can I come all this way without seeing the city where my grandmother could possibly have lived as a young girl?'

I broke my promise to Tiana. Somehow she found out, back home in New Zealand. She had a premonition of some kind. She saw a laughing boy, playing in blinding lagoons. At first she thought it was my brother, Mana. Then she saw a floating city and, hovering above it, a malevolent bestiary. That's how she knew I had disobeyed her.

But she broke her promise too. The promise was never to come to me in her dreams. This may be difficult to understand but Maori people believed that you could travel in your dreams, most often when your yearnings of aroha, of mokemoke, one for another, needed to be expressed. Even in these great days of change, when nobody believes in these things, Maori still travel this way to talk with whanaunga about old ancestral matters that must be resolved, about breaches that should be healed, or to tell of taonga, family heirlooms, that need to be found. When they are dying they travel to embrace, mingle tears and say farewell to all those they have loved.

Or they journey to protect or warn a loved one of some malignant star or malevolent sign. Whatever the travel, all had to be achieved within the space of the dream. So, if they were in a hurry, or had to journey far, they called upon their family protector, or kaitiaki, to help them. In Tiana's case this was the merwoman, Hine Te Ariki.

I know now, but I didn't know it then, that when Tiana realised I was in Venice, she sent Hine Te Ariki ahead to warn me to get out of the city. When I didn't heed any of the warnings, she came herself. My father told me that one night, when they were readying for bed, she told him, 'On no account must you wake me. Promise me.'

Once he had agreed to her command, she put on her long flannel nightgown and brushed her hair with deliberate, even strokes until it gleamed with the hidden fire inherited from her ancient ancestors of Te Tira Maka. She took her knife and strapped it to her left arm. Around half past eleven, her face became remote and still. Her eyelids began to flicker. With a hiss of anticipation she saw the sea of her dreams opening before her. Her feet began to paddle, her toes circling faster and faster in a motion that propelled her forward. Using an overarm crawl she approached the high cliff rim of her dream. The sky was blood-red and the sea was a thousand kilometres beneath her, swirling, opalescent and luminous, and as deep as a constellation.

She took a deep breath. Looked to her sacred mountain, Hikurangi. There and *mark*. Arms outstretched, she thrust herself over the cliff and dived, her flannel nightgown billowing. As she was falling, she called for Hine Te Ariki.

Knifing into the water, she plunged downward. The sea of dreams was the colour of pounamu. The infinite ocean was shafted by eternal sunlight.

Something was swimming towards her. Something was approaching.

It was Hine Te Ariki. She was six metres long. Her face had the form of a woman's but the features were inhuman and unearthly. Her skin was dark and mottled like an eel and the eyes were dark green. Her mouth was wide and huge in that alien visage. At her chin was a beautiful moko.

As she reared up and joined Tiana, the thick ropes of Hine Te Ariki's hair exposed her neck where her gills were dilated. She had rudimentary breasts and thick hair at the armpits and groin. Her lower body gleamed with scales. Layered like diamonds, the scales sparkled in that timeless sea. At the extremities, the scales became splendid crystal flukes of immense power. They were out of proportion to the rest of Hine Te Ariki's body, flicking back and forth, to maintain her upright position.

The two women, human and kaitiaki, greeted each other. Hine Te Ariki took Tiana in one hand to her breast like a doll. She turned slowly to face the north.

'Me haere taua,' Tiana said. 'Let us go.'

～

The tangihanga, or period of mourning, is the most important Maori ceremonial of the modern age. In the old times, this public display of death and grief often continued for a week or longer; European definitions of hygiene and its conflicting values system about death and bereavement changed all that. Since the early twentieth century, the tangihanga has been celebrated over a maximum three-day period.

The tangihanga allows for the last farewells to be made, in a formal context, to the deceased. The tupapaku is addressed as a living person and usually lies in state on his or her marae; in these days of rapid urbanisation, the body may lie in a chapel or church for the first day until the marae is ready to receive the deceased. The first day of the mourning period is usually reserved for the family and the next two days for mourners who come from afar. On the afternoon of the third day the body is committed to the earth.

Depending on the mana of the dead person, the tangihanga can be anywhere up to 2000 strong, and when our beloved Auntie Ngoi Pewhairangi died at Tokomaru Bay in 1985, 4000 arrived on the last day, including a special government delegation which flew by air force aircraft to pay respects to this extraordinary woman.

The tangihanga is not a wake. It is a formally conducted series of encounters between whanau and mourners, where the deceased is remembered with affection and relish, and the tribal affiliations and allegiances are redrawn and recommitted to memory. It is ironic that a death has now become the major way of binding ourselves together. At the tangihanga tribal memory is shared and blood ties are reinforced in a passionate and impassioned letting go of the emotions. It is a catharsis and, in its enforced acceptance of death itself, it is a way in which death is conquered. But the ultimate fear should not be of death and, rather, of our individual judgement before God.

On the second day of the tangihanga, Grandfather Ihaka was moved from the chapel to Poho o Rawiri marae, as had been his request. He had wished to lie there on the marae which he had loved as his second home. When he was being carried from the chapel the pallbearers, who were young men, went to take him out the glass doors head first. Abraham, the elder who had welcomed me the previous evening, reprimanded them.

'Turn the casket around,' he said, 'so that Ihaka can go feet first.'

Poho o Rawiri was already crowded with mourners when Grandfather Ihaka arrived. It was astonishing to see and hear the acclamations that were made to him as he was taken into the meeting house and placed on the stage. Floral wreaths and old photographs were banked on either side of his casket. Aunt Floria, Aunt Hiraina and other Mahana and tribal women seated themselves around him, weeping as the visitors arrived.

The first ope arrived from Tuhoe, the tribe of Ihaka's birth. The karanga came like an arrow through the air, cleaving the world with extraordinary beauty. The group of kuia, including Aunt Floria and Aunt Hiraina, stood to welcome them. The ope was 500 strong, and they brought such pride to our clan in their coming. I marvelled at the tribute of their members and the strength of their kinship for this man who had been one of their own. The weeping began, the exchange of tears, and then the whaikorero, and I was again caught up in the beauty of the language and the lyricism of Maori farewells to the dead. Ihaka was referred to in the highest of terms—as a chief, leader of the people, protector of the poor and the weak.

The next group came from Kahungunu, from hapu around Nuhaka and Wairoa. The numbers were large, 300 or more, and they included many whom I knew by sight. Again I was not prepared for the aroha which they expressed for Ihaka. They praised him with an extravagance beyond my comprehension. They wept tears of real feeling. They requested that he be allowed to travel to one of their marae before his burial. In reply, Abraham referred to Rongopai as being one with Kahungunu links, and to *Takitimu*, and the ope accepted this. However, during the korero, one of the mourners in the ope, emotionally wrought with the sadness of the tangi, collapsed from a massive heart attack. Erina was near the old koroua when he died. 'His eyes were streaming with tears,' she told me. 'I have not seen so many tears shed for anyone. He came to farewell Grandfather and, now, he has become Grandfather's companion in death.'

By the time the third group had arrived, from Whakatohea, it was clear that the tangihanga would be of considerable proportion.

'The visitors pay our father and his iwi such tribute,' Aunt Floria whispered. 'All of us should feel proud, Tamatea, that your grandfather was so loved.' Even so, I could not help but notice the occasional veiled references from those of the Ringatu faith to Grandfather's defection after Riripeti had died; they began to kiss my hands, saying, 'So many years have passed since we saw you, Beloved of Riripeti.'

Abraham took me aside. 'I don't care what your relationship with your grandfather was like, boy,' he growled. 'I'm telling you that you must fulfil your obligations. If not to Ihaka then to your grandmother. Come and join the elders.'

I had no option but to comply. Very soon, a steady stream of visitors created a pathway towards me. 'We come to honour your grandfather,' they said. 'We also recall the great lady who was his wife. When we see you, Tamatea, we see her. She gave you a destiny, Beloved. Return to it.'

Always the same entreaty. Return to it, return to it.

A second ope arrived from Tuhoe. I realised that fortune was attending me and that I had been invited to join the elders none too soon. They had brought Toroa with them, coming into the hall with his wife and three children.

A loud murmur echoed through Poho o Rawiri. Immediately, Teria came to me. 'What will you do?' she asked. 'Can there be peace and reconciliation?'

I should have anticipated his arrival. He was entirely within his rights to come to the tangi. There was nothing I could do to stop him but, when I saw him, I looked at Grandfather Ihaka.

'Even in your death, my grandfather, you still attempt to challenge me and my birthright.'

⌒

Just as I was named after the captain of the *Takitimu* canoe, so too was Toroa named after the captain of the *Mataatua*, the canoe from whom have descended the Tuhoe, the Children of the Mist. As such, it was only logical that Ihaka should have taken Toroa's side against me; after all, they were both of Tuhoe descent. But they had the benefit of numbers, for when Riripeti died and they challenged me, I was alone in the battle.

It was Vanessa who, in 1965, was the first among us—Te Ariki and Tiana's children—to be introduced to Toroa. She had just finished school; I was twenty-one and studying law at Victoria University in Wellington.

What happened was that Aunt Floria took her to the South Island as a trainee fleeco in Grandfather Ihaka's shearing gang. 'I had a really neat time,' Vanessa told us later, 'and I enjoyed getting paid too.' The gang didn't work during weekends and Vanessa loved going out on the town and dancing with the South Island boys, under Aunt Floria's strict supervision. Then, quite out of the blue, 'Oh, and guess what, I met our brother,' she told us.

Our brother?

I can't recall precisely how I felt when Vanessa said those words. I was home for the holidays and we were all in the living room at

Palliser Street—Teria, Erina, Vanessa and myself—sitting around the table after dinner. We were playing cards, five hundred I think, and Vanessa said the words in such an ordinary manner, as if conjuring up a brother from out of the air was a daily party trick: first there were the four of us, now there were five. The fact is that we were accustomed to such rumours about Dad. Here was another one to add to the list.

'Oh, that father of yours,' Teria said to us with a sigh, excluding herself. 'Eight no trumps,' she added.

'But it's true,' Vanessa protested. 'Grandfather introduced me to him. It happened on my fourth day at the shearing shed—'

Apart from Aunt Floria, there was a strange boy in the shearing gang who kept acting like her chaperone. At a party, she had been having a small sip of beer, not even enough to make a fly drunk, and he had come over and taken her glass away. What a cheek! And when her cousin Sammy had wanted to take her into town, this boy had said, 'Be back by twelve, Sammy, or else.'

'Who does he think he is?' Vanessa asked Sammy as they drove into Dunedin on the truck.

'You should know,' Sammy answered. 'If you don't, ask your father.'

The emphatic way in which Sammy responded bothered Vanessa; she became more curious about the boy. His name was Toroa and he was twenty-one too.

'You and Toroa,' Vanessa said to me, 'could have been twins. Then, on my third week in the shearing gang—'

It was Ihaka who had thrown the spear. After dinner, he brought Toroa over to Vanessa. He had been cruel. Tactless. Dismissive. 'It's about time you met your eldest brother,' he said. 'Your father is Toroa's father but his mother is my niece Awhina. She was the one your father was supposed to marry before he met your mother.'

In the eyes and presence of all who were in the room, and with Grandfather's words acknowledging him, Toroa placed his arms around my sister Vanessa and kissed her. By that act, both he and Grandfather challenged us all. In particular, they laid claim to the birthright that was rightfully mine, for, when I was born, Riripeti had acknowledged me as the eldest grandson. But Ihaka now had the mantle that had descended to him at her death and was moving to overrule her decision and give the birthright to Toroa instead.

Thus began Grandfather Ihaka's campaign to have Toroa recognised as the true heir to the Mahana clan. Just as Grandmother had taken me to all the hui and other meetings when I had been a child, so too did Ihaka seek to establish Toroa's credentials in a similar manner. At twenty-one, Toroa was able to take an active part in the campaign; I had only been a passive participant as a young child, relying on Riripeti to act on my behalf. What dazzled the family, in particular, was Toroa's brilliance in the art of whaikorero and marae debate. My own knowledge was seriously flawed because, in the years following Riripeti's death, and alienated from her great dream for me, I had to strike out for myself and find an alternative destiny in the Pakeha world. Perhaps this was why, increasingly, the Ringatu faithful and the iwi came to regard Toroa with respect and admiration and to call him 'son'.

They wanted to believe Grandfather. They also wanted to put destiny back on track by installing Toroa in my place. They abdicated from my side. Grandfather Ihaka called them to heel and they trotted obediently behind his assertion—'This is the eldest. This is the heir, Toroa.'

After the holidays I returned to my university studies in Wellington. I was supporting myself at university on a legacy left to me by Tamati Kota, Riripeti's priest; Grandfather Ihaka had refused to support me and I was too proud to ask Te Ariki for help.

At the time I had a Maori girlfriend, Tepora, and we were living together in a small flat in Karaka Bay. I had met Tepora through a friend, Hamiora; the three of us were students. The first time I saw her she was wearing a dress of Grecian design, off the shoulder, and she had threaded pearls into her hair at the nape of her neck. Her resemblance, even if only superficially, to Riripeti took my breath away.

Those were halcyon days when our little house was like a nest floating in a forever solstice. We swam in the freezing water of

Wellington Harbour, and at night we made love again and again and again. Our physical need for each other had always been frightening in its intensity; being apart felt so unnatural. We had managed to separate for Christmas, me to go to Gisborne and Tepora to her mother in Auckland—I never met her mother—but we flew back into each other's arms as soon as we could. I have never been able to understand what chemistry in the skin or soul could make two people so reactive to each other.

Tepora seemed to take the threat to my mana more seriously than I did. I told her when we were lying in bed together. We had been giggling over something that had occurred earlier in the day; someone had stolen one of her evening gowns off the clothesline and that day, in Cuba Mall, we found out who it was. Tepora had lurched against me. 'I think I'm going to be sick,' she said. She pointed at an Amazonian transvestite, flouncing past. 'That man's wearing my dress.'

Now, all was stillness. When she finally spoke, Tepora's voice seemed to come out of the past. For a moment I thought I recognised it. 'You must do something,' she said, 'before it's too late.' Mystery drifted across her voice.

But I delayed my action. I was trying to come to grips with those mystical things called moots and torts. At the time, Magna Carta and King Edward seemed as remote as Olympus to a young man from a place called Waituhi; I was finding it by turns difficult and boring and, worse, irrelevant. But I knew that I had to become versed in Pakeha law. Only then would I be able to understand how the Pakeha had used the law to dispossess Maori of the land. Once I had that understanding of how the law could be manipulated, perhaps I would be able to use it to get the land back.

In those days there were very few Maori students in the university system. Most had been streamed away into middle- or lower-class occupations, automatically failed because of the colour of their skin. Those of us who succeeded did so not because we were privileged but because we were driven to. In my case, Riripeti was like an owl perched on my shoulder, an unspoken presence whispering in my ear. I dared not fail for if I did I had the feeling that the owl would also become executioner and peck at my jugular until it was beyond repair. I would have loved nothing better than to have given it all up and taken a lesser occupation.

I did not feel any sense of threat until nearer the end of the year. Toroa had been living in Rotorua. As a postscript to one of her letters Teria added, 'Oh yes, I should tell you that Toroa, you know, the one that Grandfather keeps saying is our brother, well, he's moved to Gisborne.'

The first territorial incursion had been struck.

I flew back to Gisborne for the weekend, intent on sorting the matter of Toroa out. I had wanted Tepora to come with me but, at the time, she felt it would be best to keep our relationship a secret.

My first objective was to confront Te Ariki. As usual he was at the airport to meet me. My father and I had a great love for each other. It made up for the disturbing relationship I had with Tiana. Of course, as usual, he wanted to bring me up to date on the family and his and Grandfather's joint leadership of the iwi. However, at no time did he mention Toroa. 'Dad,' I began, 'can you tell me about this boy who is being championed by Grandfather Ihaka?' I formulated the question the way a lawyer would ask a client.

Immediately the mood changed. 'You embarrass me by asking that question,' he answered.

I went for the jugular. 'Is he your son?' I asked. 'Is he your eldest?'

Te Ariki's face had a frightened, angry look. 'You are my son. You are my eldest. As for this other boy, let me handle it my way. I will settle it with your grandfather.'

I took Te Ariki at his word. I returned to Wellington, expecting that Dad would tell Ihaka that what he was doing was wrong. I expected that Grandfather would then cease championing Toroa. But a month later, Teria telephoned me, 'Toroa is still here. Grandfather still claims he is our father's eldest son.'

At Tepora's insistence, I returned to Gisborne again. I didn't tell Te Ariki I was coming back. I asked Teria to meet me at the airport. She was waiting with Meri. When we spoke on my arrival, I discovered the matter was more serious than I had expected.

'The family is closing ranks against us,' Teria said. 'You remember how they were with Aunt Helen? It's all happening again. Mum, Dad and I went to a Maori cultural concert last week and Toroa came in with Grandfather. Te Ariki didn't notice what was happening, but I did. Wherever Dad walked, Toroa would walk behind him or next to him. When Dad sat down, Toroa sat down next to him. When Dad went in to supper, so did Toroa. By simply being seen with Dad, people assume that Dad has accepted him. Why doesn't Dad do anything?'

'I had a stand up fight with Aunt Floria,' Meri chimed in. 'We were in the shearing shed and she asked me why I was hostile to "your brother". I told her that he wasn't our brother and she said our grandfather said he was. I saw red and asked her, "Was Grandfather there when Dad was supposed to have put his thing into Toroa's mother?" She blushed like mad but I was insistent. "Well, was he?"'

I had to laugh, because there was a certain irrefutable logic about Meri's argument.

'Of course Aunt Floria couldn't say yes or no, so I said to her, "Well, my father was there and he said he didn't." Anyway, Mum heard us arguing. She knew what it was about. Mum said to Aunt Floria, "I want a word with you Floria, right now." Then she let her have it. "If you want a fight, Floria, you pick on me, don't pick on my kids. Or else come and have it out with me." Lucky for Aunt Floria that Mum didn't have a knife in her hands.'

I asked Teria and Meri to drive me to Palliser Street to drop off my suitcase.

'What are you going to do?' Teria asked.

'If Dad won't tell Grandfather Ihaka and the rest of the Mahana family that Toroa is not his eldest son, I will.'

Tiana wasn't at home when we arrived. She turned up just as I was going out the door. I was so angry that all I could do was to confront her too. 'Why have you not forced Te Ariki to sort out this business about Toroa?'

'Oh? And you think any of the Mahana clan will listen to me? Including your father? To them I am a woman of no account. And your father, well, he is a Mahana like the rest of them.'

Sometimes Tiana never made any sense. I grabbed her arms and pinned her to the door. 'Whose side are you on?' I asked her. 'You've always been against me, haven't you? Haven't you!'

She gave me a look. Her voice rose out of her, striking back. 'Wrong question, Tamatea. The question is really, whose side are you on?' She struggled in my arms. All I could feel was elation that I was now physically stronger than she was. No longer could she mark me, ritually, as she used to do when I was younger.

'Let Ihaka and the Mahana family acclaim Toroa as their eldest son,' she said. 'Perhaps that way I can reclaim mine. I owe no allegiance to the Mahana clan and I have paid my dues many times over to the woman who made you her Beloved.'

I went to Uncle Manaaki first.

'Uncle,' I began, 'I have never asked you for anything, ever, and I am not asking for anything now. Rather I am asking you on behalf of my father, your brother Te Ariki, not to take the side of this boy Toroa.'

My uncle thought that the whole affair was a great joke. 'That brother of mine,' he laughed, 'he always was one with the ladies. You know, he should have married Awhina, she was a beauty. When Te Ariki jilted her we were all surprised because frankly, boy, your mother couldn't hold a candle to Awhina.'

I flared at his sneering putdown of Tiana; she was my mother, after all. But I didn't want his remark to deflect me from my purpose. 'Toroa is not my brother,' I said. 'I have Te Ariki's word on this.'

Uncle Manaaki laughed again. 'You are taking this much too seriously,' he said. 'Toroa is a fine young man. You know, of course, that both Awhina and your grandfather say Te Ariki is the father. Why fight it? Even if he isn't your brother I can do nothing against him for that would mean confronting my own father.'

Next on my list was Uncle Pita. 'Uncle,' I asked, 'I understand that you have the boy, Toroa, staying with you.'

He paused and, then, 'Yes, I have your brother living with me,' he said. 'But you know he's on marae business today with your grandfather—and your father. He's not here at the moment but I know he'll be glad that his younger brother has come to see him.'

My uncle always enjoyed having the upper hand and I sensed him relishing our conversation. 'He is not my brother,' I responded.

'Oh?' Uncle asked. 'Your grandfather says he is, and that's good enough for me, Tamatea. It was at Dad's request that I took Toroa in. Your argument is with him, not me.'

I could feel my lip curl. 'As usual,' I said, 'you hide behind that old man's coat-tails. Hasn't Te Ariki spoken with you yet?'

'Not yet,' Uncle Pita answered. 'I'll listen to him, Tamatea, but not to you. You're just a boy doing a man's job. Let your father do it—if he dares.'

I turned next to Aunt Floria. As soon as she saw me walking up the path to her house she tried to turn me away. 'Your grandfather is not here, Tamatea,' she said, 'and even if he was I wouldn't let you bother him. You and him are always arguing, and you should know better. Don't you think he's got enough on his plate looking after everybody without you harassing him as well?'

I tried an oblique approach. 'Do you love your brother Te Ariki?' I asked.

Her eyelids flickered. 'Yes, of course I do,' she answered.

'Has he ever lied to you?'

'No.' Then she saw where I was heading with my questions. She folded her arms. 'You think you're so smart with your university education,' she began. 'Well, Dad's outsmarted you this time. Even if Toroa wasn't your brother, he is now.'

I was puzzled. Aunt Floria drew herself up, triumphant. 'Your grandfather has adopted Toroa. Made him his whangai.'

I staggered back. I went to Aunt Hiraina to see if it was true.

'Your grandfather doesn't mean you any harm,' she wept. 'The trouble is that Mum put you before Dad and he can never forgive you for that. As well, he is firmly convinced that Toroa is the best person to succeed him. He must have his reasons.'

I took a deep breath. 'Reasons? Then he can explain them to me,' I said. 'Do you know where he is?'

Hiraina could never keep a secret from me. 'He's at Takipu marae, Te Karaka. Toroa is with him—and so is your father.'

I don't know what the meeting was about on Takipu marae. I parked the car at the gateway and strode in. Whatever it was, the marae was crowded. Good. If I was going to make a declaration about Toroa, let it be as publicly as possible to all within listening range.

As soon as people saw me, they began to smile and greet me. They were puzzled when I pushed through them towards Te Ariki. His face broke into a joyous smile. 'Tama,' he said. 'Why didn't you tell me you were coming home?'

'Which one is Toroa?' I asked him. My eyes were already searching the crowd.

Immediately, Te Ariki stiffened. 'If you've come to make trouble, this is the wrong time to do it.'

'When will there ever be a right time, Dad?' I asked him.

'This is my business, Tamatea. I will handle it in my way. Stay out of it.'

'Sorry, Dad, but it is my business. If you can't handle it, I will. My mana is at stake. And after all, what have you got to lose by telling the truth? Is Toroa my brother?'

'I have already told you, no.'

'That's all I need to know. Now which one is he?' But I had already seen him. I would have recognised him anywhere. Although his hair was tied in a topknot and he was stockier than I was, in every other respect, yes, we could have been twins.

I threaded my way towards him. There was no doubt that he was handsome in the old Maori way. His bearing was regal and his neck and ear ornaments were redolent of the classical Maori. His happiness in seeing me was so unguarded that I faltered. All this time I had fabricated an enemy in the abstract. In the reality, he appeared softer, kinder, somebody who under different circumstances I might have been friends with. But my victory lay in crushing him entirely and forever. To accept him would have been to acknowledge and sympathise with him and, perhaps, also to suspect that Te Ariki was not telling me the truth.

You could have heard a pin drop when I pressed my nose with his. Tears began to run down his cheeks. He tried to embrace me.

Instead, I pushed him away. Gently. But with firmness. 'Tena ra koe,' I said. 'I know who you are. I know you as a boy named Toroa whom my grandfather has adopted. But in this public place, I renounce you. You are not my brother. There is no blood connection between us.'

'Tamatea, no—' Te Ariki shouted.

Somewhere in the universe I heard a snapping sound as if a thread had broken.

'Tena ra koe,' I said the second time. 'I, and my father, have nothing to offer you because nothing we have is rightfully yours. I renounce you, Toroa, you are not my father's son nor heir to anything that is his.'

'Pokokohua, Tamatea,' I heard somebody shout. 'Taurekareka.'

I felt a sudden discontinuity, as if a million lives had suddenly been extinguished. But Toroa lifted his head, proud.

'Tena ra koe,' I said the third time of the formal renunciation. 'All here are witness to my words. Toroa. Find peace wherever you can but do not expect to find it with me and mine or my father and his. You are neither my brother nor his son.'

As I stepped away and turned from him, I heard a primeval scream like a cyclone shrieking in my blood. But it was too late, it was already done.

It was then that Grandfather Ihaka arrived. He raised his walking stick and began to rain blows on me. He was quivering with rage.

'You, Tamatea,' he said. 'How dare you—'

His attack stunned everybody. Caught unawares, I was slow to react. But one of the blows slashed the skin just below my left eye and I felt blood splash across my face. 'Grandfather, I warn you—'

'—intervene against my whangai, Toroa. You know nothing. You—'

'—to stop this attack. Toroa? I will fight him and you, Grandfather.'

'—are of no account. Do you hear me? That boy, Toroa, is my heir. He is your father's eldest son—'

'—you will not win against me, although you have tried all these years and particularly since my grandmother died. You wouldn't have had the guts to try anything while she was alive—'

'—and your eldest brother. The rights are his, not yours. And your grandmother has nothing to do with this. This is just between you and me, Tamatea—'

'—but now that she's gone you make your move. Well, Grandfather, I'll fight you both, and on the marae if I have to.'

Always talking past each other. Always at war. Always the bitterness, the hurt, the anger, the viciousness. Until Dad, shocked, separated us. Grandfather Ihaka was panting with exertion.

'So,' he said to Te Ariki, 'see what you've done?' And then he turned to me. 'You want a fight, Tamatea, eh? Eh? Alright, let's see you fight Toroa.'

I knew I was blindsided. Grandfather Ihaka knew it too.

Only Toroa interceded on my behalf. 'Grandfather—'

Ihaka turned to him. 'No, Tamatea brought the fight to the marae. Let him pay the consequences. Let it choose who is the heir and who is the pretender. Let it be done now. Let it be tested here.'

My heart was thundering with fear and anger.

My own passions had created a situation in which I would in all likelihood fail. I had foolishly provoked a public contest. I had risked everything. The winner would take all.

Grandfather Ihaka strode into the middle of the marae and signalled that he wished to interrupt the proceedings. He spoke in Maori, a long superb speech acknowledging the visitors and making references to tribal genealogy. Then, just as I had done in my formal renunciation of Toroa, Grandfather made a formal statement of his case. 'I wish to pronounce publicly that this boy, Toroa, is the eldest of his generation, and upon him will fall my mantle when I am gone.'

It was a statement which nullified my renunciation and consigned me to the ranking of lower status. I looked at Te Ariki. Why did he not support me?

'You started this,' he said. 'You finish it.'

I took the position which had just been vacated by Grandfather. The marae can often be the loneliest place in the world. I could feel the currents of sympathy for me but I sensed that they would not be enough to sway the power of Grandfather Ihaka.

'Why have you all taken Grandfather's side? I asked. 'Just because he says a thing is as it is, is it? I am very sorry that it has come to this.' I could feel the loneliness like acid eating my heart away. 'I am the eldest son of this generation,' I continued. 'I claim no mantle from my grandfather. I have the mantle of Riripeti, and that is enough. Should Grandfather wish to give his mantle to this boy, then let him do so as to his adopted son. But I warn you all, let him not call that boy my eldest brother.'

'Is that all you have to say?' Grandfather Ihaka mocked. 'So which weapons do you wish to fight with? The club or the spear? Mere or taiaha?'

I was not an exponent in either. I felt drained and defeated already. Grandfather Ihaka made the choice. 'Let it be the taiaha.'

'You brought this on yourself,' Dad called. He would not intervene.

Toroa was brought a taiaha. He made some expert moves. He would defeat me in a trice.

A taiaha was brought to me. I went to accept it. Suddenly I had a recollection from the past, a memory:

Then Riripeti was there. She struck Grandfather Ihaka across the face and pushed Awhina to the ground. Toroa began to run to his mother. Riripeti, turning to him, raised her hands and—

I looked at Grandfather Ihaka. 'Foolish man,' I said. 'Let your whangai try to defeat me with his puny wooden stick. I have no need of a weapon.' My voice was not my own. It was guttural, the voice that Artemis herself would speak in whenever she wished to invoke the power of the whare wananga and of the natural world. With such mana I could stop the sun, call on spiritual forces, even take on the spirit shape of the black spider with the red moko on its back. I had the power of life and death.

A look of shock passed across Ihaka's face. Quickly, he motioned Toroa to begin the attack. As Toroa advanced on me, I knew what I had to do.

'So be it,' I said.

I put both hands into the air and began to squeeze.

Toroa halted. He started to gasp. He dropped his taiaha.

I squeezed even tighter. He was forced, choking, to the ground.

People rushed to help him. Horrified, Ihaka, looked at me.

'*No,*' he cried.

'Enough, Tamatea!' Te Ariki said.

I stopped. I walked towards Grandfather and said in a voice that only he could hear, 'You wanted evidence and now you have it. Give Toroa your mantle, I have no need of it. But cease to place him above me. Next time, I will kill him.'

27

Ten years later at Grandfather Ihaka's tangi, Toroa had come again.

There had been so much opposition and conflict in my life. Had the *mate* begun because of what Grandfather Ihaka tried to do when he wished to put Toroa above me? Was it for this rather than any other reason that the family's misfortunes began?

When would there be an end to it?

Te Ariki did not seem aware that Toroa was there, but the rest of the family knew, oh yes, they knew, and they kept looking my way to see what my reaction would be. I realised that if I did not act quickly, the assumption would be made that we, Te Ariki's children, wished a reconciliation. Any such act would mean acceptance of him as our brother. I looked at Tiana; you would have thought that my own mother would support me but obviously she, like Te Ariki, was standing apart. Whatever way destiny was swirling, they would not oppose it.

Toroa now had a wife and three children. As he came into Poho o Rawiri, he was welcomed by some of the elders and embraced with tenderness. I crossed the floor to talk to Te Ariki.

'You have told me that Toroa is not your son,' I said. 'He has come to the tangi. You cannot welcome him.'

Te Ariki's lips quivered. He gripped the chair until the knuckles of his hands grew white. I thought the bones would burst through the skin. His eyes sought out Toroa who, at that moment, looked up at us both. His face was suffused with grief.

'You cannot do it, Te Ariki,' I repeated. 'If you do it, you take mana from me and my brothers and sisters also. Let others welcome him as a mourner to the tangi, but do not welcome him as one of our whanau.'

'Surely,' Te Ariki pleaded, 'after ten years there can be forgiveness? Surely, all that is past now?'

'No, Te Ariki.'

Toroa's wife began to weep, sensing the implacability of my will, and the children clutched at her skirt, not knowing what was happening. Te Ariki looked at them again and his eyes, also, filled with tears. Why?

Angry, I asked him, 'Te Ariki. You have told me the truth, haven't you? Toroa—is he your son?'

My father shook his head.

'Then the way I have chosen is the correct way,' I said. 'You cannot welcome him.'

At that moment, another ope arrived, this time from Ngati Porou. 'Haere mai, haere mai . . .' Aunt Floria called, her voice echoing through the meeting house.

'Toia mai te waka,' Abraham and other men chanted.

In the foreground, I prepared my father for his encounter with Toroa. He came towards us. I could hear the indrawn breath as the Mahana clan watched my greeting.

I interposed myself before Te Ariki and pressed noses with him. 'Haere mai, whangai of Ihaka,' I said. 'I welcome you on behalf of my father and the Mahana clan.' I felt no exultation as I said the words. I knew that by doing so, I was consigning Toroa forever from the embrace of the family. His face was calm with resignation. He shook hands formally with Te Ariki and my sisters and brothers.

'By your leave, Tamatea,' he said, 'I have come to farewell the great man who adopted me. Allow me to farewell him. When that is done I leave him in the care of the family whom he has loved.'

He was contained and correct. I admired his dignity. I gave my assent and, together with his wife and children, he went forward to Grandfather Ihaka and stroked his hair. The tears, falling from his eyes, splashed on Grandfather.

'Thank you, Tamatea,' Toroa said. 'You will not see me again.'

As he was leaving the meeting house, Tiana came to my side. 'So you banish him just like that, eh? You think you know everything, Tamatea. You don't.'

The third day dawned clean and bright. Grandfather Ihaka was carried from Poho o Rawiri. The wind brought the salt scent of the soughing sea. The sun spiked the hills with its light.

'E Ihaka,' an old man called, 'on mornings like this you and me used to go out to catch the koura and to net the flounder. But, aue, my friend, now it is you who have been caught in the net of death. Haere ki te Po, e hoa.'

The cortege drove out of the awakening city and along the sea road towards the crossroads at Matawhero. We made a quick stop at the beach. One of the old women brought back a lustrous strand of seaweed which she draped over the casket. 'He loved the sea,' she said. I looked at her, not able to comprehend her affection. As the journey resumed I wondered whether I had misjudged the mana of the man. Ahead were the diamond-shaped hills that he had loved. It came to me that the time of taniwha, of vivid personalities striding over the landscape, had not been that long ago.

We took the road to Waituhi. The smoke of many fires cast a dark wreath on the morning sky. Waituhi was crowded, and mourners were commenting that they had not seen such a large gathering in the village since the days of the Matua. The mourners came to weep with me and to talk about Ihaka, and I began to feel claustrophobic, hemmed in by this aroha for him.

'Will you speak at the graveyard?' Te Ariki asked.

'No,' I answered. I felt that I could not be hypocritical about my enmity for Ihaka and I suspected that Grandfather himself would not have wished me to pretend that I loved him.

I went to turn away from Te Ariki. I realised he was under great emotional stress but I was taken aback when he gripped my arms and pinioned me to him. I pulled away from him. Couldn't he understand? 'How can I speak when, once, Grandfather dressed that other boy, Toroa, in animal skins to make him smell like me, and claimed he was your son and my eldest brother. He tried to take my birthright from me. I owe him nothing. If I had not beaten him at Te Karaka, he would be the one standing here and I would be the one who was turned away at Poho o Rawiri.'

My father gripped me harder and I should have known then. 'You've already caused enough pain with your retribution. If it was anyone's fight, it was mine.'

'Yes,' I nodded. 'But you never took up the fight, so I had to act in your place, to protect you—'

Mourners standing nearby were becoming aware of our argument.

'I never asked for your protection.'

'—for the sake of my sisters and brothers—'

'They did not ask your help.'

'—no wonder,' I said, 'Grandmother Riripeti wanted me to lead the iwi and didn't pick her own son to do it.'

It was a terrible thing to say. And Te Ariki looked at me, tears running down his face. 'You say that to me?' he asked. 'Your father?'

The sun climbed slowly to midday. The priest arrived. The time had come to close the coffin.

'No,' Aunt Hiraina screamed.

Her passionate outcry set off a storm of grief. It was not until she had cried herself out that the final moments could be embarked on.

My father beckoned me to join the Mahana kin. We filed past Grandfather where he lay in his casket. As we did so, my aunts bent to kiss him, for soon he would be closed away from the light. He was looking calm and serene and, oh Lord, believe me, I really wanted to kiss him in farewell. I was holding my sisters Teria and Vanessa. I could see Grandfather's face as I approached, and I could smell the floral wreaths surrounding him. I wanted to do this, to kiss him, because I had finally come to a repentance of some sort.

But I heard a young woman calling to Ihaka from afar. I turned to the source of the voice and was dazzled by the sunlight. A car, glistening with mirrors, had driven to the edge of the marae. It looked like a crystal casket falling though the many changes of the night. The rear window was slowly being wound down, opening a gap in the mirrors.

I saw a face blanched with grief. It was a face half-veiled, and at the nape of the neck was a cluster of pearls. A shadow began to lower across the face until it was completely in darkness, and

when I looked back at Grandfather Ihaka the lid of the casket had covered him and I saw Grandfather's face closing away from the light. The lid was shutting him away from us and

Tiana was shaking me, asking, 'Ko wai te wahine na? Ko wai? Who was that young woman? Who was she?' But when I looked to confirm her identity the opening in the mirrors had been closed and the car left the marae. Yet, still Tiana's voice called to me, 'Ko wai? Ko wai?' Who was she? Who?', as if she had seen something fearful, something prophetic, and

I saw Toroa's face closing away from the light. The lid was shutting him away forever from us and

I prayed for him, Toroa, he who had tried to take my rightful place as the heir of the family. I had thwarted all his plans and all his dreams and here they would be laid to rest with Grandfather. The priest intoned the last rites and the pallbearers took up the body of Grandfather, but I was not among them. They carried Grandfather up to the graveyard. The sun was burning through the blue of the sky and

I saw Te Ariki's face closing away from the light. The lid was shutting him away forever from us and

I watched Te Ariki weeping at the summit of the hill where the graveyard was. Slowly, the casket was swung out on ropes above the hole where Grandfather would lie, and let to descend. Overcome, Te Ariki chanted a haka of farewell. Until that time I had not cried a single tear. But tears sprang to my eyes as I watched my father, for there was no doubt that he loved his father and

I saw my face closing away from the light. The lid was shutting me away forever from the clan and

I looked down at the casket where it had come to rest. The clay was brown and dry. People cast flowers into the grave. Then the gravediggers shovelled earth on the casket. All around me, grief was raging. My tears were flowing like the sea and my heart was thundering and I looked down at the casket and

I saw the clay falling and

I was being closed away

from the light.

And who had been the young woman in the car?

'Ko wai te wahine na? Ko wai?'

If I had not been so overcome with the turmoil around me, I would have sworn it was Tepora.

⌒

'No wonder Grandmother Riripeti wanted me to lead the iwi and didn't pick her own son to do it.'

It was a terrible thing for me to have said to my father. After the tangi, when he took Regan and our children to the airport,

I apologised. 'I didn't mean it,' I said. 'I love you.'

'I know you love me,' he answered. 'But don't say you didn't mean it. You did.' He hugged me fiercely.

And I remembered that I had said words, almost similar, to Ihaka during his visit to Wellington. They had been terrible words to say to him, a fragile old man who had wanted to give me his blessing. But the words, once said, could never be recalled, and they went beyond forgiveness. They were dark words, black, merciless.

It had been time for me to leave Grandfather Ihaka. I had sat so far away from him, in that little room at Uncle Alexis's home. The space between us was an eternity apart. I stood up and reached for the door. Grandfather Ihaka began to weep. His body was wracked by deep sobs and the room was filled with the sound of his pain.

Yes, cry your heart out, old man, try to move me with your tears. But none of your tricks will work on me. I know them all, Grandfather, trickster, actor in the grand style, thief.

'No, mokopuna,' he said. 'Do not go yet. Can there be no reconciliation between us?'

I looked down on him, my shadow sliding around him like coils. 'We have been at battle with each other ever since I was a child. How can there be any reconciliation?'

Oh, he could make his tears seem so real. He could make himself look the epitome of sadness. 'But I wish to give my blessing to you,' he said.

His mantle. His blessing. His life. I felt myself trembling on the brink of indecision. Then I thought of Toroa, the one whom Grandfather Ihaka had tried to stand in my place. I heard a voice inside my head saying, 'If you bend to your grandfather he may place his hands on your head and take your power from you, your mana. Or he may utter an incantation against you and render you an empty husk of a man. Do not trust him.'

That is when I said the words. I smiled at him and sat back on the bed and embraced him. He mistook the action for forgiveness and he hugged me fiercely—until my coldness came to him. I was still smiling as I kissed his forehead and then both cheeks.

'There, there,' I said. I got up and went to the door. The words.

'I can never forgive you, Grandfather,' I said. 'You tried to take my mana from me when Grandmother was alive and you could not do it. You succeeded in alienating me when she died and when you and my father took over the leadership, but I developed my own mana by walking in the Pakeha world. Then after many years, you dressed Toroa in animal skins and you brought him before the iwi in Waituhi, and before the family, and you acclaimed him, saying, "This is Te Ariki's son, this is Te Ariki's eldest son and therefore the rightful heir of the clan." Oh, how I had to fight you then, Grandfather. You tried to set him in my rightful place. You did not succeed then and neither you nor he will ever succeed because I am too strong for you both. Give your mantle to him, Grandfather, because he will need it if we ever come to the battlefield. I have Grandmother's mana. I need none else.

'Ah yes, Grandfather,' I breathed. 'You were like Rakaihikuroa who schemed the deaths of the twin sons of Kahutapere so that his own son, Tupurupuru, would have ascendancy in Turanga. You said to the people, and to the family, "Waiho ra kia tu takitahi ana nga whetu o te rangi; let there be only one star shining in the sky." And you tried to set that boy up to be one star in the family heavens.'

'I was wrong, mokopuna,' he said.

I went on, heedless. 'Oh, how I had to fight you. And I won—but only just. And I was merciful—but only just. I could have speared that boy through the head, just as Tupurupuru was speared, and watched him staggering and wriggling like a fish at the end of my spear—but I did not. Instead, I let him go.'

'Please mokopuna . . .'

'And now you want a reconciliation? You, who wished to deal the death blow to my mana? No. No such forgiveness is possible. And if there is ever another challenge to me, Grandfather, then I swear to you that the next time there will be no mercy. I will spear Toroa and hang him by his plaited hair on the end of a swaying kahikatea bough. And you can come to see him as he dances in the wind.'

The wind whistled through my words.

'Goodbye, Grandfather,' I said. I left the room. I walked down the passageway to the sitting room. And I felt like turning back and taking that old man in my arms and saying, 'Forgive me, forgive me.' But no, this was how it was meant to be played out, our last moments with each other—here in Uncle Alexis's house in a windswept street of a dark city settling into sleep.

It is said that in death the spirit or wairua of a high chief leaves the husk of the body and sets out on his journey to the land of the spirits accompanied by a servitor and provided with ample provisions.

The wairua travels to the most northerly point of New Zealand called Te Rerenga Wairua. It is from this place, near North Cape, that the wairua departs Aotearoa.

The promontory is bounded by a cliff, and at the edge of it there is an ancient pohutukawa tree with blossoms like dark blood. The tree has an exposed root which extends down to a flat platform below. The spirit descends the root and waits at the edge of the sea until a deep hole appears in the surging water. The hole is fringed with seaweed. As the waves flow in, the seaweed sweeps over the hole. As the waves recede, the seaweed sweeps back to clear the entrance to the wairua's sea journey.

The spirit leaps into the sea's opening and, from there, proceeds to Ohau, in the Three Kings group, on the horizon. The last farewell to Aotearoa is made from Ohau (and visiting Te Terenga Wairua in 1983 I had a sudden premonition of my own death in old age). The wairua then sets its course to join the western trail of the setting sun. It is said that this is the trail that leads to the place of spirits.

So, farewell Ihaka. Farewell to the Long Night, the Night Unending. Farewell to Paerau, the star of the night sky. Farewell from Te Tai Rawhiti, from the East Coast. Travel across the Great Sea of Kiwa to Hawaiki, Distant Hawaiki, Hawaiki Far Away, Hawaiki the Joining Place of the Spirits.

Go to join the multitude of your people, who are like a million stars in the heavens, waiting to embrace you in the other world.

Oh, my grandfather, farewell, farewell, farewell.

Gisborne Airport. Grandfather Ihaka's tangi was over.

It was evening. 'It's time for you to get on the plane,' Te Ariki said.

As usual, he had come alone to farewell me, Regan, Bianca and Miranda; we'd said goodbye to Tiana and my sisters and brothers at Palliser Street. This was the way Te Ariki and I preferred it. No matter what we said or what we did to each other, there was a great love between us.

'We'll leave you alone with Dad,' Regan said, 'and get on the plane now. Bianca, Miranda, give your grandfather a kiss.'

'Goodbye, Papa,' they chorused. They embraced him and waved as they walked across the tarmac with Regan.

The last boarding call was made. 'I love you, Te Ariki,' I said. I was exhausted and I hated long goodbyes. But I also wanted to clasp Dad in my arms forever.

'I know,' he said as he broke our embrace. 'Now go, Tamatea. But never forget, all that I have ever done has been for love of you.'

I walked away from the terminal to the plane. I didn't look back. When I took my seat beside Regan she squeezed my hand. She was already reading a book. Bianca and Miranda were sitting, self-important, opposite us. As the plane took off they waved and waved. For a brief moment I saw Te Ariki, silhouetted in the lights of the terminal. Then we were climbing steeply in the night sky.

As always, I felt a sense of disorientation about leaving. Departing one world and going to another. Leaving the past behind and going forward into the future. Departing home, the Waituhi Valley.

Going home, Wellington.

Regan knew how I was feeling. She pressed my arm. 'Can I have my husband back now?' she asked. She always knew how to normalise my life and bring me back to sanity.

'Yes,' I nodded.

'Good,' she said. She opened her book again.

'So what are you reading?' I asked her.

'Wilkie Collins,' she answered. 'His novel, *The Moonstone*. TS Eliot called it "the first and greatest of English detective novels". It's about a famous yellow diamond that's stolen by British soldiers during the siege of Seringapatam, India, in 1799 and the way it finds its way back to its Indian owners.'

'Are you enjoying it?' I asked.

'I've always loved it. It's regarded as the first mystery story ever written in English. What I especially love is that the resolution of the mystery is not the main thing. Rather, it's the process of getting there.'

The plane broke through the clouds.

Above, the dazzling stars.

Below, the dark slumbering earth.

28

My Uncle Alexis, who had set me in quest of the matriarch, died a month after Grandfather Ihaka. His blindness had made him into a recluse, a person who would not go out of the house, the windswept and self-imposed prison of his in Hataitai.

My Aunt Roha told me that she had actually got Alexis out and down the path and as far as the car. She was going to take him for a drive. But at the door of the car, he stopped and would not get in. Instead, he began to swing his walking stick around his head, faster and faster, like a dazzling sword, and his mouth cracked open in a soundless, agonised scream. She could not get near to stop him. All she could do was wait until he calmed down. When this happened, he jerked his head towards her and said, 'Take me inside, girl.'

From that time onward, this man who had been so devilishly handsome and debonair doomed himself to die. His home became a fortress. At first, his old gambling friends made the effort to keep seeing him, but luck depends on the living and not the dead or dying, and the word got around that Alexis had the hoodoo on him. The visitors trickled away, afraid or driven from him, and that is how Uncle preferred it to be. In his own mind he was already dead.

Clinically, his body still functioned, but he had unplugged himself from life. He grew bloated and grey, his body puffing up with poisonous gases. It was as if he was willing his body into dysfunction. Every day he waited for death's radiant angel and, when it came, he ran to the embrace of its dark enfolding wings with a terrible, unseemly joy. I was in Canada at the time, spending a few days after an international First Nations conference on land rights, visiting Inuit friends in Saskatoon. Te Ariki sent me a telegram:

YOUR UNCLE ALEXIS HAS DIED. SEND FLOWERS. YOU ARE TOO FAR AWAY. LOVE TE ARIKI.

When my friend Hinuk found out about the death she arranged for a memorial service, in the Inuit way. After it was over I stood out in the snow and looked for the Dog Star.

I returned to New Zealand and went around to see Aunt Roha. The house was as closed up as ever. Just as I was leaving, she gave me a letter. 'He told me to give this to you,' she said. I took the letter out to the car and opened it. Inside were two notes, each to the value of $100, and a scrawled letter which Uncle Alexis had written himself in his blindness. It must have cost him great effort and great pride to put pen to paper, knowing that it would look shockingly damaged and crippled.

The letter read, 'I never did repay your grandmother when she made that bet about you. You know, when she said that you would never accept any money from me. Well, she won and I didn't. I like to repay my debts. Please take this money on your grandmother's behalf. Your Uncle Alex.'

I smiled to myself. I thought of my uncle with affection. Even now he was still trying to tempt me. I couldn't take his money, I just couldn't. I drove down to Evans Bay and then over to Seatoun. The wind was blowing out to sea. I took the hundred dollar bills, tore them into tiny pieces and scattered them to the sea. They were like dreams disappearing on the whim of the wind.

ب

'Tutakina te tatau,' Maui said.

It was 1949, Wellington, and the door to the meeting house began to shut, enclosing the people within the stomach of the whare runanga.

'Let the door be closed,' Maui continued, 'for the Prime Minister and all those who have come to the hui are inside.' But the people knew that the Matua, Riripeti, the ariki of Te Whanau a Kai, Te Aitanga a Mahaki and of Rongowhakaata, was still in the darkness of the night and had not yet entered.

'Bring me the axe,' she said. Her voice was filled with fury. Grandfather Ihaka made a gesture of apprehension, saying, 'Hei aha.' She would not be swayed. Tamati Kota also tried to intervene, but she pushed him away from her with beautiful hands which etched flames in the night.

'Homai te toka ki ahau,' she said again. There was a firmness now. 'All of you, my ope, gather closely around me when I have the axe in my hands.'

('And so the door was closed,' the journalist said. 'An atmosphere of unease prevailed. Some of the people were openly hostile to Maui and the other elders for shutting Artemis out. "Haven't you already done enough?" someone yelled at Maui. "Must we divide ourselves against each other in this manner? If anyone should remain outside it is him," he said, pointing at the Prime Minister.

'The elders, however, decided to take no notice of the furore their action was causing. Maui signalled to a tohunga to begin the meeting with a karakia. The tohunga stood up and began to intone the prayer. We all bowed our heads and closed our eyes, and people chanted along with the words.

'Then, in the middle of the prayer, I heard a voice saying something in Maori. It was Artemis's voice, as clear as crystal, cutting through the prayer. Yet it couldn't possibly have been her because she was on the other side of the door. The prayer, my God, it suddenly stopped. People looked at the door.

'"What is it?" I asked. "What is happening?"

'"Didn't you hear?" an old kuia said. "The matua has called for an axe. She wouldn't dare, but I think she's going to chop down the door."')

'Don't do it,' Grandfather said.

Riripeti looked at him and the firelight danced dangerous flames in the depths of her eyes. 'Don't do what?' she asked. 'You know nothing. Only he, my grandson, knows, don't you, e mokopuna?' Her veils swirled around her as she knelt down beside him. 'Ah yes, e mokopuna, you and I were born in the same manner and I was there to see you take your first gasp of air and—'

Her eyes shifted away from him. They were luminous with flames, the irises pitted with torchlight and, then, they became like a green river.

From far off the child saw something undulating, like a silver star swimming, swimming, swimming through the flaming river. As the star came nearer it began to shimmer and to dissolve into a lustrous green fish, which took its final appearance in the form of a beautiful greenstone. The child saw water streaming like moonstones from its sharp approaching head.

'Ara, te toka,' Riripeti breathed.

Swimming through the darkness came a supernatural axe, the same sacred adze which had cut down the tree from which *Takitimu* was fashioned, and which later chopped a way for the waka through the sea. The priest, Ruawharo, had only to touch its blade to the water and the waves were seared apart. The axe came undulating through flames, carried on a feather cloak of incomparable beauty—a rich woven kakahu of many colours and many hues, shimmering indigo and carmine and turquoise, like a celestial rainbow. Its companion adzes had been Te Whironui, Rakuraku o Tawhaki, Mangatirei and Hui te Rangiora; it had been kept hidden away by its people only to be used at moments like this. It came as the living treasure that it was, on its cloak of feathers, and it took light from whichever source was available, the stars, the flaming torches, the burning souls of its bearers. It was wondrous to look upon.

And as it came, Riripeti called out its name.

('And again,' the journalist said, 'Artemis's voice came to us as we waited inside the whare runanga. It announced a name and, at the disclosure, a number of people began to keen in lament. An old man next to me was nodding his head in acknowledgement and wonder.

"The Matua has brought one of our sacred taonga with her," he said, "but the door is closed."')

The axe was large and wedge-shaped. Its dimensions were of such magnitude that it could only have been wielded by the strongest of men. The pounamu blade itself was dark green, almost black, and its cutting edge was ground to sharpness. One could believe that such an axe as this could chop through waves or mountains. Within the dark greenstone there were darker shapes and shadows which moved and changed and flowed from one shape into another.

'Bear the toka to the doorway,' Riripeti commanded. As this was done, she began to sing a chant, her voice elemental, her words spinning like birds of fire and igniting the night with flames.

('I cannot describe to you,' the journalist said, 'the intense emotion that gripped the people in the meeting house. We heard the chanting of your ope as they bore the greenstone adze to the closed doorway. We heard Artemis call out its name, once, twice, three times. People in the meeting house were weeping quite openly. One old lady said, "It is the greenstone that is singing to us. It is telling us its name and its genealogy. It may have the voice of the Matua, but it is the voice of the greenstone."')

The song was of the creation of the greenstone adze in Hawaiki and its creation, together with others, by priests in that land. The greenstone and its companions had been made extremely tapu, so it sang of its pride in its common parentage with such sacred toka. The waiata was about the making of a sacred canoe and the part that the greenstone had played in that creation. The honour of cutting down the tree had been given to the axe. In a trice the deed was done, the noble trunk seared in two as if by laser. Oh, how proud the greenstone had felt at being chosen for the task!

'Ko Takitimu, ko Takitimu, ko Takitimu.' This, the greenstone said, was the name of the waka which, one evening when the stars were cascading into the well of heaven, received the cargo of gods which would be taken to the new land far to the south. The gods were wondrous to look at and their going was marked by supernatural farewells. Above, in the dark sky, fiery birds protected the altar with flaming wings. On either side, as the gods were carried to *Takitimu*, many taniwha appeared to make an avenue of tall, rearing serpents of awesome beauty. Far out to sea, the tipua of the deep made ready to escort and to protect the gods on their journey. The new land had to be made sacred and only the gods could do this.

The song was a magnificat. Joy of joys, the greenstone found itself being lifted from its place and taken also onto *Takitimu*. It wept many tears of gladness, and these were solidified in the roimata of its depths.

('That,' the journalist said, 'must have been one of the most poignant moments of my life, listening to the greenstone telling the story of its coming to the new land.')

Ah yes, the greenstone sang, and the journey had been long and perilous. The song changed and became drenched in loneliness. 'They have all gone now,' the greenstone sang, 'all my companions. And I am the one who remains. I have searched for them everywhere but they have gone from the land and from the sea. I am alone.

'Aue, for many years I was enclosed in darkness. Then strong hands found me and I was brought into the world again. I have served the gods. Now I serve the children of the gods. I yearn to be warmed by you, for I belong to you. Will you not let me enter?'

('All of a sudden,' the journalist said, 'people began to stand up and shout at Maui, "Forget the Prime Minister. There is a more important guest waiting at the door. Huakina mai te tatau. Huakina mai te tatau mo te pounamu. Open the door. Open the door for the greenstone."')

'No,' Grandfather cried.

With an anguished cry Riripeti picked up the axe.

'I will go in uninvited,' she said.

She raised the axe against the door. She became the greenstone herself, wavering in and out of focus, phosphorescent, glowing.

('The voice of the greenstone was calling stronger and stronger. People were screaming and wailing, oh, it was pandemonium. Until an old man could stand it no longer. He pushed the elders away from the door and pulled it open. And—')

Riripeti was at the doorway.

She was holding aloft a wondrous greenstone toka. At first there was simply a pulsing, glowing presence. Then small needles and chips of light began to flicker in the greenstone, vivid and urgent. The needles transformed themselves into soft rays of exquisite beauty, illuminating and compelling, merging one colour into another.

There was a whirl of colour, like shifting harmonies, and a sublime interplay of crystalline shapes—pyramidal illuminations, orbs of intoxicating brilliance, meteoric starbursts, spiralling and blinding coils—hologrammatic images of staggering virtuosity.

('I have already said how theatrical Artemis was,' the journalist said. 'But this was overpowering. As she walked into the whare runanga, by some trick of light, the greenstone adze seemed to flood it with intense brilliance.')

'Anei te taonga tapu ki a koutou,' Riripeti said. 'Te Awhiorangi, te toka o aku tipuna. I bring you Te Awhiorangi, the taonga of our ancestors.'

At her words there was a thunderous roar from the iwi assembled therein. While the acclamation resounded around her, Riripeti motioned the child to stand by her side. With the axe in her hands she offered it to the iwi.

'Let Te Awhiorangi, which chopped the way through mountainous seas for our ancestors to come from Hawaiki, this night chop a way for all of us so that we can regain our lands and go on into the future together.'

The light from the greenstone became stronger and more brilliant. Awesome rays shot interlacing lightning strikes throughout the whare runanga, rays of dazzling power spinning from the adze, so that one had to look away or else be blinded.

The magnificat of the greenstone swelled and burst in ecstasy.

Hui e, haumi e, taiki e.

Let it be done.

⌐

The matriarch, my grandmother Riripeti Artemis Pere, who married Ihaka Mahana, died in Gisborne on 19 July 1957.

I remember vividly looking down at that beautiful face, so artfully made up by some funeral director. She appeared to be eighteen and her cheeks held the blush of an adolescent. Her hair was like sable, thick and curling down one side of her face into her cupped hands. Around her neck was a greenstone pendant. Her bracelets lay still around her wrists.

She was dressed in white silk, as if for a bridal ceremony. Around her shoulders, and draped over the casket, was a huge feather cloak of red and brown hues which glistened like the wings of a giant moth.

I had never seen my grandmother in anything but black. She looked transfigured now and, in her death, she confounded all my expectations of decay and aging. This was not an old woman at all. This was a woman who had conquered death. Her madonna smile, the gleam in her hair, the blush in her cheeks, the aura, remained undiminished.

This is why I could not comprehend when finally, after the tangi-hanga, she was closed away into the fold of earth.

'You and I will never die,' she had whispered.

Wrapped in the red wings of a giant moth she was triumphant.

'I doubt if any of your family,' my psychologist friend said, 'will ever be able to escape the influence of your grandmother. Artemis made a religion out of herself, that's what she did. She had the clan as her congregation. As a consequence you all venerated her and you turned her into a goddess.

'Nor had I ever fully realised the extent to which the concept of mana still controlled Maori motivation. I guess there is still a great gap in our knowledge of psychological differences between Maori and Pakeha. But you are more than a Maori; you are my friend. I know you, not as an ethnic oddity but as a person, an individual, of intelligence. You are much in control of yourself, your inner as well as outer world. So I am going to say something to you which you may not like.

'It has to do with your grandmother. But it also has to do with your grandfather Ihaka, and your relationship with him, and the reason for its deterioration, particularly the attempt on your mana when he introduced Toroa to the family as your father's son. It's all well and good, but it is too good. It is too logical or watertight. Everything fits too nicely for me to believe in it.

'My own view, therefore, is that you're rationalising what really happened, and you have used your intelligence to make it so believable that you believe in it yourself. I would say you hated Ihaka long before the attempt on your mana, and that this hatred stems from some primal event which you have buried in your subconscious. I doubt if you would even recognise it as such.

'What could it be? I don't know, but I would suggest that you were jealous, sexually, of your grandfather. Until the onset of your own puberty, Ihaka posed no threat to your adoration of her. Your feelings of love became confused with sexual longing when you reached adolescence. Nobody, in your eyes, would have been worthy as her consort except, perhaps, one person. Yourself. But it was your grandfather who slept with her, who shared her bed and took her body.

'That's my diagnosis. But, I repeat, there is some small incident which triggered your sexual jealousy. Perhaps, one day, you might recognise it, and when you do, you might begin to forgive Ihaka for having been the matriarch's husband.

'Then there's the matter of your mother, Tiana. All I can say at this point, on what you have told me about her, is that she is at the very heart of the darkness at the centre of your soul. The answer may lie in Venice.

'What have you called the darkness? Te Kore? The abyss? Be careful of what you find there, my friend. After all, a greater person than I, Nietzsche, has warned of the danger.

'When you look long into the abyss—

'The abyss looks long into you.'

epilogue

'Everything about Venice is extraordinary,' wrote Lord Byron. 'Her aspect is like a dream, and her history is a romance.' Indeed, Venice is a dream like no other and thousands of people have fulfilled their fantasies of love, sex, ambition and death in that city of the seas. People have flocked to her because she is gay and sensual, the carnival city of E.T. Hoffman and Robert Schumann; but others have come in search of the secret mysteries of Venice, as I must, in my search for Riripeti.

Regan and I first saw the Serenissima Republica in 1973 when I decided, on the spur of the moment, to take a break from my work at the Commonwealth Office in London.

People told us to approach by water taxi as only then would we fully experience its indescribable refulgence—the quality of light that it tapped as its source of illumination from the earth, sea and sky. Venice was how Hawaiki nui, Hawaiki roa, Hawaiki pamamoa must have looked: a halcyon citadel of aquamarine, gold and azure anchored at the navel of the universe. As well, the illumination tapped another source: the residual energy of a city that historically had been one of the first great powers of the western world. In its heyday, the winged lion of Venice had rested triumphant in all the capitals of the earth. Venice itself had once maintained all the diplomatic missions of the civilised world in the city.

Not that everything about Venice was like a vision by Turner. Nor was our procession across the lagoon to the Square of Saint Mark as splendid and triumphant as I had imagined it would be. When the water taxi darted swiftly into the canal system to take us to our hotel, the water colour was an impenetrable indigo, holding gases of rotting sewage. The proud gondolas that we jostled with were no longer queens of the canals, having been joined in the new world by plebeian vessels of all description, like the vaporetti—the ubiquitous omnibus that transported the out-of-pocket tourists from jetty to jetty. We negotiated the city in fits and starts, zigzagging our way into the heart of Venice within an aquatic traffic thick with barges, gondolas, steamers and launches, piloted with nervous irritation, shouted obscenities and muttered imprecations by swarthy captains; the only song to be heard that day was a tape-recording of 'O Sole Mio' issuing from a forlorn gondola endeavouring to pilot its pallid tourists from one side of a canal to the other.

In this turmoil, the Rialto Bridge was like an apparition from a disturbing dream—a hunchback man carrying jewels in a sack. Above the jewels the pedestrians and loiterers snapped photographs of us and we snapped back. I saw a beautiful woman reflected in the water; I looked to locate her on the bridge but she was not there. Yet, when I checked again, there she was, a drowned woman, sliced in half as our water taxi stabbed beneath the bridge.

Disorientation, so I had been told, was a familiar sensation to all travellers to Venice. Perhaps it was because Venice was an unreal world. I felt as if I had left the real world and crossed some threshold between reality and fantasy where the senses were heightened by the conjunction of both. Venice, it seemed to me, was a product of two worlds in collision, the supernatural with the real, the fantastic with the natural, the bestial with the sublime—and it had me in its thrall. I had entered a timeless place, rather like Rongopai, whose very buildings, stones and statuary communed with men. Gods were in attendance, conjoining with the lives, passions, ambitions and deaths of the Venetians.

Our friend Gerard, who met us at the landing stage at the C'a Foscari, explained it to Regan and me in this way. 'Venice is like a huge amplifier,' he said. 'It feeds on the way you are thinking or feeling, processes the information, decodes it and then socks it back to you, but fivefold. If you're feeling happy, Venice boosts your happiness to ecstasy level; and if you're feeling bad, then it makes you go way below the baseline. But Venice also adds something itself: it senses your disturbances and adds its own resonances from the canals, the stones of the buildings and the history of its humanity. It conjures up what you want to see and makes you feel what you want to feel. That's why people either love Venice or hate it violently. Some people do not like being exposed to their dreams and nightmares.'

We were standing on the balcony in the sunlight. From here the canal was gilded with silver like a stream of mercury in constant flux with the traffic. When looked at from the middle distance, Venice maintained itself as a picture postcard. But I made the mistake of tilting my head too far back and the sun struck into the darkness behind my eyes, rendering me temporarily blind. My vision swam with tears.

There was a strange piece of statuary on the wall of the palace. It was a chimerical lion with jewelled eyes. I could swear that for a brief moment those eyes flashed and sparkled with hostility.

We had looked forward to Venice, Regan and I, and I guess that was why Venice amplified our expectations. In many respects, though, Venezia Vecchia, as the central city was called, was not at all beautiful. The houses and palazzi around the working class area of Canareggio and the castelli in the derelict Arsenale were boarded up or crumbling away, their foundations succumbing to the slow slap of the seas. The city was in fact only beauteous where the turisti congregated and, there, it had a ruined loveliness of the kind which dared you to imagine how it once looked. It asked you to clothe the island of San Giorgio Maggiore with loveliness, make the mists swirl artistically around the domes of Santa Maria della Salute, invest the Square of Saint Mark's with gentle orchestra music, cause flocks of pigeons to circle over the Ducal Palace, and listen for tears at the sentimentally named Bridge of Sighs. Ah yes, Venice was a mistress of deception for she asked us to substitute our objectivity with melancholia and, once in the grasp of that most romantic of senses, only then could the possession begin.

On my part, I kept thinking that I had only to turn the corner and I would see Caterina Cornaro, who became the last Queen of Cyprus, Jerusalem and Armenia, Lady of Isolo. I might come across Shylock slowly walking home among the warrens of canals, bridges and alleys. In the hushed peace of Saint Mark's I expected to hear the ballad singer, La Gioconda and her mother, La Cieca, praying for sanctuary from Barnaba. I would look up from the vaporetto, so I thought, and see Canaletto capturing on the canvas the church of San Simeone Piccolo.

I would not have been surprised at all to witness them, mingling in the present with the tourists and other visitors to the city of the sea.

In this respect no other city in the world evoked this feeling of the past and the present, of life as a continuum. Of Goethe taking notes, or Giovanni Bellini enshrining the glory of the city, or Turner transforming the colours of Venice into his special English Romantic vision. Or Stravinsky composing from a window above the canal, Peggy Guggenheim opening her garden to visitors, Baron Corvo drinking in front of Florian's, Wagner writing the third act of the luminescent *Tristan and Isolde* at the C'a Foscari, or Renata Tebaldi singing her way into history at La Fenice.

And looking down on them all, from the parapets and towering minarets and spires, were those stone members of the Venetian bestiary—the winged lions, phoenix, cuttlefish, griffins, octopuses, swans, basilisks, hawks, centaurs, dragons, golden stallions, cats and other monsters—all presided over by Saint Theodore and his crocodile, like a circle of mythical spirits. These were the monsters of the Venetian myth, tapping a source as deep as the Maori and displaying the reality in the light of the world. Perhaps that, also, is why I felt so akin to Venice, for here were the manaia, the marakihau and the taniwha of my own culture far to the south.

Quite by chance, I saw a mermaid shape in the Giudecca and cried out, 'Hine Te Ariki.' I let go of Regan's hand and ran to a small bridge to verify my sighting but all I glimpsed was a slow swirl of silver coiling down into the depths of the water.

For the first few days Regan and I absorbed the delights of Venice and the Lido with unaffected and unabashed delight. But the tourist season was ending. It was strange how, so quickly, Venice began to empty of its seasonal visitors and enable the Venetians, impatiently, to return. Nothing was lonelier than to see rows of deckchairs and portable dressing rooms being dismantled on the Lido and stored away for the next summer. Or empty gondolas and vaporetti holding on for one more day, just in case.

But we revelled in it because it allowed us to indulge our passion for aloneness, for wandering the canals and streets without being impeded by tourist tours. Regan loved nothing better than to read from Henry James' *The Aspern Papers* or, when we went to the Lido, from Thomas Mann's *Death in Venice*, where we imagined Gustav von Aschenbach and Tadzio on the beach.

Venice had us in its thrall, so much so that in the last days of November I asked Regan, 'Shall we find a room in the old city and stay on?'

'Oh, yes, yes, yes,' she said. So I rang London to say that I was extending my leave, and Gerard found us a small student apartment in the attic of Canareggio 2617. The students who owned it were away for two weeks: 2617 was simply one of a number of doorways in a white wall of houses fronting a small canal. It was ideal for our purposes, and we had a window overlooking a small piazza and bridge across the canal. In the mornings, we were woken by the merchants taking their wares to market and, in the evenings, we joined the workers returning home.

One evening, although the weather was cold, I noticed warmth in the night wind.

'The sirocco is coming,' Gerard said. 'It blows from the Sahara.'

Perhaps the sirocco accounted for my sudden feeling of oppression. Looking back, I can recall a growing sense of unease as we wandered through the streets of Venezia Vecchia. The wind from the direction of Africa seemed to be a harbinger of some happening. It lifted the blanket of sumptuousness from Venice so that I could see what had to be seen—my dreams or nightmares, but magnified fivefold.

Day in and day out, therefore, although Regan and I continued to enjoy our sightseeing, I had the sense of waiting for something to happen. At dusk, at the landing stages of gondolas, I saw a strange ferryman beckoning me; but when he glimpsed Regan with me he began to row his boat upon the turbulent water until he was no longer there. The following morning, as we were journeying along the canal, I kept catching glimpses of a beautiful young girl in a Renaissance gown, running between the rotting palazzos and below the fading arcades, and in her laughter was a ghost of memory. 'Quickly mokopuna, haere mai, we must escape them.' One evening, as Regan and I were walking back to the attic apartment, a grotesque harlequin detached himself from the blackness and ran at me as if to capture me in his blood-red cape.

So it went on, mild disturbances in the normal order of things. Increasingly I felt concerned for the safety of Regan and myself. I saw menace where there was none in the gilded horses of San Marco. I grew fearful, in our daily journeys by vaporetto, of witnessing that beautiful young girl in her flight through the mazes and across the small bridges of the city. I was easily startled in the evenings, wandering the cobbled streets, when people appeared and disappeared like silent shadows.

Both Regan and Gerard were amused at my agitation. 'The sirocco always affects people,' Gerard said. We were having dinner in the attic, and this was our farewell to Venice, for we would be leaving the next afternoon. Gerard had promised to take Regan to the ornate Ca'd'Oro in the morning. I had decided to visit the ceremonial bucintoro at the Querini.

'No,' I responded, 'it's not the sirocco. It's—'

At that moment the candle went out. Gerard laughed and asked where I kept the matches. While he was getting them I went to shut the window.

I saw a familiar shape silhouetted in the canal and, for a second, recognised Hine Te Ariki. At the time I didn't realise that Tiana had sent my kaitiaki to warn me that I was in danger. She had swum all the way from Aotearoa on the other side of the world, out into the ocean of Te Moana Nui a Kiwa, around the horn of Africa, up the coast and into the Mediterranean towards a city guarded by a winged lion.

She must have had urgent reason to warn me, if it meant swimming halfway round the world.

The dinner concluded around one in the morning.

'I'll come by at ten,' Gerard said to Regan. They were looking forward to their visit to the Ca'd'Oro. Regan was so animated about it that she did not sense my own growing unease. It was late by the time we got to bed. As for me, I couldn't go to sleep. Then, around three o'clock I had the dream.

I heard the sound of weeping outside the attic. With beating heart I left Regan's arms and went to look. I opened the window and the warmth of the night enveloped me. There was a full moon, overripe and silver, and it shone in a cloudless sky. The Canareggio was enveloped in a miasma of mist, and the water in the canal was at high tide. I listened again for the weeping and I saw firebrands lighting the mist with flame. Dark shapes began to issue from an alleyway and glide along the path to the canal.

At the same time I heard the splash of oars. I looked down the canal. An elaborate barge was approaching, rowed by two oarsmen in black tam-o'-shanters. The barge was draped with black cloth and its beak of shining steel cut through the water. It came to a stop at a jetty near the small bridge. There was a lantern at the stern and, in the light of the lamp, I saw wreaths of flowers. I looked again at the dark shapes as they approached the barge, and saw a shining casket being carried by pallbearers. Death had brought a rictus to the otherwise smiling face of Venice.

I walked softly from the room and drifted silently down the stairs to the front door. As I opened the door I was dazzled by the firebrands. The casket had been laid on the funeral barge, and mourners were stepping into small gondolas. An elderly man in black mourning clothes beckoned me towards him. I knew I had to go, and I joined him. He smiled kindly and indicated that I should sit next to him; it was, of course, his tears which had woken me. As I seated myself two boatmen, one at the prow and the other at the stern, pushed the gondola away from the canal and thrust their paddles into the black water.

I heard a voice cry, 'No, son,' but there was no turning back.

The dream made Venice a surreal city, as dark and suffocating as a raven's wing. Above my head was a moonlit track of stars, disturbed only when the funeral convoy slid under the small bridges of the canal. On those occasions the firebrands would light up the bellies of the bridges, exposing the decay and rot of the ages. The only sounds to be heard were the dipping of the oars and the soft weeping of the old man beside me. He held my hands and, every now and then, dabbed at his eyes with a handkerchief.

Five gondolas accompanied the barge on which the casket lay. The firebrands were like fiery wings fluttering in the water and against the houses lining the canal, beating silently for a way out of the maze. Every now and then they flamed across the heads of the bestiary—the stone animals of Venice—in malignant contortion. A wolverine shape gnawing at a gorgon bird. A misshapen gryphon being strangled in the coils of a monstrous serpent. A degenerate winged lion struggling with a malevolent crocodile. Hideous half-human half-beast creatures, they were all mute witnesses to my journey. As we passed by, they came alive and plunged into the canal to accompany us.

The funeral cortege began to pitch and sway and I knew that we were in the sea's swell. The miasma dispersed as we floated free of the tall palaces of Venice. The boatmen became more purposeful, fighting the night tide as it surged against and over us. I saw the casket shift in its bed of flowers and glisten with spray.

We approached a far-off island. The gondolas glided to a landing stage. I helped the old man from his seat. He motioned that we should join the other mourners at the barge, where the casket was being unloaded. Among the mourners were six women, one taller than the others. They were swathed in black, and they were chanting in a strange, high-pitched way. As I approached the group the chanting stopped. The tall woman in the middle of them turned to me.

'Tena koe, Beloved of Riripeti,' she said.

The moon struck the earth and I saw that I was on an island cemetery. The island was crisscrossed with avenues lined with cypress trees. On each side of the avenues were headstones like daggers thrust into the ground. In the distance was a great dead city of marble vaults and mausoleums.

I became afraid. I tried to run but the mourners encircled me in a tightening space. The tall woman motioned to her women to pinion my hands by my sides.

I heard a voice calling again, 'Son, son.'

I had no option but to go with the mourners along a wide moonlit avenue lined with cypress trees. I fell and my hands clutched at the casket. Grave robbers were lifting bodies from the ground as if they were flowers in a deathly garden. Whenever I tried to get away I was pushed back behind the catafalque carrying the casket. I looked up into the night sky. The air was possessed with the presence of spirits. My heart was thundering. Ahead I glimpsed a dead city. I saw thousands of monumental tombs. One of them was a huge vault of black marble veined with gold. The door to the vault was open, like a huge mouth.

'Son, so—'

I was pushed through the door and into the darkness. With a booming sound the door closed behind me. The firebrands were applied to braziers on the walls of the vault. I was in a huge room. The walls had square holes in them, resting places for bodies of the dead. Photographs and fading flowers were hung in small votary niches. The smell of death, stale air, and candle wax was everywhere.

The room was filled with thousands of people; I could not tell who were alive and who were dead.

All were mourning the statue of a beautiful goddess. Stunning, life-sized and made of marble, she was like a poutokomanawa, a centre post of a meeting house. I thought she was asleep, but when I looked at the statue's face again, I realised she was blind; there were holes where her eyes should have been. She held in her arms emblems of the natural world, like offerings to her iwi: leaves, vines, birds, fishes and a bestiary of her own. In a fold of her dress, a spider.

The tall woman hooded in black turned to me. 'You are the price that has to be paid,' she said.

And I was falling through the many periods of Te Po, spiralling out beyond the reach of the gods, back through Te Po and the twelve changings of the night. The light began to diminish, ever diminish until all was utter and complete darkness. I knew that I was in Te Kore, the Void. And other gods and spirits, as depicted in the stone frescoes of the floating city, began to hover over me.

I cried out for help.

Immediately, as if in answer to my call, there was a shuffling sound outside the vault.

Silence.

Then sounds of shuffling again.

The iron door to the vault reverberated with a heavy booming sound. The mourners were transfixed at first, and some backed away. Others ran to the door to push back and keep the door from opening. The booming was so loud that even when I put my hands over my ears I could not lessen the deafening sound. The reverberations were so strong that at every thud against the door my body was wracked with the vibrations. At every blow the dead were disturbed from their sleep. The bones and other funerary objects scattered in the firelit gloom. Dust swirled thickly. The mourners backed away. There was a short silence, shocking in its intensity. Then the sound of heavy breathing. Slowly, a three-fingered webbed hand slid around the door, hovered, and wrenched it violently open.

It was Hine Te Ariki, pulling herself into the vault with her hands, searching the gloom. When she saw me her eyes caught fire in recognition. She reared up and advanced, her lower body curling her flukes into the room. Some of her side fins were ripped and torn.

Once she was there she surveyed me with love. Beyond her, I saw the enormous gouges she had made in the earth to get to me. Bloodied and ripped though she was, she was indescribably beautiful. Panting, she reached out for me.

Then a voice said, 'Oh, my son.'

Tiana had come with her.

Slowly, Hine Te Ariki uncoiled from the figure of Tiana.

She looked like a sleepwalker and was dressed in a long white nightgown. Her hair was brushed back from her face. There was sweat on her brow. Her feet were paddling, as if she was caught in one of her dreams. Her eyes were wide open, but it was as if she was still asleep. She looked at me and, although her face was calm, her lips were trembling.

She turned to the tall woman and her mourners. She had a way of lifting her face to the light. In her hands she held a knife. She began to bargain.

'I have come for my son,' she said. 'If you allow me to take him I will be your instrument of restitution from she who has gone before us all.'

The Venetians surged forward to stop her.

Tiana cried, 'Hine Te Ariki.' My ancestress swept her flukes back and forth, keeping them at bay.

The Venetians tried to charge again. But a voice called, 'Stop.' The tall black-garbed woman stepped forward. She threw back her hood. She wore pearls in her hair and although she looked like Riripeti, she wasn't her. She took counsel with her followers. There was disagreement but she overruled them.

'Tiana,' she said, 'you are a mother of great courage. We ourselves cannot make right what took place here, and while the sacrifice of the Beloved of Riripeti may arguably appease us, I therefore accept your bargain.'

My mother nodded. Although she bowed to no men or women, she inclined her head. 'We have your leave to go?' she asked.

'Yes,' the tall woman said. 'But be warned, Tiana. If you cannot do what you have promised to do then you, and not your son, will pay the price.'

The price? What was the price? I was chilled with fear; I had the feeling that it was beyond imagining.

And so my mother, Hine Te Ariki and I escaped that place, the vault on the island of the dead and, when we exited, we fell in a terrifying vertiginous descent through the many Changes of the Night towards the Dawn.

The sky was lightening. Venice floated serene on the water. I was standing with Hine Te Ariki and Tiana on a cliff on the island of the dead. Below, the sea surged against the rocks.

Tiana was breathing heavily, sucking the breath in. She looked to the south. Then she turned to me, her feet still paddling, and caressed my face.

'I told you never to come here,' she said.

'And I told you never to come to me in your dreams,' I answered.

'You were in danger,' she argued, lifting her face to the light. 'Even when in danger, you keep me to my word?'

'Yes,' I said. 'Whatever Riripeti's transgression when she was in Venice, and I refuse to believe it was intentional, I stand by my own actions. I have no need of you, Tiana.'

That is when she pricked my skin, tenderly, ritually, with her knife. 'No need of me?' she asked. 'Regardless of the anger between us, you and I are bound together by blood. Although you were already dead in my womb when Riripeti came at your birthing, you will always be mine.'

My head reeled. 'I was already dead?' I hadn't known that fact. Why hadn't I been told earlier? I refused to believe it.

'Why else would I have let you go to her?' Tiana asked. 'Therefore, although I have been opposed to her on other matters, on that matter I bear her no ill will.'

The dream began to implode. Tiana became rigid. It was as if, far away, my father had placed his hands over her feet, trying to wake her, forcing her to surface from her sleep.

'No,' she commanded. 'No.' She was furious, and looked at me with great longing. For a moment I thought I saw tears in her eyes. But I have never known my mother to cry and there have never been tears between us.

'You were my firstborn, Tamatea. I held you in my arms.'

I reached out for her. I saw her reaching for me.

Our fingertips almost touched.

But Hine Te Ariki bent down and, holding Tiana to her breast like a doll, dived into the sea. With dizzying speed, she was soon on the horizon. There, she looked at me.

'Hoki mai ki te wa kainga. Hoki mai.'

A crystal splash, and they were gone.

I woke. It was after ten, and I was drenched with sweat. I went to the shower and then returned to waken Regan. She sighed and pressed herself close to me. Her eyelids fluttered open.

'Can't you sleep?' she asked.

'It's ten,' I said. Hoki mai ki te wa kainga.

'Oh gosh,' she answered. 'Gerard.'

'It's time to go home,' I said. 'Back to Aotearoa.'

Later that year Regan and I left Europe and returned to New Zealand.

In July of the following year, 1974, I went to see my Uncle Alexis who was going blind in Wellington.

Auckland,
October 2008

author's note

THE MATRIARCH *REDUX*

The Matriarch began life as a short story called 'The Mother'. It marked the end of a ten-year embargo I had placed on my writing.

Three hundred pages later, I knew I was in trouble; even when the novel was published in 1986, it was only half of a manuscript approaching a thousand pages and still growing.

This situation explains why I have returned to the original novel and tried to resolve some of the issues surrounding its publication. For one thing, the structural pattern I deployed was by no means complete and I was not able to see its totality until fourteen years later, when I finally published the rest of the manuscript in what might be called a sequel to the novel, *The Dream Swimmer*, in 2000. With both *The Matriarch* and *The Dream Swimmer* I had devised a structural framework for all the material, based on the Maori concept of the koru, or spiral. To achieve what I set out to do—to write a work (or two works as it turned out) that would truly capture the metafictional and metaphysical vision I had in mind for it—only the spiral would work. This enabled me to thus 'spiral' from past to present, from personal to political, from history to myth, from reality to fantasy, from fiction to non-fiction and, as far as methodology was concerned, to use autobiography, biography and historical documents, including parliamentary Hansards.

However, the spiralling narratives in *The Matriarch* particularly (I was more in control of them in *The Dream Swimmer*) were often dangerously imbalanced, in my opinion, and time has revealed a lack of congruence with the connecting spirals in *The Dream Swimmer*. In other words, the 'join' between both books, as you would expect of two works written fourteen years apart, was not exactly seamless. I've made attempts to rebalance the two books accordingly and, while still honouring the discontinuous narrative, to 'throw' some of the spirals over to *The Dream Swimmer* so that they both become the one holistic book that was originally intended.

Other rewriting clarifies referential linkages that should have been better made in *The Matriarch*; there are a lot of interconnections between, for instance, history and the fictional text. Thus, I have reinserted a short reference piece on the Italian revolutionary Giuseppe Garibaldi (1807–82) and the Italian Risorgimento (1815–61, leading to a unified Italy); I had written a large fifty-page section on both to clarify their relevance to Te Kooti Arikirangi Te Turuki (the Maori Garibaldi, c.1814–91) and the Land Wars (1845–72). Given the central conceit of the novel—that Riripeti may have lived in Venice (which didn't join unified Italy until 1866)—and given that the operas of composer Giuseppe Verdi (1813–1901) feature prominently in the book, I also wanted to indicate more clearly in this new edition why Venice and Verdi are so much a part of the story.

Italy, Venice and Verdi are among a number of references that are made in *The Matriarch* and are resolved in *The Dream Swimmer*. For instance, I have inserted a reference to Wilkie Collins' *The Moonstone*; the very end of the saga presented in *The Dream Swimmer* draws its inspiration from the restitution motif of Collins' novel. Again, I have revisited the set-pieces involving the *Takitimu* canoe and the adze, Te Awhiorangi, to make them more appropriately what they were supposed to be: homages to Maori oral literature as well as to the inventory of the Anglo-Saxon literary tradition. Those readers who have already read the original version of *The Matriarch* will notice other changes. One of these is the greater and, I think, better handling of the spider imagery.

The Matriarch reflects my own personal involvement in the tumultuous years of Maori protest during the 1970s: the rise of Nga Tamatoa, protests over the Treaty of Waitangi, the Maori Land March of 1975, protests at Bastion Point in 1977 and Raglan in 1981. I became a founder member of the Maori Writers and Artists Society and I was the first Maori member of the Queen Elizabeth II Arts Council of New Zealand; in that capacity I established what became Te Waka Toi, the Maori funding arm of the council. I joined the Ministry of Foreign Affairs as one of their first Maori diplomats and established policy practices and a marae, the first in any government department. By 1976 I was third secretary at the New Zealand High Commission, Canberra, Australia; I joined fellow Maori writer, Teremoana Pehimana, in the vigil with Aboriginal activists the evening before the bulldozers arrived on their sacred ground to begin building the present Australian Parliament. On my return I became the secretary for the Pacific Affairs Coordinating Committee, working with my mentor Ken Piddington to assist Pacific Island communities in New Zealand. Further activist work took me up to the Springbok Tour (1981); I marched, gave speeches and was banned from Parliament Grounds for interrupting the business of Parliament. Whatever experiences I became involved in influenced the writing of *The Matriarch*.

With this new edition of the novel I maintain my personal commitment to rewrite all my five first books: *Pounamu Pounamu* now exists in a new edition (2002); *Tangi* was rewritten and expanded to include a sequel (both books were published together as *The Rope of Man* in 2005); and a totally reversioned edition of *Whanau*, twice the length of the original, was published as *Whanau II* (2004). *The New Net Goes Fishing* awaits. I am grateful to Geoff Walker of Penguin Group (NZ) and Gillian Tewsley, who heads the Raupo imprint, for their act of faith in enabling me to continue my rewriting commitment.

Finally, I wish to thank my parents Te Haa Ihimaera Smiler, Julia Ihimaera Smiler and my whanau. In particular, I am, as always, grateful for Jane, Jessica and Olivia, who constantly illuminate my life and give it meaning.

Witi Ihimaera
Auckland
October 2008